ENCELADUS

ENCELADUS

Terminus Strain: Book 1

Chase Gluch

ENCELADUS

Cover illustration by Talia Gluch

ISBN (paperback): 979-8-9940072-0-4
ISBN (ebook): 979-8-9940072-1-1

www.chasegluch.com

First Edition: December 2025
Printed in the United States

For Carlie.

Who gives me way too much credit,
And way too much leeway,
And way too much support.

TABLE OF CONTENTS

CHAPTER 1

ENCELADUS

"Welcome, ladies and gents, to Enceladus."

Di glanced up from her glass-like infopad, sparse mission dossier open on its screen and reflecting in the glass of the window beside her. She peered out the port side view of the bridge at the pockmarked, white celestial sphere, ribbons of light blue snaking their way across the moon caused by the various sub-surface ocean patterns. Geothermal vents blasted particulate into the atmosphere at its southern tip; a phenomenon exacerbated and made more violent by excessive ice mining operations. The deep scars left by those operations were slowly refilling since they had moved deep below, aided by the near constant snowfall.

It had been years since Paragon, the mining corporation that owned drilling rights on the entirety of this moon, had transferred their teams below the surface. They had spouted their typical empty PR platitudes about the safety of their crews, but everyone knew the corpos were sick of losing equipment to the sub-zero temps, fierce winds, and ceaseless moisture on the surface.

A gentle churning had settled in Di's stomach, a growing unease the closer they came to their destination. Paragon had offered her crew the job with very little in the way of details. Find out why communications are down and where their missing assets— employees – had gone. One did not say no to an all-powerful corporation like Paragon if they wanted any sort of future as a mercenary-for-hire, but she had been more than willing to stick their offer up their ass. In the end, the astronomical payday had been too great a temptation for even her, and the crew had been more than willing to agree.

"And if you look out your left side, you'll—"

"That's enough, Hazel," Di said, turning away from the window.

"Aaaaand Captain said it's time to shut my yapper. Ship-wide conference on the main deck in ten." The comm system clicked off with a final harsh, staticky buzz as Hazel, her trusted pilot, turned toward her with a sly grin. "Need any help, Cap?"

"Thank you, Hazel. I'll be fine." Di brushed a strand of dirty blonde hair behind her right ear, a nervous habit she had begrudgingly never broken. She turned back toward the window for one final glance at their destination before shifting to the task at hand.

Grabbing her infopad, she marched from the bridge, down the hall past quarters, and into the mess hall where two of her crew members, Gene and Gerald, were just finishing up their meal.

"And here's the thing about it," Gerald said, words

blasting forward at breakneck speed, much to the chagrin of his crewmate, or rather, current victim. "The science just *doesn't make sense!* How is it that a *laser* can be shaped into the form of a *sword* without any sort of reflection or reflective system in place? Now if they had claimed it was a form of plasma or—"

"Did you hear the announcement?" Di interjected. "Main deck. Now."

Gene locked eyes with her, exaggeratingly rolling his eyes and nodding in appreciation. His thick, salt-and-pepper beard was looking more and more salt than pepper these days, his hair having gone the way of grey years ago.

Gerald, the polar opposite of Gene in terms of looks with his thin, gangly limbs and chocolate, bouncing curls flopping awkwardly, gulped uncomfortably, adjusting his thin rimmed spectacles higher up the bridge of his nose.

"Yes, ma'am. Sorry ma'am." He hastily scooped up his unnecessarily heavy stack of voluminous texts, despite the ability to recall any written word in the known universe with a swift tap on his infopad, and hastily stumbled out of the room.

"Thanks as always, Captain," Gene muttered, slapping his pronounced gut. His aging features and broadening belly did nothing to stem the whispered nickname of 'Santa Clause' that followed him these days, though a quick flex of his abnormally toned and muscular arms quieted all but the bravest.

"You can always tell him to shut up," Di said, the hint of a grin tugging at the corner of her mouth.

"You don't think I've *tried* that?" he asked, a wide smile

breaking.

Di shook her head and grasped his outstretched hand, pulling him to his feet with an audible grunt. "You're losing your touch."

"Don't I know it," he muttered, placing thumb and forefinger on the bridge of his nose. "Just don't let anyone else hear you say it."

"Never," she said. As long as she'd known Gene, and that was a very long time, he had always held himself as the ex-military, tough-as-nails, no-nonsense hard-ass. It wasn't until she had witnessed him at his lowest, the one time he had let his shell crack, that she understood him for what he was; a loyal, soft-spoken man who would die to protect the ones he loved. Di was fortunate enough to count herself among that tight-knit circle.

"I need you on the main deck as well," she said, placing a hand on his beefy shoulder.

"Of course, Captain," he said sternly. Gene always reverted to that hard ass when it was time to work. She would expect no less from her second-in-command.

He stumped away, lightly favoring his right leg. Di shook her head. It looked like his old injury was acting up again. That was never a good sign.

After a quick sweep of the few remaining empty rooms, she made her way to the main deck, a large, open area where their tightknit crew often held important meetings. And this one was about as important as it got.

"Captain on deck!" Gene shouted, the babble of various

conversations petering out. Di nodded appreciatively and glanced around at her small, hand-picked crew. Well, all but the corporate shill in the corner. She struggled to hold back her scowl at the not-so-deft-handed insult of insinuating their need for a babysitter, but now was not the time to reopen *that* wound.

"You've all been briefed already, so I'll spare the deep dive," Di began, dropping her pad at the command desk. "Paragon has hired us to determine the status of their mining operation here on Enceladus. Their crew out here has been radio silent for several months now; no status reports, no calls home to weeping mothers. That includes the ground team and the team in the sky."

Di glanced out the large bay window at the massive floating orbital station connected to the surface via an interplanetary elevator. It was apparently easier maintenance than a fleet of shuttles, though she suspected it had more to do with budget than any feigned care for their ground crew's quality of life. Either way, she had strong suspicions those freezing temperatures and the constant snowfall was a bear on the elevator system. She did not envy the ones responsible for keeping that thing operating or the ones forced to use it.

"Conditions are harsh on the surface, so I need everyone at their best. First and foremost, we need to ensure the safety of our crew."

The sound of a throat clearing gave Di pause, and she shot a withering glare toward Liam, Paragon's hired goon. No one else would dare interrupt her opening speech, at least not someone sober. And that had happened only once.

His smug attitude plastered on his too chiseled, plastic-y, clean-shaven face spoke all too well of a man who got what he wanted. Hell, even the impressive way he filled out his standard issue bodysock that *no one* found appealing emitted pompousness.

Ignoring his obvious attempt to hijack her op, she bulled forward. "As I was saying, average surface temps are -200 degrees Celsius, or -330 degrees Fahrenheit for you cowboys who refuse to let an outdated, nonsensical system die."

That elicited a round of hardy chuckles, bringing the mood of the room up from tense frostiness to slightly relaxed, though still on a razor's edge. Everyone present was well aware of the risks of accepting a mission like this. Travelling to an outer system station, where the nearest help was anywhere from five hundred million to over one billion kilometers away, was a risk in and of itself. Tack on the inherent dangers of a mining outpost, the natural hazards of surface-side weather patterns on a moon with constant snowfall, and the very real possibility of a self-governing system of rough miners, both men and women, who hadn't integrated with normal society in what could be decades viewing your interference as an opportunity to brush up on some target practice. No, Di didn't believe anyone could be truly relaxed at those prospects. Even so, her crew held up marvelously. They always did. Besides, it didn't hurt that the pay was nearly triple what their last job had paid out for supposedly a quarter of the work.

"Luckily, most of the actual mining operations, including living quarters, are several kilometers – yes, Lucas, kilometers, you're going to need to learn to calculate that one on your own – below the surface. So we'll likely be sitting at a balmy -165 degrees Celsius."

Another round of laughter and a few good-natured slaps on the back of the ship's mechanic, Lucas, brought a smirk to Di's lips. She could almost forget the ever-looming presence of their corporate overlord smirking in the corner, perfectly coiffed, raven locks reflecting the sterile, white cabin lights above.

"Just remember to keep an eye on your newfangled suits—" Another blatant cough from 'his majesty' ripped her smile away, prompting an old twitch at the corner of her eye she had thought long gone. Leave it up to a corpo to bring back in seconds a tick that had taken years of therapy to get rid of.

"Excuse me," Di continued, dipping her torso in a mock bow. "Your newfangled *E.I.A.P.S.L.*, graciously provided by Paragon."

Essential Interplanetary Apparatus for Preservation and Sustainability of Life, Di scoffed internally. *Damn eggheads and their overly complicated acronyms. It's a damn space suit, call it what it is.*

"An 'eppsul'?" Emma asked, rolling her eyes and pointedly shooting a patronizing glance toward Liam. "What the hell's an 'eppsul'?"

"Not 'eppsul'," Gerald said, his enthusiasm already rising at the prospect of explaining something overcomplicated and only interesting to someone who, like Gerald, studied quantum mechanics as a de-stressor. *"E.I.A.P.S.L.* is an acronym. It stands for Essential—"

"Gerald," Gene interrupted, with a slight shake of his head.

"It's… Well… Oh." Gerald's face flushed and he slumped back in his chair, shooting Di an apologetic wince. Leave it to Gerald to misinterpret blatant sarcasm for a genuine opportunity to enlighten someone on one of his many topics of interest.

"You've all been thoroughly trained in the use of your *E.I.A.P.S.L.,*" Di continued, putting an emphasis on the acronym. "I'm fully confident in you all to keep yourselves alive. Also, please keep in mind that our wonderful and trusting benefactors are monitoring everything we see, speak, or do. So try to keep mutinous, anti-corpo language to a minimum." She raised an eyebrow as though daring Mr. Roberts to comment. He, unfortunately, didn't take the obvious bait.

"I will say, however," she continued, "that once this brief is over, I expect you all in your gear at all times until we are safely away from this rock. Stupid mistakes lead to stupid deaths."

Hells below, she had seen plenty of those. She and Gene had purged more than a few ship locks full of enemy combatants back in the day. Deaths easily counteracted had they just thought to keep their damn suit on.

"Before we go through final checks, I want to make this abundantly clear. Everyone, and I mean everyone," she said, slowly enunciating the second *everyone*, "has a job to do. As long as we do those jobs, both individually and collectively, we're gonna do just fine. In and out."

She took the time to meet each and every one of her crew members' eyes; silently reaffirming, encouraging, bolstering.

Gene, her long-standing companion-at-arms, who returned the gaze with a brief nod. He had loyally followed her through many a bad decision without so much as a grumble or gripe. Well, maybe a gripe or two here and there.

Gerald, the greenest on the crew. Too many in their line of work dismissed him outright, all because of his encyclopedic memory and thirst for knowledge. Di had come to learn that having a certified genius was advantageous in many scenarios, and she could find no one smarter or more willing to lend a helping hand. Even if it was done with a non-self-aware smugness. He audibly swallowed but gave her a crisp nod as well.

Gayle, a no-nonsense gun nut with an aim that rivaled any self-respected automated system. Hand her a rifle and point her at a target, it'll be gone in an eye blink. Give her a paperclip and point out the obnoxiously buzzing fly in the room, it'll be pinned to the ceiling before your coffee is cool enough to drink. A perfect trait in a security officer. Gayle's bushy, blonde eyebrows wiggled up and down, an eagerness suggesting her hope that things went just a little wrong allowing her to show off her skills. She pulled her stick-straight, short, golden hair back into a tight ponytail at the nape of her neck, green eyes glazing as she mentally entered her own personal warzone for self-analysis.

Hazel, who had been around almost as long as Gene,

winked, her deep brown eyes sparkling, and returned Di's nod. There was not a single pilot that matched her. Sure, there were *better*, more *skilled* pilots in the system, but her willingness to do what needed to be done coupled with more than a hint of daredevil insanity meant she succeeded where others failed or dared not even try. Her dark skin wrinkled at the corners of her mouth as she flashed her bright white teeth in a mischievous grin.

Lucas, an old soul trapped in archaic ideals and obsessed with the "good ol' days", even though he was at least half of Di's own age. Still, there wasn't a single mechanic more gifted than him. Two jobs previous, he had jerry-rigged a siphon filter out of a used newsreel and sealed a cracked conduit with gum and moustache wax. A regular modern-day MacGyver, as he often said. Whatever that meant. He merely shrugged and popped another wad of chewing gum in his mouth, clasping his hands behind his neck and rubbing the stubble of his black crop top hair.

Finally, Emma. The promising up-and-coming assistant pilot. Where Hazel was experienced, Emma was naturally gifted. She had plenty to learn, especially in *this* crew's line of work, but Di had no problem believing in her capability. Emma returned a twitchy smile accompanied by an involuntary nervous giggle. Her pale cheeks flushed pink, and she pulled back behind her curtain of auburn hair, bangs falling in front of her eyes.

Di nodded again, silently praying to whatever god was out there among the stars that she hadn't just lied to these wonderful men and women. Her family. Despite her outward bravado, that creeping, unspoken hesitance twisted in her gut. She had never been one to doubt her instincts, but the looks of confidence and support from her team pushed aside her lingering sense of unease.

"There will be two teams," she continued. "The first, Alpha Team, will be surface side. Bravo will be on the orbiting station. Alpha will be led by myself, accompanied by Gene, Gerald, and Emma."

Gerald visibly blanched and started blinking furiously, taking a moment to wipe the inner corners of his eyes.

"Gerald, I may need your help with the scientists. It's not just miners down there; there's a whole slew of your kind right alongside them. You can reminisce on whale mating patterns, or the theory of relativity, or whatever the hell it is you talk about." She met his eyes again and gave an encouraging nod.

Gerald had never been surface-side before now, always relegated to the ship. The 'safe side,' as he liked to call it. But not this time. Di needed her Science Officer at her side, and what better way to break him into a life lived dangerously than taking him to a potentially hostile ball of ice?

"Bravo Team will consist of Gayle, Lucas, Mr. Roberts, and Hazel who will dock at the—"

Liam cleared his throat, and Di slammed her hands down on the table in front of her, causing more than a few crew members to jump in their seats.

"Mr. Roberts, I feel as though you have something to say. So if you wouldn't mind using your *words*, feel free to come up to the stage, here, and share your wisdom with the group at large. That is unless, of course, you simply have a tickle in your throat, in which case you will find the lozenges back in the Med Bay. Beneath the counter. Third drawer down on the left." Di shot him her trademark, icy glare, the small, tight smile tugging at the corners of her mouth struggling not to evolve into a full-blown scowl.

"I apologize, Diane," Mr. Roberts said, smooth, coolly controlled voice showing no hint of intimidation at her hostility. "I'm just a little concerned with your division of labor. I merely noticed that I am not to accompany you to the surface, despite my corporate mandate giving me full authority over this mission."

Di bristled at his openly smug attempt to pull rank, struggling to keep her seething anger in check and her voice calm. "Mr. Roberts. While I appreciate Paragon's involvement, I am captain of this ship, and as such, I am in command of all operations performed by its crew."

"Yes, but—"

"Liam," Lucas interjected with a raised finger, much to the annoyance of Mr. Roberts and the enjoyment of everyone else. "Li. Can I call you Li?"

"I would prefer Mr. Roberts."

Lucas leaned back in his chair, a look of feigned, patronizing concern plastered across his face. He lifted his clunky, well-worn, black combat boots to the small table in front of him and clasped his interlocking fingers across his plump midsection. If it weren't for his youthful, wispy facial hair and lack of wrinkles, his stocky, short build would have been the picture-perfect representation of a wizened parent giving fatherly advice.

"Right. So, listen Li. Your company may have sent you out here to nanny us and given you the impression that you matter. But out here? You don't. You *really* don't. Di is in charge, and what she says goes. It's best that you learn that sooner rather than later. It will save you a few headaches."

Di choked back a smile at Mr. Roberts' look of pure indignation. She was pretty sure no one had ever told him no, much less spoken down to him like he was a toddler.

Mr. Roberts locked eyes with Di, mouth pursed. "I assure you; Paragon will hear about—"

"Yeah, yeah," Hazel interrupted, standing and striding to Di's side. "You'll write up a report, they'll give us a sternly worded reprimand, maybe dock our pay. We get it. Can we do this already? I get antsy with all this waiting around and talking."

"Wheels up in five," Di said, putting a thankful hand on Hazel's toned, muscular shoulder.

Liam raised a finger, frustration marring his perfectly chiseled jawline and smooth, glowing skin. "I would like to remind everyone of their E.I.A.P.S.L.'s experimental artificial intelligence module. Paragon has graciously allowed you to field test their new neural implant interface and would like you all to complete a brief, fifty-two question survey upon completion of the mission..."

Before he had finished his announcement, the room had emptied of all but Di, each crewmember going their separate way to complete whatever individualized ritual their superstitions wouldn't allow them to skip.

Di raised an eyebrow and shot him a scathing glance as she, too, strode past him to head toward her quarters. She reveled in watching the weasel flounder helplessly in his own pool of self-aggrandizing superiority.

Hazel stood waiting as Di rounded the corner, ready as always for final mission prep notes.

"I'm going to need you to be vigilant with the ship's comms," Di said, Hazel joining in lock step with her purposeful stride. "The ice will be too thick for anything to get through over the air. I'll ask for the comm ports and the correct channels when we touch down at the surface base, assuming someone's there to greet us, but no guarantees on what we'll find down there. We may be guessing at things for a bit. Just keep an eye on your radio."

"Will do, boss," Hazel said, offering a mock salute. As the pilot, she was often left with the ship for an emergency getaway and, as such, was the go-between when the crew had to split up over long distances or where comms were spotty. She peeled off toward the cockpit to complete her own preparations for the final approach.

Di glanced over her shoulder to find a stern-faced corporate suit in her wake with what was surely another complaint. Before Mr. Roberts had a chance to suck in a breath, she picked up her pace and threw up her hand.

"Sorry, Mr. Roberts. Your concerns will have to wait. I've got too many things to prepare before we launch and not enough time to do it. If you'll excuse me."

The rage-filled crack in his business-like facade was enough to elicit an actual smile as she turned into her cabin, door sliding satisfactorily shut behind her.

CHAPTER 2
SURFACE

Di checked and rechecked the readings on her heads-up display, or 'HUD.' For the fourth time since donning the suit, she went over its functionality and diagnostics, making sure her vitals were reading accurately, performing comms checks.

Despite her distaste for the man, Liam *had* kitted them all out with state-of-the-art tech. Pre-market shit, the kind that eggheads would drool over if they could get their hands on it. It was a testament to just how nervous Gerald was that he wasn't giggling like a kid in a candy shop. He had spent nearly the entire trip begging Mr. Roberts for just a little more hands-on time with the suit. The corpo hadn't acquiesced to his request until Saturn's rings had nearly entirely encompassed the cockpit's viewscreen. Even then, it had just been another test fitting and the final neural-sync to the crew's surgically implanted controllers at the nape of their necks.

Di experimentally commanded her suit's comms functions to activate with a passing thought. A dim, red recording light flickered in the reflection of her helmet as

Paragon's second babysitting function triggered, and the sporadically recording suit cam flared to life.

Temporary experimental neural command access has been granted for... Diane Eastwood. *To accurately and effectively perform your requested mental command, please remember to use specificity and —*

"Forget it," Di mumbled, pulling up the screen imbedded into the suit at her wrist and manually punching in the command for open comms. "Testing, testing. Do you read?"

"Loud and clear, boss," Hazel replied, her voice crystal clear in the internal speakers of Di's helmet. "Same as the last six times you asked," she muttered under her breath.

"Come again, Hazel?" Di asked tersely. Gene harrumphed beside her in his muted attempt at a laugh.

"Nothing, Captain. Nothing." Hazel waved at them through the cockpit window as their landing shuttle remained in a hold position beside Di's ship, the CS Katana.

The number of comments and jibes she had endured over the name of her ship had lessened over the years as her crew's reputation spread, taking on jobs that no one wanted or were too dangerous for most mercs. The more missions under their belts, the more the name seemed to fit. Even the sleek, narrow shape of the craft was reminiscent of the ancient battle weapon, warning off would-be attackers like the raised hood of a king cobra. Yes, the name fit the ship just fine. Besides, swords were badass. Everyone knew that.

"Alpha Team, comms check," Di said, switching over to

local short-wave comms.

"Read you," Gene replied, still holding a finger up to his ear despite the fact he had his helmet on and comms hadn't required physical contact in decades. He quickly recognized his mistake and sheepishly lowered his hand.

"You're good from here, Captain," Emma said, giving a wave from the pilot's chair.

"I... I can hear you," Gerald stammered. "Can you hear me? I mean... do you read? Copy? Ummm..."

"You're good, kid," Gene said, slapping him on the shoulder. "No need to be nervous."

"Easy for you to say," he mumbled, then blushed. "Is my mic still on?"

Di grinned and Gene chuckled. They shared a knowing look. It had been years since she had experienced more than simple pre-mission jitters, but the memories of near overwhelming panic were all too sharp in her mind. Even now, butterflies were steadily waking from their slumber in the pit of her stomach.

Something about this mission had raised her hackles the closer they had come to Enceladus, like a dog who sensed a coming storm. Following her instincts had never led her wrong before, and she once again hesitated for a reason she couldn't quite put her finger on.

It was more than just facing imminent danger. Those particular butterflies were exciting, invigorating. They filled her with purpose and heightened all her senses. But the butterflies that refused to go away, these soured her stomach. Distracted her. Made her hesitate, and hesitation got you killed.

"All set, Captain?" Emma asked, swiveling in her pilot's chair.

Di froze, the wrong butterflies surging. She almost called it all off then and there. Her questions, the ones she had fought with for months as they had made their way toward Saturn, rose again in her mind. Paragon's request, the facts of the case; something wasn't adding up. Who loses a crew of over one hundred and fifty experienced miners and scientists, the vast majority of which were well-versed in interplanetary survival? Either this was a case of deliberate sabotage by a rival corporation, possibly even the workers themselves, or something had happened to them. Something bad.

Part of her, a core part that had often led her into trouble, yearned to find the answer. The more sensible part of her brain was quietly sweating in the background, begging her conscience to see reason. Either way, her gut was telling her they wouldn't like what they found when they got to the surface.

"Captain?" Emma repeated, a questioning eyebrow raised.

"Di, you ok?" Gene asked quietly, placing a steadying hand on her shoulder.

Di blinked, breaking free from her introspection. "How many extra firearms are aboard this shuttle?" she asked Gene.

Gene's eyebrows furrowed, picking up on her apprehension. "Five rifles, fifteen extra mags. Same amount for sidearms. Everyone has their standard issue boot knife and pistol, plus I have Florence." He lovingly patted the butt of his prized semi-automatic rifle magnetically locked to the back of his suit. Even in the low light of the shuttle, it's slate-grey metal gleamed like a brand-new weapon despite its ancient history with the man, light scuffs a little too deep to buff out the only indicator of its well-worn usage.

"There should also be a few explosives available in the weapons locker. EMP blasts, flash charges, standard hand grenades." Ever the professional, Gene provided a professional report despite the blatant concern written on his face and the fact he had given the exact same report thirty minutes prior.

"Good," Di replied, resolve hardening. "I want everyone armed at all times. If I see you without a gun in your hand or strapped to your waist, I'm docking your pay. Understood?"

Everyone nodded, though Gerald had turned three shades whiter and was actively attempting to wipe the sweat from his brow through his helmet.

Gene brought her attention back to him, locking eyes and asking the unasked question; *You sure you want to do this?*

They had come too far to turn back now, at the precipice of what would be the most lucrative payout in decades. They had voted as a crew back when Paragon had first sent out the encrypted infoblast requesting mercenaries for an important, secretive task. Four to one in favor, abstaining her own vote. Though she was the captain and had final say, it was clear what her crew wanted. They needed to see her confidence; to know they could rely on her.

"Emma, take us down," she said, meeting Gene's eyes once more and nodding. He didn't look any less on edge, a hint of a question on the tip of his tongue, but he was professional enough to drop it publicly once her decision had been made.

"Aye, Captain. Setting course for provided coordinates. Estimated arrival in t-minus four minutes."

Di opened comms to Hazel and the wider team at large aboard the Katana. "Mission is a go. There will likely be interference once we've hit the atmosphere, but after we've touched down, we'll connect to the base's comms and hail you from there if we need to."

"Heard," Hazel responded. The Katana changed course, pointing toward the giant space station floating menacingly above the moon. "Have fun. Out."

Emma accelerated their landing shuttle, dipping the nose toward the white, crystalline surface. The faintly luminescent ball overtook their view completely.

"Steer well clear of those thermal vents on the southern pole," Di said, pointing toward the cloud of particulate blasting from the surface.

Those subsurface thermal vents had been the initial catalyst in man's search for life and sustainable environments in what were now the outer territories. It hadn't taken long to discover just how inhospitable Enceladus was for humankind, but that hadn't stopped those greedy enough to see dollar signs at the prospect of near limitless ice, especially at a time long before the water shortages. It had been a gamble, a long game, but it had paid off in spades. That is, until every single miner and scientist had gone inexplicably dark.

Emma dutifully pulled the yoke ever so slightly to the right. "Adjusted trajectory leaves us with an updated estimate of t-minus five minutes."

Di nodded, glancing once more at the clouds of water vapor roiling up and out of the atmosphere. Tiny speckles of refracted light sparkled in the wan, distant sunlight, adding to the already large clouds hovering at the far fringe of the moon's atmosphere. With gravity just $1/100^{th}$ that of Earth's, the icy water vapor coalesced like a perpetual fog bank covering the southern portion of the moon rather than a true snowfall. It was breathtakingly beautiful, though there was also something off-putting about it. Something alien.

The ring vents, as some had come to call them, were mainly responsible for one of Saturn's distinctive rings, part of the vapor and silica remaining trapped in the planet's orbit rather than replenishing Enceladus' atmosphere. Without that replenishment from the constant spew, the surface of the moon would be a pitted, unsightly thing, pockmarked with massive, man-made, mined-out pits. Yet despite the decades of abuse inflicted by Paragon before they had moved their operations below ground, it looked pristine all thanks to the limitless snowfall.

For all its beauty, looking at this celestial ball of ice sent a strange shiver down Di's spine. For something so natural, it gave off an unnatural aura.

"Entering atmosphere now," Emma called. "Switching to thermal readouts."

The view out the cockpit became hazy, as they dipped through the cloud cover this close to the southern pole. Anyone ballsy enough to try and land a vessel rather than using the massive elevator system connecting the surface to the space station relied almost solely on their instruments.

"How does it feel, Emma?" Di asked, hand claw shaped in a viselike grip on the back of the copilot's empty bucket seat.

"Not bad, honestly," Emma replied, glancing back. "I've trained in zero visibility situations before. At least I can sort of see if we're heading toward a mountain. Maybe not fast enough to stop us from crashing, but still."

"Eyes forward," Gene muttered. He shot an amused glance at Gerald who had just instinctively grabbed a motion sickness bag.

"Sorry," Emma said, blushing. "Honestly, it's practically on autopilot at this point. I'm just here in case that fails, which is like a one in sixty-five chance."

"Not helping," Gerald said, ineffectively holding the bag up to his helmeted face.

Di glanced his way, second-guessing her decision to bring the kid along. Yes, her own stomach was clenched as they flew nearly blind, but it was more in excitement than fear. Gerald, on the other hand, looked as though someone had poisoned his mess kit. Then spun him around two dozen times. Human skin was never meant to look that particular shade of green.

"Emma, ETA?" Di asked, brow creasing as Gerald hyperventilated.

"Actually, we're here," she replied.

On cue, the retro thrusters kicked on as the icy ground came rushing up to meet them. Hot jets of exhaust kicked up a roiling cloud of snow. Faint flickering lights encased in thick ice flashed around them signaling the designated landing pad, though it looked like it hadn't been maintained in some time. The shuttle lightly touched down accompanied by Gerald's audible exhale. The corner of Di's mouth twitched upward as she locked eyes with Gene who visibly suppressed a knowing smirk.

"Give me a moment to handshake with the landing system. It should trigger the automated clamps to keep us in place." Emma typed several commands into her screen, frowning. "Odd. It's registering our arrival, but I don't see the clamp engaging."

"Probably too much ice," Gene said, craning his neck to try and catch a glimpse of the landing pad beneath them.

"Makes sense," Emma replied. "I guess I'll have to manually tie us down then. Don't want the ship floating away on us." She gave a chittering, nervous laugh, glancing back at the three solemn faces behind her. "Sorry."

"Everyone, make a final comms and suit check before we open the doors," Di said, choosing to ignore the uncomfortable tension. As she stood and made her way to the hatch at the back of the shuttle, she once more attempted to issue a mental command, this time distinctly asking for a diagnostic rundown of the suit's systems. To her delight, a pleasant chime rang in her ear as the corner of her HUD began to fill with green checkmarks next to vital functions. As her suit finished processing, she manually felt for the pistol at her waist and the knife on her ankle. Green lights flashed signaling all systems go, and she glanced around at her team. "Everyone good?"

"Aye, Captain," Gene said, grabbing Florence from over his left shoulder and checking the magazine.

Gerald merely nodded, assumedly because he didn't trust opening his mouth. Though he was a few shades lighter, the green tint still flushing his cheeks indicated it wasn't just from motion sickness.

With Emma's thumbs up, Di nodded. "Good. Everyone, grab a rifle and an extra mag or two from the weapons locker. Keep your helmets on and be wary of your surroundings. Once we've left the artificial gravity field of the ship's interior, we're going to need to buckle into the safety line beside the ship."

To demonstrate, Di gripped the die-cast carabiner at her waist, pulling it out a short way and unraveling the tightly wound cord coiled beneath the outer layer of her suit. "I'll secure the ship to the landing pad, then we can follow the safety line to the surface shuttle bay. Once inside, artificial gravity should kick in again. Clear?"

All three returned her 'clear' and she gave them an encouraging smile. "Should be fun, yeah?"

Gene snorted, Emma returned her smile, and Gerald

continued to stare a hole through the floor between his boots.

Di pulled a rifle from the locker at the rear of the ship and slapped it across the magnetic holster on her back, the others following suit. When she was sure everyone had a firm grip on one of the safety handles and with a glance out the window at their hazy surroundings, Di waltzed to the rear of the shuttle and yanked on the hatch release lever.

As the audibly grindy gears chugged, lowering the walkway to the icy surface, a blast of bone-chilling air overwhelmed her. In all likelihood, it had been a mere fraction of a second between the air hitting her and the suit's internal thermals kicking on to deaden the effect. Yet that momentary exposure had felt like dunking her entire body in a tub of pure ice water, buck naked.

"That'll wake you up," Gene said over comms.

"'Advanced' suit my ass," Emma muttered, walking up behind Di while placing her loaded pistol in the holster on her belt. "What's wrong with kicking on *before* we're blasted in the face?"

"Eyes forward," Di said, bringing focus back to the task at hand. "Emma, hook into the safety line before taking out the cable. I'll try and find a decent anchor spot."

"Yes ma'am."

As Di took a hesitant step out onto the exposed walkway, the all too familiar feeling of weightlessness roiled in her stomach. She clutched desperately at the handrail on the side of the ship's opening, terrified of the sheer helplessness welling up inside her. It was only made worse by the complete lack of visibility brought on by the snowy fog around them. A red warning message flashed on the corner of her HUD informing her, most helpfully, that due to her elevated heart rate she was likely in distress. Yeah, no shit.

A heavy hand enveloped her own around the metal rail, and she looked back into Gene's calming emerald eyes.

"Let me take lead on this one, Captain," Gene said. Even through tinny speakers, his voice was calming.

"Thank you, Gene," she said, sure that her false sense of security had not fooled anyone. Di's heart rate slowed as Gene hooked his line on to the anchor spot and shoved out into the dense fog, cord unspooling behind him.

She had long since moved past embarrassment of her fears, having conquered many of them. And yet this one still clung to her, refusing to relinquish its hold on her heart. Of all the things for a spacefaring bounty hunter to be afraid of– lack of gravity. The universe was ironically cruel.

"Unhook me!" Gene called from somewhere close by. Di unlatched the carabiner, and it whisked silently away from the ship.

Di glanced back at Gerald who, credit to him, was now curiously gazing at the naturally occurring wonder around them. She could see his inquisitive, scientific mind whirring away, attempting to calculate how and why the snowfall behaved the way it did.

Gene suddenly loomed out of the bright white

surroundings, catching himself expertly on the handhold. "There's definitely a lot of ice buildup, but the line should be fine."

Di met his eyes, conveying her gratitude. "Thank you, Gene."

"'S nothing, Captain." He proffered a gloved hand, and she took it. "You ready?" he asked.

Di didn't trust opening her mouth at that particular moment, so she merely nodded.

"I won't let go," Gene said. And with that he pushed off, following his line through the haze and towing her along with him.

To her astonishment, a thick, metal bar quickly materialized in front of them, to which Gene guided her hand. He grabbed the carabiner at her waist and buckled her into the guide cable securely attached to the safety rail. Glancing back, she saw nothing but white. If she hadn't just come from the damn thing, she would have had no idea a ship sat a few meters away.

"I'll be right back," Gene said. "Just hang tight. Hold on to the cable here, and I'll be back with the others in a moment, but I'll keep my comms channel open."

As he disappeared yet again, her mind grappled with the surreal nature of her surroundings. She was alone, but for her own rhythmic breathing in her ear. Di fought to keep the panic down, choosing instead to focus on her breaths, matching her wavering inhale to her steady exhale.

"Here we come," Gene said in her ear, accompanied by a

dark shape looming toward her. Gerald unceremoniously bumped into the steel railing, shooting Di a nervous grin as Gene buckled his safety line in beside Di's. His mouth was moving, but no sound accompanied it. Di pointed to her mouth, then her ear, shaking her head to indicate she couldn't hear him. Gerald blushed, eyesight temporarily losing focus as he issued the mental command to open comms.

"Sorry," he said.

"You're new at this," Di responded. "It took me a few tries to get used to switching comms. What were you saying?"

"Oh! I was saying it's fascinating, isn't it?"

"What is?" she asked.

"The snow! It's like it's frozen in the air, but it only *looks* like it's not moving." Gerald held out his hand flat. "It's ever so slight, but there's just enough gravity here to pull it toward the surface. We may not feel it, but it's still there."

Di couldn't help but flash a self-satisfied grin. She knew Gerald would start enjoying himself once he had been distracted enough to forget his nerves. His face had a much healthier pink hue, and behind his eyes reflected the child-like wonderment and curiosity that had drawn her to him in the first place.

"We ready?" Emma asked on the public comms as she gracefully alighted next to Di, hooking in beside her.

"Depends on you," Di replied. "Is the ship secure?"

"Should be. I used a torch from the tool cabinet to melt some of the ice, just enough to snake the ship's cable through two of the bolts. It'll hold."

"If you're comfortable with it," Di said. "Alright everyone, stay close. It shouldn't take us too long to get to the surface outpost."

She started forward just behind Gerald with Gene in the lead position, pulling herself hand over hand along the thicker railing below the safety line.

"They expect *everyone* to make this trek when they come in?" Emma asked from the rear.

"Most people dock at the station and take the elevator down," Gerald chimed in. Gene paused a moment to clear a particularly thick encasing of ice so their lines could slide easier, and Gerald leaned out and away from the railing to catch a glimpse, his safety line snapping taut preventing him from drifting off. "And on the rare occasion they needed a freighter to come down with loads too big for the elevator, the base met them at the landing bay with a shuttle to take them all back."

"So that's what these big rails are for, right?" Emma asked. "The shuttles must run along them."

Gerald nodded enthusiastically. "I guarantee it beats pulling yourself along like we are."

"How do you know all this?" Emma asked, leaning out to catch his eye.

"It was in the report," he replied as though this were the most obvious answer, completely oblivious to the fact that he had been the only one, other than Di herself, to read the damn thing cover to cover.

"Keep moving," Di said, glancing up at Gene who had

finished clearing the ice and was waiting expectantly for the rest to follow.

She could feel her knuckles whitening with her death grip on the railing. Sure, she was plenty confident in the mechanisms of her safety line. But there was knowing, and then there was *knowing*. Who knew if there had been a flaw in this particular line that would snap in intensely cold temperatures, or the quality assurance inspector happened to glance away as it came down the conveyor? In her highly analytical mind, she wasn't willing to risk her life on something she "knew".

Gerald continued to jabber away on the public comm, going off on one of his many intellectual tangents. Facts and history about the mining operation, Paragon's assessment of the situation, the makes and models of the transports. Di would have been impressed if she wasn't so preoccupied with trying not to piss herself as her fingertips slipped.

A great, intimidating shadow suddenly loomed large as if appearing out of thin air. Gerald clamped his mouth shut as he caught sight of it, and everyone watched as the cargo bay slowly materialized through the snowy fog.

"Hold up, Gene," Di called over comms. "I'm going to try and hail the Katana."

Bringing up her wrist, she carefully removed her other hand from the comfortable safety of the railing to clumsily switch comms from local to long range.

"Katana? Katana, do you read?"

Her calls were met with nothing but empty static.

"Katana, if you read, please respond."

A faint break in the white noise gave her momentary hope, though it never materialized further than a blip in the signal.

"The snowfall in the atmosphere is causing too much interference," Gerald said, glancing up. "It's like a snowstorm, but nearly uniform and frozen in time. I doubt you're going to get much unless you have a really, really big booster."

"Di?" Gene asked, glancing back. "We good?"

Di clicked her tongue in frustration. She had anticipated it, but being cut off from half of her team didn't feel great. "Let's get inside and see if we can find a hardline to tap into."

Gene nodded, continuing forward toward the large bay doors that stood ajar. One shuttle lay forgotten near the entrance attached to the guide rail, and another was ratcheted down to what appeared to be a service lift.

"Why is it open?" Gerald asked. "Shouldn't this be closed?" No one responded, though it didn't bode well for whatever awaited them inside.

The group followed Gene inside the open bay as he kept one hand near the pistol at his waist, tugging himself along the line. They crossed a thick, visible metal line at the edge of the garage and Di felt her boot knife lean away from her ankle for a brief moment. Wrenches, drills, and other various machine shop tools were haphazardly attached to the line along the floor, up the wall, and even a couple on the ceiling.

"Watch your step," Gene said, keeping his eye trained on the closed sliding door just up the stairs in the back of the shop.

"And keep your firearm close."

"Fascinating," Gerald said, glancing all along the magnetic strip. "Ingenious, really. It keeps everything from floating out of the garage in the low gravity. Well, most things." He kicked at a large wrench with his boot, sending it spinning away toward the back wall.

"Focus, Gerald," Gene muttered as he drifted up the steps to the door.

"Right, sorry."

Di patted his shoulder and gave him an encouraging nod. She reluctantly detached herself and felt her pulse spike before quickly reattaching to the railing along the stairs.

An eerie feeling had settled over the group. They had been briefed on the situation, they had known that Paragon had lost contact with their crew, yes, but knowing and seeing were two very different things. Di had half expected to be greeted by rifles shoved in her face and demands to turn around and go. Hell, she would have *preferred* that. The stillness that stretched over them like a heavy blanket was oppressive and ominous.

Gene approached the door, glancing back and giving Di a nod. "Listen up. The artificial gravity generators may or may not still be on, and they may or may not be working correctly. Just in case, make sure you're upright as you cross the threshold." To emphasize his point, he pulled his body in close using the handle of the door and planted his feet.

"On your mark, Gene," Di said. She placed a hand firmly on the butt of the pistol at her waist, still maintaining her stranglehold on the handrail with her other. There was no telling what was waiting for them inside, but it was best to be prepared for violence when experience told her violence was the norm and not the outlier.

The door hissed as it gratingly slid partially open, releasing a barely visible puff of built-up pressure. A good sign that the basic functions were likely still working at least. Gene squeezed through out of sight.

Gerald moved to follow before Di placed a hand on his shoulder. "Wait a moment," she said. He glanced back and nodded, green tinge returning to his pale skin.

"We're clear," Gene called. "Come on in."

Di released a breath she hadn't realized she had been holding and patted Gerald's shoulder, giving him the go ahead to follow. They all unlatched from the railing and pulled themselves inside the doorway.

Lights flared on as Di entered, glancing at Gene who stood at the control panel beside the opposite door. It was a small utilitarian room with cubbies and lockers lining the edges for the mechanics to place their belongings while they went out to work.

"Close the outer door," Gene said pointedly to Emma who snappily obeyed. Small particles of ice crusted along the edges of the door and inside the trough where it was housed, but after a few brief seconds and several awkward, jerky movements in the near-zero gravity, the door snapped shut.

"Everyone ready?" Gene said, glancing around the room.

"Ready for what?" Gerald asked as he wobbled unsurely,

struggling to keep himself upright.

"Gravity in 3… 2… 1."

Gene flipped the large, manual switch on the inside of the panel. The overhead lights faded, flickering between dim and off as the walls buzzed with energy. In one swift motion, gravity returned, and Di's boots comfortably clunked back to solid ground. She couldn't help the sigh of contentment as her body weight blessedly returned to normal. Gerald flopped awkwardly, falling to one knee with arms flailing to catch himself.

"I hate the transition," Emma muttered from beside the outer door, shaking her head and putting a steadying hand on the handle. Gene grunted, rubbing his right knee with a carefully veiled grimace.

"Take a moment to reorient, but we don't want to take too long," Di said, unstrapping the rifle slung across her back and checking the slide and magazine. Her confidence had returned with the gravity, and she was eager to distance herself as far as possible from the outside. "If there *is* someone looking for a fight in there, we just let them know we're here."

Gerald stumbled to his feet, pulling his pistol from his belt holster and gripping it awkwardly in two hands. At least he was pointing it skyward this time. Emma also removed her pistol, checking the round in the chamber and nodding, then holding it up in a ready position close to her chest.

Di glanced toward Gene who was staring at her intently, waiting for the go-ahead. She gave him an encouraging nod.

Though she was nervous about Gerald's inexperience, prolonging the inevitable was only going to make his nerves worse, and with it the increasing likelihood of a preventable accident. Still, she took a moment to adjust his grip so he didn't accidentally shoot himself.

"Everyone, keep comms chatter to a minimum," she said, turning back to the group. "Only switch to public comms in an emergency. Otherwise, just use the hand signals."

Confirming with each member of the crew, she switched off her own comms and watched as they all followed suit. Eerie silence followed, with nothing but her heavy breathing reverberating in her ears. Her heartbeat quickened as Gene hit the button, and the door slid open.

Gene was first out the door, rifle up tight against his shoulder. He pointed it to either side of the darkened hallway before motioning the 'all clear'. Di gently nudged Gerald out, followed quickly by Emma, and Di took the rear, closing the door behind her.

Motion sensors triggered automatic emergency lights that flashed on along the top edges of the wall as they traversed the empty hallway. Not a single thing looked out of place, nearly as pristine as it must have looked the day after construction had completed. Spotless white walls occasionally broken up by sterile stainless-steel doorways. Two, three, four branching hallways, right-angle corners hiding what was bound to be identical immaculate hallways beyond.

It wasn't too dissimilar to the many corporate offices Di

had had the displeasure of touring on and off Earth. Soulless. Professional. Meant to keep people focused and avoid distractions. Even so, empty room after empty room left a steadily growing pit in her stomach. She hadn't known what to expect when arriving, but this was far, far down on her list of possibilities. A group of grizzled miners barricading themselves in? Sure. A station overrun by pirates? Understandable. But an empty ghost town, not a single soul, alive or dead? It sent chills rolling down her spine.

Ahead, Gene paused holding up a closed fist. Gerald nearly bowled into him before stopping himself, stifling a muted gasp. Gene glared over his shoulder and shook his fist again, emphasizing his command to stop. Gerald hunched his shoulders and craned his head abashedly back at the rest of the group, holding up a hand and mouthing, 'I'm sorry.'

Di peered around their bodies through an open doorway with flashing lights lazily blinking in the room beyond. Gene held up a single finger pointing forward, then a flat hand, palm down in a circular motion, followed by another closed fist.

I'll check it out, everyone else remain where they are and watch the entryway until I give the signal to follow.

Gene readied his rifle and cautiously moved toward the doorway. Before Gerald could move after him, Di gripped his shoulder and pulled him back, shaking her head as he glanced worriedly back at her. As smart as the kid was, he was a tactical moron.

Di held her breath, feeling the tension oozing off of Emma

and Gerald as they all waited for Gene's signal. Seconds ticked by, the suspense stretching longer and longer. This was nothing new to her, waiting on bated breath for an 'all clear' signal. Yet all it took was one time, one wrong step, and that 'all clear' would be replaced by shrieking sounds of death.

A memory flashed briefly in Di's mind, taking her back to a time before mercenary work, before her crew and her ship. One wrong step. One mistake. A missing signal, a hurled friendly insult. That was all it took for hell to break loose. It was deathly quiet then, too. She lost sixteen people that night. Likely would have been lying in a ditch herself if not for Gene's quick thinking and fast hands.

A single bead of sweat rolled down her forehead, sliding along the creases of her furrowed brow and catching in her eyebrow, momentarily hitching in the outer corner of her eye before continuing down her cheek. She moved to wipe it away, forgetting her helmet and bumping her hand into the clear visor. Di blinked rapidly, her HUD flashing another warning sign at the sudden spike in her heart rate, reflected by her quick, shallow breaths.

"We're clear," Gene's deep bass voice rumbled on the comms. He appeared in the doorway, gun pointed harmlessly at the floor. They locked eyes for a moment, Gene's brow creasing in concern. Di's private comms crackled. "You good?" he asked, lips barely moving.

"Just need a moment," she replied, stepping past him and into the room beyond.

Her HUD showed her BPM at 187, and she sucked in a deep breath through her nose. Therapy sessions came reflexively to her mind, a measure forced on her by desk jockey superiors who had no idea what actual combat looked like. Even so, these exercises had proven useful throughout the years. A gleaming desktop beckoned to her, and she marched up to it, placing her hands firmly on top next to a stack of instruction manuals. Closing her eyes, she counted one, two, three, four, five seconds in, five seconds out. After four rounds of breaths she opened her eyes, feeling her heart steadying in her chest. Her heart rate on her HUD flashed gradually from red, yellow, and finally to a light green.

It was only when she had brought her body under control that she took the time to observe their surroundings. A wide, seamless bay window opened out to the dim grey-white haze of the surface, taking up the entirety of the far wall. Nearly a dozen computer stations dotted the moderately sized room, screens black and lifeless. Just like the rest of the facility, there wasn't a single item out of place.

Di switched to group comms. "Circle on me," she said, spinning around to address her team.

Gene shot her a questioning look, one eyebrow raised, to which she merely nodded. While panic episodes like this were rare, this was not her first rodeo. Gene had learned long ago when to administer help, desired or not, and when to leave well enough alone. This was clearly the latter.

"Gene, what's your analysis?"

"No hostiles in the immediate vicinity," he said, clicking on Florence's safety and re-holstering it on his back. "No obvious signs of struggle. No indication they left in a hurry. Hell, there's barely an indication anyone has been here at all."

Di nodded. "Anyone else have anything to add?" she asked. Gerald raised a hesitant hand, and she nodded toward him.

"Since the shuttle was still on the track in the garage, I doubt they left that way," Gerald said, shrugging noncommittally.

"Good," Di said, nodding.

"Could they be sheltering below?" Emma asked. "Or taken the lift up to the orbital station?"

"We can test both theories," Di said, turning to Gerald. "The easiest would be to hook into the station's tethered comms and contact Bravo Team to see what it looks like up above. Gerald, can you check on that?"

"Yes, Captain," he said, moving to the nearest station. After a brief scramble, Gerald fell comfortably into his element. The screen flared brightly, and he began fiddling with the keyboard.

"While you're in there, can you check on the station's necessary systems? Oxygen, gravity, heat. I don't want to be taken by surprise if we find ourselves in a tense situation only to have it made worse."

"Of course. Once I've re-established connection with the station and got comms online, I'll do a diagnostic check."

"Thank you," Di said. "Gene, Emma. While he's working on that, I want you to search for any weapons lockers. If they're full or empty, I want to know."

"Yes, ma'am," Emma said. Gene merely nodded and moved toward the door.

"Don't go farther than two rooms. I don't want us to split up more than necessary."

Gene unholstered his pistol and gave her another nod. *I've done this a thousand times, Di,* he seemed to insinuate with that simple movement. "Emma, on me. Take out your gun."

Emma unholstered her pistol and instinctively checked the magazine and the slide before following Gene out the door.

"How are we doing on those comms?" Di asked, turning back to Gerald.

"I've got connection to the ship, but I can't seem to wirelessly bridge the gap between our suits and the station." He turned back and grimaced. "You're going to have to manually connect."

Di scoffed and patted his shoulder. "You say that like it's so horrible."

Gerald's eyes widened. "Are you kidding me? *Physically* connecting to something?"

"Honestly?" Di asked. "I'll bet some of this equipment is at least a hundred years old, technologically speaking. You think a corpo is going to risk bleeding-edge tech on an outpost this far out?"

"Fair." Gerald turned back to the desk. "The port is on the

wall over there," he said, pointing toward a box attached to cables that ran up into the ceiling.

Di walked over and flipped open the lid, revealing a small circular port. "And what am I supposed to do with this?" she asked.

"These suits have physical comm capability," Gerald said matter-of-factly. "Just issue the mental command, '*access communication cable, connector J-6.3*'"

Di turned to the small screen on her wrist that flared to life as she brought it up to her face, not even bothering with the mental command. In just a few short seconds she had found the command to produce the appropriate cable, at which point a small plug protruded from one of the ports at her waist. She pulled on it, revealing a coil of cable with plenty of length to connect to the socket on the wall. As she plugged it in, a staticky burst assaulted her ears before the line went silent once more.

"No signal," she said, turning her neck and glancing back at her man-in-the-chair.

"You have to input the code to where you want to dial in. Give me a second, I'll look up the station's code list."

Di glanced down at her wrist computer which now displayed an old-fashioned number pad.

"Ok, try this," he called out. "Zero-six-seven-six-three."

Di punched in the code and heard a click, followed by light, rhythmic buzzes. She waited, anxiety rising as the call continued unabated, her mind racing through scenarios. She had told them to find a comms station first thing; she was sure of it.

They likely wouldn't have taken as long as the surface team had to reach it unless something had gone wrong. If the station was inoperable, systems malfunctioning, they likely would have attempted to recover the comms anyway to send word to her down below.

Di glanced out the window, straining to see past the snowy haze. This far out, sunlight struggled to illuminate their icy sphere. It was a land of perpetual twilight. Coupled with Enceladus' impenetrable weather, she could barely see up past the first few meters of the interplanetary elevator outside the window. Forget about all the way up to the orbital station.

"Damn it," she muttered. "Damn it, pick up." She shot Gerald a questioning look. "The line isn't getting through."

"That may be the wrong code," he said, squinting at the screen. "Try this—"

"What do you mean the wrong code?" Di interjected. She forcefully yanked the cord out of the port and re-socketed it.

"They don't really have these things effectively labeled in their system. There's, like, sixty-four different codes labeled 'Station-1,' 'Station-2.'"

"Well, did you check for a map or a key?" she replied testily, straining to keep the anger out of her voice.

"Of course I ran a search," he said, snapping back. "Like you said, we're not exactly working with top-of-the-line tech, here." Keyboard keys clacked as Gerald furrowed his brow, moving to push his glasses back up his nose before realizing he still had his helmet on. He sighed and rolled his eyes, focusing back on the task at hand.

"Ok, I think I have something," he replied, eyes fluttering rapidly as he read some of the text on the screen. "Yes, try this one. Zero-six-nine-four-nine."

Di punched it in and waited as the buzzing began anew. Within three buzzes the line clicked, hissing with a familiar voice on the other end.

"Captain?" Lucas asked. "Is that you?"

"Midnight oil burns brightest," Di said, parroting her side of the 'all clear' pass phrase.

"What?" Lucas asked.

"Midnight oil burns brightest," she repeated through gritted teeth.

"Midnight… Oh! Right."

Sounds of shuffling and muted whispers came through the receiver and Di rolled her eyes.

"Ocean waters hide secrets," Lucas finally said, to which Di released a pent-up breath. "Sorry, Captain."

"What's your assessment of the station?" she asked, choosing for the moment to ignore his flippant ignorance of protocol.

"It seems pretty nice, from what I can tell. Lots of old tech—"

"Lucas, put Gayle on," Di interrupted as Gene and Emma waltzed back in the room carrying a single, handheld device. "That's all?" she asked, nodding to what looked like a miniaturized jackhammer.

Gene shook his head. "We found several weapons lockers, but they were all cleared out. No ammo, no guns. Just this one mining tool."

Gerald glanced up, a look of excitement on his face at the prospect of a new toy. "Can I see it?" he asked. Gene shrugged and handed it to him.

Gerald leaned close, flipping the device in his hand. "I believe this is a portable plasma cutter, used to cut the ice into more manageable chunks. Very hot, very dangerous."

"What's the distance on it?" Gene asked, interest piqued much more now that he saw a potential new weapon.

"Probably not that far. Maybe a foot or two." Gerald grinned, adopting a far-off look. "Think Star Wars."

Gene gave him a flat stare before rolling his eyes.

"Hello?" Gayle's voice came back clear from the other end.

Di silenced the room with a raised finger, turning her attention back to the call. "Gayle, give me a sit rep," she said.

"No signs of resistance or struggle. Station looks completely deserted. No bodies either, though we've barely cleared this section. Still quite a bit of ground to go, and more than a few locked down areas to figure out how to open."

"We're looking at the same down here, but we're still on the surface. Gerald is working on getting the station off of supplemental emergency power to get the elevator working so we can check below."

"Are your normal comms working?" Gayle asked. "We couldn't hail you earlier."

"We're hooked into the physical line," Di replied. "I think the weather is giving off too much interference which we somewhat expected. It's like the densest fog I've ever seen, but it's snow."

"It's only going to get worse when we've got ten kilometers of ice between us," Gerald said, focus locked on the screen in front of him.

"Gerald said it's going to get worse once we go below, but there's bound to be comms ports down there." Di turned back to Gerald. "Do you still have this code?" she asked.

"Zero-six-nine-four-nine," he replied.

"Good. Our first priority once we're down there is to secure our position and find the nearest comms port. Can you find a map of some kind? Make our job a little easier?"

"One second," Gerald said, leaning closer to the computer monitor, the faint glow casting shadows that accentuated his glasses and slender nose. "I've been running a trace on security backups to find out what's been going on and I think I found something. Looks like conduct logs or some other entry from the workers posted up here. I—"

Speakers blared deafeningly overhead with a garbled, unidentifiable mess of conflicting sounds, a hellish mixture of static, reverberating interference, and what might have once been human voices.

"Turn it down, Gerald!" Emma yelled, barely audible over the cacophony.

"Captain, what is that?" Gayle screamed on the line.

"It isn't responding!" Gerald shouted, furiously typing.

"Well, if there *was* anyone around, they know we're here now," Gene shouted, wincing.

The sound abruptly lowered, Di's ears still ringing. Even though her suit had dampened the sound, the sheer volume and tenor of the strange noise had been overwhelming.

"Sorry, everyone," Gerald said, cheeks blushing. The muddled noise continued, though at a much more tolerable level. "I don't know what happened. I just opened a folder, and the system booted into a data dump or something. I think it played the first file in there."

"Is it a recording?" Di asked.

"A recording of what, a beached whale crushing an out of tune orchestra?" Emma said a little too loudly, hands on her helmet and eyes squeezed shut.

"It does look like the audio file was sped up somehow. It's dated…" Gerald paused, clicking a few keys. "Just over three weeks ago."

"Three weeks ago?" Emma asked, squinted eyes peeking open. "Wasn't that when—"

"When the outpost went dark," Gene interjected. He shot Di a knowing look.

"Gayle?" Di said finally returning her attention to the call. "We're fine, but you're going to have to hold on a second." Gayle's background jabbering stopped, and Di turned back to Gerald. "Can you slow it down?"

"I think so. Just give me… one… more…"

The audio above abruptly changed, no longer spewing unrecognizable, ear-splitting noise.

"There," Gerald said. "Not like it made a whole lot of difference. I still can't tell what's—"

Garbled voices echoed in the background, the shouts too faint to make out any intelligible words. But that wasn't what any of their attention was focused on anyway.

Di's blood ran cold, shivers running down her spine and goosebumps rippling along her arms. No, the distant voices were second fiddle to the ear-splitting, throat-rending screams that reverberated around the room.

CHAPTER 3
DECISIONS

"GET BACK! GET BACK!"

"SOMEONE CALL ORBIT!"

"LOCK IT DOWN! DON'T LET THEM—"

The recording abruptly ended, followed by the stunned silence of all in the room subjected to its disturbing message. The hum of the comm line sizzled next to Di's ear, its trance-like electronic static accompanied by Gayle's breathing.

"Was that screaming?" Gayle finally asked, shaking Di out of her reverie.

"Gerald found a station recording," she replied. "It... doesn't sound good."

"Heard," Gayle said, her immediate shift to a militaristic tone giving her response a no-nonsense edge. "Exfil imminent?"

"Negative. Once we get the elevator up and running, we'll head below to look for survivors. Or, at the very least, sufficient evidence for Paragon to know their outpost is scrapped."

"We're going *looking* for whoever that was?" Gerald asked, giving Di an incredulous look.

Di took a steady breath. It was moments like this where a captain either lost or earned the respect of their crew. The obvious, sane response was to get the hell out of dodge, but they were not known for taking the obvious, sane approach. It was why she had been hired on countless missions. The crew of the Katana were willing to go where no one dared go, do what no one had the courage to do. They had known, *Di* had known when she took this job that it wouldn't be easy, yet each and every member had been willing to blast off to the ass-end of nowhere to follow her.

Di's superior motivation and ultimate objective was the safety of her crew, orders be damned. Next in line, however, was the mission. A mercenary crew who couldn't finish what they were hired to do was not worth hiring, and though Paragon was universally despised by virtually every man, woman, and child, they unfortunately held sway. One word from the corporation that owned half of everything, from drinking water to ball bearings, lubricant to instant meals, and they could kiss their lucrative careers goodbye. They would inevitably drift apart, some crew members joining other freighter crews, some taking positions as personal guards for the wealthy elite. And herself? She had no idea where she would end up.

Stuck between a rock and a hard place, as the old saying went.

"This is not a dictatorship," Di said, keeping the comm up so that Gayle could listen in. "I've said it before, and I'll say it again; a crew is a family, and we don't make major decisions solo."

Di locked eyes with all those in attendance. Gene, Emma, Gerald. Admiration, anxiety, courage, and a whole mess of fear in Gerald's case, reflected back. She knew what answer they would give before she even uttered her next words, despite Gerald's initial hesitation.

"If we go down there, I'm betting there's a high chance we're going to have to shoot our way back out," Di continued. She thought of the empty weapons lockers and that chilling final recording and shivered involuntarily again.

"That's option one. We can also head back to the shuttle and get the hell away from this frozen rock. You all already know the consequences of that choice, but I don't want someone at my back who is second guessing themselves."

Though she remained silent, Di could hear Gayle's snort of affirmation. That was nothing new. Gayle was first into the fray, and Di could tell it was killing her not to be down on the surface where the action was assuredly about to kick off.

"You know my answer, Captain," Gene chimed in. Always reliable, always loyal. It was no surprise he was first to voice his affirmation.

"We need something to send back to Paragon," Emma said. "I don't see the harm in at least taking a quick peek." She flashed a nervous smile that wasn't reflected in her eyes.

"Gerald?" Di asked, turning back. His face was bathed in the reflected computer screen's harsh glow, bright white light not at all helping his pallid complexion.

"What if I can pull information off their system from here?" he asked. Even before posing the question, his shoulders were slumped in defeat. He had known before even voicing it that Paragon wasn't going to accept a spreadsheet. Video proof. It was edict number one on their exaggeratedly long list of requirements.

"I think that's a fantastic backup plan," Di responded, placing her call with Gayle on mute and taking several steps forward to place a gentle hand on Gerald's shoulder. "But I think we both know what Paragon's response would be."

Gerald nodded, audibly gulping. "It's not enough. I know."

Di knelt, bringing herself down to eye level with Gerald who hesitantly met her gaze. "This isn't your realm of expertise, I know that," Di said, words chosen calmly and carefully. "We all know that. We were all in your position at one time or another, so you can believe me when I tell you that we all understand. I understand. And no one will hold it against you if you choose not to join us below."

Gerald raised hopeful eyes to glance at Gene and Emma, but Di grabbed his helmeted head and brought his focus back to her.

"I'm not going to lie and say we don't need you down there, because we might. But the safety of this crew is my top priority, and if you can't guarantee me your one hundred percent when the shit hits the fan, I need you to tell me now."

Gerald sucked in a deep breath, eyelids fluttering, and

nodded several times. "I understand Captain. You can count on me."

Di's chest swelled with pride. Though she had never been a mother, she imagined this was what it felt like to have a child make a difficult decision despite fear or hesitation. Her bravado had nearly waivered for a moment, not entirely sure which way Gerald would go. As it turned out, she had been right about him all along.

"Thank you, Gerald," Di said, standing and roughly patting his shoulder. Gene gave him a stern nod and Emma an encouraging smile.

"I'll get to work on the elevator," he said, turning back to the console. It may have been her imagination, but Di thought she heard a newly hardened sense of purpose behind those words.

Di unmuted herself, switching the call to public comms so everyone could hear more than just her one-sided conversation. "Gayle, let Bravo Team know we are heading below to check on the status of the crew and to locate potential survivors. Gerald is going to send you the recording we found after he gets the elevator working. I want you to transfer that to the Katana's systems as part of our Paragon file. They'll want to hear what's on it."

"Yes, Captain," Gayle said. "And our primary objective up here? Still the same?"

"Yes. Search for survivors, but be careful. This recording is… disturbing." Di shuddered. Those screams. "We have no idea who or what attacked the crew, and we don't know if it made it up to the station."

"We'll keep watch for anything strange." Gayle lowered her voice to a barely audible whisper. "What about company boy?"

"What about him?" Di asked.

"Well, he's acting as though he's in command up here, diverting attention away from securing the area and searching for survivors. Seems more occupied with trying to find and collect some sort of research data."

"I thought this was a mining operation?" Di asked sarcastically, glancing back at her crew who were attentively listening. They all knew Paragon was hiding something, had known it from the jump. No corpo would go to these lengths just for employees. Human lives were expendable to them, nothing more than a dash of red on a ledger.

"That's what the brief indicated," Gayle said diplomatically. Di suspected Mr. Roberts was still within earshot. Gayle continued, dropping her voice even lower. "Something isn't adding up, though. I don't like it when we're not given all the details, especially if it affects our decision making."

"Neither do I," Di responded. "We're going to head down below, peek around a bit, and come back up. I don't plan on moving farther underground than necessary."

"Glad to hear it, Captain," Gayle said.

"If *Mr. Roberts*," Di sneered, "has any further off-target requests, kindly remind him we go by the mission brief.

Survivors first, any non-mission-critical objectives second."

"Just so I'm clear, do I have authority to…" Gayle paused, and Di could tell she was mulling over her words carefully. "Supersede certain corporate ambassadors should he put up resistance?"

Di smirked. "Yes, Gayle. You are the most senior member on Bravo Team. I give you full authority to 'supersede' as you see fit."

"Thank you, Captain. Out."

Di could hear the ear-to-ear grin, and it temporarily lifted her spirits as she disconnected the call, despite their dire circumstances.

Though she chose to put on a brave face, something she was well practiced in doing, the audio recording had been more disturbing to her than she cared to admit out loud. That visceral fear was not a response to raiders, not for a group of grizzled, veteran miners. No, this was something else entirely, and one thing Di hated when on assignment was an unknown variable. It was nearly impossible to plan for an unknown variable.

"Gerald, any E.T.A. on that elevator?" she asked, turning and beckoning Gene with a quick jerk of her head.

"Maybe. There's something preventing me from hailing it, but I think I'm close."

"Good, keep working on that."

Di grabbed Gene's elbow as he approached and towed him a short distance away, opening up a private comms channel. "I don't like this, Gene."

"It doesn't look great. But you know as well as I do, we can't show up empty-handed with nothing but a half-fried recording."

"I know," Di replied, nodding her head. "I know. I just needed to hear you say that." She raised a half-cocked eyebrow. "Would you be doing the same thing? In my position?"

Di had often wondered why Gene had not taken a captaincy after the war. He had damn sure been offered more than his fair share, well before Di herself had leased the Katana and gathered her group of misfits. She had long suspected it had something to do with the accident that had brought him back into her life some fifteen years ago, but it was an unspoken truce that she didn't ask for what he didn't want to share.

"We would've been gone hours ago," Gene mumbled, letting a sly grin loose. "Hell, I wouldn't have taken the job in the first place. Can't trust corpos."

Di shoved him playfully and he raised his hands in mock surrender. She had learned to cherish his playful moments, that spark that reminded her of who he had once been. They were few and far between in recent years, not like it had been when they'd first met in military basic training back on Earth. The younger Gene had been more than a touch arrogant and had lacked a single serious bone in his body; a stark contrast to the no-nonsense, stern, somber man the rest of the crew knew. Part of her was saddened they had never known him the way she had, flaws and all.

"Captain, we have a problem," Gerald called out.

Di's attention snapped back to the present and she rushed to Gerald's side, hand instinctively moving to the butt of her pistol riding in the holster at her hip. "The elevator?" she asked.

"Yes," Gerald responded. "It looks like it's about one hundred meters down the shaft, but it's stalled out. There must be a manual brake engaged on the car. I can see where it is in the system, but I can't get it to move." He sighed heavily and glanced up over his shoulder. "If we don't want to manually climb ten kilometers down, someone is going to have to get down there and unstick whatever is… stuck."

"I've got this," Gene said, already moving to unsling Florence from his back.

"Stop, Gene," Di commanded. "You really think we can belay your weight down a hundred meters?"

"You don't need to belay me a hundred meters. Artificial gravity should dissipate pretty quickly the further down I get."

"And if you can't get the elevator going? You gonna just climb up the walls?" Di shook her head. "I'm going."

"I'm lighter than you are," Emma chimed in, cheeks rapidly flushing at her unintended insult. "Captain, sir."

"I'd rather you stay out of harm's way as much as possible. I can fly, but not like you, and I'm not comfortable with our chances without you at the helm given all this damn snow hanging in the air."

Emma nodded, looking mildly relieved. Di glanced at Gerald and raised an inquisitive eyebrow. "What, no offer?" she asked.

Gerald flushed and shot her a forced grin. "I should probably stay by the computer in case something goes wrong with the elevator after you release it. Besides, if we're mostly considering the weight, I weigh more than you do."

"Not by much," Gene muttered, shooting Gerald a wink.

"You didn't happen to find any climbing cord when you were looking for weapons, did you?" Di asked.

Gene shook his head. "Negative, Captain. We'll have to use our EIAPSL safety lines." He typed a quick command into the computer at his wrist and a thin port opened at his waist. The small length of thin steel cord attached to a carabiner protruded from it and he began pulling, looping it loosely around his hand. "We each should have around thirty meters which should be enough to get you down there safely."

Di and Emma followed Gene's example, punching the command into their wrists and pulling out their cords. Gerald had already pulled nearly half his line out having issued a mental command before Gene had even finished speaking.

"Anyone here a Space Explorer?" Emma asked, reaching the end of her cord and disconnecting it from her waist. "I was never great with knots."

"I got a few badges, but it was never my thing," Gerald chimed in.

Gene finished with his own and held out his hand for Emma's cord, which she gratefully provided. "Di, disconnect yours and wrap one end around your waist. We can use the clip to secure it a little better after the knot."

Though initial instinct was to let herself dangle from the fully connected cord at waist level, she understood Gene's instruction. These safety lines were not meant for prolonged stress in a gravitational environment. Though it was likely strong enough to hold her if she were to dangle directly from the suit's port, it wouldn't last forever. Better safe than sorry.

Di reached the end of her length of wire with a hearty tug, then disconnected it and did as Gene asked, wrapping it twice around her waist before cinching it tight in a simple knot.

Gene glanced at her, raising an eyebrow. "You sure you want to do it that way?" he asked.

"What's wrong with the way I tied it off?" she asked incredulously.

"Nothing, if you want to cut yourself in half."

"Quit being a smart-ass and tell me how to fix it," Di replied.

Gene had never and *would* never openly disrespect her in front of the crew, nor would he directly contradict something she did in her capacity as captain. He did, however, believe in offering sarcasm when it was warranted; a backhanded way of letting her know she was free to do what she was intending, but that it was a stupid decision and would likely get her and/or everyone else brutally maimed or killed.

"Can you tie a bowline knot?" he asked, laying the other three loops of steel cable on the table beside Gerald and meandering over to stand beside her.

"Yes, Gene. Which is why I tied it *this* way instead."

Di was just as adept with sarcasm, especially when sparring words with Gene. A sly grin tugged at the corners of his mouth as he took the carabiner in one hand and a decent length in the other, making a loop and threading the clasp through in a series of complicated patterns until a tight knot formed. She was well aware the bow-whatever knot was not very complex, but knots had never been her strong suit. A knot was a knot. If it held, it was good. If it didn't, hopefully whatever she was tying up wasn't very important.

"Thank you," Di said, shooting him a patronizing grin.

"Of course, Captain," he said, holding the knot out to her. They shared a look; the same look they had given each other thousands of times over. Like a silent joke of which only they knew the punchline. "Take this knot in your left hand. You'll use your right hand to steady yourself against the wall of the shaft."

"Right," she replied, quickly shifting away from their friendly back-and-forth ribbing to her formal, in-command self. Grabbing the knot firmly in her left hand, she moved toward the still-sealed elevator shaft. "Gerald, how's the artificial gravity in the elevator shaft?"

"The shaft itself shouldn't have any gravity, but you will still likely feel the station's effects for some distance."

"Some distance?" she asked. "Any solid estimate you can give me?"

"I'd say you should feel less of the pull a few dozen meters down. It'll be a gradual loss."

"Thank you, Gerald." Di sucked in a deep breath,

releasing it shakily.

"This is not going to be very comfortable, even with the added layers of your suit," Gene warned, grabbing the other end of her cord and using a different knot to secure it to the other three end to end. "At least at first. Having lesser gravity as you travel down will help at least."

"Understood," Di said. Thoughts and fears flashed across her mind as they often did right before engaging in a stressful situation. Particularly anything that involved minimal gravity.

It's fine. This is fine, she thought to herself, pushing her negative thoughts away and focusing on maintaining her breathing. *It's an elevator shaft, an enclosed space. It's not like I can just float away into the nothingness of space in there.*

"You ready, Captain?" Gene asked, looping the cable once around a vertical support beam close to the elevator doors.

Di paused, taking a moment to close her eyes. She took one deep, long inhale, held it for a count of five, and released it feeling a portion of her anxiety leak away with the exhaled carbon dioxide. "Ready."

"Gerald, can you open the doors to the shaft please?" Gene asked. "Emma, take position behind me as a safety for the belay."

Both crew members jumped into action, Gerald clicking a few keys and Emma grabbing hold of the cable behind Gene. It was a comforting thought to know her second-in-command could be first-in-command should anything happen. The crew listened to him just as much as they listened to her, if not more so considering his intimidating, prickly personality and gruff exterior.

After another long calming breath, the thick steel doors slid noiselessly open behind her. Di couldn't help but lean over to look down into the black nothingness that awaited her, the gaping maw of the unknown opening wide to swallow her whole. Just like the rest of the facility, it was unremarkably bland and unadorned with no distinguishing features. It was surprisingly clean for an area reserved only for the eyes of maintenance workers. The shaft itself was significantly wider than she had expected, at least a few meters to the other side.

For a brief moment, she had the desire to reach out and see if she could touch the wall opposite the opening and felt the vertigo kick in, her startle reflex jolting her off balance.

"Hold on, not yet!" Gene shouted, noticing Di tipping precariously over the edge. Steel cord wrapped twice around his hands in an instant, his legs bent and braced to keep her from falling.

Di spread her arms out wide, angling them back. Her fingers brushed the frame of the elevator door, and she gripped it like the lifeline it was, her body swinging wildly to the left. Face and chest slammed painfully into the inside wall of the shaft, the tips of her left fingers and the toes of her left boot holding on for dear life.

"I've got the line, go pull her in!" Gene shouted from inside the room.

Di felt the line at her waist grow taut. A rush of footsteps and a helping hand snaked around the opening, latching on to her waist. In a moment of pure faith in her team, Di let go and swung her body toward the doorway. Momentum from her awkward leap, Gene pulling on the safety line, and Emma's guiding arm sent her collapsing in a heap on top of Emma inside the control room.

"What happened?" Gene said, straining to keep his voice calm as he straightened from his half-collapsed crouch.

Di rolled off Emma. Her heart rate warning flashed in the corner of her HUD, the spike of adrenaline still pumping through her veins sending the number skyrocketing. For the second time in as many hours, she had to rely on her breathing techniques, closing her eyes and taking deep, steady breaths.

"I lost my damn balance," she finally said with a heavy exhale. Eyelids fluttering, she saw her heart rate gradually dropping and accepted Gene's outstretched hand as he pulled her to her feet.

"I know you're excited and all, but you should wait for us before diving in headfirst," Gene growled, bringing his annoyance in check.

"Noted," she said, wincing and offering an embarrassed, apologetic smile.

"At least we know the knots will hold, right?" Gerald said from his chair, glancing unsurely over his shoulder and flashing her a quick awkward grin.

"Sorry Emma. You ok?" Di asked.

"I'm totally fine, Captain," Emma replied. "Like you said, you're the lightest one here."

It wasn't often that Di was made the fool, and she was appreciative of her crew's willingness to make light of a dumb mistake rather than turning an awkward blind eye, afraid to upset their superior. It was truly how a family would respond to her idiocy. At least, that's how she imagined a family would act. Hers hadn't exactly been all that normal.

"Round two?" Di asked, taking the cord back in her left hand and warily approaching the open doorway to the yawning blackness below.

"Yes, Captain," Gene said, readjusting the cord around the pillar and taking it in both hands. "Remember, look for sure footing before taking each step. Go slow."

Any remaining moisture in her mouth quickly evaporated as she turned her back to the yawning, midnight-black chasm. Her legs shook as she bent her knees, heels hanging out in open space. The bare environment of the command room increased her anxiety, giving her nothing in the space to attract her attention, nothing to focus on to distract herself.

It was now or never, and she was afraid her knees might give out if she waited any longer. With a brief nod to Gene, Di slipped cautiously over the edge.

"I'll be with you the whole time over comms," Gene said in her ear as she dipped below the lip of the floor and out of sight of the others.

Moving one foot behind the other, she leaned heavily against the taut safety line, its hard steel biting through her suit at her waist. No doubt her clenched knuckles were white beneath the fabric of her gloves as she clutched desperately to the one thing keeping her anxiety at bay.

I wish I could see a little more than just this wall, she thought.

With that wordless mental command she hadn't conscientiously intended to make, her helmet's headlamps flashed to life revealing the plain metal wall with plain metal support beams before her face. Turning her head, she saw the thick steel ropes of intertwined cables leading down into darkness, the elevator car somewhere below her. Step after step led her down further into the fathomless beyond.

"Talk to me," Gene said. "Tell me what you're seeing."

"It's an elevator shaft, Gene," Di replied. "I see walls and cables."

"Copy," he replied, choosing to ignore her nervous retort. "Any loss in gravity yet? You should be a few meters down now, so the gravitational effect should be lessening."

"I think so? I still feel a pull, but it isn't as strong."

"Great," Gene said. "Try pushing off the wall a little bit to gauge it."

"Copy." Di bent her knees a bit more and lightly pushed herself away from the wall. She felt a brief moment of weightlessness before swinging back toward the wall, bracing for the light impact against the soles of her boots.

"How was that?" Gene asked.

"Still pretty normal," Di replied.

"I need you to go down a few meters at a time and push off the wall. Once you feel like you're at a little below half of normal gravity, stop."

Wordlessly, Di continued to gradually descend, pausing to push off the wall every fifteen steps. Counting off each step between jumps pulled her mind away from the unbidden images of phantom 'what-ifs' that attempted to flood her mind, conjuring dangers just beyond the light of her headlamp.

Thirteen. Fourteen. Fifteen.

Knees bending, Di pushed off yet again, pausing much longer at the apex of her swing before coming back gently to the wall.

"I think I'm close," she said.

"What's your estimate for the percentage of gravity?" Gene asked.

"Good hell Gene. Forty percent? Thirty-five?"

There was a long pause while Di hung motionless, feet firmly planted. Glancing around, she took a moment to look for signs of distress, indications that the elevator stall may have been an involuntary mechanical failure rather than someone physically pulling a manual brake. If there was damage to the track or the car itself, she wanted to know before putting her life in its hands. However, just as it was above, everything was pristine. As far as she could tell there was nothing out of place. No frayed wire, no misaligned tracks. Nothing.

"Di," Gene suddenly said in her ear, startling her. "I need you to switch to group comms real quick."

With a mental command, she switched over to the comm channel with Gene, Gerald, and Emma. "I'm here," she said.

"Good," Gene replied. "Gerald?"

"Captain, it's Gerald."

"I know who it is, Gerald. What am I doing here?"

"Sorry, Captain," Gerald said. Di could practically hear his cheeks flush. "Um... we may have hit a slight snag."

"What do you mean a 'snag'?" Di asked.

"With the diminishing gravity, it may be a bit harder for your descent to maintain speed. We aren't exactly sure how the steel cable will react, seeing as part of it will be in full gravity and part will be in microgravity. It's definitely something I should have thought of."

"Ok?" Di said. A gurgle in her gut indicated her body was one or two steps ahead of her brain on what Gerald was suggesting, and that she wasn't going to like it.

"For safety purposes, it may be best for you to maintain a steady, downward trajectory before you—"

"Gerald," Di snapped.

"He's saying you're going to need to drop before you hit zero gravity to maintain enough downward momentum to safely get to the elevator car," Gene said.

"Excuse me?"

A warning chime sounded in her ears as the red alert of her elevated heart rate popped up in the top right of her HUD. 164 and climbing. Annoyed, she sent a mental command to shut off the audible chime when her heart rate spiked, met by not one but two warnings that doing so may result in additional harm. Confirming both, the obnoxious tone stopped, though the gradually increasing number remained in the corner of her vision.

"You'll only be in freefall for a few moments," Gene continued. "As soon as you approach the car, I'll slow you down with the cable."

"Yeah, Captain," Emma chimed in. "It's just like a spacewalk."

Di heard the comms cut out for a few moments, no doubt Gene telling Emma to shut her trap. Emma had a hard time understanding Di's fear of zero gravity and tended to forget at the most inopportune times.

Emma's voice suddenly buzzed in her ear. "Err, sorry Captain."

"This is less like a spacewalk and more like a controlled fall," Gene chimed in.

Di exhaled heavily, hands starting to shake. "What do I need to do?"

"Give yourself a little distance from the wall, but don't push away from it or you'll likely end up throwing off your trajectory. We don't want you smashing into anything or tangling up your line. You just want to be centered enough in the shaft that you don't hit a wall on your way down. Once you're hanging, let me know."

Gingerly, Di dropped her left foot, letting it dangle in open space. Then, with one hand still clutching the knot at her waist and the other pushing lightly against the wall, she took her right foot off. Already it felt as though she were floating despite the fact she still had some limited gravity.

"Ok, I'm ready," she said. Her breathing increasingly shallow with anticipation.

This is nothing. I'm in an enclosed space, and I can't float away, I have control.

"I'm going to lower you at a steady pace," Gene said. "Let me know if it's too fast."

"Copy."

The rope jerked in her hand, her stomach plummeting much further than the rest of her body as she descended at a brisk pace.

I'm in an enclosed space. I have control.

Di clutched at the cable with both hands now, looking up as the small square of light above, her bastion of safety, shrank and shrank until she was alone in the dark. Her headlamp glinted off riveted metal walls as they whizzed steadily by.

In mere seconds, gravity was entirely gone as she no longer felt the pull against her limbs. Still, she clung to the cable, a literal lifeline connecting her to the control she craved.

I can't float away. I'm in an enclosed space. I have control.

"Any second now, you should be able to see the elevator car below you."

Gene's voice startled her, jolting her back to her terrifying reality. Gathering her wits, she looked down and saw the barest glint of metal amongst the inky black.

"I think I see it," she said.

"Good. When you're ten or so meters above it, I'll slow

you down."

Di's heart pounded heavily behind her ribcage, heart rate monitor silently flashing red. Paragon's eggheads had clearly never seen real action; having a bright flashing warning across her vision did nothing but distract her. It was more likely to get her killed than to save her life. She would have to ask Gerald how to override the suit to get the damn warning removed entirely when she wasn't dangling precariously from a thin metal cable.

Like a lumbering beast looming from the darkness, the elevator car grew clearer and more in focus the closer she drew. Just as Gene had predicted, she fell at a steady rate which was simultaneously comforting and disconcerting, defying all terms of logic in her brain.

"Ok, slow me down," Di said. Immediately, her falling decelerated alarmingly quickly. "Not so fast!"

"Sorry," Gene grunted. "Hard to gauge. It just feels like a dangling rope."

Though she was still travelling downward, it took a full thirty seconds for her feet to touch sweet, solid matter. Immediately, Di grabbed onto the frame of the elevator car with one hand, stomach lurching as she felt herself begin to drift away with the opposite force her feet touching down created. She instinctively flattened herself as much as she could against the roof of the elevator, comforted by the feeling of control she now felt.

"Touch down," she said, breathing heavily.

"You need to undo the knot in the cable at your waist and

let Gene pull it up," Gerald chimed in. "We can't risk it getting caught in the mechanism when we get the elevator going."

"Copy," Di responded. "Let me get inside the box first. I think I'll feel a bit better with some walls and a ceiling."

Shifting slightly, she used both hands to pull herself along toward the maintenance hatch on the farthest side of the car. The tug of the cable at her waist as she shifted along the roof was a gentle reminder that she was still in good hands up above. Even if, heaven forbid, some catastrophic disaster occurred, she had her safety line to pull her back up to solid, gravity-affected ground.

As she approached the hatch, Di's stomach lurched as if the car itself had dropped a few meters. Though it had appeared closed from her vantage point as she had descended, she saw now the handle turned clockwise and the thick, metal door slightly ajar. A strange, blackish substance streaked away from the edge of the door. As her headlamp's piercing white light flashed across it, she discovered it was more of a mildly translucent, deep shade of blue, warping and altering the image of the metal behind it.

"Gene, I've got something."

"Body?" he asked. It would have been her first question, too.

"No," she replied. "The emergency hatch is open, and there's some sort of dark blue goo around the edges and along the roof."

Di glanced up along the closest wall of the shaft, her lights flaring against the dull metal. Streaks of dark smudges, what she assumed to be more of this blue substance, led up the wall a short way, then disappeared for a short distance before appearing again. It left a streaky stain all the way up the wall until it vanished at the edges of her light.

"Is it blood?" Emma asked. She was not a fan of blood. This was one of many reasons why she had chosen to be a pilot rather than a physician.

"It can't be. Wrong color, and I think wrong consistency." The temperature reading outside her suit flashed on her HUD, a crisp –156 degrees. This far down in the middle of an elevator shaft, who would put in heating? It was slightly insulated from the thick layer of ice by the metal walls, but if Paragon was unwilling to shill for artificial gravity, they damned-well weren't going to heat it.

"I'm reading –156 degrees down here. If it were blood, I think it would be frozen. This looks almost... gelatinous."

"If it isn't solid, it can't be blood," Gerald said. "Blood freezes right below zero. A good portion of it is made up of water, after all."

"Thank you, professor," Emma said in her dry, sarcastic tone.

"This is definitely not blood," Di replied, interrupting before either one could pitch a fit at the other.

"Can you confirm it isn't in a solid state? Can you get a sample of it?" Gerald asked, sounding a touch too enthused.

"I'm not touching this with my hands, even with my suit.

You can collect whatever you want when I come back up with the car." Inhaling deeply, she placed her right hand on the hatch's handle. "I'm going in."

"Be careful," Gene said.

Attempting to avoid the mysterious ooze as much as she could, she flipped the hatch open and pulled herself toward the opening, her legs flipping upward and away from the car as though she were doing an elaborate handstand. Ignoring the terror threatening to claw its way loose from her throat, she slowly pulled her head through the hole and into the car itself, wanting to gauge the surroundings before throwing herself in.

The austere, silver walls and sterile metal paneling were entirely coated in spatters of deep crimson red, bordering black itself, ice crystals tinging it with a thin white layer.

That was what frozen blood looked like.

CHAPTER 4
DESCENT

Di froze, fists clenched against the edge of the hatch. After the initial shock had worn off, senses sharply returning, her fight or flight kicked into overdrive.

The sharp, metallic, coppery smell normally associated with blood was nowhere to be found, either because this blood was old and frozen over or because her suit's filtration system was doing its job. Even so, she still felt the taste on her tongue making her gag.

Her headlamps swept the small, enclosed space of the elevator car. Di's muscles bunched in anticipation, ready at a moment's notice to kick away, microgravity be damned, at the slightest movement or indication of danger. Spatters of rich red blood intermingled with patterns and swirls of an unnatural dark substance dotted the walls, floor, and even parts of the ceiling, tiny rivulets and streaks peeling away from the larger pools.

It wasn't until then that she realized what was missing. A body. There was no body.

"Gene?" Di called, using her implant to switch to private

comms. "We've got a situation here."

"Go," he replied.

"The interior of this car has a new paint job. I'm talking at least three or four liters of blood, maybe more. All over the walls."

"Is the area clear?" he said, a hint of worry tinging his words.

"I'm fine, there's nothing here."

"Good. How many bodies?"

Di, finally feeling comfortable enough to pull herself fully in, lightly pulled on the lip of the hatch. She tucked her legs and rolled fully into the car, planting her feet on the floor and catching one of the few remaining blood-free spots on the handrail that lined the entirety of the space to keep herself from floating off.

"That's the thing," she said, double checking each corner as if there were any chance of a body somehow hiding in a seven-by five-meter space. "There are no bodies."

"None?" Gene asked. "Were they taken out at the bottom maybe?"

"It's possible," Di said, hesitating. "But then, who threw the brake to stop the car? And why was the hatch already open?"

An uncomfortable silence on the comm stretched giving Di time to digest what her brain was just now beginning to comprehend. Judging by the sheer volume, there was enough blood in here for several bodies, or a single significantly deflated one. But if that were the case, where were they? It's true that they could be piled up just outside of the elevator down below; it's what made the most sense. But then, how did the elevator's manual braking system engage partway up the shaft? And why was the emergency hatch open? And what were the dark blue streaks moving up the wall?

"Di?" Gene said, breaking the silence. "Still there?"

"Where else would I be?" she responded, tremors in her voice betraying her false levity.

"Do you see where the manual brake is located inside the elevator?"

Di glanced toward the main sliding doors and noticed a small compartment opened in the paneling just below the 'up' and 'down' buttons. Inside was a switch and a lever striped in black and fluorescent yellow, though it was so caked over in blood she could barely make out those original colors.

"I think so," she said, moving cautiously closer.

"There should be an access panel with a lever and a switch," Gerald chimed in. "Close to the doors. See it?"

"Yes, I see it."

"You'll need to turn the switch to 'active' and manually push the lever back into the vertical position. That should reactivate the car and let me take control."

Pulling herself closer via the handrail in the near zero gravity, she hooked a foot underneath the rail to keep her in a relatively secure, horizontal position while she inspected the small space within the panel. Sure enough, the switch and the lever were labeled 'Manual Override', though most of the lettering was obscured by blood. Hesitantly, Di reached out a probing finger, wiping it along the face of the lever. Unexpectedly, a small streak was left behind in the blood. It congealed on her glove, looking like a similar consistency to a frozen slush, large chunks of icy, crystallized blood coating the tip of her finger.

"Gerald? How quickly does blood freeze?"

"In these temperatures? Basically instantly. Why?"

"This blood isn't completely frozen," Di responded, wiping her finger along a small bare patch on the wall beside her.

"That's impossible," Gerald responded. "It's been three weeks and four days since this place went quiet."

Di glanced at the corner opposite her beside the large door, noticing the small, electric heater for the first time. "Is there climate control in the elevator?" she asked. "Could it have been heated in here for a few weeks after everything went silent?"

"No," Gerald said, computer keys clacking in the background. "No, there are no climate controls, no heating. They were cheap, remember? And besides, the second the temperature in there dropped below zero, which would have been shockingly fast once any heating source expired, the blood would have frozen over entirely."

"I'm looking at a personal heater in here," Di said, pushing herself over to the opposite wall to inspect the small device. Moving gingerly to pick it up in one hand, she found it was solidly stuck to the floor. "It's frozen to the floor."

"Di, I need you to move back to the panel and disengage

the brake," Gene said, cutting through the nonsense as only he could. "We can discuss more when you're safely up here and we can inspect it together."

"Yessir," Di responded. She couldn't help but grin. Try as he might to put on the tough guy act, Gene couldn't always hide his concern for his fellow crewmates, her in particular. His strained, curt command was as strong a tell as a poor card player scratching his nose when he had a particularly good hand.

Gliding toward the small panel, she turned her focus back to the switch and the lever. Grasping the key in her left, she had to temporarily let go of the railing beside her and grab the lever with her right. They both felt slick in her gloved fingers, and the reminder of what she was touching sent a tiny shiver racing along her spine. Bracing herself as best she could beneath the handrail and against the wall, she attempted to turn the switch. It fought her hard, whether from the sub-zero temps or the muck gumming up the mechanism she couldn't tell.

"It's stuck a bit," she said, straining. The handrail dug into her back and shoulder blades, the only brace she had to keep her from spinning ineffectually away.

With a guttural grunt and a surge of strength, she flipped the switch to the 'armed' position and pushed the lever up until it was vertical once more. Overhead lights blared blindingly above, and a vibrating hum rattled the car as it came back to life.

"Got it!" she shouted in between several deep breaths.

"I see it on the system now. Good work. Just detach your safety line and I'll send 'er up," Gerald said.

Di slipped the steel loop over her head and gave it a quick tug as a signal they could pull it up. As the cable disappeared through the ceiling hatch, the car jolted to life. It began moving up the shaft, slowly at first but gradually picking up speed. Di felt a small force pulling her down to the floor as the elevator climbed reminding her that she was about to re-enter the artificial gravity above. As her own weight began to return, she righted herself until her feet were below her, the soles of her boots mercifully connecting with the ground. Before long, the thick, metal doors slid open to reveal three relieved faces waiting to greet her.

"Good job, Captain!" Emma said, clasping Di's hand and pulling her free from the blood-soaked car.

"Where did you say this blue goo was?" Gerald asked, seemingly having forgotten his previous fears in search of satiating his scientific curiosity.

"Look around in there, you'll find a lot close to the ceiling hatch," Di replied, moving to shake Gene's hand. "Thank you, Gene."

"Thank *you*, Captain," he replied.

"For what?" she asked, cocking her head.

"For not dying. I'm not ready to take command quite yet." He grinned and swatted her upper arm to which Di responded by punching his shoulder good-naturedly.

Gene's face fell slightly, eye twitching. "*Mr. Roberts* is on comms for you."

"Great," she said. For a moment, she hesitated. She really

did *not* want to deal with whatever corpo bullshit he was about to try and force down her throat.

Sighing, she trudged over to the comm receiver and plugged herself in. "How can I help you, Mr. Roberts?" Di asked in a sickeningly sweet, blatantly sarcastic tone.

"Diane," he replied. "I've been waiting on this line for some time. Is everything ok?"

"Yes, everything is just fine," she said curtly.

"What is your status? Are you below? Have you found any Paragon personnel?"

"We're still on the surface. There was an issue with the elevator."

"Issue? What kind of issue?" he asked.

"It was stuck partway down the shaft. I had to climb down and manually release it."

"*You* did it?" His tone marked an indignation at the mere thought of not delegating such an inferior task to a subordinate. It was the epitome of corpo cynicism at its finest.

"Yes, Liam," Di replied. She was getting tired of his snobby elitism and was one more snide comment away from disconnecting, consequences be damned.

Mr. Roberts snorted dismissively, boiling Di's blood further. "Fine, fine. As long as you remain on mission, I don't much care how you accomplish the tasks you were paid to do. When will you be descending?"

"Mission parameters have changed somewhat," Di said, eyes shifting back to the blood-soaked elevator car, doors hanging ominously open to give a clear view of the carnage. Gerald had apparently found and enabled the emergency heating system as tiny pools of defrosting blood mixed with the unknown blueish goo were beginning to gather at the inner edges of the elevator where the walls met the floor, tiny rivulets leaking out into the room itself. Her suit's automated regulation meant it barely made a difference to her personally.

"I don't believe you have the authority from Paragon to change mission parameters, Ms. Eastwood," Mr. Roberts clucked.

"Something isn't right," she replied, turning her attention back to the conversation. "The elevator was soaked in blood, and the emergency hatch was already open, but there were no bodies."

"It is my understanding you had prepared for casualties. You all but guaranteed it in your preparation meeting on your ship. I don't see how this changes anything at all."

"It's not the casualties that's the problem," she said through gritted teeth. "It's the lack of a body and the unnatural circumstances that—"

"You were hired to do a job, isn't that right?" Mr. Roberts interjected, oily smugness oozing through the speakers.

"Yes," was all Di trusted herself to say.

"Then do your job. The job for which you were contracted. The job you will be paid quite *handsomely* for, I might add. Find out where Paragon's assets have gone. It doesn't matter if they're alive or dead, just find them."

Di ripped the comm cord from the port on the wall. It snapped back, automatically retracting into her suit, the port closing behind it. She switched comms to local.

"Asshole!"

"I take it he still expects us to go down?" Gene asked.

Di moved to brush her hair behind her ear, fingers bumping ineffectively against her helmet. She snarled and clenched her fists, sucking in a calming breath before responding. "Unfortunately, our corporate delegation does not believe our current situation warrants a change in the mission parameters."

Gene nodded, picking up his gear he had placed on the table and strapping it all back on. "Heard. Let's get this over with."

"Wait, we *are* still going down there?" Gerald asked, eyes widening. "I feel like a bloody elevator lets us know where the crew is, right? There's no way anyone is still alive. If they were, they would have contacted Paragon or the authorities or something."

"That's what common sense says, yes," Emma said, sighing. "But we're not dealing with common sense. We're dealing with a corpo."

"This stinks like more than just a manhunt," Di said, popping the magazine out of her pistol and pulling the slide back, checking and rechecking that there were no obstructions. She then slid her rifle from her back and did the same. A warning in her gut told her this may be one of the last calm moments before shit went sideways.

"You think they're after more than just information on their crew?" Emma asked, approaching the elevator and peering in.

"Mark my words. Once we get down there, I'm betting *Mr. Roberts* will change mission parameters himself." Di spat the name like the foulest curse that had ever graced her lips.

She had never liked corpos or their slimy slugs that greased the wheels and kept the cogs turning. Liam Roberts, however, was among the worst she had had the displeasure of working for, and that was saying something considering at least half of her crew's temporary employers were enjoying twenty to life in varying prisons across the galaxy for one heinous crime or another.

"Everyone ready?" Gene asked. He stood at attention next to the open elevator doors, his beloved Florence in hand.

Gerald stood shakily, blinking far more than necessary as sweat beaded on his brow, but he nodded and went to stand by Gene. His gait was more aligned with a death row inmate than a mercenary, but he wasn't the only one who felt the impending doom. Di approached him and placed a comforting hand on his shoulder, pushing her own fears aside for the moment. Confidence, not fear, was what Gerald needed.

As Emma moved to enter the elevator, Di stopped her with an outstretched palm. "Emma, I'm gonna need you posted up here in case there's trouble below and we need a fast exit."

"Are you kidding me?" Gerald shouted. His momentary outburst startled even himself, the shock evident as the blood drained from his face. "Sorry, Captain."

"I'm sorry, too," Di replied. "But we need a pilot up here, someone who can fly hot and under pressure, or if… if we're detained below." She tried to say it as delicately as she could, though it sounded like a pathetic attempt even to her own ears.

"Are you sure, Captain?" Emma asked, trying and failing to keep some of her relief from showing.

"Yes, I'm sure." Di stood at attention in front of the group, resuming her captain-esque stature. "Mission parameters are clear. We are to ascertain the status of Paragon's mining crew with documented certainty. It does not, however, demand that we sweep this entire base. Once we've determined that no survivors remain, we will haul ass off this damn ice ball and never look back. Clear?"

"Yes, Captain," all three replied, voices overlayed like a strange echo.

Di nodded and walked past her crew, the first to enter the carnage in the elevator. Her footing was a little more unsure, the floor's surface now slicked with a thin layer of thawed blood. She glanced up at the hatch, focusing on the smears of mystery blue goo. As she did, she noticed faint movement and dodged out of the way as a thick globule fell, sizzling on the ground at her feet.

"Captain?" Gene asked, striding in to stand beside her.

Di knelt down, getting as close as she dared to the bubbling liquid beside her. She pulled up the ambient external temperature of the room on her HUD which read a balmy five degrees.

"What is that?" Gerald asked, momentarily forgetting his nerves for the sake of his curiosity and crouching to inspect it. "Is it *boiling*?"

Emma poked her head in to catch a glimpse. "How can something boil at just above freezing?"

"Actually, there are a fair few elements and compounds that boil at even sub-zero temperatures. Ammonia, methyl chloride, methane." Gerald continued rattling off various items before Emma cut him off.

"Any of those look like that though?" she asked.

Gerald paused thoughtfully before responding. "No, no I don't think so. Do we have any vials for samples by chance?"

"I'm sure we'll find some below," Di said, straightening from her crouched position. She nodded at Emma who returned the nod before striding over to the computer and taking a seat.

"We'll be in contact as soon as we've found a comm port," Di said. Emma attempted an encouraging smile, but it came off as more of a grimace. The doors slid slowly shut.

"It's probably best if everyone braces before we leave the gravity well," Di said, taking a position in what appeared to be the cleanest corner.

"I believe our *E.I.A.P.S.L.* suits have a magnetic function," Gerald said. His gaze became unfocused, eyes darting back and forth as he combed his eidetic memory. "Yes, the suit provides several magnetic settings for the boots. We should try the one that allows for movement, I think."

"Everyone ready?" Emma asked over comms.

"Hold," Di commanded. Turning her wrist to access her suit's menu screen, she began to scroll through the settings. It was probably advisable to use this as an opportunity to practice with her neural link, but she had always preferred the real feel of touch.

Though it took her a tad longer, Di eventually found the option she needed under the 'gravity' menu, selecting the 'spacewalk' option. Though the setting was green, she felt no difference. Lifting her foot, there was no telltale magnetic pull, and she wondered whether she had done something wrong.

Double checking her settings, she turned to Gene and Gerald and nodded. "Suits on?"

Both nodded, also testing their steps.

"Fascinating," Gerald said. "The magnetic function adjusts the strength automatically as you lift your foot to make it feel like an actual step, even in low or no gravity."

"We're clear, Emma," Gene finally replied.

The car shuddered as it began sliding down, delving deep below the surface. In mere moments Di felt the gravity shift, her arms instinctively floating around chest height. True to their function, her boots held. She hesitantly raised her right foot, feeling the conflicting forces of magnetism and gravity pulling her leg in opposite directions. The sensation made her stomach lurch uncomfortably and she firmly placed her foot back on solid ground.

Though Gerald's scientific curiosity held for a few seconds, the gravity of the situation won out against the gravitational function of his new toy. Gene remained at attention facing the door, methodically checking and rechecking his rifle's action, muzzle, trigger, sights, and magazine. Anyone else may have called it neurotic, but Di knew it for what it truly was; Gene's meditation, his zen, his calm collection before the inevitable storm.

Uncomfortable silence hung thick in the air as the elevator car continued its descent. This was not the type of discomfort from a first date gone wrong or a socially inept uncle asking inappropriate questions at the dinner table. This was heavier. More dangerous. The kind of uneasiness one felt on the cusp of an inevitable disaster. It was not an unfamiliar feeling for Di, though it was still one she had never quite gotten used to.

Pulling up her HUD, she queried their travel speed, altitude, and estimated arrival time. They were traveling at nearly sixty kilometers per hour, meaning it would take them roughly ten minutes to reach the lower station. She watched as the numbers plummeted, moving from -1,100 meters elevation to -1,200 and so on. It was oddly soothing, the numbers slipping by in a steady, meticulous gait.

Di had been on dozens, if not hundreds, of jobs in her career as a hired mercenary. She had led most of them herself. Everything from escorting important officials to bounty hunting wanted criminals. Hell, they had once been house sitters for a particularly paranoid, but extraordinarily wealthy, czar of some city-state or another. Her life had been on the line numerous times, in active warzones and seedy underbellies. Yet she had never felt what she was feeling now. Not even during her time in the military.

Sure, she had been anxious before a battle, hands shaking in nervous anticipation. Di had always pictured herself as a little bit of an adrenaline junkie. Damn it, she was proud of it. She often looked forward to putting her life on the line. But never, not once in the two and a half decades as captain of the CS Katana and her crew, had she felt such a strong aversion so deep in her soul. Nervous. Anxious. Terrified. A sense of utter *wrongness*.

They had taken jobs of questionable morals, done things especially early on that she wasn't proud of and likely wouldn't do today. These had been stepping stones for all of them, lessons to be learned that she wouldn't trade for anything. But this? She had never felt so blind. No one knew what this was, what to expect. The mounting dread of the unknown taunted her, enticing her to move further and further into the darkness where light couldn't penetrate and where nightmares took shape. And Di, try as she might, couldn't seem to shake the feeling that this time she had been wrong to take the job.

"Slowing on approach," Gene called out, widening his stance and bringing his rifle up to his shoulder, flicking off the safety.

Di followed suit, reaching for the rifle over her shoulder, checking the mag, thumbing the safety, and holding it tightly against her shoulder.

"Gerald," she said. "Weapon."

"Right," Gerald shakily replied, reaching an unsure hand

to the pistol at his belt. He looked at it sitting in the palm of his hand like it was a snake, moments from taking a juicy bite out of his neck.

"Take it off safety," Di said, giving an encouraging nod.

Gerald nodded, turning off the safety and holding it barrel down in a loose grip. He may be terrified, but at least he finally had the good sense to remember his training and keep a live weapon trained away from friendlies without a reminder.

The gravity began to shift and her arms felt heavy again, the elevator finally close enough to the lower station for the artificial gravity to take effect. Well, at least there was some good news. It meant basic functions down here were still working, so it couldn't be all bad. Could it?

"Thirty seconds," Gene called out, though Di was still watching the ETA via her HUD. It counted down, innocent and ominous all wrapped into one.

Twenty seconds. Di's heart began pounding in her chest, beating a deep, rising rhythm against her ribcage. The all too familiar red warning of her spiking heart rate flashed in the corner of her vision. She closed her eyes, focusing on her deep, purposeful breaths.

"Ten seconds. Prepare for arrival."

Gene's steady voice calmed Di's nerves. She could do this. Just another job, one that could pay for the Katana three times over. In and out. Get visual confirmation and haul ass up to the surface. That's all they needed to do.

A haunting 'ding' echoed in the confined space of the

elevator car. Di's eyes snapped open, releasing the breath she hadn't realized she was holding. With it, she let her worries empty like the CO_2 leaving her lungs.

The doors slid open.

CHAPTER 5
DISCOVERY

Blood pounded in Di's ears as the small room beyond the silently sliding elevator doors was revealed. Though her breathing was calm, every muscle in her body tensed at the prospect of the horror that would greet them. If it was reminiscent of what had awaited her in the elevator car, she wasn't particularly eager to draw this out further. As she had said on the surface, best to get in and out as quickly as possible.

It took her a moment to realize the entry room was empty and clean, just like the facility had been above. Her brain refused to register the normalcy of the situation. At any moment, some horrifying creature or band of bloodthirsty cutthroats were bound to jump out of their concealed hiding place. Yet her brain refused to corroborate the truth her eyes were conveying.

"Clear," Gene called after stepping out of the elevator and sweeping the corners of the small, nondescript room.

Gerald hesitantly followed, gun visibly shaking in his hand as his fingers flexed on and off the grip of the pistol.

Di's attention shifted to the sealed automated door on the

far side wall. Gene was of a similar mindset as, following the careful sweep of the three small closets on the left and right side, he turned his rifle to the doorway. He shifted fluidly to a position just to the left of the doorframe.

"Gerald, to the side," Gene called out on comms, dipping his head in a jerky motion.

Gerald blinked furiously, shoulders heaving up and down. Despite the state-of-the-art anti-condensation coating on the inside of his helmet, a small circle of fog was fading in and out in front of his partially open mouth. Though his body tensed as if to comply with Gene's command, his feet hadn't gotten the memo.

With as comforting a grip as she could muster through her own anxiety, Di grabbed Gerald's left arm, the one without the gun, crossed in front of him, and led him to a corner.

"Gerald," she said trying to get his eyes to focus. "Gerald, I need you to look at me. Focus on me."

"We're taking too long," Gene muttered, though thankfully he had the sense to do it on a private channel. "We're too vulnerable like this."

Di ignored him as Gerald's unfocused eyes slowly slid over her face, recognition finally registering.

"Good," Di said in a stern but calm tone. "Focus on me for a moment. This is just like before; we're going out that door and your job is to stay low and cover Gene and I. Understood?"

Gerald nodded weakly, though his grip on the pistol in his right hand flexed once and then steadied.

"Do not fire unless Gene tells you to." Di kept her focus on Gerald, willing her command beyond their two helmets and directly into his brain.

It was oddly comforting, seeing someone so utterly in need of a commanding hand. Her own nervousness faded to background noise as she focused on getting Gerald back to a mentally stable place. They needed every hand on deck. The gun in his grip paired with the trembling jerky movements of his extremities was a bit more concerning than she cared to admit, but she wasn't about to leave him weaponless. That would no doubt send him into a spiral of which she wasn't prepared to pull him out. Still, a firearm in the hand of someone who couldn't wield it properly was just as dangerous as a firearm in the hand of an enemy, if not more so.

Di turned, again taking up her position beside the door. "Line up on my six," she said, to which Gerald thankfully complied. Nodding to Gene, Di located the manual override for the automatic sliding door, a small wheel with a handle. Cautiously, she spun the wheel and opened the door a crack, just enough for Gene to squeeze through. He led out with the muzzle of his rifle and quickly disappeared for a moment before Di followed, moving to the left side of the hallway. She felt Gerald's presence sucked to her back hip and felt another surge of pride. He would make a fine field member yet.

Automated lights flickered on overhead in response to their movement, just like they had on the surface station above, revealing yet another sterilized hallway. This one was significantly wider with various sealed doors that lined the left side. The lighting was dim enough that they could only see two or three doors down until the hallway faded to nothingness in the dark. None of the doors had viewports, and there were no windows at all to allow a view into the many rooms. Though the hallway was empty and barren of any signs of life or struggle, there was no telling what awaited them inside.

This was a nightmare scenario for defending against an unseen attacker. Any one of these doors could open at a moment's notice, and at that point it would realistically come down to Gene's reflexes to determine who lived and died.

Di glanced at Gene who still held his rifle at the ready, eyes trained down the hallway. "Assessment?" she asked.

"Not optimal," he replied without looking at her. He was doing his job, keeping them safe, focus solely on what lay in front of him. "I don't particularly enjoy the idea of manually sweeping each room, but I don't see another choice."

"It's your call," she said, bringing her pistol down to chest height.

Without a word, Gene crossed in front and triggered the first set of sliding doors. Di tapped his right shoulder letting him know they were ready, and they filed into the room.

As the lights came to life up above, Di saw it as an unremarkable square room. A simple storage area, something that made sense so close to the elevator. Shifting anything from above, whether it be large equipment or boxes full of testing supplies, was a time-wasting hassle to say the least. Best to drop it off quickly and sort it later.

Shelves lined the walls from the back to the front leaving little to no cover. Unmarked metal boxes and plastic totes were stacked three deep on each shelf with various open and empty spots dotted all throughout the room. Two massive wooden crates sat in the far-right corner, faint grey lettering labeled, "PERISHABLES" stamped across each side.

"Gerald, watch the hallway," Gene said, taking several slow, methodical steps into the room.

Di stuck close behind him, scanning the room while Gerald took position just inside the door. "I don't see anything in here," she said.

"Which is what concerns me," Gene replied, picking up speed as he moved toward the center of the room.

Di peeled off, exploring the shelves all the way to the back of the room. "We need to move on, Gene," she called, turning to face him.

He lowered his rifle so that the tip was pointed away from her, though still nestled strongly against his shoulder. "Captain," Gene replied, a terse, one-word response that conveyed both compliance and annoyance at not being allowed to perform his customary full and complete sweep of the area.

"If someone were in here, we would know it by now. We need to move on."

Gene nodded and moved swiftly to the door, taking a moment to check the hallway before exiting the storage room. Di followed with Gerald at her heels. His grip on his pistol had loosened somewhat, a sign that his anxiety was either lessening or merely wearing him down. It could be exhausting maintaining such a high level of stress, but his eyes were still wide and his head jerked back and forth, jumping at shadows.

"Next room," Gene called, already taking position beside the second door several meters down. Di stacked behind him, and he opened the door, lights flaring on behind it.

As she moved to follow, Gene stopped abruptly nearly causing her to run into his back. Gerald stumbled a bit but managed to keep from tumbling over her. It only took a moment to see what had caused him to pause.

A large, wet streak of crimson blood splashed colorfully along the white tiled floor just inside the doorway. Small splotches became gradually larger pools moving deeper into the room with more spattered along the shelving to their right. The trail led ominously to a small space with a door in the far corner, barely bigger than a clothes closet.

Gene smudged the slushy blood streak with the toe of his boot. "It's fresh," he called, quickly sweeping the corners with his firearm before landing on the closet door. "Still wet."

"You think it's one of the miners?" Di asked, pistol held at the ready before her eyes. She scanned the room, a space not dissimilar to the one they had just come from save for the closet. And, of course, the fresh streaks of blood.

"Don't know. Watch my six." Gene moved cautiously forward until he stood directly in front of the door where the blood trail ended. With a deep inhale, Gene flicked on Florence's flashlight attachment and pushed open the door, moving in as Di shifted to guard the doorway. She glanced inside.

A middle-aged man in a well-worn, grey coverall lay slumped against the wall, beard stained deep red around his mouth and down his chin. The front of his shirt was soaked in blood, though Di could see no visible wound or tear in his clothing where one could be hiding. The blue and white Paragon patch on his breast pocket, now flecked with crimson, sat proudly above his name patch, cursive lettering spelling out 'Patrick.' His chest rose and fell in shallow bursts, and his glazed eyes tried desperately to focus on the beam of light from Gene's gun.

"He's still breathing," Di said. She moved past Gene and knelt intending to check his pulse.

The man's eyes flared, and he dove violently sideways away from her touch. Gene grabbed Di's bicep and hauled her back as the dying man flailed along the floor, desperately pulling himself away from them and leaving another ghastly streak of blood along the floor.

"We're not here to hurt you," Di said, though the man didn't appear to recognize her gentle assurance, or even the fact she was there at all. With a hesitant mental command, she activated the small but powerful speaker system located near the bottom of her helmet. "Did you hear me? We're here to help, we're not going to hurt you."

"Don't..." The miner's words were garbled, as though he were attempting to speak through a mouth full of jelly. He hacked up a thick globule of blood and continued to crawl away.

"Patrick? Is that your name? Where are you injured?" Di asked, reaching forward again. She stopped, however, as his eyes tracked her movement and widened again in his maddened scramble to maintain his distance.

"Don't…"

"Ok, ok," she said, putting up her hands in surrender. "But we need to do something about all of this blood."

She turned to Gene who still held his gun trained on the suffering, huddled mass now pushing himself as deep into the far corner as a human body could be. "Do you think it's internal?"

"I don't really see an external injury to account for this much blood. It seems like it's all coming from his mouth and nose. Gotta be internal."

"Go…" Patrick gurgled.

Di shifted to look at the dying man as he tried desperately to convey his message. Small streams of blood began to pool at the corners of his eyes, dripping gruesomely down his cheeks and running in the creases around his nose, combining with the steady flow from his mouth.

"Where should we go?" she asked. "Are there others who are alive? Are there more injured?"

A barely perceptible shake of his head left him wracked with another deep, heaving cough that sent renewed waves of blood across his sprawled body.

"There aren't any other survivors? What happened?"

"Don't… touch…" His breathing quickened, chest rising

and falling in shallow bursts. "Leave… Leave… while… you…"

With a final shuddering wheeze, the last vestiges of life escaped his lips in a burble of blood, the light leaving his widened, bloodshot eyes. His tensed muscles relaxed, and his body slumped fully to the floor.

Di crouched down, ducking her head for a closer look. A small stream of dark blue, nearly black sludge dribbled from the dead man's lips, mingling with the crimson streams. She reached a hesitant hand forward, as if to tilt his head to feel for a pulse.

"Stop," Gene commanded, striking forward with lightning reflexes and snatching her arm away.

"It's just like the stuff I saw in the elevator." Sure enough, the deep purplish goo quickly began to boil once it touched open air leaving the regular blood behind.

"Did you not hear what he said?" Gerald asked. Di turned and saw Gerald standing just beyond the closet's doorway, staring wide-eyed at the bloody corpse.

"He told us to leave," she replied, standing from her stooped position and pushing past her gawking crewmate.

"Yeah. And specifically, *'don't touch'*!"

"I heard what he said," she replied, forgetting their safety protocol and rushing out into the hallway. She could already hear Gene's reprimand dying on his lips with an exasperated sigh.

Ever since landing, her instincts had been warning her. Over and over, despite her hesitancy, she had ignored them, pushed them aside. Yes, she had put it to a vote. But it was her job as captain to see that her crew was kept safe, and she'd be damned if she was going to let greed corrupt her moral duty to them. She was finally going to listen to what her gut had been telling her all along and get herself and her crew the hell off this moon.

Striding briskly back to the elevator bay foyer, she quickly found what she was looking for. Typing the command into her wrist computer, the thin comm cable sprouted from her wrist, and she jabbed it into the port beside the elevator door. An inlaid screen on the wall flared to life with several options available, topmost being the surface. Jabbing it fiercely with her pointer finger, she waited as the staticky buzz sounded in her helmet.

"Captain?" a familiar voice said. "Is that you?"

"Emma, is everything up there alright?"

"Yes," Emma replied, then hesitated for a brief moment. "Wait, why? What happened? Is everyone—"

"Just listen," Di interrupted. "I need you to patch me through to Gayle and then get to the shuttle and start preparations for launch. We're getting the hell out of here."

"What about Paragon?" Emma asked.

"Screw Paragon. Something isn't right here, and I'm not sticking around long enough to find out what it is."

"Aye, Captain. Patching you through."

Dead, empty air hung like the executioner's blade over Di's head for what felt like an eternity, but in reality had only been a handful of seconds, before an oily voice greeted her from the other end.

"Captain? Can I assume you have good news?"

His slimy corporate tone immediately raised her hackles. "Mr. Roberts, we are abandoning this mission."

"Excuse me?" He feigned shock, but Di could see straight through his piss-poor acting. "You have been commissioned by Paragon to discover the whereabouts of their employees and property, and you have yet to do either."

"The safety of my crew is the highest priority, and I no longer deem this mission safe."

There was a moment's hesitation wherein Di could hear the faint clacking of computer keys. "Ms. Eastwood, need I remind you of your contract—"

"Damn your contract! Damn Paragon! Damn Enceladus! If you're so hung up on 'completing this mission', we'll leave your ass on the station!"

She violently ripped the comm cable out of the port, and it slithered back into her suit. Turning to face Gene and Gerald, she found the latter staring wide-eyed at her outburst while the former merely raised a single eyebrow, a self-satisfied smirk tugging at the corners of his lips.

"Get in the elevator."

"Yes Captain," they both replied in unison. As everyone turned to enter the elevator car, it shuttered and dropped a handspan past the open doorway. Di froze, barely daring to breathe as a deep groan echoed along the shaft and the lights within the car flickered and died.

Nobody moved, waiting for the other shoe (or rather, the car itself) to drop. Di's lungs burned as she held her breath, seconds ticking by with an accompaniment of metallic groans. After a tense thirty seconds, Gene gingerly poked his head inside, glancing side to side as if to ascertain what had caused the elevator to move and shake of its own accord. He tested the control panel with a few exuberant pokes.

Di released a shuddering breath. "If that thing falls and your head gets sliced off, I'm not going down there to get it," Di said, gently pulling at his elbow.

"Fair enough," he replied, ducking back into the room. "We need to get back on comms. Maybe Emma hasn't left yet."

Di moved to the port, once again pulling out the cable and fastening it to the wall before dialing the surface. Light buzzing filled her ears, but the line rang empty.

"Damn it," Di cursed, pulling out the cord yet again.

"Figures." Gene turned to Gerald. "Any ideas?"

Gerald blinked, as though it were the last thing on his mind that he would be addressed in a crisis like this. "Excuse me?" he asked. "Ideas for what?"

"Well, unless you're willing to get on that elevator—" Gene began, to which Gerald furiously shook his head. "We're going to need a new route to the surface."

"How am I supposed to know?" Gerald asked, fear pitching his voice up an octave. "I've never been here. I've never seen this facility. I've never been on a mission like this. *You're* the ones with the experience!"

"Settle down," Gene said holding up a friendly hand, palm out. "Just asking if you had any ideas, that's all."

"Gerald, breathe," Di said. "We're going to be fine. I'll try to get the station on the line."

She plugged her suit's cable into the port for a third time, hoping the old adage would turn out to be true. It took her a few moments to remember the correct station code, but she hurriedly pressed it when she did.

Di had never been particularly religious. She had never really put much thought into a god, a creator, or whatever force was responsible for placing humanity in this universe. Even so, she found herself fervently praying as the quiet buzzing ringtone continued unabated, hoping it wasn't going out into the ether with no one there to answer.

"Captain?"

Di's tense shoulders dropped at the sound of Gayle's voice. "Gayle. Thank God."

"I don't know what you said to Mr. Corpo, but he's sulking."

"Gayle, we have a situation."

Gayle's tone immediately shifted, adopting her signature no-nonsense professionalism. "What can I do, Captain?"

"This may be a long shot, but can you check on the status of the subsurface elevator?" Di asked.

"Isn't that something Gerald usually handles?"

"We don't have any system access at the moment." Di shot Gerald a quick glance. "But we may be able to move further into the facility to find one."

"I'll be honest, none of these computer systems look like

English to me. I think you'll have quicker success finding Gerald a terminal down there."

Di chewed on her lower lip, already regretting her next words. "Is Mr. Roberts familiar with the system?"

Gayle's exhalation hissed in her ear followed by a moment of dead air. "One second, Captain."

Di wasn't particularly hopeful. After screaming at the man, a corporate shill whose ego bruised quicker than a week-old banana, she was pretty sure he was more likely to file a written warning than he was to help, regardless of whether he knew the installation's computer system or not.

"Captain?" Gayle's voice sounded terse and restrained. Not a good sign.

"Yes?" Di asked.

"Mr. Roberts..." Gayle began through audibly gritting teeth. "Mr. Roberts feels that, as we are now retracting acceptance of the Paragon contract, he, as representative of the company as he so eloquently reminded me, is unable to assist any further with non-company business." She exhaled loudly. "I'm sorry Captain."

"Shit," Di muttered. She was going to strangle that man-shaped ball of greasy slime the second she could get her hands on him.

"Honestly, he's probably too proud to admit he has no idea how to work this system," Gayle whispered. "Asshole."

Di's mind whirled, instincts automatically shifting her thought process to analyze their options. In a matter of moments, their situation had morphed from tenuous to serious to perilous. They had little functioning knowledge of the mining base's current status at large beyond this hallway, no personal access to the base's systems, and no reliable method of transportation back up to the surface. Try as she might, she could only see one way forward.

Glancing at Gerald, unsure what his reaction to her next words would be, her face hardened in resolve. Like it or not, this was the hand they had been dealt, and she'd be damned if she was going to fold now.

"Gayle, I need you stationed at this comm port until further notice. If I hear that bastard's voice the next time I call, the comm port may not survive."

"Aye, Captain."

"We're moving further into the facility. There has to be a terminal not far from here we can use to access a map or emergency procedures to figure out how we're getting back to the surface."

"We're going—"

Di cut Gerald off with a single raised pointer finger, not even deigning to glance his way as she continued her instructions to Gayle. "I will contact you when we've found a terminal. If you don't hear from us in one hour, I need you to get off the orbital station and back on the ship. If you don't hear from us in two, leave."

Gerald inhaled sharply. Di watched from the corner of her eye as his knees buckled and he slumped against the wall, sliding down to a seated position.

"Heard," Gayle replied with only slight hesitation. "Good luck, Captain."

"Thank you, Abigayle."

The line disconnected, and she pulled her comm cable out one final time, turning fully to Gene and Gerald. "If you have grievances, now is the time. Because once we walk out that door, we are a team. We move as a team, we work as a team, we survive as a team. Our lives depend on it."

Gene nodded, bringing his rifle back up to his shoulder, muzzle pointed at the floor. She hadn't expected anything from him, though his eyes indicated he may have one or two things to mention on private comms once they had left the relative safety of the elevator foyer. He understood that this statement was not intended for him.

Di turned to Gerald, hands clasped behind her back, expression hard and unforgiving. She had been understanding before, perhaps even gentle, but that moment was dead and gone. Emergency situations called for action and obedience without a moment's hesitation. You hesitated, you died. It was that simple. She had drilled that concept into every one of her crew members' brains from the moment they stepped foot on her ship, but hearing it and experiencing it firsthand were two very, *very* separate understandings.

Gerald blinked, finally registering both his captain and his senior officer were standing at attention waiting for his response. With a shuddering breath, he gripped his pistol tighter. "Ready,

Captain."

Di's face relaxed from a deep scowl to a mildly perturbed frown. "Stand up, Gerald. We're shifting formation. Gene will remain in front, but you will now be second. I will cover the rear. Understood?"

"Understood," both men said.

"Gene, we don't have time to check every room." She saw his mouth pucker into a tight line. "I know it isn't ideal, but we need to get out of here. Time is of the essence. The longer we're down here, the more tenuous this gets."

"Understood, Captain."

Di inhaled deeply, expecting her heart rate monitor to spike and the flashing visual alarm to fill her HUD. Surprisingly, it remained at a steady 75, fluctuating up and down only slightly. Maybe she was growing. Maybe those breathing exercises had finally allowed her anxiety to level off and her mental health to become a touch more stable, providing acceptance for who she was. Or maybe she knew they were screwed no matter what they did.

Either way, it was what it was.

Lining up at the door, they entered the hallway again moving single file along the lefthand wall with guns at the ready. As they passed the open door where they had found the dying miner, Di poked her head inside. She craned her neck to get a look into the closet at the rear, door still ajar.

The miner was gone.

"Gene, stop," Di commanded.

Gene held up a closed fist and stopped, but remained facing forward, eyes scanning the darkened hallway. "What is it, Captain?"

"Where's the Paragon miner?" The words sent a chill down her spine as she spoke them aloud.

Gene's head whipped around, concern heavy in his gaze. "Gerald, watch the hallway for a moment."

With swift, succinct movements, he moved past Di into the storage space, once more sweeping the room. When he got to the closet, he paused at the empty spot on the red-soaked floor where the man had died moments ago.

Di remained standing in the door frame, head on a swivel. She wasn't entirely sure whether she should be watching the room or the hallway.

As her light passed back through the room, she froze on a newer, fresher streak of blood in the far corner. "Gene," she called out on their private channel. He glanced at her then followed her beam of light to the partially concealed area behind one of the large crates stacked haphazardly against the back wall.

"Watch the room," he called out, moving slowly toward the obscured corner.

His slowly roving light attached to the barrel of his rifle revealed small streaks of blood along the wall, as though left behind by fingers gently grazing it like the tips of tall grass. Smaller boxes were strewn around the larger one, their contents of single cell batteries, petri dishes, soap dispenser refills, and individually wrapped cotton swabs spilled across the floor. Gene carefully maneuvered his footsteps around the objects as best he could, though the crinkle of plastic and paper wrappers was unmistakably deafening in the silent atmosphere.

Di quickly swept the rest of the room with her gun finding nothing out of place. No other errant blood streaks, no shifted boxes. Nothing.

Gene glanced over his shoulder attracting Di's gaze. With a silent finger display of 'three, two, one', he booted aside the box blocking his way, gun drawn and finger poised on the trigger. Di couldn't see past him, though his body language was no longer as tense. He leaned down to peer at something just beyond her sight behind another stack of crates, then turned back toward her, stepping aside to give her a clear view.

Where she had expected a corpse, she merely saw an empty vent, screw holes torn open where the metal grill had been ripped off. Dark splotches covered the opening reflecting a deep purplish-blue in her light.

"Gone?" she asked, anticipating the obvious answer.

"Gone. Do we know where these vents lead?"

Di shook her head. "Unless you're planning on squeezing through that tiny hole in the wall, I suggest we move,"

Though he had asked the pertinent question of where the man had gone, Gene had left the more obvious question unasked. Who, or what, had taken the miner?

Without hesitation, Gene marched swiftly back to the hallway, taking up position just outside the door. Di followed, shifting back to her place at the rear of the pack.

She ground her teeth, kicking herself for not thinking of having someone cover the hallway in their hasty return to the elevator. Maybe if she had they would have heard the poor man being dragged off.

What was wrong with her? Ever since they had touched down on Enceladus, she had been the direct cause of one failure after another. Her inability to tether the ship. Nearly falling down the elevator shaft. Ignoring proper protocol and basic mercenary instincts to station a guard as lookout. Sloppy mistakes that, had her head been properly clear, could have easily been avoided. So far, she had been lucky. Her failings as a captain hadn't gotten anyone injured or killed.

"Ready?" Gene called out on the open comms.

"Ready," Gerald and Di replied, guns rising to cover Gene.

She exhaled, pushing past her self-abuse. Now was not the time. She would have plenty of empty moments on their return trip home to analyze every little detail, but letting herself get distracted in the field was a surefire way to let the small mistakes become bigger ones.

They moved swiftly and silently, hugging the left wall again as they slipped down the silent, barren hallway. Overhead lights flickered to life above them. Other than the brief moments Gene took to ensure the doors they passed were securely closed, they didn't hesitate for anything. The hall itself continued its linear, nondescript existence as it was gradually revealed ahead of them by the automatically triggered harsh white lights.

Di rotated, pistol firmly gripped in both hands close to her chest, elbows out for stability, checking for signs of movement from the doors they had already passed. All was as it had been, nothing out of place. If she hadn't seen a dead man with what amounted to a near full body's worth of blood covering his jumpsuit, the atmosphere would have felt serene. Instead, it was oppressively eerie, bordering psychosis-inducing. The peacefulness juxtaposed what they knew to be true; a large colony of miners and scientists had abruptly disappeared with no trace but for the small crime scenes they had found. It was terrifying.

"Coming up on an open area," Gene whispered, slowing their pace.

Di turned back and saw just beyond the furthest light what appeared to be a large open atrium, the entrance dimly lit.

"There are a set of benches up against a half wall just inside. I'll go left, Gerald right, Di center. Find cover quickly."

"Heard," she said as Gerald nodded. She could hear his gulp over the mic.

After a moment's hesitation, Gene swept forward, quickly peeling off as he hit the corner where the space opened wide. Gerald, less gracefully, shifted to the right, immediately huddling behind a polished metal bench. Di moved forward to the bench in the middle, ducking down behind it.

"I don't think we're far enough in to the room for the lights to register our movement," Gerald said over comms.

Gene nodded. "Use your suit's infrared layer in your

helmets. Scan the room for anomalies."

"What kind of anomalies?" Gerald asked.

Di glanced over as his helmet flashed slightly more opaque, the infrared vision initializing instantly. She brought up her own with a concentrated thought to her internal implant, the dark room suddenly flashing a dull blue. Maybe she was getting the hang of these non-verbal commands after all.

Gerald's form registered as a lighter green, his suit reserving and recycling his own body heat to keep the warmth in rather than letting it escape into the air around him. She knew her own form would look similar in his view.

"People. Dead things. Anything that seems out of place." Gene swept his rifle up and over the edge of the wall in front of him, sweeping side to side.

Di stowed her pistol at her waist and reached over her shoulder to grab the rifle stuck to her back, swiftly clearing the chamber and bringing it up in a ready position. She followed Gene's example, shifting up just high enough for the barrel of her gun and the top half of her helmet to peek above the wall. Strange, barely identifiable objects swam in her thermal vision, though all of it was a hazy blue reminding her just how cold it still was in the facility the deeper they went. If anything living lay in wait for them, it would register as a splash of warm color; shifting reds, oranges, and yellows. That is, assuming they didn't have high-tech suits like hers.

After a tense thirty seconds of constant surveillance, gun shifting back and forth, eyes peering intensely at every crevice,

Gene lowered his gun. Following suit, Di shifted her vision back to normal, welcoming the change.

"Gerald, you see anything?" Gene asked.

Hands still shaking, Gerald's visor cleared revealing a sweat-soaked forehead and wide, erratic eyes. "Nothing," he said, refusing to lower his weapon.

Gene shot Di a sympathetic smirk and stood, walking cautiously around the edge of his half wall. The lights in the large, open space finally triggered bathing them in that same sickly white glow.

They were standing in what could best be described as a crossroads, an atrium large enough to shuttle large equipment with more hallways branching off in a dozen different directions. Though the ceiling was higher than the confined spaces they had been traversing so far, it couldn't have been more than six meters high. Plenty of space for freight, but surprisingly wasteful for a corporate facility. Every single corporation she knew of would have balked at increased construction costs for something so frivolous as a space not quite so claustrophobic. Never mind the mental wellbeing of the dozens of workers stationed here years at a time, trapped in a building ten kilometers under the surface with little to no interaction with the sky, weather, or much of anything beyond the thick layer of ice looming ever present above their heads.

As her gaze travelled from above to below, she noticed a glass circle, roughly five meters in diameter, set into the floor in the very middle of the room.

"Gene," she said, nodding in that direction as he glanced her way.

"Looks like a window," Gene replied, taking a cautious step toward it. He was not the biggest fan of heights, and the prospect of standing on glass was enough to make him hesitate.

"A window in the ground? Seems a little strange."

"Don't ask me," he replied, closing his eyes and taking a step back.

Curious, Di walked forward. As she moved closer, what lay below opened up to a breathtaking view. Through the dim light, she could just make out a circular shaft which had been drilled through the middle of the facility leading straight down to the subsurface ocean below the thick layers of ice. She thought she could make out the undulating water below the surface of encrusted ice several dozen meters beneath them. Faint breaks in the wall and thin balcony-style walkways indicated where each of the floors connected back to this central hub. Di counted at least twelve more floors.

Paragon had started out on Enceladus as a simple ice mining operation, stripping the moon of its constantly replenishing resource. She imagined this shaft was left over from one of the cores drilled out of the moon's surface, the massive ice cylinder that had once been here later being chopped into smaller, more manageable chunks to then ship back to Earth. It wasn't until the company had confirmed the existence of the liquid ocean below that they expanded to more scientific endeavors. Or so their advertisements boasted. Nobody really knew what it was they were studying out here, and being one of the big three corpos, Paragon wasn't about to divulge their secrets.

Gerald whistled, sauntering up behind her and staring down at the intimidating drop below the glass. "This place is bigger than I imagined." Though he was attempting to show bravado, his voice quavered uncertainly.

"I thought you read Paragon's file on this place?"

"Yeah, but they would never put in writing just how much they had out here. At least not in documentation an outsider could get his hands on. Besides, all it said was that this was a 'big ice mining facility.' You know how much corpos like to embellish things."

Di nodded in appreciation. Despite the circumstances, Gerald was still Gerald, and he couldn't resist sharing his intellectual observations. Many people took that as a sign of his arrogance, a chance to show off his vast knowledge on anything and everything. She knew it for what it really was; a simple attempt to connect to people. It wasn't *his* fault his IQ was twice as high as his audience.

"The sheer volume of payload that must filter through this facility has to be astronomical. I can't imagine the amount of fuel it must take to shuttle it between the surface and the orbital station, let alone between here and Earth. This drilled out core alone must have taken..." Gerald's eyelids flickered as he mimed counting on his fingers. "at least a mid-sized freighter to haul it all back home, assuming the height is roughly fifty meters, and the diameter is roughly eighteen meters, meaning the volume would be over one hundred thirty-seven thousand..."

He stopped mid-sentence, eyes refocusing to register Di's raised eyebrow and friendly smirk.

"Sorry."

"No need to be sorry for who you are, Gerald." She shot him a genuine smile which he gratefully returned.

"You two done? I've found the way down."

Di glanced over her shoulder at Gene who stood just inside a set of doors inlaid in the far wall. Over his shoulder she saw the floor disappear, stairs leading to the levels below. His rifle was back in a ready position, butt pressed firmly against his shoulder. He was inspecting Florence's slide and power source, a nervous tick that to anyone else may have appeared to be a routine function check. Di knew better. Florence was as well-oiled, perfectly polished, and pristinely lubed as any gun could be. Better, even, than the day he bought it. He had no need for double or triple checks, though when he did, it was a sure sign to her that he was concerned. She even felt herself getting antsy standing in one spot for this long.

"We'll follow your lead," she responded, lightly pushing Gerald in front of her to line up at Gene's back.

Gene nodded in appreciation and pointed at the nondescript map on the wall beside the doorway. "It looks like the lowest floors are their dedicated science wings. If we're going to find any working computers, that's probably our best bet."

"Agreed." Di nodded and took up her place in the rear.

With a final nod, Gene took his first steps into the stairwell. They moved carefully and silently; not exactly slow, but not quick either. Just as the hallways above had registered their presence, bulbs flared to life on each flight as they passed beneath them, shooting their glaring fluorescent light bouncing across the sterile white stairs and walls.

After descending to level B8, Di hailed Gene on the public comm line. "Which floor are we starting on?"

"B10 was labeled as 'Research and Development'. I think we should start there."

Though she tried not to show it, the plummeting pull in the pit of her stomach had returned in full force. They were moving further and further away from their intended escape, traveling lower and lower down in the moon's icy crust. Though she preferred it to the relative helplessness of microgravity, having hundreds of tons of frozen water above your head that could hypothetically crash down at any minute was not exactly comforting.

"Take positions," Gene called, taking his customary point position to the left of the sealed doorway leading to level B10.

Di and Gerald did as commanded, shifting themselves to the right of the door. With a single nod, Gene triggered the doors and pushed through. Di followed closely behind Gerald, sweeping her rifle left then right before crouching behind another half wall similar to the one on the top floor. As before, the motion sensor lights had not yet been triggered.

"I think I spotted the right hallway on the opposite side of this atrium, but we'll need to circle around. We shouldn't cross through open air." Gene indicated with his gun toward the center of the dark space before them and Di nodded. Gerald poked his head up ever so slightly, pausing for a moment before slumping slowly back down against the wall.

"Gerald, you circle right with me. Gene will go left," Di said, placing a hand on his shoulder.

Gerald didn't respond. Di glanced up to see a concerned look on Gene's face. Though she didn't have a clear view of Gerald, she sensed something wrong. His breathing had increased, shoulders heaving.

"Gerald, what's wrong?" she asked, leaning forward.

His eyes were wide, skin a pasty mixture of ghostly white and olive green. He opened his mouth to respond but apparently thought the risk of retching was too great to speak. With a single pointer finger, he indicated beyond the wall to the atrium.

Gene's gaze hardened. He brought his rifle up, finger back on the trigger. Di, fear building in her chest, raised her head above the half wall. It was at that moment the motion-sensors finally caught their movement, flooding floor B10 in bright light.

Di's stomach dropped at the sight of the veritable river of bright red, frozen blood coating every inch of the atrium floor.

"I think we know where the crew went," Gene muttered.

CHAPTER 6
EXPERIMENTS

"How many people were stationed here?" Di asked. Not for the first time, she was extremely grateful for her suit's olfactory filters. Despite the advanced technology, her mind was now convinced she could taste the thick coppery cloud emanating from the frozen lake of blood.

"Around one hundred and fifty according to the records," Gerald said, voice wavering as he slumped down.

"This seems like a lot of blood for a hundred plus people," Gene replied, rising above the half wall to continue scanning the room.

"An average adult human body contains roughly five liters of blood," Gerald said. Even with his eyes squeezed shut against the horror, he couldn't resist spouting pertinent facts when prompted.

"The miner we found was leaking blood from every orifice," Di chimed in, standing and approaching Gene. "And five liters is a lot when you're talking blood."

Gene grunted. "Maybe." Temporarily satisfied that

nothing was going to ambush them, he lowered his gun and paced along the edge of the round room, carefully sidestepping the blood as much as he could. "Even so, where are the bodies?"

Di, stomach thankfully now settled, peered around the room, desperate for clues. Red spatters dotted the various hand railings and columns throughout the atrium. A macabre, frozen waterfall of red draped off the edge of the floor and down the open center circle, only falling a meter or so down before coming to a sharp point far above the ocean's encrusted surface. But as Gene had said, there was no sign of a single body. Not a bloody smear of one being dragged elsewhere. No body parts. Other than the grotesque, gory blanket of icy blood, not a single sign that any living thing was or had ever been there.

"I think Paragon will have a hard time arguing this isn't the 'proof' they were looking for," she said, carefully approaching the railing that lined the steep drop to the water below.

"It's a corpo," Gene muttered, head swiveling to glance at the various avenues branching off from the atrium. "They'd argue even if you dropped the bodies in their lap."

Di snorted, glancing beside her at a shining chrome table with a mirror finish, pristine but for the crimson flecks dotting one side. She glared at her reflection; eyes slightly bugged in a maniacal way, light purple bruising along the bags of her eyes, thin lips pursed against the urge to scream. The woman staring back looked like a crazed copy of the woman she had bade farewell to mere hours ago in the ship's bathroom mirror. The eerie feeling as though she were merely a bystander in a stream of horrifying events was new as well.

Di leaned down close to the reflection looking side to side to see if there were any grey hairs tinging her temples yet. Her fingers moved instinctively to brush an errant lock behind her ear, but she caught herself before they bumped ineffectively against her helmet, a sign she was finally readjusted to life in a suit. She sighed.

"Anything for an excuse to lower the payout," she said. "But if this isn't enough, they can shove it up their asses."

Di manually checked to make sure her suit's monitor cam captured footage of their surroundings, but not before smirking and flipping the bird to her frazzled mirror image reflected in the table. A conspicuous red dot appeared in the top right corner of her HUD accompanied by a 'Recording In Progress' notification.

Paragon was constantly monitoring and gathering data through recorded video from each member of the crew while wearing these *precious* E.I.A.P.S.L. suits. Sporadic notices of 'random' recordings for 'quality assurance purposes' had popped up from time to time while training with the suit. Those had just been the moments Paragon had *wanted* them to know they were being watched. There was no doubt in her mind, Paragon had more than just a handful of clips of her in this suit. If she ever made it back to a place where she could upload her data, she planned on capping it off with a delightful stream of foul-mouthed expletives.

"This looks like the way we should go," Gene said. Di

glanced up to find him already at the mouth of the closest hallway entrance, cautiously sweeping his rifle back and forth. A small plaque on the wall read *Data and Records* with a helpful arrow directing them further down the passage.

"Following your lead," she said.

Without prompting, Gerald stood and took up his position in the center of the pack, a sign of progress in the kid's field abilities.

This particular hallway was narrower and not quite as long as the others they had already traversed, though the overarching dread still coated every inch of its similarly pristine condition. Before long, they reached another opening leading to an expansive area at least a dozen meters across, though not as large as the atrium. Thick, corrugated, plastic-looking conduits lined the far wall, coalescing from various ports around the room. Many of them separated into bundles of colorful wiring both massive and miniscule leading to industrial generators in the far corner taking up an entire wall and a half. The area was accompanied by a handful of brightly colored signs warning curious onlookers away.

"These cables must lead all the way to the turbines at the southern pole of the moon," Gerald said, forgetting protocol and leaving his position.

So his field abilities still needed some work.

At an exasperated look from Gene, Di lowered her gun and moved to scope out the rest of the room. "Do you think these power the entire facility?" she asked.

"I have no doubt these are the main generators with how many conduits lead to and away from them, but I would imagine there are backup generators in a different portion of the facility. Possibly some emergency generators in a third spot, especially considering these don't appear to be on at the moment, but we're not stewing in complete darkness."

"What's in these ones?" Gene asked, already across the room and examining several small cubbies and nooks. He pointed to a large cylindrical pipe that went from floor to ceiling.

"Ah yes," Gerald replied, attempting to fall into his role as self-proclaimed know-it-all despite his shaking hands and quavering voice. "Those are the cryoducts. They carry liquid water from the subsurface ocean and use the force of the cryovolcanoes to propel it through their machinery to cool it down." Gerald waltzed over to examine the innocuous tube. "Relatively ingenious, to be honest. It would take significant electrical power to heat this facility to a livable temperature, but pumping water through their incredibly hot machines and then distributing that excess heat around the facility is comparatively simple."

"Fascinating. Can we find a functioning terminal please?" Gene nodded toward the side room he had located having already done his preliminary security sweep.

Inside were rows of desks and stacks of cabinets, doors securely shut to hide their boring reports and statistical analyses. Three or four computer monitors dotted the room, a promising prospect, along with a wall lined with test tubes, beakers, and other various scientific equipment that did who the hell knew what. A set of swinging double doors leading off to another portion of the facility sat motionless between two of the desks housing more complicated-looking equipment.

Di strode purposefully to the back row of tables, pushing a slightly indented button on the corner of one of the monitors. It momentarily flashed a bright white before a familiar image of a login screen appeared.

"Gerald, come work your magic," she said, moving aside for him as he sat heavily in the chair before the computer.

"What exactly am I looking for?" he asked.

"Emergency procedures, blueprints, anything that we can use to find a way out of here," Gene said approaching from the opposite side of Di.

Gerald nodded, fingers flying across the keyboard, computer mouse flicked effortlessly in his right hand. "It might take me a second. There are a lot of files in here, and none of it is organized." His faced scrunched up as if the mere concept elicited a horrible taste in his mouth.

Di took the momentary reprieve to wander to another station in the room, one particularly cluttered when compared with the pristinely immaculate stations everywhere else. A stack of papers peeked out from a hastily closed cabinet door and, allowing her curiosity to momentarily steer her, she moved to inspect the contents.

As the cabinet door slid silently open with the barrel of her rifle, her anticipation was dashed at the sight of binders upon binders carefully labeled chronologically. She wasn't entirely sure what she was expecting, but she should have expected exactly what she found. Yes, these were scientists, but scientists on a barren ice world with little to examine other than the ice itself.

Di pulled a binder from the far-right side and opened it. A tiny circular disc slid down from an open pocket, no bigger than her palm and about as thick as her fingernail, which she caught deftly in her left hand before it fell to the floor. *Exp. 5-217* written in hasty penmanship was scrawled across the top.

"What is that?" Gene asked from over her shoulder causing her to jump.

"Good hell Gene. Don't sneak up on me."

He smirked and gave an innocent shrug. "What is it though?"

Di flipped it over and found nothing of note on the opposite side. "Let's see if one of these terminals can tell us."

Approaching the nearest one, she placed her rifle on the desk beside her and woke it from its comatose state. As the screen flared to life, she was presented with a generic login screen. "Gerald, what password should I use to get into this?"

"Try leaving it blank. You'd be surprised how many people don't bother setting up a password."

Di hit the 'enter' key and, to her surprise, the screen came to life. "You'd think with the number of degrees these guys have they'd be a little smarter," she muttered, eliciting a chuckle from Gene. "Gerald, where do I insert this disc?"

"Disc?" he asked, standing and glancing curiously toward her. He sauntered over and plucked the object from her hand. "Ah. It's a data disc." He placed it on a small, inset square on the table below the edge of the monitor which glowed to life with a muted white light. A window appeared on the screen.

"So, it's like NFC?" Di asked, crouching closer to inspect the disc that lay inert on the table. Though she wasn't particularly adept with cutting edge technological advancement, she considered herself a dabbler. Curious enough to ask, do a little research here and there, but she mostly left it at that.

"Sort of," Gerald said, clicking on the solitary folder located on the disc. It opened to reveal various documents, videos, and data files with complicated non-names, like *E-5-217-870920.1* or *PV07109*.

"Let me take a look," she said, scooching Gerald aside and clicking on one of the documents. The screen filled with script in miniscule print listing dates, names, and words she could barely pronounce. Scrolling down, she found a break in the wall of words, a start to a more manageable and understandable summary section. She began to skim through the text, catching on important words like 'test subjects,' 'cryovolcanoes,' and 'organism.'

"They were conducting unsanctioned experiments on animals?" Gerald asked, disgust tinging his question.

"They were conducting unsanctioned experiments on everything, Gerald," she replied.

"Humans?" Gerald asked, aghast.

Di shot him a patronizing, 'oh, you poor innocent moron' look. "What regulations do you think are enforced way out here?"

"And when they're discovered back home after it's all said and done, Paragon gets a slap on the wrist, a minimal fine, and everyone moves on with their day," Gene interjected.

Gerald's face scrunched in disgust. "Except for the ones they experimented on," he muttered as he returned to his terminal to continue searching for a way to the surface.

"These experiments *do* seem a little dangerous," she said, returning attention back to her screen.

"How so?" Gene asked, interest piqued.

"They were conducting dives close to the cryovolcanoes near the southern pole of the moon," Di said, scrolling further down. "Apparently when testing the water that flows through these heating pipes, they found something interesting. A microorganism of some kind."

"So they wanted to see if it was another resource they could exploit?" Gene guessed.

"They wanted to see if it was another resource they could exploit," she replied, shaking her head. "Paragon wanted a closer look. Never mind the three scientists who suffered from hypothermia and the one who nearly died from a blast of water to the facemask."

It didn't surprise her to see such blatant disregard for human life. Ever since the corpo lobbyists had sunk their claws into the international trade systems and relaxed galactic employment regulations, countless people had mysteriously suffered from jobsite accidents conveniently 'caused' by their own negligence or inexperience. With a quiet payment of a pittance to the grieving family left behind, a pathetically rote statement, and a spokesperson's plastered-on display of remorse so fake and plastic it would take five hundred years to decompose in a landfill, the rich got richer and the working man stayed reliant.

Closing the currently open report, she picked a different file further down. Another document flared white on the screen, this one dated nearly two months after the previous one. Rather than scientific calculations or observations, it appeared to be a medical report. Some sickness had started spreading among the scientists and the miners, though it wasn't particularly lethal. No one had died, but it didn't seem like anyone was getting better either.

"What exactly were these experiments about?" Di asked rhetorically.

"Why do you say that?" Gene asked.

"From what I can tell, they jumped pretty quickly to animal and human testing after discovering this thing. It just seems stupid to think they were exposing themselves to an unknown alien organism without doing thorough testing first." She was no scientist, but even she recognized how irregular and dangerous it was to jump headfirst into something you didn't fully understand.

Curious, Di opened the binder again, noticing a pocket in

the back with a thin square lump. She attempted to fish it out, noticing the wording as it began to slide free of its plastic sleeve.

URGENT! T-

"Captain," Gerald called out. "I think I may have found a way back to the ship."

Momentarily forgetting her discovery and tossing it on the desk, she rushed to Gerald's side and peered at the screen. A rudimentary map of the facility was open on one side with some text on the other. She recognized the atrium on the top floor and the singular hallway leading to the elevator they had taken to get down here. It wasn't promising, as all offshoots led singularly back to that corridor.

"What am I looking at here?" she asked. "Is there an emergency exit I'm not seeing?"

"Not exactly," Gerald replied. "There's only one shaft up to the surface for this facility, and that's the elevator we came down in."

"So we're trapped," Gene said grimly.

"It only appears that way. Just beside the door there's a small opening for maintenance access. It appears to go all the way up to the surface, but it's a much tighter fit than the elevator shaft."

"We're going to have to *climb* all the way up?" Di asked incredulously.

Gerald shrugged. "Look, I'm clearly the one in this group who prefers cracking a book to taking a run. But if this is the only option, I'll be happy to get the hell out of here any way I can."

Di glared at the screen, her mind spinning. Manually climbing nearly ten kilometers was going to be brutal, but it wasn't impossible. If they could find a comm port down here in this lab, they could hail the station and make sure Bravo Team didn't leave without them. It was still risky taking such an exorbitant amount of time to climb what was essentially the galaxy's tallest building over ten times, but they would have to take what they could get. Besides, as much as she dreaded the fact, the microgravity along most of the shaft would be immensely helpful to preserving energy and maximizing speed.

"Ok. Gerald, I need you to find a comm port. We're going to notify Bravo Team of the plan and move out as quickly as possible." She turned to Gene. "I need you to maintain security. Don't go far, we're leaving fast. I'll try and collect some of these data discs. Maybe we can figure out what the hell was going on down here from a safer distance."

"Aye Captain," Gene said.

"Gerald, when you—"

A loud crash echoed beyond the double doors beside them.

Gene's gun flew up to his shoulder, barrel pointing unwaveringly at the doors. Di's hand flew to her pistol at her waist a hair slower than Gene's reaction, whipping it up toward the direction of the noise.

"What was—"

Di shushed Gerald quietly. He was the only one who had not been quick to the draw.

Another clang of something metallic bouncing off a solid surface clamored like bells in an empty church. Whoever this was, they weren't trying to be discreet.

Di glanced at Gerald who had once again gone white as a sheet, eyes bulging and perspiration dripping down his temples. She silently got his attention and opened their private channel. "Comm port," she whispered, bringing her pointer finger to her mask in a shushing motion.

Shifting positions until she was right behind Gene, she placed her left hand on his right shoulder, the signal for 'you take lead.' Gene nodded and gingerly nudged one of the swinging doors silently open with the barrel of his rifle. Di, pistol aimed just over his shoulder, followed in lockstep.

Beyond the doors lay a medical lab like the kind she had only seen in movies. Gurneys lay sprawled around the room, more than a few overturned and scattered haphazardly across the floor. Every single one was dyed red, drenched in dry blood that had soaked through the white sheets. Medical equipment on wheeled trays were pushed to the sides of the room as though shoved in a panic to get away from the epicenter. Except there wasn't anything in the center of the room. No bodies. No signs of life or death.

Opaque mirrored windows lined the far wall. She guessed it was a viewing gallery, a more comfortable position for the higher ups to monitor whatever disturbing experiments they conducted in here. One pane was cracked near the bottom, spiderweb-like fissures branching out from where something hard and heavy had impacted it.

The door to the gallery was open.

Gene noticed it just as she had, signaling to take position beside the door. Another sound like tinkling glass issued beyond the open doorway. Di silently crept through the room, carefully weaving her footsteps around the various metal tools, paper products, and broken shards of glass strewn around the floor.

This was risky. If whoever was in there happened to be looking out the one-way glass at that moment, they would have a front row seat to two strangers attempting to catch them unaware. Their best chance was to take the person by surprise. She hoped, assuming it was just another survivor, they could resolve this peaceably without bloodshed. If it wasn't a survivor... Well, that's why they had guns.

Crouching low to obscure view of her position, she leaned gingerly against the doorframe. Gene silently spun across the gap in the door taking position on the opposite side. His eyes narrowed as he peered into the slightly open doorway, gun still raised. Without taking his eyes off the room, he issued two succinct hand motions; 'follow' and 'go left.'

Gene eased the door open and entered the room, Di wordlessly following. The lights above were already glaring, their sterile white light illuminating a room full of overturned, cushioned, navy blue chairs. Another door lay across the room sealed tightly shut.

Recognition dawned on her as she saw the blood-stained grey overalls, the matted dark hair, the stubby fingers and slightly pudgy middle of the man standing beside an open vent in the wall. Though he wasn't facing her, her mind struggled to comprehend how this could be Patrick, the dead miner they had found above.

It didn't make any sense at all. She had watched that man die, struggling and gasping his last breath. Yet here he stood, limbs trembling and body swaying gently as if in a nonexistent breeze. His fingertips had developed an unhealthy grey tint, and the exposed skin on his arms and neck was pale white, bordering on blue.

"Patrick?" she asked, succumbing to her shock and immediately realizing her stupidity.

The man whipped around, eyes bulging and teeth bared. His lips and the tips of his nose and ears were grey just like his fingers. His face looked cracked and dry, and his cheeks lacked any hint of a rosy hue. She had seen cadavers that had looked more alive.

Then Di noticed the eyes. Glassed over and hazy white with a tinge of blue; it reminded her a bit of her grandmother's severe cataracts. But these eyes were different somehow; more cognizant, more aware. She shifted to her right and the eyes followed her, head shifting slightly like a predator marking and analyzing its prey.

"Diane, don't move," Gene hissed.

He rarely used her full name in the field, and when he did it was for good reason. Her hackles had already been raised, but with Gene's three words the fear lying stagnant in the base of her stomach began to boil over.

Patrick's grey lips curled back further, and he opened his jaw wide, accompanied by little cracks and creaks like the joints of an old wooden rocking chair that hadn't been properly maintained. A soft sound emanated from deep within his throat, a chilling mixture of a snake's hiss and the whistle of a boiling kettle.

Slowly, right hand shaking, she began to raise her pistol toward the creature, convinced that this was no longer Patrick the human miner. Whatever had happened, there was no humanity left.

The otherworldly sound cut off and it cocked its head as if curious about the steel barrel now pointed at its chest, unaware of the danger. It took a hesitant, jittery step toward her, moving faster than Di had anticipated. The sudden movement triggered her reflexes, and a bullet rocketed out of the pistol accompanied by a brief muzzle flash. The small shard of metal pierced just over the right breast, a perfect kill shot. Dark blue, viscous liquid spattered out of the hole in its chest, painting a grotesque streak across the ground between them. The bullet ripped itself out of its back near the spine, pinging off a metal panel behind and sending sparks briefly flashing in the air.

It didn't flinch, barely moving, gaping hole in its chest oozing purplish-blue across the red-stained coveralls. All Di could hear was the heavy sound of her own breathing pounding in her ears and a faint tinkle as the bullet casing came to rest at her feet.

The entire eyeball flushed dark blue, the same color as the 'blood' dripping from its wound. Its mouth opened impossibly wide, issuing an ear-piercing shriek. Di flinched despite her suit's sound dampening. Without further warning, the creature charged, launching itself directly at her chest and closing the three-meter gap between them in a single lunge. She only had time to squeeze off two rounds, both shots swinging wildly and only one connecting with the outer flesh of its arm, before impact.

The two of them tumbled heavily to the ground, skidding across the floor and taking out two chairs behind her. One hand gripped her right wrist, bony grey fingers squeezing like a vice to prevent her from raising her pistol. Even with her suit's ability to regulate temperature, she could still feel a chill where the creature's palm rested. Her left forearm strained against the creature's chest, struggling under the impossible weight and strength bearing down on her. Dark blue 'blood' dripped from the open wound above her, splattering against her face mask and partially obscuring her vision. It raised its head, neck bent back, jaw unhinged like a snake, and howled another unearthly scream.

And then the head was gone. The howling cut off instantly as Di was showered in blue viscous liquid. The body collapsed on top of her, all fight gone from its limbs. In moments it was hurled off her, Gene extending a helping hand to get her to her feet.

"What the hell was that?" she asked. Gene just shook his head.

As the adrenaline of the situation left her body, her limbs began to shake. Di sucked in quick shallow breaths, unable to let the air escape her lungs. The silent heart rate monitor flashed red in the corner of her vision, spiking dramatically. Her vision swam and her knees buckled.

Due to her copious amounts of field training, she recognized the signs of shock setting in. Even so, she was helpless to stop it.

"Sit," Gene commanded, cautiously directing her toward one of the many empty cushioned seats dotted around the room which she gratefully accepted.

"I... I..."

"Relax. Take a deep breath and exhale."

She did as she was told, taking a stuttering breath as he picked up her legs and placed them on another chair.

"We... need..."

"Di, stop. We need to take a minute is what we need. I'll not have you collapsing on me as soon as we set foot out that door." Gene glanced up, checking out the one-way glass to ensure nothing else was in there with them. "We have a minute. You're gonna be fine, but you need to breathe."

The contents of her breakfast hours before churned uncertainly in her belly, threatening to come up. The smeared 'blood' across her suit and visor didn't help much. Though as she thought that, gentle steam began to rise from the streaks of blue obscuring her vision. Gene leaned back, hesitating for only a moment before scanning her suit. A small cable extended from his wrist, and he plugged it into the port in hers.

"Your pulse is still pretty elevated. Just keep taking deep breaths, as deep as you can." He paused a moment, eyes flicking up and down on his feed inside his helmet. "It doesn't seem like anything is broken. Your suit looks uncompromised. No tears. Does anything hurt?"

Di sucked in the biggest breath she could, held it for a count of five, and exhaled heavily, ejecting as much of her fear as she could. "No, I'll be fine. We need—"

"Captain?" Gerald called from the doorway, gun in hand. "I heard a screeching sound and came to—" His eyes bulged as he caught sight of the headless corpse lying beside them.

"Gerald, we need to go," Gene said. "Do you have what we need?"

Gerald didn't answer, eyes transfixed on the steaming body.

"Gerald!"

His focus snapped back to Gene as if waking from a dream. "I... Yes, I think so. But I think you need to come see this."

Gene squinted, glancing back at Di. Gerald's uncharacteristically serious tone, despite the fear in his eyes as he glanced back toward the dead body, conveyed an urgency she had rarely seen in the man.

Gene leaned in, locking eyes with her to gauge whether her next response was genuine or not. "Are you sure you're ready?" he asked on their private channel.

Inhaling shakily, exhaling strongly, she nodded. "We

need to go."

She swung her legs off the chair and hesitantly stood, knees wobbling. After another few deep breaths, she felt her body begin its steady recovery processes. She knew it would take some time until she felt truly stable. Hell, she didn't think there was any surefire way to come back from what she just saw, but at least her legs wouldn't collapse underneath her for the time being.

"Lead the way," she said, sweeping an open palm toward Gerald.

Though it was a short walk back to the terminal glowing brightly in the next room basking the desks in a more sinister light, her mind flashed through what she had just experienced.

It wasn't possible, was it? She had watched Patrick die, seen his chest stop inflating and his final breath shudder past his lips. The sheer amount of blood that coated his clothing, still oozing and bubbling from every orifice as they found him, should have been enough to kill him. And yet he was standing in that room. Moving, breathing, acknowledging their presence. Until they had killed him for a second time.

But that wasn't Patrick. That wasn't *human*. Not anymore.

They really needed to get off this damn ice rock.

Gerald plopped heavily down in his seat and began scrolling through the open folder on the screen. "I found that second data disc in the folder you were looking at. The one marked *'URGENT! TAKE ME!'* I couldn't resist taking a peek."

The screen flipped rapidly past documents interspersed

with pictures and video files, all full of men and women in lab coats holding tablets and various instruments. Di briefly noticed pictures of mice held in clear, acrylic containers before they flew past in a flurry of motion.

"That microorganism they found?" Gerald asked. "You were right. They were experimenting with it. They tested it on mice, introducing it to their blood streams just to see what would happen."

Gerald paused on the next picture, a gruesome scene of a dead mouse lying rigid on its back, paws curled and pointing up. Flecks of dark blue liquid oozed from its mouth, nose, and eyes. "Look familiar?" he asked.

Di nodded, stomach plummeting. The same 'blood' she had found in the elevator. In Patrick's reanimated corpse.

Gerald began cycling through pictures once more. Mice, rats, and rabbits flashed past, each one briefly appearing healthy before the inevitable follow-up picture of their lifeless bodies, dark blue material oozing from their faces.

"They kept experimenting, reintroducing the microorganism to new hosts and getting the same results. Until one test subject fought back."

He paused on a blurry photo of a large rat mid-flight, teeth bared in its attack on the nearest scientist.

"The scientist it bit got really sick and eventually died the same way the animals did."

The next photo was one she had seen plenty of times before. A dead body on a metal table, bottom half covered unceremoniously by a clean white sheet, top half bare. Eyelids closed and sunken in, skin waxy and cold. The only difference was the telltale purplish-blue 'blood' that had poured from his nose, mouth, and eyes.

"Let me guess," she said. "The body got up."

Gerald nodded and clicked on a video file, finger shaking.

A haggard man appeared on screen, purple bruises beneath sunken eyes hiding behind thick black-rimmed glasses. A touch of gray at his temples marked him in at least his mid-forties.

The room behind him looked like a disaster. Dark streaks across the wall, random objects strewn across tables, cabinets open with large stacks of paper spilling out.

"My name is Doctor Spencer McTavish," the scientist began, voice shaking. "And as far as I can tell, I'm the last one on this god-forsaken rock left."

CHAPTER 7
FLEE

"Whoever is watching this, I beg you. Do not take what I say lightly. What we've unleashed here is..." Doctor McTavish exhaled heavily, pinching the bridge of his nose underneath his glasses before continuing. "It is imperative that this information make it off Enceladus. No one can come back here, not anymore. I pray to God that the person who finds this isn't destined for the same doom that we are."

Di blinked several times in rapid succession, attempting to process the scientist's words. The one and only question now forcing itself to the forefront of her mind; were they already too late?

"About four months ago, our team discovered the microorganism during a routine particle test of the water pumped through the ducts throughout the facility. The OHMEGA-97 parasitic sample, or the "Omega Parasite" as it was later monikered, presented itself more as a virus than a parasite. It was small and round with seemingly simple genetic makeup, but when left to its own devices it began to slowly multiply on its own. Upon further inspection, it indeed had a clearly defined nucleus, though it was infinitesimally smaller than any known parasite any of us had ever seen.

"Our excitement at a potentially massive scientific breakthrough, not just on parasitology but on the potential for life on outer planets or moons, led to shortcuts. Not just in scientific procedure and study, but security as well."

"Of course they did," Gene muttered. It had long been his very openly shared opinion that if people would consider security and safety upfront rather than as an afterthought, eighty-five percent of the human race's problems would be solved long before it escalated to the point of actually needing that security. It was an ideal Di and the rest of their crew had come to share wholeheartedly. The only reason they had all made it out alive through the hundred or so jobs they had taken was owed almost solely to Gene's overly cautious zealousness, and, to a similar degree, Gayle's mildly unhealthy paranoia as the Security Officer.

"We spent a mere seventy-two hours after discovery conducting tests on the Omega Parasite itself before advancing to test subjects," the video continued. "Introducing it to other living organisms; tests that started with rats and rabbits which seemingly led to nothing. The test subjects showed no symptoms or signs of infection and upon further review, their blood showed only a handful of living samples of the Omega Parasite. However, starting with test thirty-two, the test subjects began exhibiting uncharacteristic behaviors; loss of appetite, gaunt features, and strange, dark subdermal pigments. These symptoms worsened leading to a coma-like state and, eventually, the test subjects' expiration."

"Can we skip forward?" Di asked, simultaneously enrapt in the scientist's explanation and cognizant of their imminent danger. While she knew they needed to move, this video file felt important. If they could understand what they were up against, even just a fraction, it could mean the difference between survival and death.

"Sure," Gerald said, placing a tremoring finger on the 'forward' button highlighted below the video.

Doctor McTavish sped forward jerkily as the video advanced, head bobbing sporadically. He suddenly left the screen for a moment before reappearing, holding what appeared to be documents and pictures.

"Stop," Di commanded.

Gerald lifted his finger and the video resumed regular playback.

"—ubjects, upon reanimation, exhibited violent tendencies and seemingly sporadic behavior. It was only upon further study that there appeared to be synchronous, or at the very least highly similar, behaviors between the subjects. It was hypothesized that, upon reanimation, test subjects gained the innate ability to communicate, though it was never proven."

A strange groan echoed distantly in the background of the video causing Doctor McTavish to freeze, glancing cautiously above and behind himself. After a brief pause with no further sounds around him, he continued, though his voice was a touch softer.

"Shortly after these tests, people throughout the facility began to show symptoms. At first it was misdiagnosed as the common cold owing to the constant sub-freezing environment. That is, until the symptoms worsened. It was gradual, with only one or two requiring medical intervention in the first week. Then it cascaded into dozens needing hospitalization with more than half succumbing to a comatose-like state similar to our test subjects.

"Once we had finally admitted to ourselves what was going on, several colleagues, along with myself, tried to warn the executives of what we assumed was happening. They asked for proof, and when we could only provide loose conjecture according to our limited studies on the animals, they ignored us. We went to the medical staff next, but by then it was too late. People began dying. Miners, scientists, cleaning crew; it didn't matter, and with limited space they had no choice but to store bodies in the open."

He shuffled through his stack of papers while he continued. "The first human reanimation took longer than we had guessed it would. It gave us temporary hope that maybe we were wrong. We weren't, of course."

Finding what he wanted, he brandished a physical photo from a security camera of a cordoned off hallway full of bulging body bags. "This was taken three weeks ago when the epidemic was just beginning, before any human reanimations had occurred."

Doctor McTavish produced a second photo of the same hallway, now completely full of corpses. The majority were still in the black plastic body bags, though those on top had not been properly zipped up. Several bodies lay on top of the piles without even the decency of a bag.

"This was two weeks ago. In one week, the Omega Parasite had wiped out nearly one-third of the station's inhabitants. It was around this time the first reanimation occurred. Unfortunately, it was in the presence of one of the janitors who was... rather violently attacked."

Flipping to a third photo, Di recognized the same hallway, though it was now full of people, black body bags discarded under their feet.

"This was taken three days later. We attempted to seal off the medical wing, but it didn't matter. It was merely a desperate effort to keep the reanimated from attacking those of us still around to care.

"The parasite's ability to adapt and learn was astonishing. The first victims were slow upon reanimation. I hypothesize this had something to do with the parasite's requirement of a sub-zero environment to flourish. Since blood coagulates and freezes just below zero, I assume this was the main hindrance. Shortly after the first few reanimations, the Omega Parasite adapted yet again, forcibly ejecting the blood from the body of its host and replacing it with a dark viscous liquid better suited to freezing temperatures."

Di immediately thought back to the dark blue, purplish goo she had found throughout the facility. Glancing down at her own suit, she saw the faint stains of the parasite blood splotched across her chest, the liquid itself long since evaporated. An involuntary shiver ran down her spine and her eyelids fluttered in response.

"I've named this final mutation the Terminus Strain." Dr. McTavish grimaced. "It's only fitting for a parasite we so brazenly monikered 'the end.'" He shook his head, placing the photos from his hand on to the desk in front of him and rubbing his eyes beneath his glasses. "By the time we had fully grasped what was happening, it became nearly impossible to stop. The hosts could move quickly and communicate across vast distances. And now—"

A crash echoed in the video much closer than the previous noises. Doctor McTavish visibly blanched, his protruding Adam's apple bobbing as he swallowed. His speech quickened, taking on a hint of hysteria.

"I've made several copies of the important documentation of our research, some physical and some digital. Evidence of what we found, what we *caused*. As far as I know, I'm the only one left. I aim to make it to the orbiting station to commandeer a shuttle, or at the very least reach the long-range transmitter to send what I can off-world. If I somehow don't make it, I pray the poor fool who finds this video can do what I could not."

The video abruptly ended leaving a ringing, hollow absence. Di's stomach churned, egged on by both fear and anger.

"Comm port," she hissed.

Neither Gerald nor Gene needed further explanation. Gerald pointed to a far corner of the room and Di purposefully strode to it, summoning her comm cable from her wrist port while she fumed.

Jamming the cable in, she quickly found what she was looking for and summoned the orbital station's comm line. One and a half rings later, her call was answered.

"Captain?" Gayle asked.

"Put him on."

Again, with no need for further promptings, the line quieted for several seconds giving Di time to collect herself. It would do little good to fly off the handle if she was going to get anywhere. She took two deep breaths before his voice reached her ears.

"Diane? I hope this is good news."

Not Di. Not Captain. *Diane.*

"You sonuvabitch."

So much for diplomacy.

"Excuse me?"

"How long has Paragon known what's been happening out here? How long have *you* known?"

"I have no idea—"

"Stop bullshitting me Liam!" she screamed. Her heart rate monitor spiked to 146, familiar flashes of red warnings in the corner of her HUD. She forced herself down, blood beating behind her temple as she strained to control herself.

"The parasite, Liam. The Omega Parasite." Her words, moments ago influenced by fiery primal rage, now replaced with a steely cool resolve, effectively conveyed the threat that it was. It was not a question; it was a demand.

"Ms. Eastwood, I—"

"Captain," she interjected.

"Captain. Yes." His voice quavered, the tone of her accusations having the cowing effect she had hoped for. "The... the Omega Parasite is a classified trade secret owned by Paragon, and—"

"You piece of shit," Di interjected with an incredulous chuckle. "Hundreds are dead and you're spouting some corporate-fed fu—"

"Dead?" he asked. "What do you mean hundreds are dead?"

Di paused. His tone had changed, taking on a genuine note of surprise. While he may have known about the parasite, even he apparently hadn't been told everything.

"This *trade secret* you've been sent to recover has killed everyone at this base," she spat. "It's created monsters, reanimating corpses that are roaming around down here where *you and your goddamn company sent us*!" She hadn't meant to shout the last part, but it had grown and evolved from her increasing sense of frustration and disbelief. Did human lives mean literally nothing to Paragon?

"That's... that's not possible."

A faint screech echoed from somewhere within the

facility. Di, Gerald, and Gene all instinctively turned toward the noise. Her rage was instantly chilled by primal fear, turning the blood in her veins to ice.

"Captain? Captain, are you there?"

Di would have hung up if not for Gayle's voice.

"Gayle. Contact Emma." Di struggled to keep her voice monotone and collected, fighting her growing sense of panic. "Tell her to keep the ship primed. We're going to attempt to climb the elevator shaft."

"You're going to climb it?" Gayle asked. "What happened to the car?"

"Too risky. Tell Emma to take off if we're not there in an hour, but to keep the lines open. If we can't make it to the ship, I'm going to try to figure out a way to transfer something important. Whatever happens to us, we cannot lose this information."

"Heard, Captain," Gayle replied. Though she acted professionally, Di knew Gayle was churning inside with worry. Not just for her Captain, but for Gene. "What else can I do?" Di could hear the sense of frustration and helplessness in her voice.

Another high-pitched hiss floated toward them followed by loud clangs as something metallic hit the floor. It was close.

Without hesitation, Di yanked her cord out of the port severing the connection. Whirling around, she caught sight of Gene ducking down behind a desk, shepherding Gerald quietly beside him. The whistling screams were coming fast and getting louder. They were close. She had only moments.

A partially ajar locker stood as her hopeful salvation. In less than two strides she closed the distance, jamming herself inside as silently as she could muster. Nudging aside some folders and two dusty computer keyboards, she gingerly closed the door of the locker. The top of her helmet was mashed unceremoniously below a thin metal shelf, kinking her neck to an unnatural angle. Her arms were pinned to her sides in the tight, confining space, not allowing her to easily access her wrist module.

More than a dozen parasitic hosts burst into the generator room from the hallway leading to the atrium, simultaneously halting mid-step as if following a group dance routine to music no one else could hear. Di peered out of the small slits in the locker door that gave her just enough of a view to terrify her. Just like Patrick, these creatures faintly resembled what was once a living human, though the blackened necrosis had spread much farther up their limbs and across their faces. Bits of dead flesh hung loosely along their arms and legs revealing cords of stringy, purple muscle underneath. Though they were farther away than Patrick had been, she could see their eyes sunken deep into their skulls, flushed a deep blue.

Di's halting breath echoed in her ears, rebounding around her helmet like she was in one of the isolation training chambers in boot camp. The thought brought her momentary comfort, a sense of familiarity at a moment that was anything but.

None of the hosts had moved in what must have been a full minute. Noses slightly upturned, heads twitching minutely;

it reminded her of a pack of prairie dogs waiting, watching for any hint of danger, and triggering their chance to flee. Except they *were* the danger, and what triggered would be much more violent than fleeing.

Di mentally summoned her helmet cam feed, bringing the screen to the forefront of her visor. It was an awkward fit trying to focus it through a tiny slit rather than the rough and dented inside of the metal locker door. With the built-in retinal tracking, she focused on the blurry crack and mentally locked focus there. The hosts suddenly loomed into view in crisp, sharp detail.

Zooming in, she focused first on the face. Their eyes had lightened some, from a dark navy to a smooth royal blue. Their mouths looked cracked and weathered in addition to the blackening, more resembling leather than human skin. Di noticed their chests weren't heaving, their shoulders weren't bobbing in a steady rhythm as a normal person's would when breathing heavily. Did that mean they didn't need to breathe?

I should be recording this, she thought, issuing the command. *I'm sure Gerald will have a field day with this footage. He'll likely have three dozen theories on why—*

As one, every head swiveled in her direction, eyes flushing a shade darker.

Di's throat closed and her heart seized, lungs sucking in a single shuttering breath before catching and refusing to exhale. It took her decades of self-discipline and every ounce of will to keep her body from jolting in fear, an action that would give away her position resulting in her sudden and violent death at the hands of frozen monsters.

The recording indicator light. They had noticed the light. How the hell had they noticed the light?

Stupid, Di chided herself. The one time Paragon decided to follow GBIA's privacy procedures by including a recording indicator and it bit her in the ass. Even when Paragon feigned compliance it screwed her over.

Issuing another mental command to stop recording, she squinted her eyes in preparation hoping it wouldn't trigger another reactionary response. The hosts remained transfixed on her locker. It may have been her imagination, but she swore their eyes flushed another shade darker.

Di glanced toward her rifle sitting uselessly on the desk near the back of the room, silently cursing her stupidity. The sheer number of times she had drilled into her crew to keep their weapons close, and she leaves her primary firearm on a desk? What the hell was going on with her? She had been off her game from the jump, another indicator that she should have relied on her instincts when her gut had told her this mission was a mistake.

Di took two calming breaths. There was a time and a place for self-reflection and reform, but staring down a horde of bloodthirsty demons was most definitely not the time or place.

Turning her attention toward Gene's and Gerald's hiding spot below a desk in the far corner, she could just make out a sleeve and a boot. If anything happened to them, it would be on her head.

Her emergency messaging system appeared in the bottom corner of her visor, and she issued a simple sentence to Gene; *They've made me.*

The visible sleeve jerked suddenly behind the desk. At least their EMS worked down here. She was also glad she hadn't sent that to Gerald. If that had been Gene's reaction, there's no telling how loud Gerald would have been.

A sliver of Gene's face peeked from behind the desk, anger and worry lines standing out in stark contrast through his helmet visor. He disappeared momentarily once more before shifting as though to come out from his secure spot.

No! she commanded.

Thankfully he paused, one booted foot ready to vault himself within view of the hosts beyond the thin pane of glass that separated them. Though Gene was obedient, there was only so far his obedience would stretch. Outright allowing a superior officer to die when he believed he could prevent it was a line Di knew he would not cross.

Get ready to run, he messaged.

Di shook her head, though no one would see it, and issued another command, one that she was sure he would follow.

Wait. Watch.

Slowly, Gene eased himself back down into the crevice, shielding himself once more from her view. He shook his head in frustration, but at the very least he obeyed.

Shifting silently, Di refocused her attention on the hosts still locked in a holding position, focused on her locker. How long they would wait was beyond her, but she doubted it would be for long. The real question was why they hadn't made their move already.

A faint, echoing, hissing screech sounded several floors down, and she recalled a line from near the end of the video that sent a shiver down her spine.

The hosts can communicate across vast distances. They were *summoning more*.

Glancing back to Gene, she saw his arm stretching up near the top of the table, a thin cable extending from his wrist. She was sure it was his camera module, and he had a live feed up on his HUD.

Di panicked, heart fluttering. While she expected it had been the recording light that had triggered their reaction, she had no idea if that was the only thing that would draw their attention. If, in their altered state, they could sense something as miniscule as infrared light, Gene was about to gain their ire.

Gene, stop. It was all her mind could spew out and she hoped he would understand. Glancing back at the hosts, she noticed one or two flicking their gaze toward Gene's position. It wouldn't be long before their attention would turn fully to their newly perceived threat.

Without thinking, she flicked her camera on and off. All attention returned to her, eyes flushing a deep blue that bordered black. One, two, four of them issued a soft warning whistle. The three closest to their room took a hesitant step forward as though fighting an internal urge to act, to pounce.

Despite her dire circumstances, she couldn't help but analyze their behavior. It was clear they wanted to investigate, to attack, but something was holding them back. Whether it was an innate instinct or some external force that restrained them, it didn't have complete control over their actions. They could be convinced to break against the pack, to disobey whatever 'orders' they were receiving. All she had to do was overwhelm them.

I need you to throw something through the swinging doors, she messaged.

Gene leaned out once more, nodding his head in agreement. *Copy*, he replied.

Taking a deep breath and holding it, Di flashed her camera on and off once more. This time every single host took several steps toward the glass, their hissing whistle escaping their throats.

Now.

Gene, hefting a tablet lying next to them on the floor, launched it side arm. It flew below the top level of the desks, crashing into the right-side swinging door and sailing through. The tablet clattered noisily amongst the chairs just beyond.

Shrieks of anger and bestial fury erupted. The first three hosts smashed their bodies into the large glass viewing pane. Spiderweb cracks ran the length of it, barely holding on. Two more smashes and they were through, bounding over the jagged daggers of glass along the bottom frame. Whipping around her locker and jostling her in the process, they bolted into the next room, unearthly shrieks echoing.

Through the slit she saw Gene slowly getting to his feet, grabbing Gerald's hand and hauling him up. Feeling around the door at waist level, she found no latch or mechanism to release her and waited for Gene to set her free. Quickly and silently, he moved forward and opened the locker door.

Di nearly stumbled as she escaped her tight confines, knees wobbling. Just then she realized how tightly she had been clenching every muscle in her body. Careful not to disturb any contents that littered the desk in front of her, she leaned against it for balance and to collect herself. Glancing up, she made eye contact with Gene and gave him a silent thank you nod. She would be sure to get him a nice big bottle of malt scotch at their next port.

Sounds of shattering glass and violent destruction emanated from the room beyond, the hosts adamant on tearing it apart in search of their prey. Di was lucky her assumption had paid off. Her guess that their less intelligent primal side would take over had given them a chance, though how long they actually had before the creatures' linked conscious pulled them from their frenzy was anyone's guess.

With two quick hand signals, Gene issued the command to follow and took the lead toward the door. Gerald, wide-eyed and as pale as ever, stuck closely to his back, pistol raised and clutched tightly against his chest in his tremoring hands. She attempted to give him an encouraging nod, but she was painfully cognizant of her own fear reflecting behind her eyes.

Swiftly, the three moved in a silent line toward the door.

Di hesitated, glancing back toward her neglected rifle sitting tantalizingly on the desk on the opposite side of the room. Her pride pushed her to risk their limited escape time to grab it, but her gut warned her what would happen if they were caught between the horde of monsters currently tearing apart the room behind them and the second horde on its way. She gritted her teeth. It was time she stopped ignoring her instincts. With a final glance, she left the gun behind.

As they approached the door, Di noticed the shattered windowpane and the deep purplish stains along the edges of the sharp shards of glass that remained in the frame. Glancing down, she paused mid-step as she very nearly put her boot down on a large piece of glass. Shaking her head, she shifted around it and continued on, placing a hand on Gerald's shoulder. He jumped at the touch, head whipping around to look at her. When he recognized it was only her, he shot her a sheepish grimace.

Gerald's boot crunched as he shifted his weight on top of a glass shard.

All three paused. Di's breath caught in her throat, the garbled, frenzied ruckus behind them quieting. Time stood still. Not a single noise reached her ears. It would have seemed peaceful in comparison to the previous chaos if not for the sheer terror that gripped her chest.

Maybe the hosts hadn't noticed. Maybe they had stopped for an entirely different reason. And maybe they were really just misunderstood friends who wanted to help.

The hissing started anew. Calculated. Controlled. The

hunt was back on.

"Run," Gene muttered.

There was no hiding this time. Her legs pumped hard, harder than they had in years. She came level with Gerald as they sprinted through the generator room and into the hall. Scrabbling and screeching followed them, but she didn't dare look back. It was her turn to let primal instincts take charge.

Her quads burned. Her lungs ached. The narrow hall felt significantly longer than she remembered. She was in good shape for her age, but that was the kicker. Her age. It had been an uncomfortably long time since she had sprinted past the men in her class at the academy. That had been years ago. Decades. Now, her only chance was to channel her younger self to outrun the creatures giving chase and hope her body didn't give out.

After a slight bend, she felt a glimmer of hope. The entrance to the atrium. Salvation.

Risking a glance backward, an action she immediately regretted, that momentary hope waned. Slavering, ravenous monsters were steps behind them leaving no room for deviation. They would be overtaken and overcome before they even made it up a single flight of stairs.

"We're not making the stairs," she panted over the public comms.

"I know," Gene replied. With a sudden burst of speed, he entered the atrium, maintaining his straight course.

Like a lightbulb, Di understood his plan. Her breath sputtered in her throat, heart pumping harder.

"What?" Gerald squeaked.

"Keep running. Get ready to jump," Di said.

"Jump?" Gerald was on the verge of hysterics and his pace slowed with his hesitation.

Di instinctively gripped his upper arm as she passed, dragging him with her to keep him from stumbling. They were only a few strides away from the railing protecting the open space at the center of the room. Di's stomach churned at the thought of the sixty-meter drop to the water below, but there was no time to question. It was either possible death upon hitting the ice-encrusted water or certain death at the hands of hellish monsters. She knew which way she wanted to go out.

Gene reached the opening, scooping up a chair and placing his lead foot on the railing in a single fluid motion. Without a second's hesitation, he vaulted himself into open air and disappeared below.

Di was seconds away with Gerald half a step behind her. They were going to make it. As she jumped to place her right foot on the railing, she glanced to her left.

Gerald hesitated.

Sheer momentum threw her over the railing before she knew what was happening. Her body twisted as she reached for Gerald, but she was already hovering in midair, too far to grab him.

Time slowed. She heard a muffled mixture of inhuman shrieks, shaky breaths, and her own blood pumping behind her ears. Gerald locked eyes with her as she began to fall. The whites of his wide-open eyes were brilliantly bright as he gripped the railing, one foot up in preparation to jump. It wasn't enough. A dozen bodies slammed into Gerald, snapping the railing and sending them all careening into the open air.

Time resumed and she fell. Di's last-second lunge had altered her trajectory and sent her spinning uncontrollably. Confusing jumbles of red-stained walls, the glint of unforgiving ice, and a mass of writhing, blackened bodies flashed before her as she dropped.

Training finally kicked in and she spread her limbs to orient herself in the air. She knew she only had a handful of seconds before she hit the water. In her uncontrollable twisting, she caught a glimpse of Gene hurling the chair toward the ocean's surface several arm spans to his left, breaking the thin layer of ice on the surface moments before he pencil dived in himself.

Di knew she wouldn't wrest control of her freefall before she made impact. In an attempt to minimize the damage, she tried to tuck in her legs, forcing them where she thought was down to keep from slapping the water flat.

With a final spin, she caught sight of Gerald among the mass of squirming hosts. Tinges of red lined the opening of a deep slash across his chest, undersuit and skin exposed to the elements. Deep cracks fissured across his visor obscuring most of his face from her view. He didn't appear to struggle, but his mouth was open in a soundless scream.

With a final spin, the water filled her vision as it rushed

up to meet her.

CHAPTER 8
SHOCK

Di's eyes opened to the cold, black depths of an alien ocean, fathomless emptiness calling. Enticing her to join and become one with the inky abyss. Mind disconnected, she watched as if outside her own body as she slowly sank further and further down. The sterile, artificial lighting from the base above pierced a short way below the surface, but that harsh, wan light was fading quickly.

Her E.I.A.P.S.L. suit had saved her life, of that much she was certain. Sensing a rapid increase in speed, internal padding ballooned to cushion the blow as she hit the water. Despite the added protection, her left shoulder ached horribly as it had taken the brunt of the fall. Gene had saved their lives with that chair and his quick thinking. Tack another one on his tally. She had stopped counting the number of drinks she owed him years ago.

As she had hit the water, her suit had automatically compensated to keep her from experiencing cold shock. Unfortunately, the suit couldn't do anything for her psychological shock. While technology was poised to handle nearly every physical ailment humans could throw at it, a space suit can't erase the images of a friend being torn to shreds by a dozen crazed monsters. That's what the alcohol and the sedatives were for, and she was unfortunately fresh out of those.

In a snap moment her mind and her body collided, harshly returning her to the direness of her situation. Di was alive, yes, but only just, and she didn't have an infinite supply of oxygen at her disposal. In response, her eyes flicked to the steady countdown in the top left of her HUD display. Eighteen minutes and twenty-six seconds. Flipping around, the pinprick of light that now dimly shone above her seemed much farther away.

Flicking her wrist, she punched in a command to partially inflate the small, internal, individualized cushions around her waist to arrest her slow descent. Glancing up, she noticed a small, blinking light closer to the surface. Squinting, she recognized the simple morse code message being transmitted by what could only be Gene in a desperate bid to find her. Dot dot dash. Dot dash dash dot. Up.

Suddenly self-conscious of the surrounding blackness pressing in, she flicked on her helmet light. A beam of radiant white pierced the dark veil surrounding her, giving her both comfort and an unsettling dread. On the one hand, she could now see her path forward. On the other, the dark just beyond her saving light seemed so much more menacing than when she had been one with it.

Turning to her left, she froze at the faint streak of red slowly dissipating through the water. Blood.

A vice-like claw gripped her ankle. She screamed, kicking furiously at her attacker. After four hearty connections with her booted foot, the creature released its hold on her leg. Desperate to get away, Di increased the number of inflated cushions inside her suit and began to rapidly rise.

She glanced down expecting to meet the cold and dead navy-blue eyes of an attacking parasitic host. All she was met with were the wide and fear-filled hazel eyes of her crew member as his cracked helmet spiderwebbed and finally gave way, drowning his final bastion of hope with icy water. There were no more screams, no more frantic flailing of a desperate man in a bid to save his own life. Just fear. Resignation. Di could practically hear his accusation as Gerald sank below, dragged down by the two hosts still clinging to his waist.

You were supposed to protect us.

With a final glint off his cracked visor, he dipped below the edge of her beam of light and disappeared into the black void.

This was her fault. She had taken the job from Paragon despite it being, well, Paragon. She had pressed forward when all sense and instinct had told her to turn back. She had pressured Gerald into the surface party, despite his inexperience, despite his reluctance. It would be good for him, she had thought. He needed to be part of the team, part of the crew. She had pathetically tried to convince herself this would be a simple job for him. A little danger was a good bonding experience, and Gerald needed to feel more included.

And now he was dead. Dead at the bottom of an alien

ocean, torn to pieces by ungodly monsters.

You were supposed to protect us.

The look in his eyes as he gave up his struggle, the betrayal he must have felt. Surely, he had experienced a surge of hope finding his captain, begging for her to save him. Surely, she would help. Share oxygen. Get him to the surface. Treat his wounds. Surely, she would fulfill her promise of bringing him back home to his family alive and well.

You were supposed to protect us.

But he wouldn't be returning alive and well. He wouldn't be returning at all. His body was now unrecoverable, lost near Enceladus' core underneath the crushing weight of an unforgiving ocean.

Would they even have recognized him? Would there be anything left after the hosts were done?

Gerald's hazel eyes glared back at her, reflected in the inside of her visor. His innocent countenance gone, forever gone.

You were supposed to protect us.

A wave of intense nausea swept through, threatening to overtake her. Fight or flight cast its iron grip on her mind, overloading her senses. She had to get away. She had to escape.

Di inflated every one of the inflatable sacks within her suit, rapidly rising through the water and picking up speed. The empty black of the unknown chased her as she climbed, threatening to overwhelm her, to bring her back in its clutches. No longer was it a fascinating specimen, a scientific curiosity to be marveled at. Enceladus, this god-forsaken moon, was a monstrosity. It did not provide resources, wealth, opportunity; only death.

Two meaty hands grasped her biceps, slowing her upward progression. They were back. Back to finish her off. They'd taken care of Gerald, now it was her turn to join his bones on the ocean floor.

Her attempts to struggle were limited at best, pathetic in all reality. Di wanted to fight back, to take control like she always had. Like a captain should. Did she deserve to be a leader though, when her actions had directly caused the death of one under her command? Did she deserve to live?

"Captain! Di! Stop!"

Gene's familiar, gravelly tone brought her rocketing back from the edge faster than her suit had shot her through the water. Di's eyes refocused on his calming presence, finding solace in his chocolate brown eyes as they willed stillness from the chaos roiling inside her.

"Di? Are you alright?" Sensing her change, he briefly let go with his right hand to tap the data input on his left wrist. His eyes momentarily focused on his own HUD. "Readings say your heart rate is elevated. O2 usage is high. Suit is intact, no punctures."

"I..." She tried to respond, to summon her leader persona and take control. To be Captain Di. But it didn't come.

In every other situation she had ever faced with the crew of the CS Katana, her pride and sense of duty had pushed through in the end, blocking out her fear, her anxiety. But this time, all she felt was a hollow, empty pit.

The darkness undulating in the depths below crept up, threatening to swallow her whole. Her vision narrowed, the light above the surface of the water far above their heads fading. Just as before, she willed herself to fight, to be present, to stay alive.

But it didn't come. Gene's shouts over her comms muffled as she succumbed to the inevitable.

*   *   *

If this was heaven, she was grossly disappointed. Di's body ached as her eyelids fluttered groggily, flinching at the blaring white light above.

This couldn't be heaven. She still remembered vividly what she had done, the pain in her heart. Heaven was supposed to take away your pain, not increase its potency tenfold.

Glancing to her left, eyes blinking away the dark spots left from staring into the light for too long, she noticed a panel set into the wall above a series of drawers. It was close enough to touch. Wherever she was, it was small.

Di moved to rub her temples at the sudden onset of a pulsing headache. Her gloved hand scraped across her dry skin, bony fingertips pushing delicately into the soft spots beside her brow.

She froze. Where was her helmet?

Jolting upright, her head bounced painfully off the sterile light above her sending it swinging to the side on its articulating arm. It clattered noisily against the metal wall doing nothing to help with her now exacerbated headache.

"Captain?"

She wheeled to the left, legs swinging down to the floor from the lightly padded fold-down table she was lying upon. Gene filled the doorframe blocking the light from the passage beyond, face draped in shadow. His helmet was off as well, and a steaming cup of something decidedly pungent was gripped in his left hand.

"Take it slow," he said, gingerly approaching her with his right hand outstretched like he was approaching a wild animal.

Di swallowed, squeezing her eyes shut and willing her head to quiet. She gripped the edge of the table until the pounding behind her eyes lessened. Not gone entirely, just down to a manageable level. "Where are we?" she asked, eyes still closed.

"Exploratory submersible. We're safe for now."

"What..." The questions she wanted to ask lay jumbled on her tongue, too disjointed, too painful to slip past her lips. How was she alive? Why were their helmets off? Where did he find a sub? Settling on the summation with the fewest words, she licked her dry lips and tried again. "What... happened?"

"The long or the short of it?" Gene asked, pulling a chair from beside the table and dragging it forward to take a hefty seat. Di winced at the amplified sound of the legs scraping along the metallic floor. "Sorry," he responded, noticing her reaction.

"Why... why are our helmets off? Where *are* we?"

"Like I said, exploratory submersible. There was a secondary oceanside scientific exploration section in the facility not too far from where we went in the drink. I noticed it just before seeing your light in the water."

Di nodded, numerous questions still swirling through her brain. Leaning back against the metal wall behind her, she sighed as the cool surface pressed against the back of her neck. It was then she noticed how sweltering it felt in the cramped confinement. "Did you turn up the heat in here?"

Gene nodded, smirking slightly. "Hence why I know we're safe to remove the helmets."

"What do you mean?"

He slurped his coffee, sighing contentedly before handing it to her. Against her better judgment, she took a hesitant sip and grimaced at the overwhelming bitterness of Gene's specialty; burnt and over-brewed coffee, no cream, no sugar. Still, it felt good to send something to her empty stomach, and something boiling hot and caffeinated felt right.

"After dragging you through the water and finding this thing, I launched it from the facility," he began, patting the hull of the submarine. "Your vitals looked stable, so I took a look at those files from the doctor. Turns out his research was a bit more extensive than we first realized."

"Ok?" Di responded. "So, we're safe because of the heat?"

"Bingo. The parasites can't survive in high temperatures, anything above twenty-six degrees, really. So I cranked the heat as high as it would go just to be safe, made some coffee, and waited for you to wake up."

"How do you know we're safe?" Di asked. "How do you know this is hot enough? That we're not incubating one of those things right now?"

Gene shrugged. "I trust the doctor's research. He should know more about it than we do."

Di lowered her head into her hands, pushing against her closed eyelids with her palms. She knew Gene was intelligent, one of the smartest, field-savvy people in the business, but he could be a little too trusting at times when it came to topics he wasn't familiar with.

"Look, I'll give you what I found if it will help put you at ease."

"No, it's fine," Di replied, exhaling heavily and blinking the spots away from her vision her hands had left behind. "I trust your judgment on this. If you think we're safe, we're safe."

What she didn't voice was her concerns about the research itself. This parasite had already shown a tendency to evolve, to adapt to its environment. How old were the experiments Dr. McTavish performed? Two weeks? A month? What kinds of transformations had already occurred in that span of time? This parasite very well could already have overcome its intolerance of high temperatures enough to incubate in a live host rather than a dead one. She shuddered at the phantom wriggling she felt behind her eyes.

Pushing aside what she couldn't control, Di turned her thoughts to what she could. Their situation was far from ideal; no comms, no exit strategy, no escape route, an unknown number of hostiles with, hypothetically, the cognitive ability to converse and coordinate instantaneously. The odds were most definitely stacked against them. Hell, Gerald would have given them the exact percentage of their survival rate if he had been there.

Gerald.

You were supposed to protect us.

Di sprang off the table, shoving off the wall and clattering against the cabinets across the small corridor.

"Di?" Gene asked, limbs tensed and coiled. "I think you should sit back down."

"I... I can't. I need..." Her breaths became shallow, like she was trying to breathe the last vestiges of her oxygen tank but couldn't quite fill her lungs. The room began to spin, her brain desperately begging for air. Di willed herself to breathe deeper, but she couldn't make her lungs obey.

Images of Gerald's lifeless, bloated corpse lying forgotten and abandoned on the ocean floor strode through her brain uninvited and unwelcome. Eyes wide open, begging for help. Help she should have given.

Firm, callused hands gripped her shoulders, guiding her gently to a chair. Taking her hand in his, Gene slowly placed it on his own chest. "Breathe. Follow me. Breathe when I do."

His chest rose and fell steadily in a traceable rhythm, and she found herself instinctively responding. The edges of her vision gradually returned. Her tense, restricted chest loosened allowing her easier, deeper breaths. In a matter of thirty seconds, she matched Gene's stable pattern of big breath in, hold, steady breath out.

"Good," he said. "Good. Keep breathing just like this." He stood and began rummaging through the various drawers and cabinets, searching but not finding whatever it was he needed. "There's gotta be at least one damn teabag in here," he grumbled.

"I'm fine, Gene. I don't need tea."

"I can get you some more coffee—"

"If you're trying to keep me *alive*, I don't think your coffee is what's gonna do it." She smirked, which quickly devolved to a grimace at the vengeful return of the pulsing headache behind her temples.

Gene strode past her into what was likely the kitchen. After several moments of opening drawers, cabinets shutting, and clinking glass, he returned with a steaming mug of something, handing it gingerly to her handle first. She eyed the liquid suspiciously.

"Just water," he said. "Couldn't find any tea."

"You shouldn't have," she sarcastically remarked with a sickly-sweet smile. She cautiously sipped at the near-boiling water feeling it scorch down her throat before bubbling in her stomach. Though it wasn't much, the warmth that spread from her stomach up through her chest and down her arms to the tips of her fingers did help ease her tightened muscles.

"Keep drinking," Gene encouraged, once more picking up his own mug and sipping at his bitter coffee. "And keep breathing. Like this." He took a deep, slow, steady inhalation, nodding his head as she followed.

Di gingerly sipped at her water, soaking in the quiet that followed. She felt Gene's eyes staring through her, though she didn't meet them. It wasn't like this was the first time. It wasn't like *he* hadn't been on the end of *her* talk downs. It was part of the trade for ex-military. It didn't mean it wasn't embarrassing every time it happened. It hadn't happened to her in years.

The crew had had a relatively quiet, uneventful time of it lately. That wasn't to say the jobs they had taken didn't have their challenges; scuffles with pirates outside Mars' orbit, clients underselling the likelihood of danger, idiotic bureaucracy and red tape that had her inches from staring at the wrong side of a set of bars. The life of a mercenary-for-hire was inherently not an easy one. But they had always come out on top. Maybe a little bumped and bruised, definitely exhausted, but always on top.

But watching the light leave the eyes of a friend, a crewmate, an innocent, it changed a person. Her crew was her family, and you didn't abandon family. But she had. She'd abandoned Gerald to a fate worse than death.

"Want to talk about it?" Gene asked, stirring her from her brooding and breaking the silence.

Di grimaced, dipping her head down for another sip. "Would you?"

He shrugged. "I'm not exactly the picture of perfect mental health."

She snorted, and they lapsed into silence once more. It wasn't an awkward silence where one person had something to say but refused to say it. Gene wasn't like that. Never really had been. If he thought someone needed to hear a bit of hard truth, they'd hear it, and not always tactfully. It was one of her favorite traits of his.

Gene stretched, angling his elbows back and puffing out his chest before grunting and getting to his feet. As he moved toward the cockpit, he paused at the dining area's entrance, placing a weathered hand on the cold steel wall. Di glanced up, noticing his hesitation.

"It wasn't your fault," he said. He arched his neck, turning to lock eyes with her. "It wasn't your fault." Intensity poured through his gaze as he emphasized each word. "Di. It wasn't your fault." With that, he marched out of eyesight.

Di's eyes filled with bubbling tears until they overflowed, rivulets running down her cheeks before splashing quietly into the forgotten cup of hot water in her trembling hands. On anyone else's lips those words would ring hollow. Very few can understand the racking guilt of watching someone under your command and care die. Gene was one of those few.

Di's mind instinctively searched back to a time long, long ago when their roles had been reversed. Fifteen, maybe twenty years ago now. Sitting on hard, reflective metal chairs in a sterile room. Lights dimmed overhead, a single blaring bulb shedding light from a grungy swinging lamp shade. Gene, for the first and only time she had ever seen him this way, with his head low. Posture slumped. Shoulders sagging. Hands wringing in his lap. Like a disobedient dog awaiting its master's inevitable swift kick of retribution.

"Diane," he had said, her name lightly slurred on his lips, voice cracking.

She knew why he was there. *He* knew she knew why he was there. They had filled her in as soon as she had arrived. It had been an accident, granted one that likely could have been avoided had Gene not been plastered. But rather than place blame where blame wasn't warranted, she had gripped his hands in hers until he raised his red-rimmed, puffy eyes to meet her own.

"It wasn't your fault," she had said.

It was one of only three instances where Di had seen him cry. Now, with roles reversed, she fully understood the weight of what she had said all those years ago. What it meant to a tormented soul trapped in a self-made purgatory, begging silently for a single outlet of relief. Her heart still ached, something that may eventually dim with time, but accompanying those four words was a feeling of freedom. The courage to get up and get moving again. Wiping her eyes with her hand, she placed the steaming cup on the table in front of her and made her way to the front of the ship.

Gene sat confidently at the controls as their underwater haven plowed lazily through the clear water, dim outside lights illuminating a small sphere of light around them. Di glanced up at the ceiling of solid ice looming a few meters above the ship, oppressive and never-ending.

Gene glanced up at her arrival, another silent

understanding passing between them. There was rarely verbal gratitude when one showed up for the other. It was simply a bygone conclusion. Even so, she gave him a small nod before he turned back to the yoke, making minor adjustments with his fingertips.

"Want to share where we're going?" she asked, taking a heavy plop beside him in the co-pilot's bucket seat. Gene was never one to wander aimlessly. If he was moving, it was in a purposeful direction at the most efficient speed.

"There's an old, supposedly unused station ten or more kilometers north from the main site. It may not be active, but there should still be a way to the surface from there. If we can get topside, we may be able to hail Emma if she hasn't left already."

Di stretched toward the bright display showing a rudimentary map of the second station along with coordinates to its docking bay. "How close?"

"Should be approaching in the next five minutes. Would've gotten there sooner, but this thing isn't really meant for speed. Besides, I didn't want to push it. It barely has any fuel in the tank."

Di nodded. "I'm going to suit up and look for anything useful. Call me when we approach."

"Aye, Captain. Helmets, gloves, and boots are in the decon station at the back." As Di turned to go, Gene raised his fist, a thin metallic circle perched between two fingers. "Take the data disc. It'll be safer with you."

Di hesitated, but only for a moment before plucking the

priceless object from his grip and tucking it gently in one of her suit's padded pockets.

As she strode back through the kitchen, she swept up the cup of now lukewarm water and downed it. Who knew the next time they would have the chance to fill their bellies? Something was better than nothing. It had the pungent mouthfeel of sterilization which, while not exactly encouraging a healthy appetite, made her feel safer. Something infinitely more important.

The submersible was small, and she found her missing suit pieces lying on the floor of the shower-like apparatus at the back right where Gene said they would be. Reaching down, she hesitated before instead closing the flimsy door and twisting the knob for another round of decontamination. Call it paranoia, call it an overabundance of caution, call it whatever; the thought of those hosts made her skin crawl. Better to be overly cautious than overly sloppy.

The buzzer beeped, loudly signaling the end of the cycle. Steam hissed from around the door as she pried it open, scooping up her boots and gloves. Di leaned against the wall and strapped on her thick boots, sealing them to the bottom of her skin-tight E.I.A.P.S.L. suit. She gingerly rotated her left shoulder. No doubt her skin was mottled with black and purple bruising beneath her suit from when she had hit the water. Luckily nothing seemed broken, but her aging body was already unappreciative of the battering she had taken.

Her gloves came next, soft, pliable material sliding

comfortingly over her fingers. After having readjusted to life in a spacesuit, she now felt positively naked without her entire body covered in that protective layer. Gripping her hands several times, she noticed a slight purplish stain along her palms and several fingers. Though the hosts' blood evaporated at temperatures above zero, it left behind an imprint, a blotchy stain just like any other blood. She involuntarily shivered and moved to get her helmet. Taking one final breath of non-recycled air (at least, non-recycled air of her own), she placed the see-through dome over her head and fastened it in place. Her HUD immediately appeared, giving her the familiar readouts of vitals, temperatures, and messages.

Neural command reengaged. Greetings, Ms. Diane Eastwood. How was your well-deserved rest and relaxation?

Di nearly bashed her head through the low ceiling as her suit's mechanical voice chimed unnervingly in her ear.

"Piss off," she muttered, issuing a brief mental command to silence the assistant until it was requested.

After taking several deep, calming breaths, her heart rate had finally settled to a comfortable resting rate of 85 for what felt like the first time since entering Enceladus' airspace. Though their situation had not grown any less dire, she felt rejuvenated. Sometimes all someone needs is to face the guilt head on, have a good cry, and shoulder forward.

"Captain?" Gene called down the stunted walkway. His tone insinuated something she would want to see.

Di scooped up Gene's helmet and gloves and rushed to the

front. "We're here?" she asked.

Gene grabbed his gear and placed it on the dash. "Approaching now. But auditory sensors are picking up an anomaly." He glanced at her and pulled back on the throttle, slowing their advance. Just up ahead of the watercraft a dim circle of light shone through a thinner section of ice, likely the docking port, where the surface had frozen back over from disuse.

"What do you mean an anomaly?"

Gene shook his head. "Something is making noise up there. Loud enough for the sub to pick it up." As he centered them just under the ring of diffused light, he cut the throttle bringing the ship to a complete stop. "Orders, Captain?"

It was a miracle they had found even one station so close to their location. It would be near impossible to find another. They were running low on fuel, likely on oxygen, most certainly on time. Like it or not, this was their only shot at getting back to the ship.

"Surface, but not all the way. Let's break through the ice and get a look at what we're dealing with."

"Aye, Captain." Gene flipped two switches and gently eased the surface lever back. The submersible responded, gently rising until it bumped against the underside of the ice, jarring them in their seats. The ice didn't budge.

"A little thicker than I thought," Gene muttered, glancing at the various buttons and switches on the dash.

Di glanced below on the underside of the console, noticing

a familiar port. Plugging in, she was greeted with the unimaginative, sterile, scientific name of their vessel in the corner of her HUD.

"This hunk has to have some countermeasure for surfacing through ice," she said, flipping through her new ship menus.

In response to her voice, three switches highlighted just beyond the yoke through her visor. In green illuminated letters, it read, 'Surface Assistance' prominently. She shrugged and flipped the switch closest to her. The water at the top of their viewport began to churn in response to movement at the top of their craft. Gene glanced at her as she flipped the next switch in line. The ship responded with a high-pitched whine. A temperature gauge at the bottom right of the dash began to steadily rise. Unsure of what else it would do, she flipped the third switch and gripped her seat.

"Power rerouting," a pleasant female voice chimed through the small speaker grills at the corners of the room.

Di threw Gene a more than mischievous look. "Take us up."

"Aye, Captain." Gene eased on the surfacing lever once again. The submersible shook as they made contact with the ice, but like a hot knife through butter, they continued to rise. Di bent down to catch a glance at the large rotor whipping about beyond the viewport above them. The steadily lowering ice wall in front sweat small drops of condensation, and more than a few decent sized chunks flew spinning past. Her teeth rattled in her head, so much so she thought a few might have been knocked loose.

With a heavy jerk, Di could tell they had breached the surface, though their view was still completely dominated by solid ice. Gene flipped off the three switches and the ship shuddered still. A muffled sound echoed through the hull in the space above, though not clear enough to decipher what it could be.

"Hold on, there should be a camera up top," Gene said, pushing several more buttons. A video feed appeared on the left edge of the viewport showing a dark, nearly empty room. Piles of heavy-duty crates lay jumbled across the portside jetty and along the walls of the circular room, a thick layer of ice amalgamating them into a strange, lumpy mass. The feed didn't provide audio, but there was no sign of movement. Both Di and Gene waited on bated breath, half expecting another monster to leap out of the shadows and attack. Yet nothing awaited their arrival but the deep shadows cast by the discarded equipment dotting the spacious docking station.

"Ready when you are," Gene said, reaching for Florence propped dutifully beside him. He pulled back the bolt, checking the chamber and flicking the safety off.

"Ready," Di said. She pulled the pistol from her waist and followed as he made his way to the ladder inlaid in the wall. He climbed hand over hand and, balancing with his back against the side of the compact circular pathway to freedom, turned the wheel counterclockwise. With a final heavy breath, Di watched as Gene gripped his rifle and heaved upward with his back. A sonorous clang reverberated around the metal-plated walls as the hatch collided with the outer hull.

As the echoes died, a crackling voice issued from somewhere above.

"Please, if there's anyone who can hear me. I'm located at site 14B. Supplies are low. I am requesting immediate evacuation."

CHAPTER 9
EVOLUTION

After a short pause, the poor soul's desperate pleas began anew, the recording looping endlessly. The man's beseeching voice quavered with emotion, but not in the manic way Di would have expected of someone trapped in this dire situation. The words were correct, the inflections convincing, but something felt wrong. It wasn't something she could explain, simply her gut reaction.

"Think he's still alive?" Di asked through comms. The pleading message ended, cycling once again.

"Maybe. But Enceladus been dark for three weeks now."

She checked her pistol once more as she waited patiently, arm looped through the rung below Gene's foot. After his customary security sweep, he hoisted himself fully out of the submersible and proffered his hand to help her up, eyes never leaving their suspiciously quiet surroundings.

Di crouched on the top of the ship, feeling exposed. The room's dim lighting was focused on the thick ice hardened over the facility's docking bay, LEDS inlaid in the walls around the circular opening now almost entirely obscured by ice. Haunting shadows flickered around them, standing as menacing sentries along the walls.

"Assessment?" Di asked.

"I don't like it."

Gene was always a man of few words, but his normal persona was a regular chatterbox when compared to on-the-job Gene, especially when he sensed danger. As he was fond of telling every bar rat, new crew member, and even old acquaintances when they happened to forget, maintaining ninety-nine percent focus meant you had a one percent chance of failure, and that one percent chance felt a helluva lot bigger when you end up face to face with the barrel of a gun. It wasn't a perfect maxim, but it got his point across. You lose focus, you die.

"You don't have to like it," she responded. "We just need a way to the surface."

Gene grunted. "I'm aware."

Smart ass, she thought, grunting.

"We're still pretty close to those cryovolcanoes at the south pole where the crust is thinnest," she continued. "I don't imagine there's another station nearby either. This has to be our best bet."

"Agreed." Gene lowered his rifle, though he didn't entirely remove it from his shoulder. "We're going to need an actual map of this facility if we want to find the elevator."

Di pointed her pistol at the sole door to the docking station. "After you."

Hopping gracefully three meters down to the deck below, his right leg buckled, and he grimaced as the pain nearly sent him to his knee.

"You ok?" Di asked, her genuine concern poorly masked. He had always hated Di fretting over his old war injury.

Gene scowled. "Fine. Just old." He extended a helping hand for her own descent. She gracefully accepted, sliding halfway down the hull to grasp it before coiling her legs beneath her and launching outward in an arc to clear the small gap between the submersible and the metal flooring. Ice crunched beneath her boots, and she felt her balance shift momentarily before her boots' magnetic function sensed the metal floor beneath the ice and reengaged to give her a bit more traction. The pit of her stomach lurched nauseatingly while her vision swam. Gene's firm grip never wavered from her wrist.

"Got it?" he asked.

"Little slick," she replied, shaking her head and rechecking her pistol.

"Thermal functions were probably rerouted to the main facility once they abandoned this one. Explains why everything is iced over."

Di nodded, less out of agreement and more out of rising anxiety. Fear and doubt began to seep in like a fast-acting fungus crawling up her legs to attach itself to her chest. She missed the comparative safety of an experimental underwater craft which was saying a lot in and of itself.

Red flashes reemerged in the corner of her HUD warning

of her spiking heart rate. It was more of a familiar friend at this point anyway.

"Ready?" Gene asked hesitantly. His look of concern reminded her not to be his one percent.

"Lead on," she replied.

Light clicks echoed quietly as they switched off the safeties on their weapons. Staying less than a step from his right flank, Di warmed at the familiarity of following Gene into battle, them versus the world. If there was any way she could muster the courage and the stamina to continue forward, it was with him at her side.

As they entered the gaping maw of the facility, the dim lights from the port faded away plunging them quickly into an inky blackness. With a mental command, her helmet-mounted lights flared to life highlighting the cold, empty depths of a long-forgotten corridor. Here in the middle of a normally silent world, swallowed whole by the great, icy, metal beast, the continually looping pleas of a hopeful, ill-equipped scientist took on an eerier tone. It dogged them from the countless speakers lining the hallway, momentarily flaring loudly as they passed by empty storage rooms with speakers of their own.

The bare bones of the station were picked clean. Empty metal racks, long forgotten garbage encased in ice, and a broken hardhat shoved into the corner were the only reminders that this was once a bustling mining facility.

Di noticed this facility was less utilitarian and much more maze-like than its successor. She didn't need a map to clue her in on why Paragon had abandoned this place for much more efficient space. Twists and turns and hidden corners leading down cramped hallways set her teeth on edge. If someone, or some*thing*, wanted to hide, there were plenty of viable options here.

Gene froze in place, and she followed suit at his outstretched hand signal to 'stop'. She had heard it a split second after he had; a scratching noise emanating from a room just ahead. On a ship or a fully functional station, she could have easily attributed it to rats, but no rat could live for long in these temperatures. No *normal* rat, at least.

Gene flashed the hand signal for 'caution', and he slowly made his way toward the room with Di on his hip. Dim rustling was followed by unmistakable footsteps. Not the sporadic, jolting footsteps that she would have associated with the hosts. Normal, everyday footsteps. She followed Gene as he turned a corner and found a door cracked open, warm light spilling out into the hallway in front of them. With the tip of his rifle, he noiselessly eased the door open.

A jacketed individual with a slight frame and short, blonde hair peeking out in small tufts under his thick wool hat sat in a tattered, worn office chair facing the opposite wall. A dented personal-sized heater sat in the far corner of the room.

Gun trained to the base of his neck, Di silently split right as Gene cut left. They inched closer, now within three or four strides of the clueless man. Or host. She waited for sight of the milky white eyes that would give her permission to blow its brain out the back of its skull.

The man turned, pale green eyes widening in shock. At the sight of two trained combatants approaching with guns drawn pointed at all his soft, squishy bits, he did the sensible thing; he raised his hands. The metal, unlabeled can gripped solidly in his left hand sloshed, splashing chunky mystery meat on to the floor.

"I'm not one of them," he squeaked.

"We didn't ask if you were one of them," Gene growled through his helmet's speaker.

"But you know what I'm talking about, don't you?" the man asked. His vowels carried a hint of a western British Isles upbringing. "The monsters at the primary site?"

Neither Di nor Gene deigned to answer, though that was answer enough for him. Still, neither lowered their gun. Something wasn't right. She could feel it stronger now, and she had learned her lesson on ignoring her instincts.

"Can I put my hands down now?"

As his arms bent, Gene tightened his grip on Florence taking a threatening step forward. "Not before you answer some questions."

The stranger licked his cracked, purplish lips and scratched his patchy, weeks-old beard with his shoulder. "You *are* the ones with the guns."

"Mouth off some more, smart ass," Gene growled. "See how far it gets you."

Di held out her left hand to keep him at bay, concerned he might shoot before they got any answers. Cautiously, she lowered her pistol to waist height, making sure to maintain distance and to keep the business end pointed where it could do damage if needed.

Immediately her eyes flew to the discolored dark patch on the tip of his nose. The reminder of the hosts made her involuntarily shudder which the man instantly caught, looking down and away as if ashamed.

"The nose? I was an idiot about a week or two back. Fell asleep and the heater went out. I was lucky I woke up when I did or it would have been more than just my nose."

It was a plausible enough excuse, though she didn't believe it for a second. His response came too readily. Too smooth. Even so, words struggled to make their way past her lips. So many questions bubbled up inside, but the first to escape seemed as good enough a place to start as any.

"Why are you here?"

"Paragon hired my captain to investigate their mining site when it went dark."

Well, that confirmed her prior suspicions that they were not the only, or even the first, to attempt this hellhole.

"My name's John," he continued. "Our crew came here... I don't even know how long ago now. I've been stuck here for weeks. Weeks? Is that right?"

"How did you make it to this facility?" Di asked, ignoring his questions.

"Surface. When we landed, I was tasked with opening comms and getting vital systems de-iced and running. The right materials weren't at the site, so I thought I would pop over here to see if anything was left behind. By the time I found a comm port, almost all my crew were gone. I—"

"Where's your ship?" Gene interrupted, finger still poised on Florence's trigger. It was a good point. There had been no other landing shuttle or spacecraft at the landing dock of the main facility as far as they could tell.

"The bastards left me," John said, shrugging. "Can't say I wouldn't have done the same. You didn't happen to see them on your way in, did you?"

"Can't say we did," Di responded. "It's a big solar system."

"Fair." John's left hand twitched downward, but he refrained from lowering his hands owing to the rifle pointed between his eyes. "You wouldn't mind if I scratched my chin, would you? Beards are absolutely horrendous."

Gene tightened his grip on his gun and moved a step closer.

"Gene, stop," Di chided, pulling him back from his aggressive stance. "For hell's sake, let him scratch his face."

Sensing consent following Gene's irritated grunt and slight tilt of the gun, John gingerly lowered his arms and scratched under his chin. His arms relaxed reluctantly, shoulders slumped, posture no longer tensed as if he were a rabbit moments from bolting.

"Supplies," Gene growled all too impolitely.

"Help yourself. This is all I could find. The place was

picked apart months before I got here. Probably around the time they abandoned it." John spread his arms wide indicating the sparse boxes littering the corners of the room.

Despite his claims of spending weeks alone in an abandoned ice mining facility, there didn't appear to be much in the way of garbage. Half a dozen foil wrappers, three unlabeled cans of mostly eaten processed meats and slurry, an opened box of lithium batteries, and two hand-crank flashlights peeked out from the one opened tote beside his table. Yes, there were several other unopened boxes, but this did not feel like the rat nest she would have expected. Either this wasn't his normal base of operations, or he hadn't had enough time to stage it correctly.

"Find any weapons?" Di asked, delicately plucking an opened can of mystery sludge and inspecting it, half expecting it to burble comically like a tar pit.

"None. That was something those miners were cognizant of keeping track of, I'm guessing."

"Turn off that message," Gene said, still refusing to lower his weapon trained on John's center mass.

John leaned over in his chair, stretching his hand out to tap a few buttons. Immediately the warbling, sonorous voice that had blasted through the halls of the facility since their arrival was silenced. Absent the familiar and, arguably, comforting tones of a human voice, however obnoxiously repetitive it had been, eerie silence filled the room. Di increased the range and sensitivity on her gear, straining to pick up any noise, any at all, but to no avail. It appeared they were well and truly alone. For now.

"Where's *your* gear?" Gene asked accusatorially.

It was another good question. John had on a basic, faded, skin-tight, black body sock covering everything from his neck to his wrists and ankles that had definitely seen better days. Other than his lightly armored gloves and his heavy, militaristic boots, he looked more ready for bed than action on a frozen alien world. A fraying webbed belt with various alternating empty and occupied pouches hung loosely around his waist. The dark red knit cap that hung low on his forehead and down over his ears accentuated the deep purple bags under his eyes. Honestly, for as chipper and nonchalant as he tried to portray, he looked like he was thirty seconds from passing out.

"Punctured my O2 line and cracked my helmet screen about a week back. Stupid mistake involving a slippery railing and a bit of sleep deprivation. Luckily, I had already gotten the oxygen scrubbers, gravity generators, and atmosphere systems back up and running. There's just enough power in these old generators to keep two, maybe three major systems going at a time. I chose to be able to breathe, walk, and see. And occasionally use the broadcast network in short bursts."

John attempted a light-hearted chuckle but it died quickly on his lips. His eyes shifted uncomfortably from his wringing hands to Di's searching gaze. He was lying, she was certain about that, but about what she couldn't tell. Was it innocent or sinister? Maybe Gene was right in keeping his gun trained on him. Even if John was a perfectly lovely human being, an isolated, stranded man was desperate for a way home, consequences and rational thinking be damned.

"You wouldn't happen to have anything fresher than expired tuna, would you?" John asked, optimism creeping through.

"Afraid we're fresh out of fruits and veggies," Di replied, wincing at John's crestfallen expression. "All we had was some bad, stale coffee."

"Well, feel free to help yourselves to whatever you can find here. Although do me a favor and save a bit of liquor for me."

"No promises," Di replied, flashing him a weak smile.

She wanted to like the man in spite of her suspicions. He had a casual confidence despite the guns in his face. Even when confronted by mutated monsters, likely a few former friends, who were trying to kill him, he seemed calm and collected. It was a level of composure many would die for, *kill* for, when facing down unimaginable horrors. But it stank of wrongness. No one was this put together, especially experienced mercenaries.

Turning to feign rummaging through a box, back to John, Di flipped on her private comm to Gene. "Don't react, don't respond. Something isn't right."

A line of text appeared in the bottom of her HUD, a mentally dictated reply. *He's hiding something.*

"My thoughts exactly. But we need him. We need to get to the surface fast, and I imagine he's explored a decent portion of this facility. He has to know where the elevators are located."

"Dig all you like, you're not gonna find anything good,"

John called, attempting to break what he likely viewed as an uneven and awkward silence.

"I thought I'd at least try," she called back, briefly flipping to public comms.

You want to act buddy-buddy to get what he knows? He's going to see right through that. He's a merc.

Di shifted to a second box, shuffling through old papers and folders. "Fair point. But you think shoving a gun under his nose is any better?"

"The kitchens aren't too far from here," John replied hesitantly. "I could show you, if you'd like."

Gene's message flashed a warning. *I don't like this.*

"Keep your guard up and your gun on him."

Di turned around and stepped toward John, seamlessly flipping to public comms. "After you," she said, gesturing with an open palm and a pasted-on smile.

John shrugged. "Fair enough. I'll lead the way." A single bead of sweat appeared from below his wool hat, coursing along the ridges of his brow.

As he stood, he stumbled slightly catching himself on Di's forearm. His firm grip stiffened, and she tensed as he shook his head. Something akin to surprise flashed briefly behind his eyes before he could recover his well-maintained mask. His bewildered, apologetic smirk faded as Gene growled, and he quickly made his way out to the hallway.

"I get that you don't trust me," he called from just out of eyesight. "Hell, *I* wouldn't trust me in your situation. But is the gun necessary?"

Di shot Gene a knowing glance. It said so many things, chief among them that under no circumstances should he let his guard down despite whatever came out of her mouth.

"You'll have to forgive Gene. He's a little paranoid. Pulled a gun on *me* the first few times we met, actually." It was a true story, albeit slightly exaggerated. What she didn't mention was that they had been on the battlefield in the middle of a firefight. Plus, she had pulled her gun on him first.

Her feigned congeniality was all part of their tried and true 'good cop, bad cop' routine. Call it old-fashioned, call it corny; if it worked, it was effective, and it was amazing just how many times it had worked.

Despite a person's awareness of the truth in the tone, the words, or the actions another person conveyed, humans desperately want to believe, to trust. The humanity in everyone reaches out to cling to whatever semblance of connection they can find, and a comparatively friendly smile or a few words of confidence was often more than enough to put the average person at ease. And when the average person is at ease, the average person's falsities slip revealing the mask they hide behind. Because everyone has a mask.

The real question now was how 'average' John, the *real* John, was beneath his mask of feigned friendliness and smiles. Was he a monster willing to slit their throats the first chance he got? Or was he simply a desperate man in an impossible situation, willing to do what was necessary to ensure his survival? Either way, he was dangerous. Whether she liked it or not, the most likely outcome would be a dead body left to freeze in the bowels of a long-forgotten mine, and she sure as hell was going to do her damnedest to make sure it wasn't her or Gene. So, would she need to kill John now, or later? How cold-blooded could she be? It was an old trait, one she hadn't needed to use in years, one she knew Gene didn't approve of, but one she could slip back into should she require it.

Di waltzed out the doorway with Gene close behind. John waited patiently where their hallway connected to another, a thin smile on his lips that didn't reflect in his eyes. The facade of cheap smiles and kind words was gone.

It was going to be like that then. He had quickly seen through her attempts to put him on the back foot, though it had been worth the attempt. It had, at the very least, shown her one thing; this was not a man to take lightly. Gene was right; he was a mercenary just like them. A mercenary who had just been presented with a way out.

Mentally issuing a message to Gene, she followed as John led them deeper into the facility.

Wolf.

It was hers and Gene's term when determining a potential threat. A dog, when backed into a corner, was vicious. Willing to attack something twice or even three times its size to escape. Desperate. But a wolf would kill for the sake of the kill. It enjoyed the hunt

Affirmed.

Di glanced back at Gene visibly tightening his grip on his rifle.

"You got a map of this facility somewhere?" Di asked, warm tone forgotten. She saw no reason to continue their ruse when John could clearly see straight through it.

John disappeared around the corner as he answered. "There should be one close to the shaft up to the surface. I'll take you there now." His feigned nonchalance and warmth were also completely absent. All business, no pretenses. "We'll have to switch over the emergency generators to power the elevators first though. It'll mean losing some systems. Probably the lights."

How convenient, she thought, rounding the corner. John had not bothered to wait for them to catch up and had made significant progress down the hallway, rounding a bend.

"Captain, we should make our own way to the elevator," Gene grumbled on their private line, outstripping her pace and taking the lead.

"Where do you think he's heading, Gene? Either way, we'll have to deal with him sooner or later. I'd prefer sooner and on our terms."

"Are you coming?" John called out, voice echoing along the empty, cavernous hallways. "Be sure to keep up."

Di caught a glimpse of his coat as he rounded a corner and dipped out of sight once more. "Where are we going, John?"

"He's jerking us around," Gene growled warningly.

"No shit. Keep sight of him."

"Ah ah. Having private conversations? That isn't very

polite." The strangely playful yet sinister changes in his voice hissed like a whisper, a marked difference to the seemingly shy and nervous man he had been portraying. "Is your ship still flight ready? On the surface?"

"You answer mine, I answer yours," Di shouted, still unable to keep up with John's quickening pace. "Where are we going?"

"I told you. We need to switch the power to make it to the surface."

Their gate had picked up to a light jog, and still the only signs of their guide were the faint taps of his accelerating footsteps and the gradually fading voice floating toward them from further down the winding hallway. Di could tell he hadn't branched off any of the connecting paths which was convenient. It was also worrying. At some point, surely, they would have made a turn or two. As they travelled deeper into darkness, the lights dimming as they moved, she felt as though they should not be giving John what he wanted; and what he wanted was for them to follow.

In a flash decision, Di gripped Gene's elbow and hauled him sideways into a dark offshoot, plastering herself flat with her back against the wall. Dim lighting threw faint grey shadows down the hallway they had just entered revealing two to three meters of stark, empty nothingness but for a stack of metal containers. She slid down the hallway as silently as she could, ducking quickly behind the boxes with Gene following on her left. A half-open door sat three meters down, just barely visible as her eyes adjusted to the lower light. It was a tantalizing invitation offering a temporary refuge, yet it was nothing more than an empty promise of safety with no exits.

Di knew that John's plan was to take their shuttle, whether he dealt with them beforehand or not. The advantage went to him with his knowledge of the base's layout. She didn't dare hope to beat him to the elevator, so only two options presented themselves; contact Emma and tell her to take off without them, securing the rest of her team's safety and dooming herself, Gene, and the interloper, or going on the hunt and taking out John before he could escape.

Alpha counter, she voicelessly messaged, grip tightening on her pistol. Gene nodded, thumb flicking the fire rate switch from single to burst, pointer finger alighting delicately on the trigger.

"Captain?" John's faint voice carried from down the main hall, a mockingly sweet question. "Have you gotten yourself lost?"

Gene tweaked several settings on the scope of his rifle before bringing it back up to his eye, sighting down the side hallway past their temporary cover.

An exaggerated shadow slowly crept along the far wall. John cautiously peered around the corner, eyes squinting, mouth turned down in a scowling frown. "I'm not playing games, Captain. You and your dog can—"

Her helmet's automated sound dampeners muffled the rifle's tri-burst shot beside her head, muzzle flashes sparking dots along her vision. John fell backward out of view cursing loudly, a dark spray spattering the wall behind.

"Shoulder," Gene muttered, moving with purpose toward his downed prey. Di fell in step behind, her left hand patting his left hip to signify her flanking position. He crouched low as he moved, Di taking the high side. They reached the corner of the intersection and briefly paused to assess the danger.

Gene signaled for her to take a covering position and whipped his torso out in the open in one fluid motion, barrel searching for his target. As Di peeked around the corner, she was only greeted with a puddle of blood and a trail dripping down the hallway leading to a closed door.

"Shit," Gene spat. He cautiously crept forward, gun pointed at the door, ready to pull a shot off the moment it slid open.

Di glanced toward the dark pool of blood at her feet. "Gene, hold," she said, her stomach chilled as she knelt to inspect the puddle on the floor. Blood that, assuming her external temperature reading of –180 degrees was accurate, should have frozen over in seconds. Blood a suspiciously darker color than the red she was familiar with, purplish hue glinting in the light.

"Captain?" Gene asked, his focus locked on the door.

"He's infected."

It was impossible. She had witnessed their savage ferocity firsthand. Once infected, these monsters became mindless killing machines. And yet despite what made logical sense, she couldn't deny the cold, hard facts that confronted her. John's blood was not human. *John* was not human. Not anymore. And they needed answers.

Taking a deep breath, Di stood and quickly took up position to the left of the door frame. "We need him alive. Shoot to kill only if absolutely necessary."

"Heard, Captain."

She punched the release button and watched the door slide sluggishly open. Gene, after flicking on his mounted flashlight and checking his corners, rushed the room with Di close behind. Though reminiscent of previously explored storage rooms, this one had clearly been rifled through and picked clean of many of its useful items. Boxes and shelving spread sporadically throughout made sight lines and cover a logistical nightmare.

"You're... smarter than I gave you credit for." John's strained voice echoed somewhere out of sight in the dark storage room. Gene's narrow beam of light highlighted drops of dark, mutated blood flecking the floor and several tables near the middle of the narrowly confined space. A smeared handprint marked an opened box, useless non-medical materials splayed haphazardly around it.

"What are you?" Di called, staying near the open doorway to cover what she hoped was the room's only escape route.

John's deep throated chuckle cut short with a pained gasp. "The future," he hissed.

"Future? You're nothing but a husk. A puppet." Her words bit hard, inflected with disgust.

"I'm more alive than you could possibly comprehend." His voice sounded like it was moving, circling the room.

"Not for long, you bastard," Gene growled.

"So that's a no on talking this out I take it?"

Gene turned, sensing the voice in a different corner of the room. "I will put you down. It's the only mercy I can give."

"I will not be silenced," John barked, tone shifting. "Not before I've given my message."

Goosebumps rolled down Di's arms and legs. A message? What kind of a message could a half-crazed, half-mutated demon possibly give?

"I am chosen. I am the one who speaks for the One, the Prophet of the Seeker of Order and Unification. I am filled with a glorious purpose, a transformation of body and soul. All will be joined together, a cog in uniformity to bring about an age of perfection."

Gene circled around to the far-right side of the room and signaled Di to take the left. Her hands trembled as she clicked on her mounted light, the stark white beam jittering on the wall and the cluttered mess of sifted-through refuse. Step after hesitant step took her further from the safety of their only exit, closer toward the ravings of a madman.

"Humanity has had its time, squandered its bounty of blessings," John continued, voice echoing ominously. "The One has shown me the images gleaned from the Many. Human history and its pitiful squabbling and bickering over finite resources. No more."

Di turned a corner, gun now held tightly in both hands close to her chest. She slid cautiously along the wall, eyes trained on the various hiding places John could leap from, confident she wouldn't allow herself to be caught unaware.

"I will be Her Vessel. With the Many, I will spread the One's goodness among this universe's planets and stars. And when humanity breathes its last breath, I will finally be at peace."

Di reached the back corner coming face to face with Gene who shook his head. Still no John.

"I thank you, Captain, on behalf of Her Majesty. You are the one foretold, the catalyst to the Goddess's ascension beyond this pale, frozen rock. This is, unfortunately, where your played part must end."

Di turned, inspecting the back wall. John's voice reverberated within, echoing loudly as it funneled through the expanded cracks hidden behind old metal shelving. With the tip of his barrel, Gene pulled the shelves down, and they crashed to the floor with a deafening clang. What greeted them was a large hole bored deep within the ice behind the thin, flayed-open metal siding that was once the facility's wall. John was nowhere in sight. Though light dissipated not far along the roughly-hewn, cavernous tunnel, Di knew where it would lead. And she knew just as surely that it would lead them to her.

"Goodbye, Captain." John's voice echoed down the tunnel, sickeningly sweet. "May the One guide you gracefully to Her arms."

He called out, screeching in a shockingly violent, high-pitched squeal. His call was answered.

CHAPTER 10
OVERRUN

Di hurtled down the hallway, towed along by Gene's strong grip on her outstretched hand like a toddler dragged behind an overexuberant parent. Her pistol bounced against her thigh, held slack in her right hand nearly forgotten. Brief, panicked glances backward confirmed her fears; the hosts were gaining on them. Glimpses of flailing limbs and blackened tinges of frozen flesh haunted the corners of her vision.

"We can't outrun them forever," Di gasped. Her lungs were on fire, fueled by their dead sprint in a vain attempt to outstrip their pursuers.

"I don't plan on it," Gene replied. A faded, iced-over sign flashed past on the wall depicting an arrow atop the word "Control Room & Deep Storage".

Haunting squeals of otherworldly ecstasy echoed in her brain, reverberating between her ears like they had reverberated down the ice tunnel. It played on repeat, blocking out her own thoughts, surrounding her in a continual state of chills and goosebumps. It pushed aside natural instincts of self-preservation, honed skills that had kept her alive years longer than she maybe should have, leaving only the echoing, alien adulation and her own nothingness. It was an inhuman, haunting sound she desperately wanted to be rid of, yet knew she would never scour from the dark recesses of her mind.

Di risked another glance behind at the slowly gaining horde. Gene's left hand, gripping his pistol, swung out and back, firing off two succinct shots followed by a splash of purple blood, two hosts in front collapsing from the bullet wounds in their legs and fouling up a portion of the pack in their wake.

"Legs," he hissed between labored breaths. "Shoot. Legs."

It was now or never. Either she was going to lay down and die shredded by the mutant claws and gnashing teeth of the monsters that pursued them, or she was going to pull herself together, swallow her fears, and take out as many bastards as she could.

Her jaw clenched, muscles tightening. Teeth ground until she thought one or two would chip. Swift inhale. Deep exhale.

She was Captain Diane Eastwood, damn it.

The muted gunmetal grey was a blur as she raised it, firing off six precision shots rapid fire. Two hosts near the leading point of the mass dropped in a spray of blood, one more on each edge closest to the walls following near simultaneously. One fell mid leap as it tried to vault over its fallen comrades, further jumbling the mass of limbs and torsos. Her final bullet took another in the hip which it shrugged off to continue its dogged pursuit.

Large overhead signs announced their arrival at Deep

Storage. Di's contributory shots had given them an extra second or two of reaction time which they immediately took advantage of. A good thing, considering she was losing feeling in her burning thighs.

Gene nearly yanked her arm out of its socket as he bolted right into an open doorway, slamming it shut behind him. Shielding his eyes, he fired a single shot into the opening mechanism, sparks and smoke flashing around him.

They were in yet another room filled with rows upon rows of galvanized metal shelves, mostly empty but for a few straggling pieces of mining equipment and containers labeled with a date and the word 'SAMPLE' splashed across the front. Contrary to the previous closet-like spaces, however, this room was massive both in height and length. In the near pitch darkness surrounding the light emanating from her suit lamp, she had no idea just how far this room stretched.

"Di!" Gene shouted, throwing his body against the closest shelving. She dove out of the way as it toppled directly into the door. Following his lead, she rounded the next row and threw her shoulder into it as hard as she could, collapsing it onto the first to further barricade the door.

A loud crack emanated from behind the door, and it shuddered, threatening to give way as it met resistance from the haphazard pile of twisted metal piled before it. Frantic, ear-piercing screams from dozens of raw, mutated throats resounded as bodies piled up against the door, slamming the barrier over and over to reach their prey. Already, she could see the door bulging in numerous spots, threatening to buckle under the sheer ferocity unleashed upon it.

"That won't hold them for long," she puffed, taking a moment to catch her breath. Gene shoved another shelving unit onto the others, stumbling and clutching the old war wound in his right knee before he caught himself on a large mining drill sheered nearly in half, left to rust in a forgotten, abandoned base.

Her windedness and his near collapse were yet another reminder they were no spring chickens. If this chase continued much longer, ignoring the fact they may have already trapped themselves in their own massive, self-made tomb, their bodies were bound to collapse from exhaustion.

"What's the play?" she asked, flinching at a particularly loud and dense slam against the door.

"We're not dead yet," Gene wheezed, pulling himself fully upright and clutching his chest, wincing.

"Yet," she replied. The pile shuddered, shifting slightly against the insistent onslaught of attacks. Sucking in a deep breath, she moved to tip another shelf onto the pile, grunting as it gradually toppled. "I'm going to recon the rest of this room, see if there's another way out."

Gene shot a worried look in her direction, a blink-and-you'll-miss-it moment of genuine concern. "If there's a way out, there's a way in. Be careful."

Di reached down to grab her discarded pistol, flung to the side in haste at their abrupt entrance. Depressing the magazine release, she inspected her clip for obstructions. The last thing she needed in the heat of the moment was a jammed weapon. Four gleaming, golden cartridges caught the light of her headlamp through the thin, translucent inspection strip before she slid it into the pouch on her belt. Two full magazines at her waist combined with the mostly empty third gave her a total of thirty bullets remaining. Thirty chances to stand her ground, to take as many bastards as she could down with her. If she had known, if she had been smart like Gene, she would have kept her rifle, maybe a few more mags. But ifs would get her nowhere now. Ifs would only sink her further into the despair creeping at the edges of her consciousness, threatening to pounce at the slightest misstep.

Blinking away her moment of introspection, Di pulled out a fresh magazine and slid it home in the grip. Racking the slide back halfway to reaffirm her gun was free and clear, she released it with a satisfying clack. With a brief nod to Gene, she cautiously crept down the aisle, clangs of crashing metal echoing around her as he continued his furious onslaught to secure the door.

With the ceiling so high overhead and the open and empty shelves surrounding her, she felt entirely exposed. It was only through listening to her years of honed instinct and drilled-in muscle memory that she wasn't jumping at every clang or squeezing off a shot at every flickering shadow.

Utilizing her E.I.P.S.L., she switched her HUD to thermal-imaging infrared. Varying shades of dark indigo, deep navy, and faded teal flooded her vision. The environment was nearly uniform in temperature, but her senses felt heightened with the enhanced perspective. It provided slightly more comfort than the narrow beam of her flashlight at the very least.

Not wanting to sacrifice any advantage she had, she brought up a picture-in-picture display of unaltered feed from her helmet cam and directed it to the top left corner of her HUD. Subtle shifts of movement would register differently in thermal and light, and even the slimmest chance of her own intuition catching something a multi-million-dollar piece of equipment may miss was worth the mildly nauseating effect of having a second feed of your own sightline off to the side.

With her left shoulder pressed against the wall, she cautiously made her way toward the rear of the room. Though her primal fear was telling her to move slowly, to take precaution with each step, the relentless pounding of the horde at the door was a constant reminder of just how precarious their situation truly was. If Di couldn't find an emergency exit, a ventilation shaft, *something* to get them out of this dead end, it would take a lot more than thirty bullets to wade their way through what waited on the other side. When it came down to it, she wouldn't let them have her. Twenty-nine for them. One for herself.

As she approached the junction with the back wall, she noticed an anomaly in her thermal vision. So far, the shelves, the metal siding, everything had been a relatively even and uniform dark blue, reflective of the sub-zero temperatures around her. However, the blue paled higher along the wall. It was a subtle shift, a detail she was frankly surprised she had even noticed, but it was something. Glancing around near the top of the room, she could find no source for the mysterious temperature fluctuation.

"Gene, I may have something," she called over comms, eyes tracking the cobalt blue streak above as she inched along the back wall.

"Tell me it's a way out."

"Not sure yet. Hold."

Picking up her pace, she quickly made it to the next corner. Uniform steel panels abutted yet more uniform steel panels. A perfectly normal corner, upsettingly average and nondescript.

Frustrated, Di huffed and swung her helmet-mounted flashlight to the center of the room, stark white beam reflecting off the faded metal ceiling. Instantly, her eye caught an anomaly. A panel. One single panel. Perfectly square, each side roughly two meters long, edges welded sloppily in an attempt to make it flush with the sheets of metal beside it.

"Panel. In the ceiling," she said, trying and failing to keep the excitement from her voice.

"And?" Gene asked, grunting. Another sharp clang reverberated through his mic.

"There are temperature fluctuations around its edges. I think it might be a ventilation shaft of some kind, but it's welded shut. I'll have to climb some of these shelves to get closer."

"Don't fall."

Di smirked and rushed past several aisles before finding one directly below the outlier panel. Glancing quickly at the sparse contents on each shelf, she reluctantly convinced herself that the heavier items strewn along the bottom shelves offered sufficient stability.

Leaving herself no time to think on what a stupidly dangerous plan this was, she began to climb. Hand over hand, she clambered up five, six, seven comically enormous shelves, her confidence growing as she heaved herself up the final stretch and on to the top. As wide and as heavy as they were, the steel beneath her hands and knees wobbled precariously. Di's vision swam as she caught a glimpse of the floor six or seven meters down. Suddenly feeling unsteady, she pinched her eyes shut, flattened her body, and gripped the edges of the shelf, clinging for dear life. Though the shelving unit had stopped moving, her stomach rolled as if she were in a life raft stuck in the middle of an ocean on a moderately windy afternoon.

Get a grip, Diane, she thought, growling to herself. *There's no time.*

Sucking in a shaky breath, she hesitantly pushed herself back to her knees and then to her feet, reaching up toward the ceiling above. Her fingers barely made contact with the slick, metal surface.

The HUD's thermal vision confirmed this was the likely source of the warmer air current, fading shades of lighter blue pointing out the small gaps in the sloppy welds at various points around the square.

"I think this is our way out," she said over comms. "But I'm going to need your help to get the panel off."

And a miracle, she thought to herself.

One final clamorous peal of metal smashing against metal

rang out throughout the room before Gene answered. "I see you. Coming."

"Just be careful on the shelves. They aren't exactly stable, and I don't want to fall off." Just to be safe, she dropped slowly back to her knees, stomach fluttering at the gentle wave of her floor. She then set herself to the task of figuring out how they were going to get through a panel welded shut.

Di raised her wrist-mounted screen, lacking confidence in her current mental stability to try and wrestle with her implant. Menu screen after menu screen flipped by with a flick of her finger. Impact protection. Suit diagnostics. Environmental scan. Physical sample interpretation.

"You didn't mention it was sealed shut," Gene said, panting as he pulled himself up to the top of the platform.

"Figuring that part out now," she muttered.

Gene stood much more confidently on the gently swaying shelving, like a seasoned sailor on the deck of his rocking ship. Di noticed a portion of his visor blur, his bulbous nose becoming exaggeratedly cartoonish.

"The metals are different. Between what was put there originally and this panel, I mean. And the soldering is shit."

Di continued to desperately flick through submenus. "When they were moving out, I'm guessing they did it systematically. Shutting down sections and sealing off abandoned areas so they didn't waste heat. I don't imagine they cared how pretty it looked."

Gene grunted his assent. She glanced up, noticing his eyes

narrow. "This doesn't look right."

"Yeah. Like I said, they probably didn't—"

"Not the job itself. The metal."

Di glanced up, a small flame of hope growing in her chest. "How?"

"You need a certain kind of pre-treated steel to withstand temperatures this low. Gotta be the same type of stuff meant to withstand deep space. This solder just looks like your standard, run-of-the-mill stuff to me."

"What does that mean?" she asked, unsteadily standing. He outstretched a helping hand which she gratefully took, shifting her hand to his shoulder once she was upright.

"It means that..." He glanced at something on his HUD that Di couldn't see. "If it isn't treated metal, -168 degrees is too cold. It will be brittle."

Her eyes widened in realization. "Can we break it?"

"I hope so." As though cosmically linked to his pronouncement, a loud shriek echoed across the space. They both glanced back to the door. The haphazard pile of shelving shifted and screeched as it was pushed lazily across the floor. Di could just make out black-tinged arms flailing between the gaps in the metal.

"They pried the doors open," she said. Her momentary flicker of hope fizzled, replaced by a cold, hard stone in the pit of her stomach. In response, the pile shifted again. Inhuman, frenzied screams pitched higher, likely sensing their inevitable hunt coming to a close as they made their final circles around their prey.

Di jumped at the clangorous sound of Gene's fist smashing into the seam. Once, twice, three times he slammed his knuckles into the unforgiving metal, wincing with every impact.

She felt helpless, unable to reach high enough to be of any use. "What about your rifle?" she asked.

Gene paused, shooting her a glance like she had just suggested he toss his infant child to the monsters as a distraction. "Florence? What about her?"

"You're not getting through that with your fists."

A look of horror followed by a defeated resignation passed briefly on his face. He reverently pulled his prized possession from the magnetic holster on his back, giving the gun a soft stroke.

"I'm so sorry, baby." With glossy tears in his eyes, he flipped the rifle over and began hammering at the seal with the reinforced butt.

Tiny chips of ice and glinting metal fragments filled the air, but it was still slow work. If she could find something stronger, they might stand a chance.

Di glanced along the closest shelves surrounding them. There had to be something she could use, some discarded piece of equipment. Returning to her hands and knees, she crawled farther along the top of the shelf, scanning left and right for something other than two-ton machine parts or the empty spaces that taunted her desperation. The rhythmic pounding of Gene's gun against the panel and the repeated bashing of the horde as it made steady progress through their makeshift barricade combined to create a gruesome ticking clock, counting down their last moments.

There. Three shelves down across the aisle gap, a small pile of what appeared to be bent and broken metal piping. Before her sense of self-preservation could tell her brain how bad of an idea it was, she scrambled to her feet, gauged the distance, and leapt across the three-meter gap.

Time slowed to a crawl. Sound muffled to a dull thumping in her ears, combining with the pounding of her heart. Fear, mere moments ago threatening to pull her under its tide, mixed with the sweet taste of freedom and exhilaration.

She was fourteen again, leaping off the cape shore cliffs down the bike path from her school while Aiden, the cutest boy in her class, tried to hide his own horrified stare at being so soundly shown up by a girl. In front of no less than eight of their classmates. It had been, and likely remained to this day, the most clarifying, self-gratifying, defining moment in her life. In those three to four seconds of freefall, she could have conquered the world. It wasn't until much later in life that she would come to know crippling anxiety, the quiet killer of joy. But in that moment, she had felt no fear. The flutters in her stomach had not been indicative of fear, but of the unknown, of leaping before looking. And the shockingly cold slap as she pierced the water's surface reaffirmed that she was safe, cocooned in the encircling arms of adventure.

Di's chest slammed into the second shelf down from the

top, breath utterly stolen from her lungs. Warnings flashed on her HUD. Black and white x-ray scans of her ribs flashed in the corner of her vision, red pulsating zones indicating bone bruises or hairline fractures. Unhelpful notifications stated she should apply an ice pack to the area and encouraged her to seek immediate medical attention. All she could do was cling to the frosty metal like grim death, gasping air in, but not out of, her lungs.

"Captain, what the hell are you doing?" Gene yelled over comms.

She wheezed in response. It was a struggle just to keep her vision from fuzzing. The pain was slowly growing hot in her chest, radiating out to her spine. Her arms ached as she clung desperately to the shelf, legs kicking ineffectually in the open air.

Finally, her lungs expanded allowing her to suck in a full breath, a decision she immediately regretted. If not for the terror she felt from her momentary glance down, she might have let go then and there to clutch her right side where the impact had been concentrated. Despair filled her at the prospect of having to climb back up to the top and make the jump back.

"Pipes," she wheezed, momentary clarity pushing aside her encompassing pain. The bent and broken pipes were just to her left, two more shelves down. Gingerly, she released her grip from her right hand and slid down until her foot caught the shelf below.

"Pipes?" He paused and glanced down in her direction before realizing what she meant. "Damn it, Di! I can get those!"

"No time. Keep going." The pain was now affecting how many words she felt she could say in a given breath. Di had only broken her ribs twice in her life, and it had been miserable at the best of times. Now was most definitely not the best of times.

Though she tried to summon a mental command for 'emergency triage', mental concentration was out the window in the face of stabbing, radiating pain. Gingerly flipping up her wrist display, she scrolled through options until finding a menu for 'emergency treatment'. A short list of actions appeared, including 'Pain Medication', 'Antiseptic', 'Numbing Agent', and 'Stabilization Methods'. Numbing agent sounded like pure bliss, so she selected that first. After a short prick at the bottom of her ribcage, a creeping coolness spread outward and over the throbbing in her side. It only took until the count of three before her pain lessened and she could feel herself think again. God bless technology.

Selecting 'Pain Medication', she scrolled to the bottom for the good stuff. Not too good though. She felt like taking the edge off, not turning herself into a blathering idiot.

"Regulated narcotic selected. Authorization required."

Damn useless technology. The tranquil, robotic voice in her ear did anything but calm her.

"Captain Diane Eastwood, authorization granted," she hissed, gritting her teeth.

"Authorization required. Access code required."

"Access code? What access code?"

"Paragon representative access code required. Access denied.

Would you like a non-regulated alternative?"

"Sonuvabitch," she muttered, wincing as she accidentally rotated to peer down at the pile of scrap metal and piping one shelf below. "Whatever. Yes. Give me the highest dose."

"Alternative accepted. Now administering 500mg of acetaminophen."

"You've got to be kidding me." Another sharp prick, this time in her wrist. She doubted this would do much of anything for broken ribs, but she would take what she could get.

"Administration completed. Have a wonderful day!"

There was no physical entity to express her frustration toward, so she flipped off her wrist panel. That did more to make her feel better than the drugs had.

A loud squeal of metal scraping metal ripped her attention back toward the door at the front of the room. The massive stack of shelves was inching its way across the ground. Di could just make out the dark blue flushed eyeballs of a handful of hosts scrabbling to squeeze themselves through the tight gaps.

"Captain! Move your ass!" Gene's shout was accompanied by a renewed flurry of banging metal.

Crouching down, Di reached below her current shelf and scooped up a hefty looking pipe, slapping it gingerly along her back. Magnetic weapon locks that would have normally held a rifle or other large weapon gripped the pipe firmly against her spine. She turned back toward her hopeful salvation, Gene continually hammering away. It looked like he had made some leeway on the solder as a corner of the metal square sagged away from the ceiling.

This is gonna hurt, she thought, gingerly clambering up the shelving unit. Through the numbing agent and the miniscule pain medication, her ribs twinged painfully as she twisted her body to pull herself up and on to the top. She paused a moment on her hands and knees to take several painfully shallow breaths.

Now was the part she dreaded most. Di looked across what now felt like a gaping, insurmountable maw. As if in response, the fractured bones in her chest chose that moment to flare painfully, reminding her of the likely consequences of taking yet another leap of faith. That momentary sensation of freedom would not be felt again; she was sure of that.

"Gene," she said. "Catch the pipe."

He paused and glanced her way, exhaustion apparent on his sweaty face. This would be a race to the finish, and any advantage they had at their disposal could be the difference between a moment more to breathe and dying at the twisted, clawed hands of a horde of demons. With a pitying glance at the once pristine Florence in his hands, now covered in dents, chips, and scrapes, he respectfully placed it on his magnetic back holster.

"Toss it," he wheezed, chest heaving.

Pulling the pipe from her back (eliciting yet another painful spasm), she tossed it underhand which Gene deftly caught. He immediately set to hammering away with renewed vigor.

Now to figure out how to get across herself. Her best bet

would be to climb all the way down and back up on the other side. She would lose a lot of time, but the mere thought of jumping made her heart race and her stomach squirm. Yes, she could manage pain. No, she wouldn't intentionally inflict more if she could help it.

Di lowered herself carefully to her stomach. Her legs dangled over the edge as she propped herself gently on her left side, avoiding her injury as much as she could. Taking a deep breath, she prepared herself for the arduous journey.

"Diane!"

Gene rarely used her full name. Not good.

A flash of movement streaked below her accompanied by an inhuman shriek forcing her to instinctively raise her legs and swing her lower body back up onto the shelf. A single host fell back to the ground, its unsuccessful attempt at grabbing its prey eliciting another frustrated scream. Though its reach was nowhere near high enough, the sheer height of its leap was terrifying.

Another jump it is, she thought. Her breaths came in rapid, shallow bursts. Though perfectly warranted, now was not the time for another panic attack. She looked at Gene hoping that meeting his eyes, seeing his face, would give her the courage to keep moving.

The shelving unit she was on violently shuddered forcing her to grip the edges to keep from being bucked to the floor below. Di looked down in horror as she was greeted by two dark, soulless orbs of navy blue making their way up the side. In a flash, Gene had Florence unslung from his back and aimed at the creature below. A muffled thump, deadened by her suit's audio dampeners, accompanied by another shake of the shelf was followed by a wet slap on the floor. She glanced over the side at the headless body sprawled haphazardly over a pool of steadily growing dark blue blood.

Eerie silence loomed large, all shrieking, clanging, and shifting metal ceased. Glancing back, she saw a dozen or more warped, human-like shapes frozen in place behind beams of metal. Their heads, every single one, moved in unison to glare at the man responsible for the death of one of their own. A low, threatening rumble morphed to a chilling growl, and they flew back into motion, squirming and squeezing their way between the twisted shelving. Skin along their shoulders, arms, and torsos began to flay in their frenzy to reach the threat, injuries ignored as they oozed thick, viscous liquid making an already horrifying scene gorier.

"Captain, you need to move. Jump and I'll catch you."

Di shifted, locking eyes with her friend. Trusting eyes. Confident eyes. Behind him, the vent was nearly entirely uncovered now, panel curled and hanging limply by a single soldered edge.

Facing imminent death was an occupational hazard, one that she had mostly avoided so far in her career. There had been close calls, sure. Closer than she was comfortable admitting to herself. But there was a difference between confronting danger and confronting death. In her mind, she had always wondered how she would react when her time came. Would she cower and crumble like a blubbering idiot? Or would she brave the inevitable head-on, shoulders square, chest puffed in defiance?

In that moment, a wave of calm washed over her. Whatever her fate, she would accept it. But you bet your ass that if now was her time, she would go swinging taking as many of the bastards with her as she could.

"Di, please! Jump!"

"I'm not going to make that jump, Gene." Even from this distance, she could see the tears welling in his eyes.

"Don't give up. Please." Despite his fear of heights, he stretched his hand as far as he could, as if willing the gap to narrow would be enough.

"Gene, do you trust me?" An idea had blossomed in her brain, something too crazy to risk but likely her only avenue forward. Whatever chance she had to make it out of this room alive, however small it may be, this was it.

"Di, I can catch you. You have to jump." The last two words caught in his throat and his hand was shaking now. A loud screech of metal followed by light, quick footsteps signaled the arrival of more hosts. She didn't need to look back to know they were coming.

"Gene, get in the vent and get ready to catch me. If I miss, keep going to warn the others. We can't let the parasite leave this moon."

He gulped audibly into his mic. "Is that an order, Captain?"

Glancing down, Di saw a steady line of hosts approaching below. "That's an order. Get in that vent and try not to drop me when I jump."

The hosts began climbing, split between the two sides. Their ascent was mercifully slower now, more cautious in response to the violent death of one of their own.

"Aye, Captain." Gene slapped the rifle to his back and threw himself up into the opening in the ceiling, boots quickly disappearing behind the lip. A moment later, she saw his gloved hand appear, outstretched just below the lip of the vent.

This was it. If she failed now, it was all on Gene. She gave herself a fifty-fifty chance of making it out alive. Maybe sixty-forty. What could she say, she believed in herself.

Pulling out her pistol, she squeezed off two rounds into the spine of a host on the opposite side and watched as it plummeted to the ground. She took two more shots into the face of the creature directly below her, and it, too, fell screaming, knocking another off its position and landing with a sickening squelch. Attention was all on her now, and the remaining hosts shifted pursuit to her side, no longer hesitant in their climb.

I sure hope this works, she thought, crouching on her toes and grasping both edges of the shelf. As much bravado as she had shown, she really didn't want to die.

Throwing her weight to the right, she heaved for all she was worth, ignoring the breath-taking, piercing pain in her side. The shelf began to shift, teetering precariously before rocking back to the left.

Come on, you bastard. Moving with the motion, she heaved again on the backswing and felt the shelf hit the apex. Her breath caught in her throat as it paused. A blackened hand crested the top as the lead host fought gravity to pull itself toward its target. Her confidence plummeted, stomach roiling.

And then it fell.

Don't miss, Diane, she thought, and using the forward momentum of the one-ton steel rocket she was riding, she leapt.

CHAPTER 11
SACRIFICE

For one horrifying moment Di thought she had missed completely. Her on-the-fly calculations of her trajectory had been just that, but her momentary clarity and positive assertiveness had guaranteed her success in her own mind. That confidence, in the face of the consequences of her decision, was now lacking.

In all fairness, her launch had been as flawless as she could have hoped for; heel planted on the back edge of the shelf as it flung her forward toward her salvation. But it quickly became apparent where her problem lay; too far forward, not enough verticality.

Gene's outstretched arm strained as far down as he could, but it was still not quite low enough as her fingers brushed against his. Short-lived pride was replaced by blinding pain as her already bruised and battered chest slammed into the edge of the bent panel. Her fingers miraculously found purchase as she clung to the surface to arrest her fall. An ominous crack shook her body, and she briefly thought she had audibly broken yet another set of ribs. Then the panel shifted downward, another loud crack mixing with the clamorous clash of the shelves colliding below her.

So close. She had come so close.

"Grab Florence!"

Di's eyes flicked upward to the butt of Gene's rifle half a meter above her head. With one final snap, the panel dislodged from the ceiling. The fingers of her left hand closed on the textured stock of the gun, and her body jerked downward with the loss of her safe haven. She swung precariously before latching her right hand beside her left. Already her shoulders ached from the awkward position, a nice addition to accompany the fresh wave of nauseating agony radiating through her chest from the second impact.

"Try. Not. To. Swing." Gene's grunts were labored as he clutched his treasured weapon that, in turn, held his long-time friend.

Di could feel the sarcastic retort just behind her lips, but she was afraid that if she opened her mouth she might vomit. Glancing down, all she saw was a tangled jumble of metal, body parts, and blackish blood splatters coating the ground. A smattering of pathetic moans like injured animals and a few twitching arms and legs indicated a handful of hosts had survived. If seven tons of solid steel hadn't done it, she had no idea what would.

"Can. You. Climb?"

Di shook her head which immediately reverberated

through her body, her shoulders twinging painfully as she twisted ever so slightly. A fresh wave of white-hot knives pulsated through her torso, the sudden pain nearly loosening her fierce grip on the gun.

Gene grunted and began to slowly pull on his rifle hand over hand, grip shaking violently, face flushing a deep crimson red. After a tense few seconds, her hands bumped casually against the lip of the vent entrance, and she risked letting go with her left hand to grab it. There was enough purchase for the tips of her fingers down just past her first knuckle. It wasn't ideal, but it was what she had to work with. Gene swung her other hand close to the edge and she fully let go of the gun. Her shoulders screamed, nearly drowning out the steady torrent of pain from her ribs.

"Engage magnetics," Gene muttered, shifting back to reposition for a better spot to haul her up and over the edge.

Di paused, her brain muddling through her body's protestations, then nodded reluctantly.

Her mental command was simple, yet it took every bit of mental fortitude and physical strength to give it; *engage magnetics*. Though she didn't visibly notice any change, her grip felt stronger, like her hand was being forced down into the lip. By then, Gene had repositioned himself to his belly, shoulders over the edge with arms hanging down to grip her upper arms.

"Ok, I've got you now."

Di felt tension in her fingertips as she lifted one hand free, as though her skin-tight gloves were sticky when she pulled away. Gene's thick, meaty fist shifted from her arm to close around her wrist, and she returned in kind, her thinner hands not quite making it around his gorilla-sized forearm. He heaved her up in a single, swift jerk. The motion nearly ripped her shoulder out of her socket, but she sailed up and over landing safely beside him with her legs left dangling. If it hadn't been for the blindingly hot white flash of pain across her vision, her broken ribs may have been forgotten entirely behind her manic, wheezing laughter.

"Holy shit," she gasped between chuckles.

"You. Are. A dumbass." Gene flipped over on to his back and closed his eyes, chest heaving up and down.

"Like a fox."

He peeked out at her with one eye, eyebrow raised. "That doesn't even make sense."

Di playfully slapped his middle-aged gut. "Shut up. It worked."

"It shouldn't have. It was stupid and reckless, and you nearly got yourself killed."

Sitting up, gingerly feeling at her undoubtedly black and purple chest, she took the moment to gather herself and conduct a self-evaluation. Obviously several ribs were cracked, a few more added on no thanks to her collision with the steel plate. The good news was she didn't think any were fully snapped. No protruding bones to pierce her suit or recessed shards to pierce her lungs or heart. She flipped her wrist and navigated to the medical menu, initiating a full diagnostic rundown. A virtual model of herself appeared in the corner of her HUD, various portions of her body pulsating red to indicate injury, while a progress bar steadily counted up. She felt her suit shifting to accommodate, cushioning air adding a bit more support to her ribcage.

"Would you like me to remind you of just how many 'dumbass' decisions you've made over the years?" she asked. It had been hours that had seemed like days since they'd had a peaceful moment to banter, and she gladly took advantage. Her helmet 'dinged' softly against the metal vent wall as she lay back and closed her eyes.

"That's different."

"Oh really? Do explain."

"*I* am dispensable. *You*, as the captain, are *not*."

"Oh, sweetie. Fishing for a compliment? *You're* indispensable as well." Di blindly flailed her hand toward his head, making a connection and giving him a pandering tap.

"Di, I'm serious. Please."

With the shift in his tone, she cracked an eyelid to look his way. She could hear the desperation behind his words, the meaning behind the meaning. It wasn't just that she, captain of their crew, was indispensable. What he insinuated was that she, Diane, was indispensable.

As far as the mission was concerned, that made no logical sense. Gene had witnessed everything that she had. He had access to the files, same as her. He was more than capable of making it back to the surface and getting the rest of their team home safely. What he meant, what his eyes were trying to convey, was that she was indispensable to *him*. The meaning behind the meaning, and logic had nothing to do with it.

Though they were going on nearly twenty-five years of acquaintanceship, then cordial familiarity, and finally a genuine, unshakeable, ride-or-die bond, they had never moved beyond that point. Sure, there had been instances of potential, flashes of a theoretical life together, but that spark had never grown to commitment or romantic love. Or hell, even just animalistic lust. At least not for her. They had shared a drunken kiss in a bar on Phobos Station, a stupid moment of celebration early on in their mercenary career for narrowly making it back in one piece. It had been nice, to be honest. Lips pressed together, face held in his calloused, grizzled hands. A brief moment of what might have been. But once that moment had gone, it faded in her mind to nothing more than alcohol-fueled overexuberance. To be honest, looking back it had felt a touch too close to kissing a brother or a cousin. Not exactly something you wanted in a lifelong partner.

And yet, though she had tried to make excuses to herself, Di knew deep down it had meant more to Gene. Much more. As soon as she had pulled away, looking into his shimmering, emotional eyes, she knew it had been a mistake. This was not a casual fling type of relationship. Once that boundary was crossed, well and truly crossed, there would have been no going back. She would have either had to learn to love him in that way he wanted to be loved or leave him behind. Two options that were horribly unfair to Gene.

So, the following morning after a bitter cup of coffee and a few aspirin for her pounding hangover, she told him just that. That spark of anticipation, that happy twinkle in his eye, had faded immediately. In that moment, Di wished more than anything she could give him what he wanted. But she couldn't. And she wouldn't.

It was only unbearably awkward for a couple days before everything returned to normal. She thought she was in the clear when Gayle came aboard and took his attention away for a time. Their eventual spiral and downfall resulting in hurt feelings and bitter cold shoulders was yet another reaffirmation of Di's initial decision. Di was never told the reason for their split, but she had wondered if it had anything to do with her. Six months of squinting glares and pursed lips seemed to indicate Gayle may have thought along those same lines.

Di reached out and took his large, gloved hand in hers, eyes fully open, doing everything she could to convey her utmost sincerity. With an involuntary groan, she leaned closer until their visors nearly touched.

"Gene." Using the last of her waning strength, she squeezed his fingers as hard as she could, falsely honeyed voice dripping sickly sweet. "Don't tell me what I can or can't do."

He flinched, not so much from her pathetically exhausted grip, but from her verbal slap. Her stomach squirmed at the insensitive but necessary tough love routine. She always hated when she had to do it.

"Understood, Captain."

She let go with a sigh and flopped back against the wall of the ventilation shaft. "I made a calculated decision in an impossible situation. You know as well as I do that there was no way in hell I was making that gap any other way. And I refuse—" Di snapped her fingers, demanding his rapt attention which he reluctantly gave. "I *refuse* to let you throw yourself away for personal reasons.

"Our mission parameters have changed, of which you are well aware. Our primary objective is to get the information we have off-moon and into the right hands. Our secondary objective is to get everyone else away from this godforsaken hellhole. If leaving me behind is paramount to fulfilling objective one, you *will* do it. That is a direct order. Am I clear?"

"Yes, Captain." Gene looked paler than usual, but she knew he would follow her orders. He always had.

Di cleared her throat uncomfortably. "Now. Where do we go from here? Any idea where the elevator to the surface would be?"

Ever the professional, Gene recovered instantaneously and resumed his stoic visage and constant vigilance. "My best guess is we go up until we can't anymore."

"Seems reasonable to me." A quick lean to her right let her glance up along the perfectly vertical metal shaft above the gaping hole they had just climbed through. Jerky stirrings in the carnage below reminded her they hadn't escaped yet. As if in direct response, a high-pitched mewling echoed out from below the twisted wreckage sending a haunting shiver down her spine.

"You think the suit's magnetics are good enough to let us climb that?" she asked.

"Only one way to find out."

Gene performed a perfunctory inspection of his prized rifle and clicked his tongue in disgust. "Barrel's dented."

"You've got a helluva grip, Gene," Di joked. He grunted. "That gonna be a problem?"

"Only if I try to shoot it," he replied, lightly running a finger over the small grooves.

"I'll make sure she's fixed when we get back."

Gene took one last longing look before he slung it back on his back. The pistol strapped to his thigh that had thus far remained mostly out of action until now appeared in his hand. He performed a perfunctory inspection checking the slide, magazine, and barrel before he nodded to himself, returned it to its holster, and shifted to a hunched crouch beside her. The shaft wasn't terribly spacious, and Gene's sheer mass, huddled like a goblin shoved into a cannon, elicited a twitch of a smile; something he either missed or chose to ignore entirely.

"After you," she said.

Gene, after taking a moment's pause to switch on his magnetics, swung his legs out of the opening and slapped a hand on the metal above. The impact produced a thin, warbled ring that didn't inspire confidence in the structural integrity of their escape avenue. With an old man grunt, he flipped himself around and planted his boots firmly on the vent's lower opening.

"Give me a second to shift up and over," he wheezed. "I

think it would be safer if we climb up opposite sides of the shaft. Just in case."

"Just in case what? If you fall, you're taking me with you."

He grunted again. "Fine. It's just to make me feel better."

Di nodded and swung her legs out as he hauled himself a meter or two up the shaft. Sucking in a deep breath, she mentally flipped on her magnetics and followed Gene, crawling out and up. It took a moment or two longer for her brain to adjust to the odd sight of her hands flat against a sheer surface. She exerted genuine effort to keep herself from flexing her fingers in a vain attempt to find a handhold. Less surface area meant a higher likelihood her magnetics would fail to hold her, so she pushed her palm as flush to the metal as she could.

"Coming?" Gene asked from above. She glanced up at his expectant face peeking around his large yet toned behind, something she was attempting not to focus on but found distractingly difficult with the skin-tight features of his suit.

"And stop objectifying me," he said with a coy grin.

"How does it feel, experiencing the female plight?" she asked as she began to climb, returning her attention to the task at hand.

As she fell into a rhythm, she was surprised at how natural it felt. The motions of shuffling her hands and feet reminded her of climbing the wrong way up those old plastic slides at the playground.

Gene grunted. "Poor you. How difficult it must be to be attractive."

"It is when it drives cocky, slobbering drunk assholes to berate you while you're trying to drink alone in peace."

"Fair. Can't say I've experienced that one. Although there was the one time I accidentally found myself in a gay bar. It took me a few rounds to realize why so many guys were buying my drinks."

Di's chest pulsed painfully as she let out a strong, bark-like laugh followed by a wheeze of discomfort. "What I wouldn't give to have seen that."

"If we make it off this damn rock, you can take me to as many gay bars as you like."

His 'if' hung in the following silence, a splash of briskly cold water on their momentary levity. Though she had felt optimistic in the face of their miraculous escape, the odds really were stacked against them. There was a countless horde of demons roaming around this station specifically seeking their blood. Not to mention the unknown status of the station they had come from, their original landing area, or the rest of her crew on the orbital station. What if there was nothing to escape *to*? That haunting question had been lurking in the recesses of her mind, too afraid to face the light of reality. Even now, following the rhythm of her repetitive sliding and the empty, silent time to contemplate that likely scenario, she refused to give it space to breathe. Following that line of thought would only send her sinking into a spiral of hopelessness that she couldn't afford to entertain.

Gene's voice cut through her introspection. "We've gone

as high as we can."

Di glanced up and found the blank slab of metal with two perpendicular tunnels branching away from the main shaft. She glanced at her HUD, surprised to notice they had been climbing in silence for nearly fifteen minutes. Though their pace was slow, they had traveled far.

"Which way are we going?" she called out.

"My vote is left."

"Any particular reason?"

Gene shifted, pushing himself into the ventilation shaft on his left. "Not particularly." His voice then took on a rustic, elderly tone. "But the air doesn't smell so foul down here."

"Why does that sound familiar?"

"It'll sound familiar if you have taste. It's Lord of the Rings."

Di snorted. "Lord of the Rings? Since when do you know anything pop culture?"

"It's an ancient classic. Doesn't count."

With a heave she threw herself up into the shaft beside him. Her arms began to shake, a coalescing of the sheer exertion, building pain, and crippling exhaustion from the day's events.

"Need a minute?" Gene asked. He glanced at her concernedly.

"No. Let's just go. The sooner we get back to the shuttle, the sooner I can take that minute."

"You can take two while you're at it," Gene said before shifting to his hands and knees and shuffling away.

Almost there, Di thought. A soft groan escaped her lips as she plucked up her own courage, exhaustion be damned, and followed.

Slits on the walls whispered past granting a peek at more empty, dark rooms. The miners hadn't bothered boarding these up which she decided to take as a good sign. The higher levels of the facility were most likely boxed up last, and if she were a gambling woman, which she hadn't been for decades for good reason, she would bet they would have wanted to pack the closest to the elevator last. They had to be close.

After a sharp right turn, she nearly collided with Gene. Before she muttered a derogatory remark, she caught herself. He wasn't moving. Not a single twitching muscle, not even a shift of weight to keep the pressure off his bum right knee which had to be throbbing by now. Not even a message on comms.

A flicker of movement flashed past the slitted vent to their left. Dim shadows cast by an emergency beacon at the far end of the room sent ghoulish red light across the nearly empty shelves. A complicated console of switches, knobs, and buttons sat beneath a frosted pane of glass looking out onto the hallway. Three blinking blue lights were all that indicated the switch board still had some form of functionality or power.

Di's mind attempted to convince her that the flash of movement had merely been one of these flickering lights, but that wouldn't have made Gene pause. In situations like these, she trusted his instincts over her own.

It took a full twenty seconds for her eyes to adjust to the

inky black. When they did, the gently swaying body in the far corner of the room snatched her breath from her lungs. If she had not been so utterly exhausted, nerves already shot to hell, she likely would have audibly gasped.

What are you waiting for? Keep moving! She hoped her silent text message conveyed her spike of anxiety and minor annoyance.

I think this is the control room, he replied.

The control room. Where they would likely be able to turn on emergency power to the elevator. Shit.

We need to distract that thing and get this vent off, she messaged.

Let me check ahead. Gene cautiously shifted forward, glancing through the slots spaced judiciously apart along the ventilation shaft.

After a tense few minutes and a considerable distance, his next message flashed before her eyes.

Found an empty storage room.

What are you gonna do?

Distract it, was all he replied. The brief, tinny, gentle scrape of metal on metal felt like a blaring symphony to Di's ears, but he successfully pulled the grate back into the tunnel with minimal noise. His legs gently slipped halfway out of the vent before the rest of his body followed.

Di's heart felt like it was trying to leap up her throat and strangle her on its way out. Though she had silenced the obnoxious audible ping of her elevated heart rate notification, the eye-catching, fluctuating red numbers were still there in the corner of her vision. Taunting her. Threatening to envelop her in a horribly timed bout of panic. Images of Gene being torn to shreds appeared unbidden in her mind. Splatters of red across the walls. Gurgling shrieks of agony. Accusatory eyes. Just like Gerald.

You did this. You did this, Di.

Hallway clear, moving to intercept.

Gene's message was like a bastion of light, a calm breeze on her face. He was fine. He was capable. He was accomplishing the objective, and it would be in vain if she were to freeze now. Taking three deep breaths, she maneuvered her own grate like a deft surgeon, but one that had ill-advisedly had one or two drinks while on-call, and placed it as gingerly as she could beside her. The host still stood flinching and swaying in the corner beside the doorway with its back to her, blessedly oblivious to her presence. She flattened herself as much as humanly possible and waited for Gene's signal. It came a few moments later.

In place. Ready?

Ready, she replied. Empty silence stretched for a moment before she heard a clattering, metallic twang somewhere beyond the room. The host dropped in a feral stance, a high-pitched whistle emanating from its throat. It remained there for several seconds before leaping out of the room.

Time to move. Swinging her legs into open air, she inched her bruised and battered torso out of her relative place of safety. As an added measure, she engaged the magnetics in her gloves and lowered herself out of the vent by her fingertips. The distance to the ground was only two or so meters, but her heart pounded in her chest. With an inner 'three, two, one', she disengaged her gloves and allowed her fingers to slip free.

Despite the relatively short fall and the slight impact deadening her suit provided, the immediate jolt reverberating through her bone-weary legs caused her knees to buckle. Di's right hand shot out to catch herself from colliding with the shelving unit beside her, too late to notice the handful of screws left behind on the shelf. They jostled free and pinged softly on the smooth lab flooring.

It was primal instinct that saved her as she flattened to the floor in time to see a flash of movement through the window and the return of her rotting friend. Though she was partially obscured by a small metal crate, it wouldn't take much for the host to shift and catch a glimpse of her half-exposed body. Di's thoughts immediately went to the pistol glaringly absent from her hand, but she didn't dare shift to get it from its secure placement on her thigh. Her best shot was to hope it didn't move further into the room.

Those hopes were shattered as the host took two hesitant steps closer, face sweeping side to side, eyes flushed deep blue. Its lips had fallen off leaving a jagged, blackened line of flesh attached to its grey gums, but the teeth were disturbingly pristinely white. Chunks of its nose were missing, and its gaunt, blue-hued, pale skin clung to its facial bones to the point it was practically translucent. Bald patches randomly dotted its scalp, but enough remained to indicate the creature had once enjoyed long dirty-blonde locks.

Another high-pitched whistle bubbled in its throat before eking past its clenched teeth. The sound sent chills through Di's body, starting from her core and spreading like wildfire to the tips of her fingers and soles of her feet. As if in response, its head whipped around and their eyes locked together.

Most regulars, or in other words non-mercenaries, inevitably ask the same types of questions when they inquire into Di's career, especially after one too many drinks. One question in particular came up more often than not; what happens if you freeze in the heat of the moment? Di's reply was second nature at this point; you die. What came next was typically a jest or a jab at her stony, stern response, implying she couldn't possibly mean *every* time. Surely she had frozen a time or two. They sobered up when confronted with her patented withering glare and her inevitable retort; "Ask the men I killed."

And she wondered why she was chronically single.

Time slowed to a crawl. Di saw flecks of spittle spray from the host's impossibly wide maw as it crouched lower in anticipation of its deadly pounce. Her hand was already grasping at the grip of her pistol at her waist, reflexes acting before her mind could register. She ripped it free as the creature's powerful legs tensed to throw itself at its prey. In her heart, she knew she would be too late. By the time she swung the pistol to bear, aimed, and shot, it would already be on her back ripping at her flesh. She would become just another loss, another statistic.

Another Gerald.

A flash of steel glinted in the wan light beside the monster's head before the knife plunged to the hilt beneath its jaw, angled up toward its brain. Gene jerked it by its new head ornament, throwing it to the ground and landing on top to pin it to the floor. It made no noise in its struggling death throws other than the scrabbling clacks of its bony fingers across the floor, finally stilling with a twist of the blade embedded in its skull.

Di took a moment to remember to breathe again. "Cutting it a little close, aren't we?"

"Damn pistol jammed." He mimed spitting in disgust. "Worthless corporate shite."

The pistol in her hand rattled as she attempted to get her nerves under control, making one, two, three attempts to holster it. She was getting real tired of the constant adrenaline roller coaster, and her body seemed to agree as it drained of said adrenaline and replaced it with sheer exhaustion. If they didn't get back to the ship soon, she wasn't sure her body could handle much more.

In a mercenary's line of work, exhaustion was just part of the gig. It didn't matter which job you took; by the end, any merc worth their salt left it all on the table.

Given her now extensive experience in that field, Di was intimately aware of her own body's limitations. Every job came with moments of intense action followed by a cool down, a time for her body to register what had happened and to react as a body should. But she had never felt this kind of weightiness. It was taxing on her very bones and soaking through to her soul. It was more akin to the constant heightened anxiety from her days as a soldier, a life she had thought she had long put behind her.

A firm hand caught her by the bicep as she attempted to stand. As if sensing her mind was on the verge of throwing in the towel, Gene had appeared to pick her back up and get her going in the right direction.

She shot him a thankful smirk, though it didn't reflect in her eyes. "How did you know to go for the head?" she asked.

"That's zombies one-oh-one. Besides, it seemed to work last time."

Her mind flashed back to Patrick the miner's head being vaporized above her own, gooey purple blood coating her visor and chest. "Fair," she replied, suppressing a shudder. "We'd better hurry. If those things really are connected, they'll have sensed one going down."

Gathering her nerves, she approached the gently flashing console full of complicated buttons and unmarked switches.

"You'd think they'd have the decency to label them," Gene muttered, standing just off her left shoulder.

"We'd be so lucky." Di squinted down at the various buttons.

"I saw the elevator bays down the hall. We just need to find one that will switch on emergency power, or at least shunt what's left to the elevators. Then we can get the hell out of here."

Common sense told her to start with the switches beside the three flashing lights. It would make sense for the engineers who designed this system to make it as easy as possible to get things up and running in an emergency, so what better way than a large, obvious, flashing sign like a neon blue light? Di would have preferred a simple 'Push in Case of Emergency' sign, but beggars can't be choosers.

Muttering a constant stream of pleadings, she pushed each button in a random sequence. The lights on the board winked out, but nothing else followed. She let out a dejected sigh, shoulders and head slumping. Of course it wouldn't be that simple. It was *never* that simple.

"Di, look."

She nearly wrenched her neck with the whiplash. A single button flared to life with warm blue light. Leaning closer, she saw a faded label beneath it, various letters scratched off with use and time. It looked a helluva lot like 'Emergency On' to her. Her palm struck it a little too aggressively in response and she waited with bated breath.

The low, gentle, growing hum of power was music to her ears. Dim overhead lights came blinking slowly to life, awakened from their deep, dark slumber. They were one step closer to home.

In the next moment, her honed survivalist instincts saved both her and Gene's lives. She threw her body backward and collided heavily with his chest in reaction to a flash of movement in her peripheral view. It sent them both stumbling backward in time to see a body-shaped blur hurtling into the console at lightning speed. The host they had assumed Gene had killed flailed its limbs on impact and crumpled momentarily to the floor before launching to its feet. Di looked on in horror as it turned to face them, its head lying on its shoulder, tilted to an impossible angle. Small grey tentacles sprouted from the new hole Gene had given it in its neck, squirming like a newborn puppy searching for milk. Blue blood oozed from the wound as the worm-like parasite, or parasites, attempted to force their way free, nauseatingly wriggling and emitting a high-pitched frequency like a dog whistle.

The host's body shuddered violently, limbs outstretched and shaking. In a shower of gore, a massive, fleshy appendage the thickness of Di's arm exploded out of its neck leaving its head dangling by a few stubborn strips of muscle and flesh. It squirmed like a bait worm on the end of a fishhook, waving back and forth in the air in either agony or ecstasy at its sudden freedom. Rough, sickly grey, nearly translucent skin covered ropy blue veins that pulsed along its body. Di caught a flash of razor sharp, jagged, hooked teeth in four rows around a circular maw that distended outward with a piercing screech.

For the first time in a long time, she found herself frozen in place. No horror movie could have prepared her for the sheer cold-sweat-inducing fear that pulsated through her body as she faced down this living nightmare. As though it could sense her terror, the parasite stilled and turned its gaping jaws toward her. A collection of heartbeats later, its host body followed suit and lunged in her direction.

Her arm raised of its own volition, squeezing off nine

shots in rapid succession directly into the worm's fleshy exterior as she backpedaled wildly, putting as much distance between herself and this nightmare fuel as she could. Nine bullets ripped through the worm's spasming body painting flecks of blue and grey across the wall as they sailed through to shatter the thin pane of glass behind the console and embed themselves in the hallway beyond. With a final spasming death throw, it collapsed to the ground and slid the last meter or so to lie still at her feet. The only sound remaining from the sudden burst of violence was the rhythmic clicking of her trigger as she attempted to put more rounds in the beast from her empty clip.

Di's mind reeled. She had been lucky her body's self-defense instincts had kicked in when they had. Seconds more, and she would be nothing but a puddle on the floor. Glancing down at the glossy, slimy rows of fangs sent her stomach churning. She shuddered at the thought of those teeth gripping her neck, flesh ripping as it tore her to pieces.

Doubling over, she vomited against the inside of her visor, blessedly blurring the monster from view. Bile burned and stung her throat as she emptied her already empty stomach. The suit's self-cleaning procedures had immediately begun draining, clearing, and disinfecting her helmet before she had finished.

'Would you like to administer an antiemetic for your nausea?' her suit chimed in an infuriatingly cheerful tone.

Di chose to ignore it with several deep breaths through her mouth while the suit finished taking care of itself. Her vision cleared in time to see Gene's heavy boot come crashing down on the worm-like monster's body sending a shiver through the host's limbs.

"Didn't expect that," Gene said, a slight tremor tinging his words. "You ok?"

Di waved dismissively, hands still on her knees in a half-bent position. She couldn't trust opening her mouth at the moment.

What the hell is going on? she thought. Trauma after trauma after trauma had detached her mind from her body. She felt every ache in her chest, every muscle tensed in exhaustion. Yet simultaneously, her consciousness began to float above her as though looking down on the poor, pathetic creature she was. More and more shit piled on, buckling her knees and threatening to send her to the ground, to collapse under the weight of it all. Somewhere in the background, she thought she heard wailing screeches elsewhere in the facility. She watched as if she were a spectator of her own life as Gene gingerly approached and placed a hand on her shoulder. His mouth was moving, but no sound came out. He glanced toward the hallway, genuine fear shining through his eyes. Something was most definitely wrong, yet she couldn't muster enough mental capacity to grasp what it was he needed her to do.

It was a peculiar feeling, watching herself so detachedly. Not unpleasant. Not exciting. Not anything, really. Is this what it felt like to have a mental breakdown? If it was, it wasn't as bad as she expected. Not terribly convenient timing, but—

"Captain! I will carry you if I have to! Wake! Up!"

Gene's voice, with a tone of panic she had never heard before, was like a brisk slap to the face. Di stood straight, vision fading with the immediate rush of blood to her brain. She ignored it and locked eyes with her second in command. Her rock. She nodded.

"Elevators are down the hall," Gene said, relief flooding through and warming his words. "We need to move fast and hope the emergency power kicked in enough juice to get it going. Got any more ammo?"

Di nodded, still afraid to open her mouth. Her hands moved of their own volition, ejecting the spent magazine and popping in her last full one. Not a lot to go around, but maybe enough to clear the way should they need it.

Gene's hand was still on her shoulder, and it wasn't until that moment she noticed it shaking. He was just as terrified as she was.

Throughout the decades together, in war, in battle, in life, Di had never once seen him well and truly scared. Even at his lowest, his darkest moment in that holding cell all those years ago, his resignation at his own fate had overridden the fear of what came next.

Despite his fear, she found a confidence welling inside her. She was not alone. It brought an uncharacteristic, possibly unhinged, smile to her face. She may have finally snapped, but at least she could share her insanity with a friend.

It was infectious, apparently, as Gene's eyes softened, and he returned her smile. "Ready?" he asked.

"Ready." Her voice only quavered a little, but her resolve was now iron. She would make it, or she wouldn't. It didn't really matter in that moment. What mattered was that she had Gene, and Gene had her. He was counting on her, and she would be damned if she didn't give her all until the end. Fear lessened to a dull, but ever-present, companion in the back of her mind, accompanied by a new sense of finality.

They ran. The inhuman, hissing wails grew louder. The race was on.

Dim red light reflected against the metallic surface of the sealed elevator doors. Gene produced his knife, the same one he had impaled the host on, and pried them open just enough for Di to slip her fingers in. Muscles screamed in agony as they worked in tandem to separate the two sides. She pressed her back against the left door, boot against the right as she strained with everything she had. The pain was intense, but good. It reminded her she was alive, still alive. Still fighting.

"I got this! Get in!" Gene shouted, arms outstretched to hold the doors open just wide enough to let her slide inside. As she slipped awkwardly inside, he smoothly replaced her position with his back against the door and tilted his head to the side to peer down the dimly lit hallway.

The car itself was small, smaller than the one in the previous facility. Its roof hung claustrophobically close. Di turned to the panel on the back and was met with only dark, dead controls, the overhead lights still out. "System is still down," she said, panting.

"Emergency hatch," Gene replied, nodding his head to the roof of the elevator car.

With a kick off the wall, she launched herself up and grasped the handle, pulling it down and releasing the mechanism to unseal the entry to the elevator shaft beyond. Kilometers of empty blackness greeted her. It was a long way up to the surface by hand.

"I've got it open. Let's go."

Gene leaned out further, his neck stretched and strained. He let out a sigh, glancing down at his chest before slowly lifting his head.

They locked eyes. She knew.

"No. Gene."

"Primary objective, Di. You said it yourself."

"We can both make it, Gene."

"Get the information to the ship. I'll hold them off while I can."

"Don't be a bastard! Get in here, now! That is an order!"

"Can't do, Captain." His eyes softened, unspoken words on his lips. He didn't need to say them. She knew. With a mighty heave, he dislodged himself from the doors as they clanged shut with a ringing finality.

CHAPTER 12
WARNING

Di lunged, fingers brushing the seam as it sealed shut. "Son of a bitch!" She clawed at the nonexistent gap, desperately trying to force it open with sheer will alone. The high-pitched shrieks grew louder, dozens of overlapping screams intermingling with the thunderous slaps of stampeding feet. Gunshots rang out. One. Two. Three four five six.

"Gene!" she screamed, eyes widening.

His voice, muffled through the thick steel, sounded firm. "Go!" Three more gunshots echoed loudly in the corridor, each progressively quieter as he bolted further away from the oncoming horde.

Di's raw throat pulsated as she screamed and pounded on the door. It wouldn't matter. There was no way she could get that door open by herself. It wouldn't change anything. Yet she raged and slammed her fists regardless, hoping it would take the edge off the sting, hoping the pain in her hands and her chest could outstrip the pain in her heart and her head. It didn't. She continued anyway, stinging tears bubbling in the corner of her eyes, her vision taking on a hazy underwater filter.

After a dozen full-fisted punches to the unyielding metal, knuckles hotly pulsating, she collapsed to her knees. At least the pain was something to feel, something real. Short, quick breaths filled her lungs with recycled, stale-tasting air filtered through her suit. More than anything, she desperately wanted to rip her helmet off so she could breathe. She couldn't breathe. Damn it, why couldn't she breathe?

Her panic attacks, when they had begun some years ago, always came on slowly at first, creeping up unsuspectingly before wrapping their tendrils around her throat and chest and constricting tightly. Dozens of therapy sessions later, Di had been equipped with the tools to combat her body's reactions to fear at the onset, to tamp down on her subconscious reaction to triggers before they escalated beyond her control. Breathing techniques and internal mantras. Refocusing her attention on what was real, what she could influence, what she could control.

Over the years, having long since quit therapy (against Doctor Johnston's strongly suggested advice), she had maintained a certain level of authority over her body's occasional swinging emotions. Take some breaths. Mutter some key phrases. Focus her 'chi', or whatever. It still seemed a little silly to her, but silly or not it worked.

And yet here she sat. Abandoned on the floor of a malfunctioning elevator car half a dozen kilometers from the surface of a barren, hostile moon. Closing her eyes. Counting her breaths. Muttering her empty self-assurances. Lying to herself.

Lying that she had control. Lying that she could make it through. Lying that Gene wasn't gone.

Gene. Gerald. Both gone. One taken before her eyes, one sprinting off into the unknown alone. Hell, for all she knew her entire crew were dead. She hadn't been able to contact them in hours, and if the orbital station reflected even a fraction of the chaos they had experienced surface-side, she couldn't manage to muster much hope.

A sinister smirk tugged at the corners of her mouth, tears continuing to streak down her cheeks. If they were *all* dead, at least that included the corporate bastard, Mr. Roberts. Silver linings and all that.

Part of her, a part currently being smothered by an overwhelming sense of hopeless anguish, knew she had to move. It was fighting to rise up, like a drowning man struggling desperately to taste sweet oxygen, the tantalizing light from the surface tauntingly out of reach. Would she push to the top? Would she grab hold of her fear and kick its ass like she had in times past? Or was this it? Is this what would break her?

Gene's voice came unbidden to Di's mind. Another sweet, poignant reminder in response to her teetering on the precipice of despair.

It wasn't your fault. Now get up and go save your crew.

"Bastard," she said, choking on a mixture of a laugh and a sob. Her inner badass burst from the waves of her sorrow, gulping down life, reinvigorated for the fight. People were counting on her. *Her* people. Her family. And she would be damned if she didn't do everything in her power to get them home.

With an infusion of energy, Di sprang to her feet and vaulted herself up to the emergency hatch hanging open above. Deep down she knew her newfound vigor wouldn't last long, so she had to take advantage of it while she could. The ever-present reminder of her despair hung precariously on the edges of her subconscious, a darkness that, should she fall again, she wasn't entirely confident she could get back up from. Coupled with her physical exhaustion, injury after injury, bruise after bruise, compounding exponentially with every step, her sanity was a precariously stacked house of cards. The wrong gust of wind could send it toppling disastrously.

Crying out in pain and determination, she hauled herself up on to the top of the elevator car and slammed the hatch closed behind her. As she rolled onto her back, she stared at the never-ending corridor of darkness above. Just thinking about her inevitable trek up sent a wave of fatigue from her chest down through her limbs. Despite the promise of microgravity partway up the shaft, daunting was a light description for her monumental task.

Di closed her eyes and summoned Gene's caring face, Gerald's kind smile. She pictured Gayle's stony determination, Hazel's humorous glint in her eyes, Emma's infectious excitement, Lucas' encouraging nod. Finally, she imagined Mr. Roberts' cowed look of sheer terror facing down a horde of monsters. A genuine grin tugged at the corners of her mouth. She couldn't miss that.

Joints popping, chest aching, she begrudgingly hoisted her body off of the cold steel at her back. From a shadowed corner just beyond the cables, Di spotted a maintenance ladder in decent condition. Considering how long it must have been since a living soul had used it, she was surprised by its longevity. Here she was, assuming the corporation had cheaped out on everything possible. Maybe they had a shred of dignity and concern after all. Then again, maybe the crew who had installed and maintained the only route to the surface had wanted to make sure they had a reliable escape path. Either way, she would gladly take advantage of their consideration.

Taking a deep breath, she leaned out from the edge of the car and grabbed hold of the metal rungs. "Here we go," she muttered to herself, and began to climb.

It only took a few moments for her to find a steady rhythm. Right hand, right foot. Left hand, left foot. She only slipped twice, once on an unseen patch of clear ice that had collected on a rung and another when she grew a little too confident and attempted to skip a rung or two. The butterflies had settled long after she vowed not to try that a second time.

Darkness enveloped her as she pulled herself away from the dim lights of the elevator car below. With a now practiced thought, her headlamps flashed on reflecting the featureless wall before her eyes. After several minutes of climbing, Di felt the pull of the artificial gravity's sphere of influence lessen. Her arms and legs ached, the same ache she felt after a good session at the gym.

Having less weight to pull up the ladder would be a welcome shift, though that uneasiness that accompanied her ingrained fear was slowly growing in the pit of her stomach.

"Don't look down, Di. Simple."

With a shaky breath, she returned to her mindless, steady climb. Right, right. Left, left. Over and over. Nothing to do but push onward. Onward and upward.

"No need to dwell on what's happened below," she wheezed. "Or what waits above. Just me, this ladder, and a few hours of mindless climbing. Simple workout. I've done those before."

Repetition and physical exertion. It was comfortable. Familiar. Di used to spend hours in the gym, zoning out the world around her and emptying her thoughts to listen to the pulses of her body in motion. Some may have called it a form of meditation. Not Di. But some.

She gave in to the pattern. This was just another workout. Her bruises were an afterthought. Cracked ribs? It was just a muscle cramp. She needed to drink more water, that was all.

If she hadn't thrown a casual glance up, she would have plowed headlong into the sealed metal hatch above her with full force. Her brain lagged a second or two behind before it registered that her path was blocked, and the lack of gravity carried her body forward anyway. Her helmet bounded uncomfortably off the unforgiving steel sending a jolt down her spine.

"What the hell?" The fog of her focused mind finally

cleared enough to register a problem she hadn't foreseen; a locked maintenance tunnel. "Who the hell puts a lock on a maintenance hatch? No one's climbing up here." She let slip an exhausted chuckle. No one except her. The irony of her statement was not lost on her alongside the dawning realization of her only viable option.

"Oh shit." Di, breaking her single rule, glanced down. Far below, past the end of her shining light, she could barely make out the dimly lit edges of the elevator car. Her vision swam, and she nearly released her hold on the ladder with a swell of overwhelming vertigo before redoubling her grip.

She couldn't go down. She couldn't go through the maintenance hatch. It left only one option.

The open elevator shaft. With no gravity.

Di's empty stomach threatened a second revolt.

It hadn't always been this way. When she was a young, impressionable girl, space had fascinated her. Anything that felt like an adventure was enthralling to her, but the sheer openness of the unknown had been particularly intriguing. That was why she had joined the military. That was why she had trained to be a pilot (before bitterly flunking out in her second semester). That was why she had dreamed of purchasing a ship, gathering a crew, and sailing the open vacuum like the swashbuckling pirates of old.

It had only taken one cheap cable and a split second of inattention to break her of her fascination. By the time her uncaring supervisor had noticed her absence, she had already drifted out of range of conventional rescue options.

Two days. Two days of gentle flipping end over end, inching closer and closer to the empty void of space, before her construction employers had decided the minimal funds and effort to rescue her outweighed the mountains of paperwork and payout in the event of her death. No apologies. No paid time off. Even her corporate-mandated evaluation before she could return to work hadn't been reimbursable. We saved you, what more could you possibly want? Here's a swift kick in the balls on your way out.

Needless to say, she submitted her papers of resignation shortly thereafter, with a nice double middle finger sendoff on her way out.

It was at that point, however, she had decided she would be her own boss, set her own rules. So, while that experience had gifted her with a new, crippling anxiety of open space and the lack of control that went along with it, it had also given her a chance at life anew. A ship to call her own. A family.

Maybe a boot between the legs was what she needed after all.

"Not a big deal," Di muttered, eyes squeezed tight. "You're in a confined space. There are countless handholds. You'll be fine." She didn't think her stomach agreed with her pep talk, but she also couldn't take another round of the stinging stench of disinfectant.

Critical thinking time. Di opened her eyes and leaned out as far as her shaking limbs would allow, narrowly able to peek around the maintenance shaft that blocked her path. A dozen half-assed choices sprang to mind, but realistically there were two options; cautiously make her way along the various struts dotting the walls like a rock climber, or leap to the dangling cables in the middle of the shaft.

Sure, she could attempt to cut her way through the lock, but she had no idea where she would get the tools to do so. She could make her way back down and try to get the power routed to the elevators, but if she were caught it would make Gene's sacrifice in vain. Besides, if Gene had somehow managed to evade his pursuers, he was relying on her to bring the rescue. She couldn't do that from down here, and this elevator shaft was the only way up. Unless she was willing to dig her way to the surface through the ice itself. She didn't really have an industrial strength drill or half of a decade to spare though. Thus, two options.

Di ground her teeth and snarled. "Come on!"

Before she had a chance to talk herself out of it, she turned to face the opposite wall and let go with one hand. With a kick a little more forceful than she had intended, she rocketed away from the wall and into open air. Her outstretched fingers kept her centered in her beeline toward the thick metal central cables. She counted her lucky stars as her grip slid into place, legs and body swinging wildly around like an inexperienced dancer her first night on the pole. She pulled her chest in tightly to her lifeline and took a few moments to recover her regular breathing, eyes squeezed tightly shut.

"Damn microgravity," she mumbled. Moments were

steadily ticking away as she sat paralyzed by her own mental failings. Precious moments when the lives of her remaining crew hung in the balance.

They're dying, you know, she thought reservedly. *They're dying while you sit here like a child.*

Painfully forcing down the lump in her throat, Di shook her head to clear the negative thoughts. That would get her nowhere.

"I've got this. I've got a long way to go, and people are counting on me." Without opening her eyes, she mentally commanded her suit to release the safety line, feeling blindly at her waist until she gripped the carabiner in her fist and extended it to the thick elevator cable in her other hand. After wrapping the line around the cable, the carabiner snapped securely in place with a quick tug, and she released a quivering sigh.

In reality, the precaution was not at all necessary. But just because something isn't strictly required doesn't mean it isn't appreciated. That safety line was the only thing keeping her together, giving her the fortitude to push onward.

"One hand over the other." Di opened her eyes, focusing solely on the industrial steel braided cable in her grasp, and began to climb.

The elevator shaft rumbled ominously. She froze, knuckles white as a gentle wave rolled up the cable from below. A moment's breath later, swirling amber emergency beacons blazed to life along the corridor below. Di glanced down, the roof of the elevator car flickering in and out of view from the dim rotating lights. It shuddered and began to ascend the tracks along the walls, pulling itself up along the cable.

"You've got to be kidding me."

Without thinking, without letting her fear take hold, she lunged back to the safety of the ladder alcove below the maintenance shaft. If she could make it there, the car should pass by without grinding her against the wall. From there, maybe she could make her way back down and call the elevator.

Her safety line snapped taut at her hip as her fingers brushed the edge of the maintenance hatch, whipping her back toward the middle of the shaft and sending her spinning.

"Damn it!" she screamed. The safety line! She hadn't unclipped the safety line.

Her stomach rolled, eyes attempting to orient her location. She clutched at the cord that was gently wrapping around her waist and pulled herself back in the direction of the cable.

A risky glance down revealed the car had begun to pick up speed. Though it likely wouldn't hit a top speed of sixty kilometers per hour before colliding with her, being hit by the weight equivalent of a fully loaded freight truck going fifty wouldn't exactly feel like fluffy pillows. By the time she finally started fumbling with the carabiner, the car was bearing down. There wasn't time.

In moments of stress, when the pressure bears down and you have seconds to act, those precious seconds can be the difference between life and death. In those moments, Di thrived.

At the speed of thought, she calculated her best option at

survivability, and her body instinctively reacted. Gripping the cable in both hands, she launched herself straight up as hard as she could, hoping her safety line would slide along with her rather than catapulting her even harder into the barreling box of steel. Her faith was rewarded as the line trundled along below her.

As the elevator bore down, Di had just enough time for one more push. If she could reduce the speed of the collision as much as possible, it should minimize the damage to her already bruised and beaten body. She hoped.

Her hands briefly grasped at the cable, and she flung her body up as hard as her exhausted arms would allow. Moments before impact, she curled inward as tight as she could to protect her head and neck. Her body rotated awkwardly in the microgravity, but she resisted the instinctive urge to flail her limbs to catch herself. That decision likely saved her life.

The elevator hit. A searing stab of white-hot flame lanced up her left leg where she caught the brunt of the impact. Her back collided with an unforgiving metal surface. Di felt the safety line go taut before her vision faded and her conscious mind decided it was time for a little rest.

*   *   *

"Uunnngh."

Di's eyelids felt like thirty kilo weights. Fog clouded her memory as to why she was laying against a hard, angular surface.

And why did her knee feel like it was stuffed with Styrofoam? Her leg shifted and her eyes shot open in response to the shock of pain forcing out a wheezing gasp.

"Alert. You have been non-responsive for... three minutes and... thirteen seconds. Elevated heart rate and blood pressure indicate you have been injured."

"No shit!" she muttered, clutching at her throbbing knee.

"Please remain calm. Emergency assistance will arrive soon." Her suit's infuriatingly calm voice paused. *"Error. Unable to contact emergency assistance. Please make your way to the nearest medical facility for further first aid services."*

"You are less than worthless," she hissed through gritted teeth.

"Would you like to access the medical menu for additional options? Suggestions include: pain management medication, stabilization, cauteriza—"

"Stabilize my knee, dumbass!" She could practically hear the artificial intelligence thinking.

"Please refrain from unnecessary profanity and insults."

Di's jaw fell open. Was she being morally chastised by a robot? Leave it to corpos to program a highly advanced space suit with manners.

"I do not align with traditional definitions of a 'robot', though I have been programmed to assist my wearer in various capacities, including rudimentary medical needs."

Ah yes. And it could read her thoughts. Perfect. "Stabilize my left knee for travel and give me the strongest medication you can."

The skintight pantleg of her suit immediately hardened around her knee, though it wasn't an unpleasant sensation. It was more like it had been packed tightly in a sleeve of compressed cotton.

"Internal tracking indicates insufficient time has passed since your last dose of acetaminophen. Would you like to administer an additional non-regulated alternative?"

"I'm never wearing a 'smart' suit again," she muttered, leaning back and laying her head gingerly against the metal box behind her. "Yes. Give me whatever you can."

"Alternative accepted. Now administering 800mg of ibuprofen... Administration completed. Have a wonderful day!"

With that conversation behind her, Di finally took in her surroundings. Empty, foreboding space stretched above her. Glancing to the side, uniform rows of steel supporting joists flew past in the blink of an eye. She was still on the roof of the elevator travelling to the surface. Though it may have been her imagination, she thought she felt herself rise ever so gently off the roof as the elevator continued coasting along in zero-gravity. She scrambled to grab onto the nearby cable roller housing for security and squeezed her eyes shut.

As her thoughts cleared, she remembered the journey down and engaged her boots' magnetic functionality, immediately feeling the sole of her right foot clamp down to the roof of the elevator cab. Relief flooded through her limbs, and she relaxed her iron grip, venturing to open her eyes again.

Though this original subterranean base had been much closer to the surface when compared to the more recent, active station, it would still take some time to get there.

Pulling up her travel information on her HUD, she clocked her current speed at forty-five kilometers per hour. Her knee twinged painfully as she pictured her frail human body being smashed by the forty metric-ton freight train currently rocketing to the surface under her ass. The good news was that she had survived and had passed out for the majority of her trip. The bad news was that she had no idea how she would be fit for travel or combat in the minute and a half she had left before those elevator doors opened to whatever awaited her.

A pressing question also loomed large in her mind; who sent the elevator up? There was a chance the car below her was packed with dead-eyed creatures that wanted to rip her flesh from her bones. Her stomach rolled at the thought of a dozen half-frozen, decomposing, walking corpses separated from her by a thin wall of old steel. Her gut told her the car was empty, but if they were indeed down there and decided to check the emergency hatch, she wasn't exactly sure what she could do with a busted knee and a handful of bullets. Even so, she pulled the gun free and checked the slide. If she had to go down, she'd go down fighting.

With her remaining minute nearly up, the elevator began to fall away as it decelerated, the comfort of cold, hard steel at her back disappearing. If it hadn't been for her magnetized boot keeping her firmly attached, she would have continued on at that same rate of speed until she crashed into the ceiling of the elevator shaft.

"Guess that means the gravity generator's out," she muttered, wincing as her left foot made contact with the metal and her magnetics engaged. Her body completed a rotation to a quasi-standing position with Di hunching to protect her knee as much as she could.

Despite her earlier gripes about the suit, she had to admit it was a pretty wonderful little contraption. Having a custom-fitted brace on the battlefield would have been incredible during the war. Granted, she doubted Paragon would "donate" thirteen million dollars per soldier without some form of compensation. Maybe it would have been enough to have 'Paragon' ads plastered all over the hundreds of dead bodies littering the ground. *'This slaughter brought to you by Paragon.'*

As the cab slid to a grinding, creaking stop, Di readied her pistol and braced for an incoming fight. Though she again felt the ringing stillness below her, she wasn't willing to bet her life on a hunch. An extra thirty seconds of calm wouldn't kill her, but a snap, brash decision could.

Nothing happened. The emergency hatch remained firmly closed. No undead horrors flooded around her to envelope her enfeebled body. Phantom clicking and whistling of the creatures hunting echoed around her helmet, but no actual sound emanated from the car. Thirty seconds came and went, and though her stomach churned at the prospect, it was time to move. If Emma hadn't taken off already, she could be in danger. The rest of her crew in the orbital station could be dead and gone already. Di had to know, had to warn them if possible.

Taking a shaky, calming breath, she cautiously moved to open the hatch. Hinges squealed quietly, but to her ears it sounded like a dinner bell.

"Come and get it," she whispered in sing-song fashion. She chuckled to herself.

I've officially lost it, she thought.

As the door hit its natural stop, she peered around the edge of a completely empty car. The sliding doors lay invitingly open, leading to an equally empty hallway.

"Here we go." Di's boots unattached from the metal rooftop and she swung her legs up and over her head like a gymnast, guiding them gingerly through the opening. This would have been significantly more difficult had gravity been an additional inhibitor, and she decided to finally recognize weightlessness as a positive this one time. She needed all the help she could get.

Her feet gently touched the elevator's metal floor, magnetics engaging, and she barely refrained from putting her arms out in a large 'Y' and bowing to the imaginary judges at the judges' table.

'Despite her debilitating injury, Ms. Eastwood has pulled off a perfect routine! Tens across the board!' The nonexistent crowd jumped to their feet and roared their resounding approval, further worrying her cognizant mind of her diminishing sanity. It was good to know her body's default response to her various

pains and injuries was giddy hallucinations and not complete shutdown.

"Focus," she said, bringing her pistol up in a ready position. There was still the very real possibility of danger. If the hallways below had been full of rampaging monsters, who knew how many were waiting just around the corner? Di couldn't afford to lose focus. She was close. Too close to lose sight now.

Her right foot quested forward past the edge of the doorframe, magnetics disengaging and confirming her suspicion that the hallway floors were not, in fact, metallic. She was going to have to float her way forward in the dark with nothing but her headlamp for guidance, a fact that induced a rumbling discomfort deep in her gut. However, a swelling of personal pride filled her chest as she quickly disengaged her boots and pushed off with her uninjured right leg, gently hovering in a beeline toward the handrail along the wall. She caught it with her left hand, and her body pivoted around still wanting to continue travelling onward. Di almost lost the grip on her gun as she instinctively lunged to stabilize herself with her right hand. Shaky fingers gripped the bar tighter as she brought herself to a comfortable stop.

"Ok. I'm fine." She took two deep breaths and nodded. "This is good. One step at a time. Find a comm port and contact Emma." Verbalizing somehow helped to calm her nerves, and her grip loosened slightly. She stuffed her pistol back in the holster at her waist. She'd rather take the extra step of drawing it than risk losing it by fumbling in a panic.

"Loading dock should be nearby. They'd want a quick path to the elevator. That will have a comm port." She nodded to herself, firm in her plan. Once Di got in contact, Emma would fly over and pick her up. They could rendezvous with Bravo Team, mount a glorious rescue for Gene, then haul ass to the Katana and put as much distance between themselves and this hellhole as they possibly could. It was good.

Almost there, she thought, afraid to verbalize it and jinx herself. Better safe than sorry. Yet again extracting her trusty safety line, she clipped it to the handrail and pulled herself down the straight hallway.

Unsurprisingly, the early base was much more spartan than the up-to-date location where they had initially landed. Thick layers of frosty ice coated every surface, unprotected against the harsh surface-side elements but for the relatively thin walls themselves. Even without the added frigidity of a nonfunctioning heating unit, it was still sterile and cold all on its own. No branching hallways. No doorways leading to storage or break rooms. Though the layers of ice coated the entire ceiling obscuring its surface, she couldn't find a single overhead light source. Cheerful. At least it made navigating the facility easier.

As she reached the double doors at the end of the hallway covered in a wintery veneer, she attempted to peer through the mostly obscured windowpanes set at roughly eye level. Though she couldn't see much, see thought she could make out the general shape of a transport vehicle and a set of large rolling doors befitting of a garage or vehicle storage space.

"Now, how to get through the ice?" Di asked herself ponderously. Even if she had something to hack her way through, she had no leverage without gravity. Glancing to her left, nestled in a small alcove off to the side, a partially opened doorway led to a dimly lit room beyond.

Without electricity, what was giving off that light? she thought. Di cautiously unclipped her tether with a brief flutter in her stomach and pulled her way toward the door, peering inside.

A large bay window, almost entirely overlayed with obscuring ice crystals, let in the dim sunlight of the landscape beyond. Though it was nowhere near a sunny day on Earth, the eerie glow reflected from Enceladus' white surface and the massive celestial body of Saturn looming ever-present in the sky gave enough light to see by, like a particularly bright full moon night back home.

The snowy atmosphere was thinner here farther from the southern pole and the constantly spewing cryovolcanoes. Rather than a uniform haze blanketing the landscape, large individual flakes drifted lazily to the ground. Through the visible portion of glass, Di noticed beautiful, multi-hued refractions of light fading in and out. Brilliant haloes of pure white edged with shades of sky blue and faded emerald green dotted the skyline above the barren landscape, flaring brightly one moment and fading to nothingness the next.

For the space of a breath, a single, calming breath, the horror faded, and beauty took over. Evil roiled under the surface, brought forth by greed, ambition, and arrogance. Its tainting influence threatened to rise to the top, spilling over this pristine, picturesque portrait of tranquility. But in this moment, basking in the twinkling majesty of an otherworldly sky, Di found peace.

Her mind temporarily drifted, reminding her body of its utter exhaustion. She longed to wrap herself in this moment for a time; to grieve, to ponder, to look inward, and to dream. To remember, and to forget. But most of all, to rest.

Her heart ached as she tore her eyes away from the mesmerizing view, focus returning to the task at hand. There would be space for reflection later. Swift action was key, and there was no time to lose.

Returning her gaze to the bare room before her, she took note of the thick shadows coating dark corners. No furniture, no boxes. Just as sterile and empty as the hallway beyond except for the haphazard pile of deconstructed metal furniture. But something else caught her eye. A dim, red, circular light affixed to the wall across from the door, barely illuminating the words 'Emergency Comm'.

A flicker of hope burst in her chest, her heart fluttering in response. Gripping the frame, she pulled her thin build through the space between, just narrowly squeezing past the doors and into the room. With her growing confidence, she gently pushed herself across the room, alighting next to the comm port inlaid in the wall. It, too, was covered in ice, and she glanced toward the collection of table-sized puzzle pieces. A thin, round, solid-looking metal rod called out to her, and she plucked it from the pile, wrenching it free and sending its neighboring pieces slowly floating away. One end was threaded which she used to carefully pick at the ice covering the miniscule port.

An agonizing handful of minutes later, Di felt confident she had cleared enough away to attempt its use. Summoning her comm tether and hesitating for only a moment, she jammed it in and prayed. Five tense seconds later, her wrist screen flared to life. Relief flooded through her limbs, and she nearly collapsed.

"Let's get the hell out of here."

Navigating to the correct comm designation, she hailed the orbital station. If they could connect her to Emma on the ship, it wouldn't take long for her rescue to arrive. Tears blurred her vision in a sudden overwhelming surge of emotion. So close. She was so close.

The line buzzed. And it buzzed. And it buzzed. And it continued to buzz.

No answer. Cold fear snatched her swelling relief, sucking the air from her lungs. Flashes of unbidden images tormented her mind. Gayle, Lucas, and Hazel. Ripped apart, purple blood oozing and eyes flooded blue. Left to join Gerald. Left to join Gene.

She couldn't let this happen. Sharp, unfulfilling breaths beat a staccato against the inside of her helmet. There had to be something she could do. There had to be a way to contact Emma. She flipped through the dozens of comm location options, fear mounting higher with each passing option.

There. Landing pads. She fiercely punched it in and was greeted with seven options. Starting from the top, she punched in each one and waited, praying the stars would align. Praying Emma had stayed, had thought to tap into the landing pad's array.

Landing pad one. No answer.

Landing pad two. Endless ringing.

Landing pads three and four. Empty static. Di felt the panic rising as she punched in landing pad five. Options were running dry, and her window of escape was grinding to a close with every unanswered ring of—

"Gayle?"

A bubble of air caught in Di's throat at the wonderful, glorious sound of Emma's voice emanating from the speakers in her helmet. She tried to speak and coughed loudly instead.

"What's going on? I haven't heard from you in hours!"

"Emma!" Di finally spluttered.

"Captain! Holy shit, you're alive!"

Di let out a genuine full-belly laugh morphed from her hacking wheezes. Emma. Sweet Emma. She hadn't left.

"Where are you?" Emma asked. "I don't see anyone else coming from the facility."

She hadn't left. She was still at the main facility's landing pad. Though Di had told her to take off without them, a small part of her thrilled that she hadn't. Without Emma, she would have had only the one flimsy escape option; the interplanetary elevator.

Emma's excited jabbering faded to the background as Di registered exactly what Emma had said. Anyone *else*. Someone that wasn't her. Someone at the facility.

"He was saying we needed to take off immediately, but I wasn't just going to leave without—"

"Emma, who's there with you?"

Emma paused as though confused. "John. He's the survivor from the facility. The one you found. He approached the ship, like, ten minutes ago."

Ice flooded Di's veins sending a ripple of goosebumps down her arms and legs. He was there. That *monster* was there.

"Emma. Is he there now?"

She laughed uncomfortably. "I'm not sure. He said he had to go back to the facility and get something important. What's going on?"

"Emma. Leave. Take off *immediately.*"

"Captain, I don't understand—"

"LEAVE! NOW!" The words were ripped from Di's throat in her desperation. After a tense moment, she thought she could hear the faint whine of the engines ramping up in the background noise of the call.

"What about you?" Emma asked, her voice meeker and quieter.

"I'm not there, Emma," Di said, speaking as quickly as she could. "I'm at the alpha facility several clicks north. And while I am grateful you stayed for me, Gayle's instruction was explicit that if we hadn't contacted you within an hour—"

"Gayle?" Emma asked. "I haven't heard from Gayle since just before you went down in the elevator."

Gayle hadn't called? A new wave of concern reared its ugly head. As security officer, Gayle had never disobeyed a direct command before. Assuming her entire persona and internal code hadn't suddenly shifted, she should have hung up with her captain and immediately redirected those orders to Emma. Di was confident in her crew's loyalty, which meant she hadn't been able to reach Emma or had been prevented from making the call.

One disaster at a time. Di's current focus was to ensure Emma's safety, something she could address in the here and now.

"What's going on, Captain? You said you found something down there."

"Listen. You are not safe. John is *not safe*. Do you understand?"

Emma's voice quivered with her response. "Yes, Captain."

"Lock the bay doors down. Are the engines primed? You need to take off now, before he gets back on the ship."

An unbearable pause stretched on for what felt like an eternity. Undiscernible noises shuffled ominously in the background.

"Emma?"

Another pause. Di could faintly hear Emma's breathing quicken. "Captain. I need—"

The call cut out abruptly.

"Emma!" Di shouted. "Emma!" After twenty full seconds of no response, she knew the line was dead. In a fit of rage, she yanked her comm cord violently from the port in the wall sending her body spinning toward the window in the zero-g. She gently collided with the thick frosted pane and latched on to the edge of the frame with her left hand.

"Sonuvabitch!" In a fit of rage and lapse of judgment, her fist collided with the window sending a sharp jolt of agony through her knuckles and her body spinning backward. Hot tears once again leaked from the corners of her eyes, breaking free from her false veneer of control she had so shoddily used to convince herself she was not crumbling under the weight of her inadequacies.

Swinging herself back toward the window, she cocked her fist back once more and slammed it full force into the meter-thick, shatterproof, polycarbonate-glass compound. The pain was good, cleansing her mental frustration and agony through a physical focal point. She was helpless in so many ways, a deranged part of her relished this momentary method of control. Releasing her pent-up emotions, she held herself steady against the wall and hammered at the window until her fist ached, begging for submission as the tears fell.

First Gerald. Then Gene. Now Emma. They were dropping like flies, one by one all around her. Because she had chosen greed over sensibility, taking a contract too good to be true.

Exhaustion quickly overcame her anger. Her arm drooped to her side, and she laid her helmet against the window, looking out at what just moments ago seemed so peaceful, but now revealed its true nature. It was a graveyard. A barren tomb encasing the ones she loved piece by piece until there was nothing left.

The mangled end of her now useless comm cable floated beside her, another log stacked on her funeral pyre. It didn't matter. Di was already resigned to her fate; watching her entire life burn around her, and only once the flames guttered out and she was entirely alone would the universe be satisfied enough to let her die and fade away along with them.

The hovering snow beyond the base momentarily shifted to reveal a rare, unobstructed view. The sudden clarity gave Di a single, fleeting glimpse of renewed hope in the distance. A spark of defiance. If she wasn't going to make it out, if her crew was already dead and gone, then with her final breath she would make damn sure Paragon burned right along with them.

She searched with her stiff, aching fingers and found the pouch containing the data disc at her waist. A treasure trove of damning evidence that would ensure Paragon's demise, if not by regulatory and criminal sanctions, then at least by the fickle, swaying opinions of the public.

There was one, and only one, avenue that lay before her. To get her transfer signal out, she would have to clear the moon's atmosphere. Only one accessible possibility would have the equipment to send it long range, but she needed a way to get there. Di's focus was locked on the horizon where salvation lay.

A thin, dark, vertical line stretched past the horizon, shooting up toward the unseen orbital station she knew was floating beyond her vision. Resolve affirmed, Di looked toward

the interplanetary elevator in the distance and crossed her
fingers.

CHAPTER 13
ELEVATION

Di wedged herself between the two sides of the doorframe and, with a final explosive jab, jammed a thin plate of scrap metal between the frozen doors to pry open a space just wide enough for her small frame to squeeze through. Crunchy chips of ice ground against one another, breaking free and careening off to float aimlessly in the hallway as she forced her body between the unforgiving slabs of steel. As her upper torso made it through the opening, she paused to survey the massive warehouse waiting on the other side.

Sixteen two-man surface shuttles sat parked in neat rows along the edges of the room, secured in place with thick, dark chains. Nearly half of them sat at skewed angles. Some drifted slightly in the nearly non-existent wind. Three vehicles sat with the front tilted upward toward the ceiling despite the precautions followed to keep them secured. In the corner beside the large rolling shudder leading to the outside world, a thick stack of flat steel slabs lay bundled together, ratcheted to the ceiling with a collection of braided cables. A square rod protruded from each piece reminiscent of a trailer hitch tow bar for industrial equipment.

From the look of the place, the miners had likely used this old facility as storage or as the vehicle machine shop. Various well-worn but meticulously maintained tools were bolted to the walls on each side. Di guessed that the slabs in the corner could be attached to a shuttle and driven back and forth, shepherding supplies and equipment between locations.

She involuntarily shuddered at the thought of traveling at high speeds in a zero G environment with nothing but a thin fabric safety belt to keep her secure. Then her stomach squirmed at the realization that this was exactly what she planned to do. Before her body revolted at the thought, she pulled herself fully through the doorway and gently jettisoned her body toward the nearest shuttle.

The simple vehicle was just that; simple. It had no sleek edges, no comfort amenities. It looked like it barely had the requisite parts to work at all. Functionally, it was a squat, square box with three levers positioned in between two bucket seats, and just enough room behind the seats to strap down a personal pack or two. Each sharp edge was chock full of tightly packed, unpolished weld beads, further lending to the slapdash feel. She wouldn't have been surprised to discover the miners themselves had simply taken extra pieces of metal and made themselves a more convenient method of transportation. As impressive as that may have been, it didn't lend confidence to her next course of action.

With her improvised scrap metal ice pick and her left hand securely gripping the edge of the shuttle, she chipped away at the layer of ice around the latch securing a chain to the eye welded onto the body of the vehicle. Once it had been released, she nudged the box toward the sealed bay door. Di watched it lazily float away before its side gently bumped up against a straight metal beam a meter or so up from the floor.

Di took a deep breath in preparation for opening the massive bay door. Her phobia reared its ugly head, ready to lay waste to her nerves and wreak havoc on her steadily building, but still fragile, fortitude. With unsteady hands and trembling fingers, she attached her safety line to the bar beside the door and in front of the shuttle.

"You can do this," she said, closing her eyes and bringing her breathing under control. "For Gerald. For Gene." She swallowed painfully. "For Emma."

Di hauled on the chain shattering the brittle icy buildup. A steep wave of vertigo swept over her as the landscape beyond opened up, but she was ready and gripped the chain more tightly, pulling three more times.

A swath of frosty fog sat like a barrier between the relative safety of her little garage and the intimidating openness she would have to venture out into. Bits of ice particles, stirred to action from her disturbance of the chain, spun lazily in the air, gently drifting in dozens of directions. Again, the inherent beauty of Enceladus was a thin but effective salve for her pain. For a brief moment, suspended in the air with nothing but her safety line keeping her grounded, surrounded by a mixture of manmade contraptions and an intoxicating landscape only nature herself could provide, she could push down her fears and trepidations. She could forget the trauma, the suffering, the unspeakable horrors unleashed here. In the space of three short breaths, she felt a renewed vigor, hesitantly confident in her avenue of action.

In her moment of temporary confidence, Di turned back to her mode of transportation and inspected it more carefully. Two mechanized arms sat folded flush against the left side of the body. Attached to the ends were claw-like mechanisms that looked like they could be opened and closed, tipped with a set of round, darkened ball bearings. There didn't appear to be any engines or propulsion system, so she had to assume these strange rollers would be her sole method of getting to the elevator.

She turned to the metal beam that sat at roughly chest height bolted securely to the wall. It was roughly a handspan in height and had a thin lip on its outer edge. Glancing carefully through the haze that obstructed her view beyond the bay door, she could see the beam extended out of the garage and continued on for some distance before disappearing behind the obscuring snow. Putting two and two together, she glanced at the vehicle's arms that, once extended, allowed the shuttle to travel along that beam, carrying her the full distance between stations.

Her confidence plummeted. If the shuttle wasn't properly secured, or if the metal guide rail was damaged along the way, or if the guide rail itself didn't lead to the newer station, or if a dozen other 'what ifs' presented themselves along the journey, she could easily find herself stranded, injured, or even floating away, lost and forgotten and stuck with only her thoughts until her suit ran out of oxygen and she died alone in the cold, barren blackness of space.

Di wasn't sure how long she had blacked out from her overanalyzing, panic-induced scenarios, but her knuckles ached as she loosened her fingers gripped tightly to the guide rail. Her chest hurt, not just from her injuries, as her heart thudded painfully against her ribcage. The all too familiar constricting grip of a full panic attack was slowly loosening the noose around her lungs, her breaths gradually becoming less choppy staccato and more full and sweeping.

She could do this. She *had* to do this. It would be better for her to die in the attempt than to sit with herself knowing she could have done something to save the rest of her crew, however slight that chance might be. Her concerns for the ones who depended on her was the fuel she needed, feeding the fire in her belly that traveled along her arms and legs, wrapping around her fingers and down through her toes. It wasn't enough to make what she had to do any more palatable, but it was enough to keep her nausea at bay and the stomach acid at the base of her throat.

Di leaned over the edge of the shuttle and gripped the lever furthest to the left, hauling back on it with little resistance. A muted mechanical 'thunk' reverberated along the outer hull, and the arms were released. As she straightened them out perpendicular to the side of the vehicle, they locked into place, one near the front and one near the back. Intuitively, she gripped the smaller lever at the tip of the larger one, reminiscent of a motorcycle clutch. The claws at the ends of the arms opened, allowing her to gently guide the shuttle over the edges of the beam before locking them back in place by releasing her grip. She tested its functionality and was surprised at how smooth the motion felt as it glided along the rail.

It was now or never. With a gentle push off the ground, she pivoted her body up and over the side of the cart, guiding her feet down into the tiny, cramped crevice. Di was happy to note that the seat at least had a standard four-point harness which she gladly secured as soon as her backside touched the unforgiving surface.

Taking a perfunctory glance behind her, she noted the long, thin metal container sloppily tack welded to the frame. Painted letters stenciled in bold red stated it was for; "EMERGENCY USE ONLY." Good to know they had thought of emergencies when constructing this death trap, even if they were last minute additions. It had to be better than nothing. Painfully, she reached an arm back to unlatch the lid and take a peek at what was inside but winced at the pain lancing through her ribs from the awkward angle. With the opening barely enough to confirm *something* was in there, she returned forward-facing and rubbed her sternum. It was bad luck to mess with emergency measures before takeoff anyway.

Metal scraped metal as she gave a hearty tug on the arm attachment, making sure she was as secure as possible. Di gripped the second lever to her right and gave it an experimental tug. She heard a hefty thunk behind her confirming it was, in fact, not the accelerator, but rather something to do with the vehicle's tow hitch.

Third time's the charm, she thought. Taking the slightly curved aluminum handle in her fist, she felt a layer of ice crunch as a trigger gave way beneath her fingers. The lever felt looser in her hand now, moving much more freely, and she pulled on it gradually. The cart jolted jarringly out past the bay doors, and her left hand squeezed the frame beside her. She wouldn't be surprised if she had left a small handprint behind. After a harrowing handful of seconds passed, the ride smoothed and she cruised comfortably toward the thin black tower fading in and out of view through the snowy haze.

Despite the open air all around her and the constant threat of insecurity, being strapped to a solid piece of machinery felt right. It may have been rickety, it may not have been (hell, it *definitely* was *not*) up to code, but it was good old-fashioned engineering. If she couldn't put her confidence in herself, she could temporarily place it in a hunk of metal hurtling through the barren, icy tundra. Yes, it made no sense. No, she wouldn't think any more about it. That only risked further aggravating her already taut nerves.

In an effort to distract herself, she gazed at the alien landscape surrounding her. Subconsciously, Di knew she should watch the way forward, but she couldn't help but crane her neck around at the stretches of pure, pristine hills of glittering white enchantment. As she traveled closer to the elevator and, thus, closer to the southern pole, the sporadic yet consistent plumes of gases mixed with icy particulate spewing from the subsurface cryovolcanoes would only further obscure her vision, snow lazily falling back down to the surface over hours-long stretches. As of now she was still several kilometers out, and the weather here was tamer, albeit still with gentle falling snow drifting lazily around her. Even so, she could see for hundreds of meters out either side, and something younger, something child-like inside marveled at the gently sloping hills.

Traveling back to a simpler time, this was what she had imagined when thinking of Santa and his workshop at the North Pole. A candy cane-striped pole here. A small wooden cabin there, soft candlelight glowing through the window. Once again, she was consumed in the majesty of a wonderland only lightly marred by human hands.

Glancing down at her suit, stained with the faint remnants of dark inhuman blood splatters, she had to remind herself of what lurked below. Enceladus had the look of a pure, perfect, pristine apple on the surface, but its core was nothing but rotten, festering decay. Like a predator in the wild; innocent and beautiful when viewed from afar, but all too willing to rip out it's prey's throat and feast on the flesh if approached. She could admire all she liked, but she would suffer the consequences of coming here. She already had. Or rather, her crew had on her behalf.

Di glanced toward her destination, the thin, unending tower looming ever overhead. The atmosphere around her grew thicker; not just with falling snow, but with steadily growing emotions. Anticipation. Fear. Anxiety. Sinister swaths of inevitability swirled between her fingers and up her arms, landing as a mantle on her shoulders. Whatever awaited her, both at the base of the interplanetary elevator and the station above, it felt final. A resolution, one way or another.

Her shuttle jolted up, bouncing off a sharp, protruding patch of ice. In a panic, she gripped the accelerator lever hard, pulling it back to its apex. The cart lurched forward, swiftly increasing speed. Di's limbs were locked in shock. Another sharp impact lifted her temporarily off her seat, shoulder straps straining but holding. Ice pellets suspended in the air collided with her body and visor as she hurtled forward. The vehicle groaned ominously, arms straining to stay mounted to the guide rail.

Finally, her brain caught up to what her body's instincts and she slammed the accelerator forward to slow its now reckless speed. Bruises and broken bones flared to life beneath the restraining harness that kept her from launching out into space. A horrendous screech of metal scraping metal set her teeth on edge and sent a shiver down her spine. Steadily, the vehicle began to decelerate.

Di clung to her shoulder straps and waited for the death trap she was strapped in to slow to less stomach-churning speeds. The shadow of the outpost building and the connected landing pad lay tantalizingly close, specific details beginning to sharpen beyond a simple outline.

A boxy silhouette momentarily flared with dirty light before rising slowly into the air. The CS Katana's landing shuttle rotated, aiming toward the sky, and slowly accelerated up and away. Whether or not Emma was on it, whether or not she was alive, remained to be seen.

The cart slammed into another unseen bit of rock or ice jutting from the surface below. A loud snap reverberated through her body emanating from the side panel of the cart. Bits of metal peppered Di's back as the rear arm securing the shuttle to the guide rail was sheered clean off. The faint, distant horizon line lurched upward as Di was sent tumbling head over heels, still firmly strapped into her bolted down bucket seat. Another sound, more of a pop than a snap, shook the front safety arm.

Just as suddenly as it had happened, it was done. Contrasting the brief violence of the crash, all was now silent and still. Solid ground began drifting lazily away in her spinning vision. The surface shuttle continued to rotate as it carried on in its slightly upward, slanted trajectory, Di still securely strapped in.

It was her worst nightmare come back from the grave. She was reliving it all again. The helplessness. The fear. Spinning away from everything solid, everything secure, damned to drift into the infinite void. Except this time there was no one, not even an uncaring bastard of a shift manager, to come to her rescue.

Blaring red alerts flashed in the corner of her HUD, warning her of her rising heart rate hitting sustained dangerous levels. It did little to calm her terror. It wasn't like she needed to be told by an uncaring artificial intelligence that she was having a full-blown mental and physical breakdown.

Di's eyes flitted back and forth, unable to find purchase on any firm point of reference. The lack of focal point did nothing to keep her panic attack from taking firmer root in her chest. The horizon line came and went, appeared and disappeared in a slowly rotating whirlwind, like a carnival ride from hell. If there was any hope of getting out of this situation, it was going to take a helluva lot of concentration and fortitude. Fortitude. Something she severely lacked at the moment, her frayed nerves a near-constant reminder of her quickly drying well of courage.

"Focus," she vocalized shakily. "Analyze. Adapt. No one is coming. Find a way through."

Turning her attention external rather than internal, she attempted to let her cold, calculating, analytical side take control. Surprising herself, it appeared to work, if only temporarily.

Removing those pesky little things called emotions, Di quickly realized her forward momentum and upward trajectory were not as drastic as she had first assumed. The cart had slowed considerably before the arms had ripped free. Even the act of the arms breaking had decelerated her, though it had caused the never-ending, nauseating spinning. Although she was, indeed, moving away from solid ground, it wasn't as fast as she had feared.

Next step was figuring out how to get herself back down to the guide rail. Staying strapped into a cartwheeling box to nowhere was not going to get her to the elevator, and that was all that mattered at the moment. Getting to the elevator. Riding it to the orbital station. Saving the rest of her crew. It became Di's mantra, chanting it over and over in the background.

Elevator. Orbital station. Save the crew.

Elevator. Orbital station. Save the crew.

It was an interestingly unorthodox use of the de-escalation techniques learned in therapy, but it wasn't stupid if it worked. In response, the life-threatening alarms faded away, further dropping her heart rate and, with it, her anxiety.

Think. What are your options? There weren't many, all told. If her trajectory hadn't been skewed by the crash, she may have been able to get herself close enough to the cable structure of the elevator that she could make a leap toward it. As it currently stood, there was no way the tumbling car would carry her anywhere close. The elevator was still a good distance away, drifting further and further off to her right.

Di glanced at the car around her. Just as spartan and sparse as it was the first time she inspected it. She ducked her head between her knees and found a solid plate of metal housing what was likely the battery. No seams, no hatches or levers. Hell, not even a warning sticker. Even if there had been something to pry open, she doubted it would do her any good. It wasn't like there was some hidden emergency—

Idiot.

Di glanced over her shoulder at the flimsy metal box secured to the side of the cart behind her seat. A thin latch, still in place, kept her one chance at salvation very precariously secured. If it was nothing but a thin, silvery space blanket and a few stale, frozen nutrient bars, she was flat out of luck. She would just have to hope they had been a bit more practical. Or possibly a bit less, depending on your viewpoint.

Shoulder joints popped and tender chest muscles strained as she contorted her way around the bucket seat to get at the emergency stash. Her fingers brushed tantalizingly against the latch. She held her breath in the hope it would give her just enough reach, or possibly dull the throbbing pain radiating through her ribcage. A distant, muted sun flipped in and out of view, exchanging positions with the snowy landscape gradually and inevitably fading further and further away.

A hiss of frustration and dread slipped past her lips. There was no point. She couldn't reach that damn box while in the seat. Deep down inside, just above where her lizard brain took over, she knew what her only course of action would be; unbuckle the harness and risk losing the one solid object keeping her brain from frying. Logically, it was the only choice. Emotionally, it was a different story. The fingers on her right hand already clutched at the buckle at her chest, shaking and spasming uncontrollably, but her fear had finally caught hold of her cold analytical side and had begun strangling it passionately. The sphere of emotionless observation containing her anxiety slowly melted away, giving way to her domineering sense of dread. Her 'fight or flight' was quickly being overwhelmed by her 'freeze' response.

It was now or never. If she waited any longer, there was a

chance she couldn't physically overcome her body's primal reactions. It was between the slim possibility of freedom and the certainty of failure, and that window was closing fast.

Holding her breath, Di depressed the buckle and pushed herself lightly away from her seat. She kept a strong grip on the strap as she gradually flipped herself over the chair and into the small recess at the back of the car. Moving quickly, she fumbled frantically with her left hand to undo the latch of the emergency container while her right clutched shakily to the one thing keeping her connected to the vehicle.

Finally, the hatch flipped open, and she reached in to find something hard and bulky. It was awkward to try and pry it out one-handed, but she refused to let go of the harness. With a dangerous tug, she freed the device from its container which sent her body into a gut-wrenching spin. Her grip on the device nearly failed in her panic as her back collided with the seat, legs flipping wildly. It was only through sheer will and ingrained discipline that she held to both her potential saving grace and her current sense of safety in the bucket seat strap. As she clung helplessly frozen, letting her system reboot to regain control of her extremities, her eyes caught a glimpse of what it was she was holding.

It was a personal propulsion pack. Relief flooded her limbs, filling her with a warmth that had nothing to do with the temperature of her suit. Of all the items that could have possibly been in that container, this was the best option. Maybe these shuttles were more prone to failure than she had realized, and the miners had prepared for just such an occasion. Either way, their foresight was her salvation.

Di glanced toward the ground as it came back into view. Despite the time she had spent drifting through the atmosphere, she wasn't all that far from the surface. Her upward trajectory was much slower than her forward momentum. All in all, it wouldn't be that far of a leap to get back to the guard rail. The thought filled her with confidence. With another spin and another pass of the approaching ground, she prepared to jump.

Approaching ground?

The shuttle lurched jarringly as it collided with a protruding mound of unforgiving ice, a small hill in an otherwise pristine landscape. Shock rolled up her arm as Di's body was flung up and around her bucket seat. Though her grip remained firm on the harness, she felt the propulsion pack ripped from her fingers as it collided with the edge of the car. Her saving grace, her one remaining hope, drifted lazily through the air farther and farther from her outstretched arm.

"No!" she screamed. "No! No! No!" The collision with the ice had stopped the consistent rotations, though she was now drifting higher and higher. In her current position, Di had a perfect view of her sanity floating away in the form of a little white pack.

"No," she said, firmly rather than frantically. She rotated her body perpendicular to the car, aligned herself toward the propulsion pack, tucked her legs, and kicked. The feigned safety of the shuttle disappeared as she slipped away, sliding through the atmosphere straight as a loosed arrow.

Her arms sat rail-straight at her sides. Breath pounded loudly in her ears, increasing in tempo as her senses finally grasped what she had done. Though her limbs begged to flail in panic, she kept her elbows locked to her hips and her hands gripping her thighs. Her speed was slow but steady, moving closer and closer to the drifting propulsion pack.

Twenty meters. Her lungs felt like they were about to burst, but she couldn't manage to suck in a breath.

Fifteen meters. Blackness edged her vision, but her attention was laser-focused on her goal.

Ten.

Five.

With arms outstretched, she collided with the pack and gripped it in a tight bearhug. She had done it. The smooth, plastic-like surface put uncomfortable pressure against her bruised sternum, but she didn't care. She hugged it tighter all the same. Never had such a simple action elicited so many confusing tears of joy, panic, and pain. It didn't even matter that she was still drifting through zero gravity. This propulsion pack meant she was one step closer to leaving. To saving her friends. To home.

Blinking away her remaining tears, Di fumbled momentarily with the bulky box before she secured it in place via her suit's magnets on her back. A small tether with a metal tip protruded from the bottom corner of the pack, the interface that would allow her suit to communicate with the propulsion systems, which she gripped between two fingers. Bringing up her wrist computer, she quickly found what she was looking for. A small port at her waist opened, and she jammed the cable in.

Immediately, new settings appeared on her HUD showing battery and fuel percentages, airspeed which was currently fluctuating between six and seven kilometers per hour, and an altimeter steadily climbing as she drifted higher above the surface of the moon.

"Stabilize," she commanded. Bursts of air puffed from various vents over her shoulders spinning her around to face the opposite direction. She slowly came to a halt in the air with a final vibrating sigh.

The battery indicator in the top left of her vision ticked down to eight percent. With it that low, she couldn't trust that her pack would get her all the way to the elevator. Glancing below, Di searched for the thin, meandering line of the guard rail. The ever-present surface fog of ice and minerals clouded her view, but she found what she was looking for after a few moments.

"Target acquired. Proceed." Though her mental commands were likely faster and just as effective, she desperately needed to hear her own voice. Maintaining her sanity when surrounded by the panic that desperately wanted in was paramount, and hearing her voice echo faintly in her helmet somehow calmed and focused her mind.

A round indicator appeared before her fixated on the line below, and she felt the propulsion activate, pushing her gently back down to the sweet, solid ground. Moments ticked by in tense silence until her outstretched hand grasped the steel rail fixated to the ground. Di let out the breath she had been holding. Moving on instinct, she extended her safety line and clipped it securely around the upper handrail above where the shuttle would normally attach.

Two percent battery left. A nervous giggle escaped her throat, tears welling in her eyes. Her hands shook as she searched for something, anything, to hold on to. Fingers momentarily brushed against the guard rail, her helmet, the ice below her feet. Her arms flailed awkwardly until she gripped her elbows to keep them steady. Tiny beads of sweat gathered at her brow and slid haltingly along the bridge of her nose, joining salty tears as together they slipped around her nostrils and caught in the frown lines at the corners of her mouth. She felt the path each droplet took as though it were carving deep grooves along her skin.

The constant fluctuation of intense emotions had officially, and potentially irreparably, fried her nerves. Deep down she knew it to be true, and for some reason it elicited another bark of laughter.

"I think you're losing it, Diane," she muttered, accompanied by another chuckle.

Losing it? Or already lost?

"Does it matter?"

It depends on whether or not you think this affects your ability to save the ones that are left.

"I've come this far. I won't stop."

Even if they're already dead?

Her blood chilled at the thought. Di lifted her head and saw the faint shadow of the interplanetary elevator system in the near distance.

Elevator. Orbital station. Save the crew.

Hand over hand, she flung herself along the guide rail toward the elevator. The looming shadow darkened, lines expanding and taking definitive shape. A boxy, sharply angled building sat at the base of the impossibly tall tower. The tether itself was thin, suspended between thick, metal struts that gradually dwindled to nothing as it stretched up and up, quickly disappearing into the never-ending fog.

As she drew closer, she discovered the building was not a building at all, but rather the elevator car itself. Ice crusted thickly over its corners and along the ground leading up to its large double doors. The tether itself, along with the doors of the car and most of the metal ramp leading to them, were surprisingly free from excess buildup, though there was a thin layer of fallen snow providing a pristine white surface. Like a natural red (or, rather, white) carpet awaiting her arrival to guide her to her destination. It would have been beautiful if it hadn't been unsettling.

The guard rail branched off as one way led to the garage and storage area they had entered earlier while the other, thankfully, took her right to the lift. As she approached the doors, Di carefully unhooked her safety line with one hand while maintaining a firm grip on the rail with the other. Brushing aside a layer of snow, she found a boxy terminal set into a freestanding pillar beside the car doors. As her gloved fingers pressed unwittingly against the screen, it flared to life beneath her touch. With her luck, she had honestly expected the thing not to work. Maybe her luck was finally turning around.

Pressing the screen to open the doors, she waited on bated breath. Accompanied by thin cracks of breaking ice, the doors slid aside revealing a wide, empty space with enough room to fit the entirety of the Katana's landing shuttle. Plexiglass windows latticed with thin crisscrossing strips of metal ran nearly the entire length of the car which would offer a wonderfully unobstructed view during her ascent (assuming the fog ever cleared). The floor was covered in age-old, blotchy stains from the various cargo the miners had shipped between the surface and the station over the years.

Di pulled herself in by the handles just inside the entryway, grateful to be behind four walls and beneath a ceiling again. She punched in the command to return to the orbital station, and the doors began to slowly grind to a close. Flipping herself to face outward, she gave this hellhole a proper goodbye with a double middle finger salute.

"It's been a real shitty time. Feel free to go—"

Di's final insults caught in her throat as she caught a glimpse of a horde of hosts standing just inside the distant entryway of the base. The elevator doors slid shut as Di reveled in stunned silence, braced for the inevitable screech signifying the hunt was on.

It never came. The whirring crescendo of slumbering motors summoned back to life grew louder, the elevator gearing up for its climb from Enceladus' surface. Di peered out of the smaller porthole-sized windows set in the doors, but no movement outside accompanied the car's awakening. With a jolt, the elevator began to rise whisking her away from her nightmares and the creatures that haunted them as they quickly faded behind the icy haze.

She did it. She was leaving. It was over. If there had been any gravity, her buckling knees would have sent her crashing to the floor in relief. The fog outside seemed to penetrate her mind, clouding all thoughts and cushioning the here and now from the horrors of the recent past. Images of beautiful, distant white landscape flashed between the enveloping haze as she rose through the clouds, though her mind wouldn't, or couldn't, comment or comprehend the sights. Her unfocused eyes stared off into the distance, reflecting the numbness, the emptiness pervading her body. She let her limbs go limp, floating as though disembodied beside her.

Gradually, the dim sunlight reflecting off the moon's white surface faded leaving only a dim overhead bulb to illuminate her surroundings. The elevator cleared the thin atmosphere, and she was back in the black void of space. Di caught a face-full of Saturn's famous rings dominating the horizon as she rose higher and higher.

"Approaching station. Please stand by."

Di's brain didn't catch the announcement from the car's

mechanical, female voice until it's third repetition, and by that point the station had loomed large all around her. Guiding rings rushed by outside as the elevator gently slowed in its approach.

"Engaging artificial gravity. Watch your step."

She barely got her feet underneath her as the weight of her body increased and her boots slammed down to the floor. Her left knee buckled with a sharp, shooting pain lancing up her leg. The shocking reminder of her injury instantly cleared her mind, bringing back her long-engrained mercenary reflexes.

Di grit her teeth against the throbbing aches dotted all over her body and pulled her pistol from its holster. She checked that her magazine was full and patted the nearly empty back up mag at her waist, making sure it was present and accounted for. While she hoped this station had remained untouched, she always knew to plan for the worst. Hope was good, but preparation was better.

The elevator slid to a shuddering, nearly graceful stop.

"Please, watch your step."

The doors fluidly slid open to pure and utter chaos.

CHAPTER 14
CHAOS

Two small bursts of exploding flame to Di's immediate left shook the ground outside the elevator. Echoing, muffled taps of automatic gunfire emanated from an alcove across the wide hallway in front of her. High-pitched, whistling shrieks of enraged monsters fighting, clawing, and dying assaulted her. Smoke poured from the remnants of the explosions, distorting her view.

"Captain! Cover!"

Di recognized Gayle's voice followed by another burst of gunshots and flashing muzzle fire. She hobbled as quickly as she could the twenty meters to the alcove, diving behind a haphazard stack of crates.

In the heat of the moment where chaos reigned, she found momentary comfort. This was where she lived. This was familiar. Shrapnel flying, explosions rumbling, gunshots blazing. Here was a firearm. There was the enemy. Fill them full of lead.

Moving on instinct, Di racked a bullet into the chamber of her pistol and peered around the corner. "Sit rep?" she asked.

"We're pinned, obviously!" Gayle shouted in an unnecessarily booming voice. Those explosions had obviously not been the first, and it appeared her suit's sound dampening function couldn't keep up. "These things came out of nowhere! Crawling out of vents, boxes, whatever! We've got a makeshift barricade behind us that I'm trying to keep as a clear path to the elevator for evac in case plan A doesn't pan out!"

"The elevator? Why?" Di popped off two shots and watched as another body fell, shrieking and wriggling on the ground.

"We were coming to get Alpha Team! After you went radio silent and these things showed up, we figured you were dealing with the same thing down there!" Gayle glanced at her, worry reflecting in her eyes. "Where are they?"

Di's jaw clenched, forcing down the river of regret snaking its way from her gut. "I'm the only one left."

Gayle looked like she had been stabbed in the gut, and Di had been the one holding the knife. It almost broke her, but Di refocused her emotions to hate rather than grief and squeezed off another shot dead center on a host's forehead.

"You're sure?" Gayle asked, no longer shouting.

"Sure enough."

"But, you're sure?" She turned and faced her captain, the fight in her eyes momentarily gone behind a haze of despair.

"Gayle!" Di punctuated her name with another round fired. "Focus! Where's Lucas?"

Gayle shuddered, physically forcing away her feelings of

remorse and retaking command as the crew's security officer. Di knew it hurt, she knew it all too well, but she trusted Gayle nearly as much as she had trusted Gene, and it had never steered her wrong. Gayle was the sterling definition of a consummate professional. Never once had Di seen her break under pressure, and she needed that from her security officer now more than ever.

Gayle turned, rifle back up against her shoulder, and unloaded nearly half of a clip into the crowd. Sprays of dark blood spattered gruesomely against the walls and the remaining hosts who took no heed of their mates' downfall.

"Lucas is back behind us in the shuttle bay working on clearing a docking station for Hazel. Plan A. Corpo bastard is with him." She paused a moment, as though issuing a silent command. "Lucas? How's it going?"

Comms! Di had completely forgotten she was no longer shielded by the moon's atmospheric interference. That was one handicap gladly shed.

"I was just about to call," Lucas replied. Damn, it was good to hear his voice again. "Main docking station is complete shit. Bastards must have destroyed it when this place went to hell. But we've got some good news."

"Lucas?" Di called.

Lucas audibly sucked in a breath and whistled. "Damn, Captain. A little late, aren't we? We were just about to haul ass and leave you for dead!"

Di grinned. In the face of adversity, Lucas always had a

snarky and sarcastic comment in the pocket ready to fling as a good-natured gibe. Though he could handle a weapon just fine, he wasn't always part of the crew that saw action. A skilled, savant-level mechanic (as he so lovingly referred to himself) was typically best utilized in escape situations, not all-out combat. Losing him would have been a serious blow, and to hear his curse-riddled wit was a boon to her confidence.

"Glad to hear you're still such a coward."

"Come on now, Captain. That hurts."

"Truth often does." Di sobered herself, reunion officially over. "If plan A is shot, what's next?"

Lucas understood the shift in tone and adjusted his own to match. "Well, since you're up here there's no need for rescue. The plan is we get the hell off this damn thing."

"Any ideas on that front?"

"We *were* going to have Hazel dock for evac, but the only docking station big enough is busted to shit."

Di glanced over at Gayle who was focused on maintaining cover fire. "How'd you get in here in the first place?"

"We had to spacewalk and manually open an empty shuttle dock," Gayle said.

Di's stomach plummeted. Though she had temporarily overcome her fears of zero gravity on Enceladus' surface, it didn't mean the fear was gone. This hadn't become a 'fear becomes strength' situation; more like 'fear no longer cripples me psychologically, but I'd still rather gouge my own eyes out.' Even so, if it was their only solution, it was their only solution.

"You've got a port ready for that spacewalk back to the Katana then?" Di asked, forcing herself to hide the tremor in her voice. Gayle raised an eyebrow but didn't respond. That was not a command Di would have previously been so ready to give. Hopefully that conveyed just how deep they were in the shit.

Lucas paused. "Thought I'd have to force that one through, honestly. It's risky, seeing as we don't have much in the way of oxygen reserves."

"No station supplies?"

"None that we could find. Our suits only got a couple minutes of oxygen without actual oxygen tanks. But that doesn't matter now. That's why I was about to call. The Katana's landing shuttle is docking now. Emma hailed us just before you rang, though she didn't say why you're not on it, Captain."

Gayle's cries of surprise were muffled in Di's ears as she bolted to her feet from the word 'shuttle' and began hobble-sprinting as best she could down the hallway away from the screaming hosts. She moved on pure instinct, glancing out the ports lining the wall. Outside the station, she saw the landing shuttle completing the docking protocol, safety arms clamping shut and bursts of oxygen venting from the extended bridge.

"Lucas. Get out."

"Captain?"

"That isn't Emma. Get out now."

"I can't," Lucas replied. "The doors are sealed from the outside to keep those zombie things from getting in. What do you mean that isn't Emma?"

"A man we met below took the shuttle. He was infected with the parasite, the one that created these monsters."

You're not going to make it, Di thought. As if in response, the pain in her left knee receded to a faint throb. Without hesitation, she began a full-out sprint.

"Well, shit."

"Is there anywhere secure you can get to?" she asked.

"There's an escape pod Liam is holed up in."

"Get in and eject. Have Hazel pick you up."

"What about you and Gayle?" he asked. Di could already hear him moving in the background, following her orders without hesitation.

"We'll find a way. Just get yourself out."

Di was getting closer. She could see into the shuttle bay now through the windows as she ran perpendicular with that portion of the station. Though the panels in the hallway were smaller, the bay itself was gloriously transparent, floor to ceiling. She had no doubt it offered a fantastic view of the moon and Saturn itself as it orbited the massive planet. Right now, all it did was taunt her. Offer her a window into her own helplessness and give her a front row seat to the gruesome death of yet another crewmate and friend.

Not again. Not this time. Di picked up speed from somewhere deep within.

"Gayle, hold your position. We're probably going to need that elevator."

"Copy, Captain."

Di noticed a figure sprinting toward a bulbous pod attached to the side of the station closest to her. It sat at the end of the shuttle bay, like an unsightly wart. "Lucas. Status?"

"Entering the door code—"

The pod detached from the wall, hissing bouts of gas into the vacuum of space, and hurtled away.

"Sonuvabitch!"

"What happened?" Di asked.

"The corpo asshat left me!"

No! Not! Again!

"Lucas, get Liam on the line!"

"I'm trying! He won't respond!" From Di's vantage, she could see Lucas at the terminal next to where the escape pod had just launched. "I'm trying to recall the pod. I don't know if I have time."

The docking station across the bay opened unleashing a dozen screeching, slavering hosts bounding across the way, some half crawling on all fours like beasts.

"Lucas!" She was rounding the corner, docking bay temporarily out of sight as she ran. Lucas didn't respond, though his comms were still live. Shrieks in the background grew closer. And here she was, helpless yet again. Forced to witness another friend murdered by her mistakes.

A muffled 'thwump' echoed through comms followed by a loud rush of air. Di could see the large, pressure-sealed doors up ahead, another window port beside it. "Lucas, I'm almost there!"

He grunted. "Don't open those doors!" he wheezed.

As she passed the large window, she slowed to a stop to gaze at the wreckage spinning in zero gravity outside the station. Pale hosts floundered erratically, light wisps of steam curling off their skin and disappearing immediately into the vacuum. Shrieks and shouts escaped soundlessly from their snarling lips as they drifted every which way, limbs flailing, bodies flipping lazily. Bits of metal and broken glass gleamed in the pale light reflected from Enceladus below. Loose refuse like sheets of paper, shards of plastic, and copper wiring bounced off each other, deflecting one another and sending them slowly spinning toward the great, dark, deep black of space. There, in the middle of it all, a body in a pale grey suit sat with hands clutching his belly. Di could just make out a faint red stain slowly spreading beneath his fingers.

"Status, Lucas," she commanded. She knew the likely answer, so all she could do to help was to remain as emotionless as possible.

"Not... great," he responded, grunting between words. "Something... caught me... just above my... hip. Ripped... the suit... before I noticed."

"Give me O2 stats."

"Running... pretty low... on air," he wheezed. "Suit... is attempting... to seal itself. Don't think... it'll help... much."

Di cursed under her breath. "We're coming to get you. Just hang on. Try to breathe slowly." She switched to a separate channel and hailed Hazel, searching beyond the station to catch a glimpse of the ship.

"Go for Hazel."

"Lucas is outside the station, low on oxygen, and hurt. Can you get to him?"

Hazel paused. Di heard the distinct clicks and clacks of switches being flipped. The CS Katana drifted casually into view some three hundred meters out. "The space is too tight for me to fly in myself. He's right between two wings of the station."

"Snatch and grab?" Di asked.

"I'm getting a lot of moving pieces in my reading. Not sure how accurate I can be."

"Damn it, Hazel! Will you try?"

"Yes, Captain. Standby."

Di switched back to comms with Lucas in time to hear the tail end of some derogatory comment made by Gayle.

"—dumb bastard has it coming."

"Lucas, hold tight," Di interrupted. "Hazel is going to attempt to fish you out of there."

"Aye... Captain." He didn't sound enthusiastic, but Di told herself that it was likely the pain. His head turned toward the nearest host as it attempted to lock eyes with him in its slow spin, scrambling ineffectually to reach its prey. All thirteen creatures continued to grapple with the zero gravity, long past when a normal human would have given up the struggle and stilled, though they did appear to be slowing considerably. Luckily, none were drifting any closer to Lucas.

"What are your vitals? Don't speak too much. Save your

oxygen."

Lucas snorted, which was cut short by a groan. "BP... dropping. Suit... is trying... to—"

"Stabilize. Got it. Stop talking." She flipped back to Hazel. "Status?"

"I was hoping he would drift out, not in. He's headed toward the center."

The orbital station was set in the shape of a blocky 'U' with the edges cut inward at strict ninety-degree angles. While the elevator was dead center in the longer straightaway, the docking bay was naturally set at the outer edge of one of the arms. Lucas' self-inflicted expulsion had sent him careening toward the inner corner at an angle that would have him colliding with the station itself eventually. He had likely tried to hold on to something as the pressurized atmosphere was vented, slowing his momentum considerably. It explained why he was drifting so slowly and hadn't hit the station already.

"Try to get as close as you can," Di said. "But hurry. He doesn't have much time."

"Just dodge the literal minefield of floating shrapnel and make an impossible shot at a moving target. All while on a life-or-death time crunch. Simple." Hazel's sarcasm was meant to be light-hearted, but Di could hear the tension in her voice. She knew the stakes.

"You've got this, Hazel. There's no one else I would trust to do this."

As Di flipped away from Hazel's comm channel, she took

a moment to take a shuddering breath. Now was the time to be calm, to be the leader her crew needed. Damn her own nerves, damn her insecurities.

Will it even matter? she thought. *What if that injury was caused by a host? He could be infected.*

It was a thought that had been nagging her in the back of her mind since she had noticed the bloodstain beneath his hands.

"We'll come to that when we get him on board," she muttered to herself. Even so, she made a mental note to warn Hazel to keep him quarantined and to keep her suit on.

Buttoning up her emotions, she shifted back to speak with Lucas. "Update on oxygen. How much time left?"

"Countdown says a little more than two minutes," Lucas replied sluggishly. His words no longer sounded staccato and forced. Not a great sign. "Suit is sealed now, though."

"Stay with me here, Lucas. Cavalry is coming."

"Captain, they're making a push," Gayle shouted suddenly, sounds of gunfire punctuating her update. "I'm running low on munitions. Need to fall back to a better position, but it means losing the elevator for now."

Di hissed in frustration. Can nothing be simple? "I think I saw a security station close to this hall's intersection. Hold out at the elevator as long as you can, then I'll meet you there." Gayle didn't respond with anything but another burst of gunfire before her comms were silenced.

"Lucas? Still there?"

"Not going anywhere," he slurred. "Couldn't if I tried."

Di glanced at the Katana as it slipped closer, moving shiftily to avoid debris that could damage the hull or any one of the necessary but sensitive instruments. If they lost that, there was no ride home. No one was coming for them. They had one horse to take them off into the sunset, so it was imperative they kept that animal alive.

A port on the underside of the ship opened revealing a large, six-pronged, metal claw mechanism meant for emergency stabilization or cargo retrieval. It was typical equipment for a mercenary vessel, versatile for many types of jobs and situations. They had never used it to retrieve a live person before, however. This all depended heavily on Hazel's deft hand, something she was not particularly known for, but it was what they had to work with.

"Hazel is incoming," she said. "She's sending out the 'crane' for you, so you may need to watch for impact."

"Maybe I'd be safer staying out here then." Lucas chuckled softly.

"Captain. Move." Gayle's command was nonnegotiable, something her station as security officer afforded, and a demand Di recognized as something not to be taken lightly. When Gayle said move, you moved. With a final glance out the window, Di nodded in encouragement, something she hoped Lucas could see, and bolted down the hallway.

It was a short run back to the security office. Gunshots grew louder as she turned the corner to find Gayle already holding firm at the office's door.

"Go!" Gayle shouted.

Di complied, once again mustering the energy and pushing down the throbbing pain throughout her bruised and battered body. She sprinted down the hallway, whipping herself haphazardly through the doorway with Gayle close behind to slam the door shut. Moments later, the now all too familiar sound of thumps and howls resumed as monsters tried to beat their way in. Di collapsed on the ground beside a counter housing a glowing monitor while Gayle checked her weapons, taking the short break to reload a magazine in her rifle.

Di heaved another exhausted sigh, performing her own check. Her pistol was still gripped firmly in her hand, bullets considerably lower. Pounding throbs to the rhythm of her heartbeat thumped across her broken ribs and down her left leg. Exhaustion threatened to overtake her consciousness, her body no longer willing to maintain such a high level of anxiety, stress, and physical abuse. It was something, unfortunately, she would have to push aside yet a little while longer.

Sitting up, Di pulled her comms back up. "Hazel. Gayle and I are temporarily safe. Status update."

Silence reigned for a beat longer than Di was comfortable with before Hazel's voice came through. "Concentrating, Captain. Not great timing."

"Never is. Do you have Lucas?"

"He's grabbed on to the 'claw,' but I think something's jammed the winch. I can't pull him in through the system, so I'll have to do it manually back in the cargo bay."

When it rains, it pours.

"Hurry, Hazel. He's almost out of oxygen." Di brought Lucas in on the call. "Lucas? Still with us?"

"Can't get rid of me that easily." Lucas' voice was faint and weak.

"Not for lack of trying," Hazel retorted. She grunted and a resounding clang echoed through her microphone. "Hold tight. I'm pulling you in."

Lucas sighed. "About time."

"Alright, lazy bastard. *You* come crank your fat ass back in."

"I would if..." Lucas' voice suddenly cleared, sounding stronger. "Hazel, move the ship. You've got incoming."

"What?" Di asked, panic rising. She sat bolt upright sending a twinge of pain through her chest.

"It's one of those things. Found footing on the side of the station and launched itself toward the ship."

"You're almost out of oxygen!" Hazel shouted.

"Won't matter if you're dead before I get there! It's pointed right at the underside of the ship! It's going to hit the comms array, and—"

The line went dead.

"Hazel? Lucas?" Di looked in what she estimated to be the direction of half of her remaining crew, several walls of steel and the vacuum of space standing between them.

"What's happening?" Gayle asked, looking sharply her way as she remained at her post by the door.

"Comms are down. I can't reach them."

Gayle cursed, slamming the butt of her weapon against the door and sending the desperate hosts behind it into a renewed frenzy.

This couldn't be happening. They were close. So close.

Overhead station intercoms crackled to life. The hosts outside, who moments ago were frothing at the mouth clamoring to get in, grew quiet and still. A bad omen, to say the least.

An oily, barely human voice slithered from the speaker and wormed its way between Di's ears, invading her brain and violating whatever remaining sense of safety she may have felt.

"Oh Captain, my Captain." John, the self-proclaimed Prophet, chuckled maniacally. "It appears your part has yet more to play for my Queen. How curious."

CHAPTER 15
HARBINGER

"Who the hell is that?" Gayle asked. Her eyes squinted and her upper lip turned up in a snarl.

"He's a monster," Di muttered.

"Like these things?" Gayle asked, flipping her head toward the now silent hosts on the other side of the door.

"Worse."

John, the self-proclaimed Prophet, had changed in the hours since she had last spoken with him. His voice had adopted another layer, a second higher-pitched tone overlaid atop his own. Words were breathier, with the ends of his sentences often punctuated by a whistling hiss. It reminded her of the sounds the hosts made in their more docile form, reminiscent of a boiling tea kettle. Every word drummed up a chill along her spine, making her feel as though she could never be warm again.

"I hope you realize now that I *did* give you a choice. You could have submitted to the will of the One. Unlike *humans*," he spat, the word a curse in his mouth, "our Queen does not discriminate so prejudicially. All are welcome to join the Many, and there is always room for a Prophetess at my side."

Di involuntarily retched, nausea building at the mere thought of his offer.

"What's he talking about?" Gayle asked.

Di took a deep breath to fight down the bile rising in her throat. "He claims he's some sort of mouthpiece for the parasite. Calls himself the Prophet."

"I am *the* mouthpiece!" John shouted, speakers buzzing.

Di froze, eyes wide, mouth agape. She locked eyes with Gayle, and a short message appeared on her HUD.

Can he hear us?

Di shrugged and shook her head noncommittally. There was no way he was close enough himself to have heard their exchange. She glanced around the room, searching for cameras that he may have tapped into along with his feed to the station intercom.

"Staying quiet now?" He chuckled, a disconcerting overlap of his deep voice with the high-pitched hissing. "No matter. They will get to you eventually. You must realize that. There are only two options for you now; join us or feed us."

Di had seen too many movies to ignore the fact he was winding down his grand villain monologue, short though it may have been. As if in response, three overlapping hisses emanated from behind the door accompanied by a half-hearted thump. A threatening reminder they were locked in a tiny room with nothing but a single door separating them from a horde of hosts more than willing to rip their flesh from their bones. She had to think of something, a way to keep him talking. So she gambled.

"Tell me why I should join you!" she shouted, not entirely sure how loud she needed to be for him to hear her. The words sounded corny, too obvious, and she flinched. "How do you expect to overcome billions of vengeful humans without being wiped out yourself?"

The intercom crackled, but John's voice didn't immediately return. Di locked eyes with Gayle, sending her a brief message.

Find a map. Get us a route out of the station.

Gayle nodded, quietly slipping past her toward one of the security consoles.

"Do you know how we were introduced to humans?" John finally responded. He continued, not waiting for Di's answer. "Greed. Humanity's greed. We couldn't understand it at first, couldn't comprehend it. It wasn't until later, after the first Assimilation, that we began to grasp the extent of humankind's pollution.

"You came to harvest our moon's resources. You came to *take*. It is what you do. It is what you *all* do. We see this now. You will take, and take, and take, and take, and *take*! Until you have destroyed yet another precious resource, another moon, another planet."

Disturbingly, Di understood the venomous bite behind John's words. His anger and hateful distrust of humanity was not as foreign as he may have thought. Plenty of people felt the sting of humankind's poor decisions. Earth's surface was littered with millions of unfortunate souls who couldn't afford to escape its poisonous embrace. Natural resources, *vital* resources stripped bare. Exorbitant, overinflated prices on necessities choking the life of those less fortunate. Food had to be grown in orbital pods outside of Earth's atmosphere. Pure, clean water wasn't an option anymore, not unless you were willing to shill out half your savings on water mined from Enceladus or some other icy moon. The system was broken. She knew it. Everyone knew it, and it wasn't going to get better. Not without some drastic changes.

He isn't wrong, she thought. Chills ran up her arms forcing a shiver through her spine. The truth rang guiltily in her ears, and that fact alone scared her to death.

But he couldn't be right either. Flashes of Gerald's final moments gave her clarity. The paralyzing fear in his eyes. The pain. He hadn't been given a choice. Adapt or die, and he hadn't adapted. It wasn't right. It was simply exchanging one bully for another. The cause may be noble, or at least noble-adjacent, but the ends don't justify the means. Enslaving a species to the will of the mighty was wrong, no matter who was wielding the sword. Pretty words and self-righteous platitudes couldn't hide the fact that humanity would cease to exist if this parasite got its way.

"This is why we must save you from yourselves. You are lost, angry, spoiled children. You will destroy yourselves and everything around you if left alone. We cannot leave you alone. We will not risk our existence for your continued abuses."

Di turned toward Gayle, glancing at the wall of screens

showing more than a dozen camera feeds of the station. Though various external angles were shown, she didn't see any sign of the Katana. She half-heartedly attempted to convince herself that no news was good news. If she couldn't see them, that must have meant they had gotten away. With no comms to confirm their safety and coordinate escape, they were on their own anyway. They could worry about what happened next after getting clear of the station.

I think there's a maintenance hatch close to the hangar. Gayle's message pinged in the corner of Di's screen. Gayle pointed to a screen with a view of the large, sealed doors to the hangar. Just off to the side, partially cut off by the feed, Di saw the vent. *If we can't get through to the hangar, we should be able to use that to get clear of the station. Assuming Hazel's able, she can pick us up in the Katana.*

Di nodded. They had a destination, an end goal. All they needed was a way to get there. Through dozens of hive-minded hosts more than willing to tear them limb from limb. No problem. She glanced at the feed pointed directly at the security station. An expanded roster of hosts clustered around the door, bodies stiff and unmoving, staring blankly toward the room. Di could feel their gaze through the walls.

"Our plan is simple," John continued, apparently unaware or simply uncaring of their desperate, silent planning. Di noticed the feed to the security room itself had been cut, likely as Gayle's first act at the console. "For us to grow, to expand, we must evolve. Adapt. Extend beyond our current bounds. With your ship, we will seek others. Though we have grown in abilities since the first Assimilation, we understand that we are not yet ready to face humanity at large. But to do so, we will need more hosts. We will need more humans."

Di checked her ammunition supply, popping the mag out of her pistol. Just over half of the magazine remained, her only other option being the nearly empty mag at her waist. All in all, only a dozen or so bullets to take on a steadily growing horde at their door.

Gayle glanced over her shoulder, noticing the inspection. Di raised her eyebrow, a silent inquiry into Gayle's own weapon status, to which Gayle slowly shook her head. Not much left there either, apparently. If this was going to be a gunfight, it would be a quick one, and not one with an outcome she looked forward to.

"I will take your silence as the intelligent contemplation it should be," John said. "But know this, Captain. We do not need you to accomplish our designs. We are merely extending a hand of mercy. It has been offered this once. It will not be offered again."

An idea blossomed in Di's mind. It was crazy, reckless, and more than likely a horrible plan. Compared with an almost certain death in a gunfight, however, it was practically a 'get out of jail free' card.

"I will require an answer now, Captain."

Gayle stood, readying her rifle. Di put up one finger, shaking her head, and sent a message to Gayle's HUD.

Follow my lead.

Gayle nodded uncertainly but did not lower her weapon.

"How do I know you won't command these things to rip us apart as soon as I open the door?" Di asked, waltzing closer to the door with Gayle just behind her. She had assumed, once they had cut the feed to the room itself, that John could hear her through the hosts themselves. They were a hive-mind, after all.

"You don't," John replied. "If it helps, I have no intention of killing you. At least, not at the moment."

"And what about Gayle? Is she included in this plan of yours?"

She could sense his hesitation before he spoke. "If you wish to retain her as a pet, I see no problem with that. She will have to undergo Assimilation, of course. As will you."

Di shuddered at the word, but she pushed through to her plan. "I need to see you face to face. I won't trust what you say unless I can look you in the eye."

John chuckled in his inhuman way. "So typically human. We will cure you of that soon enough."

Gayle slapped Di's upper arm to get her attention, pointing at the camera feed showing the security station from outside. As one, the hosts parted creating a gruesome procession leading from their door down the hall toward the hangar.

"Very well. You may interact with the Harbinger. Though my patience wears thin."

The Harbinger. That was a new title, though he had thrown around so many names she had started having trouble keeping track of what was what. Maybe it represented his capacity as the so-called Prophet, the herald of his parasite

Queen. It didn't particularly matter. Her plan had tentatively worked, getting them out of the room and close to the maintenance access.

Di turned back to the wall of monitors, searching for the cameras in the vicinity of their destination.

Can you control these remotely? Di messaged, pointing out two camera feeds in the hallway outside the hangar to Gayle. Gayle approached the monitors.

I think so. We were able to bypass the system before things went to shit. There isn't a whole lot of functionality to them, though.

But you can access them from your suit? Di asked. A small but important part of her piecemeal plan relied on these cameras. She had taken a gamble in her assumption and prayed it would pay off.

Let me try. Gayle squinted at the screen, then punched in the small alphanumerical code located in the bottom corner of each feed on to the console. Next, she moved to her wrist, punching in various commands that Di couldn't see.

We don't have any more time, Di messaged. She placed a shaking hand on the door controls. If they couldn't gain control of the feeds, she would just have to hope they could either get into the hangar itself or find another distraction.

I've got it!

Di shuddered in relief. It probably wouldn't amount to much, but they needed all the help they could get.

Ok, shut off the feed and be ready for my signal.

Gayle nodded, gripping her gun tightly. Di unlocked the

door, watching as it slid silently open.

The sight before her was breathtaking. Not in a 'beautiful sunrise' way, more in an 'I think I may wet myself' way. Just as they'd seen on the camera feed, dozens upon dozens of hosts in haphazard rows lined up to provide a cleared walkway a mere two meters wide. Sunken eyes, flushed a pale blue, stared unseeingly ahead. Not the deep blue she had seen when they had been hunting, but not the cloudy white of a host unaware. They were alert, but not aggressive.

A majority of the hosts swayed gently on their feet, as though they were blissfully floating in a peaceful ocean current. The bodies were in varying states of decay and frostbite. Blackened fingers and hands, the rot creeping up just past the elbow. Sunken faces covered in paper-thin grey flesh. A missing nose here. A hand with half the fingers missing there. Though they were once human, they had long lost the aspects that made them so.

A host to Di's left shifted as she passed, leaning in as though sniffing a passing plate of delectable food. They were interconnected as one organism, but she saw this as a hint of individuality, a clue that the hivemind was not completely controlling. At least not for some. As they walked along the disturbing path, she caught the eyes of a host as its head turned with their procession, eyes flushing a shade darker. Their disturbing whistles faded in and out among the crowd. A disturbance ahead sent a rustle through the hosts, like the ripple caused by a single stone's throw flowing outward in concentric circles along an otherwise peaceful pond's surface. It was quickly quieted, and the sea of inhuman faces resumed their vigilance.

This is so wrong, Gayle's message read, flashing on Di's HUD. *They're herding us to the slaughter.*

Di shivered at the apt analogy. Her confidence, moments ago so strong, began to wane. She had not expected this many hosts, and their likelihood of breaking through to the maintenance hatch was shrinking with each footfall. Still, she plowed onward hoping her outward conviction didn't convey the sinking pit in her stomach and the creeping numbness that began to run along her arms and legs. She begged her knees not to buckle, though she wasn't entirely sure how long that plea would last.

The massive bay doors, still sealed tightly shut, loomed overhead as they approached. Small view ports at roughly her eye level reflected a calm, albeit messy, interior. Sometime after her sprint to the security office, the emergency shutters had locked in place along every single one of the large bay windows in the hangar, shutting out the vacuum of space. Seeing an empty hangar, however, gave her hope. The pathway to the maintenance door would be messy, and seeing just how many hosts surrounded them didn't fill her with confidence in that escape avenue. But if they could make it to the shuttle, they could make it off the station. She could see the one port in use by the Katana's landing shuttle, but she saw no movement inside. Wherever John was, it looked like he wasn't going to reveal himself just yet.

Di turned around to face the lightly undulating horde of inhuman hosts just as their pathway sealed shut, now clogged with more bodies pressing in. A semi-circle of cleared space a few arm lengths across was all that separated her and her security officer from a throng of increasingly agitated monsters.

"Well?" Di shouted. "Are we doing this or not?"

Another ripple pulsed through the crowd, but no verbal response was given. She took note of the maintenance door to her left, tantalizingly close with only a small army of slavering beasts between her and it.

Gayle tightened her grip on her rifle, fingers itching at the trigger, hands ready to throw it to her shoulder and unleash fiery hell. Gayle's brow furrowed, but Di shook her head. Something was wrong. Something felt off. She couldn't quite put her finger on it, but she sensed an energy building.

I don't think we're making it through this crowd. We need to get the hangar doors open.

Gayle glanced back toward the panel beside the bay doors in recognition of Di's message.

When? Gayle replied.

On my signal, I need you to switch those two cameras back on to the low-light setting. The lowest it can go.

Gayle raised an eyebrow and tilted her head slightly.

Just trust me. It should provide a moment of distraction to get us through that door.

Di thought back to her first encounter with the hosts, hiding inside a locker and attempting to get video proof of their pursuers. It had immediately alerted them to her position. She had suspected then that something within the hosts allowed them to sense infrared, and she was relying on that assumption now. If they could distract the hosts' attention away from the doors long enough for Gayle to get them open and get a few second head start, it may be just enough to let them escape.

"John?" Di called out. "Prophet? Where are you?"

A disturbance near the back of the crowd sent a ripple of hissing among the hosts, and they began to part. This was it. Something began to move through the sea of hosts, making its way toward the hangar doors. Now came the other part of her plan.

John was clearly not like the other hosts. Whether he was a puppeted mouthpiece to this Queen or if he retained some small form of his own free will, she had no idea. Whatever it may be, he was obviously an important piece to the puzzle. His presence seemed to give the hosts direction, to focus them. He could calm them, direct them, send them into a frenzy. He was a conduit, a repeater signal for the hivemind itself, she would bet her life on it. Hell, she already had. And if that signal disappeared?

Di slowly moved her hand and placed it on the pistol grip at her waist. Nine bullets. Nine chances to take him down. She had no idea if he was infected the same way as the others, unsure if he would sprout a demonic, razor-toothed worm from his neck. All she could do was take the shot she could get and hope the chaos that ensued would be enough.

Be ready.

Gayle raised the barrel of her rifle a fraction and angled herself more toward the bay doors and the awaiting control panel. Di shot another furtive glance toward the maintenance door. The more she thought about that avenue, the surer she became on their current course. Even with these distractions, the hosts would tear them apart long before they got the panel off. They had lucked out with the hangar remaining clear. She willed that luck to stretch just a little more.

Di looked back to give Gayle a reassuring nod and watched as her face visibly paled, grip going slack on her gun.

"Behold, the Harbinger." John's voice, still blaring through the overhead speakers rather than in person, sounded triumphant.

The crowd of hosts parted as a familiar figure in a grey suit stepped through. His helmet was gone. His formerly emerald eyes flushed a hazy cerulean. His grey beard surrounded blackened lips, the corners of his mouth hanging slack. Thick, meaty, yet tender hands gripped Florence, his prized weapon, in a ready stance at his shoulder.

The Harbinger wasn't John. It was Gene.

CHAPTER 16
CHOICES

It was Gene. But it wasn't Gene. It was a malformed, grossly inhuman approximation of Gene. Gone were the rosy, flushed cheeks, replaced by blue-tinged skin reflecting the alien blood now pumping through his veins. A thin, jagged line across his neck curled up around his jaw under his beard, running past his ear and nearly connecting with the corner of his eye. The skin surrounding it was still stained red, a gruesome indicator of the horror and pain he likely felt as he transformed. The tip of his bulbous nose had already started to darken, frostbite setting in too quickly.

Di glanced over her shoulder at a slack jawed Gayle, gun held limply in her fingers. Her face had taken on a sickly green pallor. Brightly glistening tears welled up at the corners of her blue eyes, a stark contrast to the flat matte blue orbs staring lifelessly back. Di could feel the wave of disbelief exuding from her security officer.

Di had already felt Gene's loss, had been forced to come to terms with his inevitable end and soldier through it. Even so, she had kept a tiny glimmer of hope alive that he had made it to a safe place, somewhere he could bunker down and wait for rescue. It was ridiculous. She knew that. It was still hope, and that hope had been thoroughly crushed by the weighty hammer of reality.

"We come before you in a form recognizable. A peace offering." The voice emanating from Gene's throat was nothing like the husky tones she knew and loved. A wispy, breathy, high-pitched resonance was overlayed by hints of his own gravelly voice. Not enough to give comfort, but just enough to hint at what once was. A stiff, emotionless, rictus grin briefly flashed across his face, skin splitting near the corners of his mouth like tiny tears in tissue paper. Miniscule dribbles of purple blood rolled ignored down his chin, lightly smoking before gradually evaporating in the above-freezing temperatures of the station. "Let our message be words of comfort from the lips of one thought lost, but merely Ascended. May we all be reunited in the One."

A strangled gasp of pain escaped Gayle's lips and she collapsed to one knee, gun clattering to the ground. Di rushed to catch her before she fell on her face, an arm wrapped below her shoulder to bolster her up.

"You think this is comforting?" Di spat, gaze shooting daggers at her once-friend's lifeless eyes. "Parading our friend around like a puppet?"

Gene frowned, brow wrinkling. "Is this not a joyous reunion of one once gone?" His head slightly tilted to a shifted angle, frown deepening. "Our continued Assimilation indicates humans mourn those who cease to be. All conjectures point to reuniting as a momentous occasion."

"*You* are not Gene!" Di hissed.

"Curious. It appears our initial assumptions have been grossly miscalculated. It is not merely the return of the flesh that incites a positive reaction. We do not understand."

"Of course you don't. You are not *human*. Humans vary. Humans change. Humans have differences in looks, thoughts, feelings. You couldn't possibly understand that. You're just a bug."

Gene's head tilted again, inspecting Di as she stood with one arm supporting Gayle.

The overhead speakers crackled to life. "How *dare* you speak to the One this way!" John cried, distorted feedback blaring at his outburst. "As the Seeker of Order and Unification, it is—"

With a wordless command exuded from every host surrounding them, a command that Di felt as an undulating wave of nausea, John's voice abruptly cut short, and the speakers went silent again. Di instinctively flinched as Gene returned his attention back to her.

"It is our desire to seek understanding of all who join the One. We would greatly benefit from an Assimilation with one such as you. Your... unique condition will be beneficial to further advancement of our Unification."

"My condition is not unique. It is what it means to be human."

The bone-chilling, emotionless grin returned to Gene's face, releasing another small rivulet of dark blood to flow along his deeply set smile lines and absorb into his beard at the tip of his chin. He did not respond further, eliciting another shiver down Di's spine.

Their plan was falling to shit. The maintenance exit was a bust. Gayle was broken, a blank slate of trauma-induced shock. They had barely any ammo left, and their backs were literally up against a wall with a hangar door that wouldn't open. Gene was gone. Definitively gone. Who knew if Hazel and Lucas had survived.

The noose was tightening. She could feel it against her throat. Slowly, steadily, the rope was cinching closed. All it would take was to let herself succumb to despair. Sure, she had fought hard, harder than most. She had gotten herself farther than was reasonably expected, farther than she had any right to be. So what if she tripped at the finish line? Di could hold her head up high at just how long she had lasted.

There's no shame in losing, she thought. *People die every day. Gayle and I could be the last surviving humans for millions of miles. That's an accomplishment, really. Right?*

Gayle stirred in her grip. Di felt Gayle's muscles tighten as if in unconscious response to her thoughts of giving in. Feelings of despair were quickly replaced with feelings of guilt. She wasn't dead yet. Gayle wasn't dead yet. As Captain, she had an obligation to her crew. They were her friends. Her family. Whatever was left, she would fight until her last breath to get them home, even if it was just Gayle and herself left.

Get that door open.

Gayle flinched as she noticed Di's message on her HUD but gave a perfunctory nod. She may have been hurting, unalterably changed, but she was still Gayle. She would do her duty.

Be ready with the cameras.

With a supporting arm underneath Gayle's armpit, Di hoisted her Security Officer to her feet. The woman was heavy, and Di's injured knee buckled uncomfortably. She pushed them both against the bay doors for stability, no acting required for her display of weakness and fragility. Di still had no clear idea how these hosts functioned, but she assumed their animalistic instincts were the same as many others; any sign of defiance, any showing of strength, and they would wipe her out. She had to time this very carefully.

Di hoisted Gayle off on to the console beside the doors, heaving a labored sigh. Gayle played her part, collapsing against it in just such a way as to give her access without revealing what she was doing to the hosts that surrounded them.

Steeling her resolve, she straightened and faced her former friend. He hadn't moved, though thankfully that inhuman smile was gone.

"What's your plan?" she asked. She needed to buy time, to bring the attention fully to herself. "Do you really think you can solve humanity's nature with a couple hundred bodies? You think you can grow fast enough before they learn your weakness and wipe you out permanently?"

"You are correct, of course," Gene said, layered voice sending fresh chills along Di's arms. "It would be hopeless with what we have on this station alone. As we reside below, our reach is limited. With distance, our grasp grows faint."

"Then you've lost already. I know your parasites can't survive above freezing temperatures. We've seen the research."

"Research?" Gene adopted a quizzical look, eyelids drooping half shut. A moment later, they snapped open again. "Ah yes. Experimentation performed on our offshoots. Many perished to teach your kind how we work, though it was immediately outdated once performed."

"Outdated?" Di asked. "How?"

"Though your kind discovered our physical limitations, you could not possibly grasp the Assimilation. It is something incomprehensible without experiencing it firsthand. You see, humans are slow to adaptation. We are not."

"I've seen your hosts die. I've seen the lengths you have to go to adapt human bodies. You can't survive in that environment."

Gene emitted a sound that could be approximated as a laugh, though its grating tone did anything but convey humor. "These hosts were the beginning. We have learned much in the convening time between First Ascension and your arrival. As we said, Assimilation is not something easily comprehended to one who has not experienced it. Our adaptation is still preliminary, as we need more hosts to continue, though we are confident we shall succeed. Thrive. Begin anew."

"What does that mean?" Di whispered. She had a feeling she wouldn't like the answer.

"With this vessel to the stars, we shall pass between the veil of shadow and light. No longer will it prevent our continuation. Even now, we feel the tendrils stretch beyond the confines of our prison."

As though in response, the station shuddered with a low rumble nearly sending Di to the floor. Though it was slight, she felt a slow and steady acceleration. To confirm her fears, she glanced through the window in the hangar bay doors.

The station was moving. Bits of refuse that had been sucked through the doorway at Lucas' exit pinged off the glass of the hangar view ports. This flying death trap full of alien zombies was moving. And it was headed straight for the moon's thermal vents.

It all miraculously clicked into place. The veil of shadow and light. It was the thermal vents. Before, the temperature and the sheer force of the vents had prevented the parasite from leaving. The moon had presented a natural barrier to keep the Omega Parasite contained. With the Assimilation, this combining of parasite and human, it had evolved to the point where it could survive the trip up the vents beyond the reach of Enceladus. Like a security update pushed through the server to each individual computer, the hivemind somehow conveyed the organic changes necessary to its trillions of offshoots.

The parasite was mobile, and this station was its carrier to take it far beyond the reaches of Saturn's moons. Toward human civilization. They were now riding in what was essentially a nuke capable of previously unseen devastation.

Humanity, in its greed and lust for power, had given its own means of destruction the tools necessary to complete it.

"We see that you understand now," Gene hissed. "You feel it. We bring change to those who require it. Though humanity does not ask, we offer salvation."

Their time was up. It was now or never, and it wasn't just their own asses on the line anymore. If this station survived, humankind, as it currently stood, would be doomed.

"What we speak is truth, however hard it may be to accept. The question now becomes, what will you do? Will you have the courage to do what must be done? Will you join in the Assimilation, take part in the redemption of humanity?"

Hard truths. The parasite presented hard truths, and Di shivered at the thought of understanding its point of view. Humanity *did* need saving from itself. The system was corrupt. It wouldn't change on its own, not without drastic measures. It was the openly held secret that every human being knew, but that no one could, or would, do anything about. Eventually, humanity would turn completely inward and consume itself, a rapid descent to utter annihilation and species extinction.

Yet despite its supposed sound reasoning and justifications, it hadn't changed a thing in Di's mind. Humanity had a chance, however slim it may be, to course correct its supposedly inevitable destiny. And it was humanity's job to do so. Enslavement to the whims of an alien parasite was not the same as redemption of her species. It was enslavement. The essence of humanity was free will and individuality. Conforming to the will of the many was functionally the same result as destruction by their own hands. What the parasite offered was merely a spin on what the corpos had been feeding them for decades. Replacing one dictator with another was not salvation. The parasite only offered one outcome; slavery. It was just another bully trying to convince her they were friends, all while repeatedly bashing her in the face with her own weapon.

And she hated bullies.

Di whipped toward Gene, pistol in hand. "Did you actually think I would join you in the destruction of my species?"

Gene growled, his rifle already at his shoulder, barrel aimed back at her in a standoff. The unfortunate truth was that he could survive a bullet or two, while she was a bit more fragile.

As she gathered her courage and locked eyes with not-Gene, she noticed something. His eyes, while still flushed an alien blue, looked different. Felt different. It may have been the desperation in her own mind, but she swore she sensed something coming from behind those eyes. Fighting. Pleading. Pushing through.

Do it.

His voice in her mind was so shocking she nearly dropped her weapon. The momentary flash of defiance in his eyes confirmed to her it was not just her imagination. Whatever tiny part of Gene remained, he was fighting. He was doing what he could to save her. He was still Gene.

She knew what had to be done. Gene's rifle, the same one he had carried since before they had met, his pride and joy. So meticulously cared for; cleaned, polished, perfected in every way. Except for the dent in the barrel, newly damaged in their flight below the surface.

Di pulled the trigger. Three shots to the chest, purple blood spraying from the wounds. He barely flinched. She could see the rage building, eyes flushing deeper blue. Whistling screeches began to rise from the hosts around them. Bodies crouched, ready to be let off the leash. To rip and tear.

Just before Gene pulled the trigger, he smiled. It was nothing like the inhuman approximations she had seen before. It was authentic, lightly reflected in his eyes that paled ever so slightly. It was a thank you. Relief.

He pulled the trigger. The rifle exploded in his hands. Di dove to the ground as bits of superheated shrapnel tore through the unfortunate hosts closest to Gene.

"NOW!" she shouted.

Small red notification lights buzzed to life from the dome-shaped bulges in the ceiling. As one, each host turned toward the nearest camera dotted along the hall, shrieking in defiance and confusion. Di had no idea how much time they had bought themselves, but the massive doors behind her split revealing an empty hangar and a single occupied port.

"Let's go!" Gayle shouted, gripping Di's upper arm and hauling her to her feet.

Di took a single moment to glance at Gene's fallen corpse. His hands were mangled strips of flesh. Bits of his precious Florence sprouted from his upper torso. His neck had been nearly completely severed. Half of his face had been shredded, a single, pure blue eyeball peeking out from darkened, bloody carnage. The gentle touch of a genuine smile lingered on his lips. Even through the horror, he looked peaceful.

Goodbye, Gene, she thought. She swore she felt a momentary surge of gratitude.

With Gayle's strengthened support, Di hobble-sprinted into the hangar, directing herself toward the Katana's landing shuttle in the docking bay. Gayle paused just long enough to attempt to seal the door behind them. It began to gradually drift shut as they turned toward their salvation at bay door seven.

Boxes, tools, shuttle parts, and various debris lay scattered across the floor; remnants from Lucas' dramatic expulsion. Ignoring the pain in her leg as it was jarred from collisions with refuse, she barreled her way through it all in a beeline to the shuttle. They were close. So close.

But what awaits you beyond the door? Di thought, her ever-present inner pessimist lurking in the shadowy corner. She shook her head, shoving down the thoughts of the murky future to focus on the very real danger of the now.

This orbital waystation was by no means small, and the hangar reflected the genuine size needed for such a large operation. Bay seven was not at the end, but it was close to it. They still had a good distance to cover, and her leg had started to seize up from the exertion, her bruised and broken chest aching something fierce as she struggled to suck in labored breath after labored breath. Right foot step, left leg hobble-slide. Right foot step, left leg hobble-slide.

"Faster, Captain!" Gayle shouted, glancing over her shoulder. Di didn't need to check. She heard the shrieks of their pursuers. By the sound of it, only a handful had made it through the closing doors. A handful was enough.

"Keep going!" Gayle stopped and pivoted, whipping her rifle to her shoulder and popping off two quick bursts of fire.

Di didn't even consider arguing as she limped her way closer. Reality trumped pride in life-or-death situations. If it didn't, they very quickly became simply death situations. Their current reality was that she was injured, and Gayle was not. Di's obligation was to make herself less of a burden, and if that meant pushing on and letting her Security Officer cover her ass, she'd do it.

Bay seven was tantalizingly close now. She could make out the extension bridge leading to the shuttle through the bay port beside the door. It was still extended, sealed to the station and ready to accept new passengers. The way things had been going, she had honestly expected it to be pulling away.

Four more gunshots rang through the massive, empty hangar. The shrieks grew more frantic and feral.

As Di approached the door console, Gayle sprinted past her to the sealed door. "I'm out. Got anything left?"

In response, Di stumbled up beside her, placing her left

hand over her right on the grip of her pistol. With a searing stab in her left knee she turned, bracing her elbow on the door frame and taking aim at the two remaining hosts. Thick, purple, ropey worms wriggled and writhed from gaping wounds in their bodies, one sprouting from the first host's chest and the other where the second's right arm had once been. Circular jaws of glinting, razor-thin teeth flexed in and out, snapping and gnashing in hungered anticipation.

Overwhelming fear attempted to consume her, just as it had below in her first encounter with this evolved predator. She wouldn't let it this time. A novice would have squeezed off a few wild, ill-advised potshots hoping to get a lucky hit. But Di was no novice. Sucking in a shaky breath, the most her broken ribs would allow, she released a steady stream of air, taking aim at the closest host. Her hands still quivered with fear and exhaustion, but that was nothing new. She had been afraid before. She had been exhausted before. She had survived before.

Di squeezed the trigger. Three heavy 'thwumps' accompanied brief, bright muzzle flashes. The parasite protruding from the first host's chest exploded, bullets tearing through its maw and cascading into the body behind it. It collapsed immediately, skidding along the ground leaving a streak of wet, black blood. Refocusing, Di aimed two more shots at their remaining pursuer. One to the knee sending it toppling to the ground in front of her in a jumble of limbs, one to the fleshy appendage squirming from its shoulder socket. It mewled pathetically, a sound somehow even more bone-chilling than its terrifying shrieks. Taking a feeble limp closer, Di coldly extended her arm and put a final silencing bullet in the worm's body. Ejecting the empty magazine, she pulled her remaining, nearly empty clip from her waist and popped it in, racking the chamber. The parasite, however, had stilled, oozing viscous, dark blue blood.

Exhaustion overwhelmed her, adrenaline fleeing as the immediate danger subsided. Her outstretched arm fell limply to her side, and she stumbled backward until her back hit the wall beside the bay door. It took every bit of her remaining strength to stay on her feet and to keep her eyelids from drooping shut.

"Let's go," Gayle said. The door beside Di hissed as it slid open revealing the darkened walkway to their waiting shuttle. In response, the massive hangar doors began to slide open, bodies straining to push through the slowly widening gap. "Captain!"

Di gratefully allowed Gayle to usher her through, practically carrying her sagging, unresponsive body. Another door opened, and the interior of her shuttle greeted her. It was unchanged since she had last boarded it. Unremarkable. Barren and plain. Utilitarian. A refreshing taste of the familiar.

Gayle dumped her into the bucket seat bolted to the wall beside the door before slamming the door locks into place. "Stay here. I'll disengage and get us the hell away from this station."

"The Katana?" Di asked.

"I'm sure she's fine. Let's get out of here first."

Di shot her a half-hearted thumbs up before she tromped off to the cockpit, disappearing around the corner.

Di's mind began to wander in a daze. Now having a chance to sit, fight or flight temporarily satiated, she allowed her body to acknowledge her overwhelming fatigue. The previous handful of hours (and not days, a fact her mind struggled to comprehend) had pushed her to her absolute limits; mentally, emotionally, and physically. Bruises, broken ribs, a torn something or other in her knee. Watching her crew, her chosen family, picked off one by one. Gene, her oldest and closest friend, mutated at the whims of an alien parasite. Gerald, ripped apart while dragged to the bottom of an unforgiving subsurface ocean. Lucas, bleeding and losing oxygen. Hazel, comms lost and status unknown. Emma, at the mercy of that deranged psychopath, John.

A thought, intrusive yet unrelenting, wriggled just behind the forefront of her mind. Elusive. Hazy. Unreadable.

Sleep. You need sleep.

It was true. Di wouldn't be surprised if she slept for the next three days straight. As soon as they had put at least a few thousand kilometers between themselves and this godforsaken moon.

Just rest. Gayle will take care of it.

Where was Gayle, anyway? Di peeked from behind her closed eyelid but saw nothing.

She's fine. She's in the cockpit.

That was true. She said... what did she say? She was going to disengage the shuttle from the station. Odd that they hadn't moved yet.

That invasive, nagging thought returned. What was so important? What was she forgetting. As much as it pained her, she went back through.

Bruises. Broken ribs. Gene. Gerald. Lucas. Hazel. Emma. John.

Emma. John.

John?

Where was John?

Why weren't they leaving?

Di bolted to her feet, ignoring the shooting pain and wave of dizzying nausea it provoked. "Gayle!" she cried.

No response.

"Gayle, answer me!"

A loud, metallic clang rang through the ship as countless bodies collided with the outer shuttle door. With the walkway still engaged, the hosts had made it through the bay door and were clamoring desperately to get to their prey within.

Di's pistol appeared in her hand, aimed and ready. She didn't have much ammo left. Three, maybe four bullets.

Her gut instinct was to rush to the cockpit, but her years of experience held a tight rein on her reactions. Di had already called out. Rushing in now would only put her in the same position as Gayle. As much as it pained her, she needed to be careful. If she was taken off guard, they were dead.

Gingerly, she shuffled toward the hallway leading to the cockpit, bad leg dragging behind her. There were three small compartments along the way, any one of which a likely spot for an ambush. As she rounded the corner, the open cockpit lay bare. All three doors were sealed shut providing no hint as to which one held Gayle.

As she shuffled closer to the first door, she heard scuffling and a cry of muffled pain from the room farthest down. Di's heart raced, HUD warnings now a begrudging familiarity she had come to rely on. Her new flush of adrenaline pushed her to act, to run down the hall guns blazing. But as much as it pained her, she would be no use to Gayle if she were caught in a trap as well.

Di clutched her pistol in both hands close to her chest and triggered the first door. Empty. She moved silently to the next one down the line.

As the door slid open, she nearly pulled the trigger. Emma sat slumped in an awkward position against the edge of the fold-down wall seat, unmoving and eyes closed. Squatting down, she grabbed Emma's wrist and quickly initiated a vitals diagnostic run. The suit looked blessedly fully intact giving Di a rising hope that the virus hadn't infected her.

Emma's suit chimed, confirming her stable vitals. She was alive, but not priority. Another muted scuffle sounded behind the wall in the third and final room. Readjusting her grip, Di moved silently and triggered the door.

"Don't move, Captain!" John's forearm tightened around Gayle's neck. A deep red stain was slowly growing from the right side of her abdomen. Di noticed a glint of light off of the large knife in John's grip as it slid from her wound and disappeared behind her, no doubt aimed and ready to puncture Gayle's spine or one of her many vital organs.

"John. Let her go." Di only caught a glimpse of his blue-tinged eyes as he ducked fully behind Gayle.

John's inherent skills as a competent bounty hunter kept him small and concealed behind his hostage so as to not present an easy target. "Why would I do that when I can simply bide my time?"

She hissed in frustration. Though the landing shuttle was well maintained and withstood regulation inspection, it was still a shuttle. Had they been on the Katana itself, Di wouldn't have batted an eye as the hosts tried to tear their way through. It was a veritable fortress. The shuttle, on the other hand, she was not so sure. Her firsthand account attested to the hosts' ferocity and strength.

Gayle, to her credit, appeared calm. Well, as calm as one could reasonably be under the circumstances. Her face had begun to pale, sweat beading on her forehead. Her fists were clenched at her chest, knees bent, back stretched backward uncomfortably in John's grip.

"I'm going to kill you, John." Di's voice sounded robotic in her own ears. It was said dispassionately, a simple matter of fact. She did not lower her gun.

"You've already lost so much. Why lose another?" His neck shifted just enough to let her see his evil grin before ducking back behind Gayle's head.

Di forced down the emotions rising in her chest. Pain. Despair. Fury. Hatred. There would be time for that later. Now was the time for cold calculation.

"You let her go, and I let you go free."

John laughed. "You expect me to believe you? You just told me you were going to kill me."

She never had been great at poker. "Then tell me what you want."

"It isn't what *I* want. It is what *we* want." He shifted backward further into the corner, and Gayle winced in pain. Di gritted her teeth.

Gayle's right hand unclenched ever so slightly, thumb gently tapping twice on her chest. It was a 'blink and you'll miss it' move. Di nearly hadn't caught it herself.

Gayle had been adamant on teaching the crew various non-verbal signs for events of every kind. Movement patterns, enemy locations. Everyone had grumbled at first, until it had saved Gene's life when a raid had gone horribly wrong. Since then, every attitude on the ship had moved to full acceptance of Gayle's teachings, much to her chagrin.

Gayle made the sign again. A gentle flex of her fingers, two taps of the thumb just above her right breast.

'Go through me. Right here.'

Di gave a nearly imperceptible shake of her head. What Gayle was proposing was dangerous in the best of circumstances. That wound in her side looked bad and shooting her through the shoulder wouldn't help. It was insanely risky, requiring a precise shot, a perfectly aligned hostage-taker, and a shit-ton of luck. It definitely wasn't something to try with an inaccurate pistol on an already wounded hostage. She had to neutralize John another way.

"Then what is it your *queen* wants?" Di asked.

"The One. Yes. It is by Her will the Many survive. Endure. Flourish. All must accept this gift unto themselves." He paused as though listening to an inaudible voice, an unheard speaker. "She wants you. She wants what you have. You will be the true Harbinger, an emissary to humankind."

Di shivered reflexively, her whole body reacting violently to his request. "What is it I have? Why am I special?"

"I..." John's word stumbled, voice going quiet. "I do not know. There are... things kept away from the Many. Even from me, Her Prophet." John shook his head as though to clear it.

Gayle scrunched up her lips, eyes narrowing, and made the sign a third time adding in a gentle twist of her wrist to signify urgency. Di cursed internally. Gayle was right. They didn't have time for back and forth.

"It... I... If *she* has... But the Vessel... My role must be *secure*..." John rambled nonsensically, focus drifting further away. It was now or never. Taking careful aim, Di waited. She didn't have to wait long. John shifted behind Gayle; his grip slackened around her neck.

Di fired, pistol kicking in her grip. The bullet entered the fleshy portion just above Gayle's collarbone, exiting her trap muscle dangerously close to her neck and her carotid artery. Gayle bucked and fell to the floor in a spray of red blood. John, face reflecting the shock he felt at being shot, hit the wall and tumbled to the ground. Dark blue blood smeared down the wall as he crumpled in a heap.

Di rushed to Gayle, pulling her as gently but as quickly as she could away from the injured madman, gun still trained on the threat. John lay unmoving, collapsed in on himself, mumbling incoherently. Gayle nodded in his direction with a painful grimace indicating she was fine enough for now.

Moving cautiously, Di nudged John over onto his back with the toe of her boot. The bullet had entered in much the same place as Gayle, a non-life-threatening wound to his right shoulder which matched the nearly identical bloody bullet wound in his left lovingly given by Gene down below. His eyes were unfocused as he continued a string of unintelligible gibberish.

Di moved to stand over his body, pistol aimed squarely at the bridge of his nose. His eyes half-focused momentarily, and he grinned.

"It doesn't matter. She is already infected."

With a flash of light and an echoing crash of thunder, John's head exploded in a shower of gore and viscera. Di remained standing above him, pistol drawn, waiting for the stomach-churning worm to emerge. After nearly a full minute with no movement, she lowered her gun and let go of a shaky breath.

"Nice shot," Gayle wheezed.

Di turned toward her, shaking out of her exhausted reverie. Kneeling beside her friend, she dropped the gun and inspected the wounds on Gayle's shoulder and side. Despite the massive bloodstain, the knife wound hadn't punctured too far. It didn't seem like it had hit any major organs, though it would be impossible to tell without scans from the med bay back on the Katana. Her bullet had, thankfully, entered and exited as cleanly as anyone could ask for, missing deflection off any bones. Both were survivable, and Di released a sigh of relief.

"We're going to get you patched up on the Katana. You're going to be fine."

Gayle's eyes softened, though not in relief as Di had expected. They reflected acceptance and sorrow. "You heard what he said."

"Yes, I heard what he said. What difference does that make?" A hard lump rose in Di's throat.

"I won't let you put yourself at risk. I won't become one of them." Gayle shifted, and Di noticed the pistol, *her* pistol, in Gayle's hand.

Di put a hand over Gayle's, forcing the gun back to the floor. "Gayle. Wait. We don't know if there's a way to get rid of the parasite. I have all the research Paragon's scientists have done on this thing." She fumbled for the data disc secured in a pocket of her belt. "There has to be something in here about neutralizing its effects, or—"

"We don't know if there's a cure, but we *do* know what happens when it takes over." Gayle coughed, a tiny spatter of blood against the inside of her visor. "If you really have that kind of information, you can't risk it being lost."

"Gayle. Please." Di's voice was a whisper. "Not another one. I can't lose another one."

"Captain." Gayle's left hand fell gently over Di's. "Di. Look at me."

Di, exerting all the effort she had to give, raised her head to look into the eyes of yet another friend she had failed. Tears welled up, and this time she didn't hold them back. They fell free, rolling down her cheeks.

"This isn't your fault."

Di let out a choked, sobbing laugh, immediately remembering Gene's comforting words in the submarine.

"This isn't your fault, Di. I am making this choice, not you."

Di blinked, instinctively rubbing at her face enclosed in her helmet and eliciting a curse at her failure to wipe away the tears that obscured her vision. She just wanted a clear look, one last time.

"You sound just like Gene, you know," Di said, forcing a pained smile. Gayle visibly brightened and returned a much more genuine smile. "He knew, in the end. What he was doing. I could see it in his eyes."

"He went out saving our asses one last time," Gayle said, laughing and wincing at the pain. "Typical."

Di glanced toward Gayle's wound in her side. The bleeding had increased, and she could see the skin growing an angry red as it puckered around the hole. The transformation was moving much quicker than she had anticipated. She desperately wanted more time, ached for it, but it wasn't hers to take. Reluctantly, she moved her hand off the gun and took Gayle's other hand in both of her own.

"I need to go. I need to undock the shuttle. Is that ok?"

Gayle read between the lines, and her features relaxed, flooding with relief. She nodded, right hand gripping the pistol. They shared a final look as Di stood.

As she moved to exit the small, intimate room, she hesitated just inside the door. Two halves warred within. One refused to accept what had already occurred, the other begged for numbness that wouldn't come, temporary relief from the ache of loss.

Let her go.

"I love you, Gayle."

"Love you, Captain."

Di left without a backward glance, sealing the door behind her. Three steps toward the cockpit, a muffled gunshot rang out in the stillness, its echo resounding in her mind long after the silence resumed.

CHAPTER 17
TERMINATION

The shuttle slowly drifted away from the docking station coming to a stop several meters above the massive orbital station as it lazily listed toward the spewing vents at Enceladus' southern pole. Though mobile, the station was massive, and the engines were not meant for speed or long-distance travel. Even so, it moved ever onward toward its goal of humanity's mass extinction.

Di felt numb. Less than numb. She felt nothing. Saw nothing. Heard nothing. Her limbs moved in the way they were expected to, her brain functioning purely on survival autopilot. She couldn't give two shits that she had somehow made it out alive, because she couldn't give anything at all. Her essence, her emotion, her will to go on was gone. Empty. Drained. She tried not to think of Gayle's lifeless body meters away, bleeding steadily, tossed aside like worthless trash. Another casualty at the hands of fate, hands uncomfortably reminiscent of her own.

Glancing out the cockpit window, she found the Katana floating stationary nearby, dark and silent. Lifeless. Empty. As far as she knew, she and whatever was left of Emma were all that had survived. Even so, she instinctually flipped on comms to search for a signal, refusing to let hope blossom to something more. The ship's comms array had been damaged, but perhaps Hazel, in her copious amounts of free time, had found a way to fix it. Maybe Lucas had survived, stabilized, and walked her through what to do. Maybe Emma was just sleeping, and Gayle would strut out of that room, happy and healthy with Gene and Gerald on the radio asking to be picked up surface side. And maybe she wouldn't need to learn to forgive herself for the terrible things she had done.

But you did do those things. You did them, and they're all dead because of it.

A choking sob refreshed the second wave of uninterrupted tears. No one was left. The Katana remained silent and still, casting an ever-growing shadow that had nothing to do with the distant, cold sun.

It wasn't safe to return to the Katana, not with the risk of a host inside. Di knew she didn't have the strength or the weaponry to deal with that, let alone the mental fortitude needed to face down yet another crew member turned host.

There was barely enough fuel in the shuttle to get her moving in a semblance of the right direction to drift her way home. It wouldn't matter anyway. She would be dead from starvation long before she made it close enough to the nearest settlement. Besides, she couldn't risk the parasite escaping in this ship. Gayle had been infected, John had been infected, and who knew Emma's status.

The long-range array of the shuttle was nowhere near strong enough to beam her damning Paragon evidence anywhere past Saturn. Spreading knowledge of the dangers lurking on Enceladus was a near zero shot. No, humanity would know the Omega Parasite once it had made its way slowly toward the center of the solar system, infesting and destroying everything along its path. By then it would be too late. By then, with no prior knowledge afforded by the months of research on the data disc on her belt and the firsthand experiences recorded via her suit feed, humankind would fall.

Hope? Hope was dead, and she might as well be along with it.

There's one bullet left.

The voice in her mind barely sounded like herself. Emotionless and resolute, the final option available to her. She could follow Gene, follow Gayle. She wouldn't have to bear witness to the fall of humanity. She could end it on her own terms before life had a chance to rip yet another chunk from her soul.

Before she had registered her legs carrying her forward, Di found herself outside the room, door still sealed shut. Gayle lay inside, the pistol held loosely in her lifeless fingers. One bullet left.

Your pain can end, here and now. Give me your pain.

Di's hand trembled as she reached for the door controls. It was easy. So easy. She deserved to rest, right? If there was nothing she could do, why prolong the inevitable?

The doors slid quietly open, and she refused to look up. Her eyes focused solely on her pistol discarded on the floor. She reached forward, straining against her own invisible mental barrier to the room. Fingertips brushed the handle, and she slid it closer to herself, taking the weapon in a shaking grip and closing the door. Racking the slide, she peeked into the chamber at the single remaining bullet. Di's stomach clenched. A quick shot, and she would be free.

Be free, Di. Be free.

Static exploded in her ears. Di flinched and clutched at her helmet, shocked awake from her self-destructive reverie.

"...Cap.... there...?"

"Hello?"

"Dia... you... shuttle...?"

"Hello! Hazel?" Di could feel a glimmer of hope deep within struggling to break free of the despair that had very nearly consumed her. She clung to it as she sprinted back to the cockpit, leaning against the dashboard and peering out at the darkened Katana, pistol laying forgotten beside her.

"Captain! Is that you?" The static interference cleared enough for Hazel's beautiful voice to break through.

Di choked back another sob, laughing and collapsing into her seat. "Hazel. You're alive."

"Captain! Oh, thank God. I wasn't sure you had made it in the shuttle. What's your status?"

Di's parched throat felt like sandpaper, and she couldn't seem to find any words. Shame flooded her as she realized just how close she had come to losing it all. It would have been a betrayal of the highest degree. Gene had died for her. Gayle had died for her. All so she could make it back, prepare the world for what was coming, and bring Paragon to justice. And she had nearly thrown it all away with her own cowardice.

"Cap? What's going on?" Hazel's voice still faded in and out intermittently, as though their connection hadn't yet stabilized.

"I'm here, Hazel. Sorry." Di cleared her throat and plastered on her confident leader facade. "Status report."

"That zombie thing hit the comms array. Busted the thing entirely. I was able to get it off the hull, but it nearly tore its way through. I had to try and seal off the lower front quadrant and power down to assess the damage. Didn't want the Katana blowing up on me."

"ETA on operational functionality?"

"I'm doing my best, but Lucas has been in and out with—"

"Lucas? He's alive?" All forced bravado evaporated, a genuine plea tinging her words.

"We got him, Captain. He's banged up, but alive. Recovering in the med bay."

Di collapsed back into her chair. She wasn't alone. Her failure had been devastating, yes, but not all encompassing. Two, possibly three crew members were alive and fighting. Gene, Gerald, and Gayle's sacrifices would not be in vain.

"Captain?" Hazel asked hesitantly. "Is... Emma? And

Gayle?"

"I found Emma unresponsive but alive. Gayle..." Di's throat closed as she tried to choke out her next words. "Gayle didn't make it."

The line went quiet. Di heard the blood pumping behind her ears as she wrestled her own demons down. She couldn't get distracted now. She had very nearly lost it all, and she wasn't about to let this final opportunity slip through her fingers. She *would* get as many of her crew home as she could.

"I'm sorry, Captain."

"We can mourn for our friends later," Di said. Her forced strength was undermined by the audible tremor in her voice. "When can you get the Katana moving again? Best estimate."

"It's hard to say, Captain. I'm afraid if I turn it on, half the ship will rip away from the stress cracks in the hull. I've got to finish sealing it all off."

Di glanced down toward the shifting station below her shuttle. It had already started to pick up speed, though it still hadn't reached the water vapor plume. It had ten, maybe twelve minutes before passing through the cloud where it would pick up billions, if not trillions, of microscopic demons rocketing from the moon's core. That station would quickly become an incubator for humanity's extinction.

Unless.

Di's mind sparked as she seized on a new plan. She had no idea if it would work, but she refused to stand by and watch.

"Hazel, first get Lucas into quarantine until you can

confirm he isn't infected. Then, you need to get the ship up and running. You have ten minutes."

"What?" Hazel shouted. "Captain, I don't think—"

"That orbital station is about to be packed with those parasites, and it's headed for Earth. I will not let that happen." Di pulled herself closer to the flight controls, plucking her pistol from the dash and placing it back into its holster. "I'm going to pilot this shuttle into the station to try and drive it down to the surface. I think if we get it close enough to the base of that hydrothermal vent, it should tear the station to pieces."

A lengthy pause prefaced Hazel's carefully guarded reaction. "You sure about that, Captain?"

"Not at all, but it's all I've got."

"Captain, I—"

"This isn't a suicide mission, Hazel. I've got vital information exposing Paragon that I'm not just going to abandon. I've also got a propulsion pack with a little charge left. When I've got the shuttle in the right position, I'll grab Emma and bail. But I need you ready to pick me up."

Another moment of tense silence. Di began to prep the shuttle for flight.

"Captain, can I be honest?"

"Of course, Hazel."

"This is the dumbest ass idea I've ever heard." Hazel sighed heavily. "I kind of love it, too. Tell me what you need."

Di heard the grin in her voice and couldn't help but smile herself. This truly was a terrible idea. A thousand separate things could go wrong, any one of which would derail the entire half-assed plan. Yet somehow, Di had a feeling it would work. A growing sense of confidence. So much had gone so incredibly wrong; the universe owed her a win.

"How close can I get but still have enough speed to affect the station?" Di asked.

"That entirely depends on how stupid you plan on being. Are you just flying the shuttle straight down into it?"

"That's what I was thinking," Di said. She piloted the shuttle higher so she could see the entire station in her viewscreen. Its angular 'U' shape pushed lazily forward, large, glowing engines located in the back at the bottom of the 'U'. The awkward shape presented a potential problem on how to hit it, but her best bet was to target the area furthest from the engines. If she could push one of the prongs toward Enceladus' surface just before it hit the vapor plume, it wouldn't have enough time to correct. One up close shot from a random, geyser-like blast of water vapor, and that station would shred apart like paper in a blender.

"I outfitted that shuttle with a little... extra kick after our last job. You should be fine a few hundred meters up. The real problem is how to line it up. If you're off and bail too soon, the shuttle won't do much."

"What I wouldn't give for a little mathematical magic from Gerald right about now," Di said. A pang of guilt thrummed in her heart. He *could* have offered his expertise if she hadn't forced him into the field. He had obviously had reservations about this job, but the peer pressure of going on his first field mission had been too much to overcome. Yet another point where, had she simply listened to her gut, listened to her crew, and stopped focusing on greed, this all would have turned out so much differently.

"Captain? You there?"

"Sorry, Hazel. I'm here."

"What I was saying is that there should be a delay of around forty-three seconds from when you hit the switch to when the boosters kick in. You're gonna want to be clear of the ship before that happens. I would suggest using the lower emergency hatch to stay away from the thrusters at the back."

"Thank you, Hazel." Di's throat suddenly closed, becoming scorchingly dry. The very next sentence, an apology, a 'good luck,' or a 'goodbye,' caught in her throat. She couldn't bring herself to do it. Not again.

"We'll see you in a few, Captain," Hazel said, taking the moment for herself. "Fly straight." It was an old pilot's term, their version of 'break a leg.' It also signified what was left unspoken between them. Focus on what remained, leave the rest behind until the mission was done.

The orbital station was slowly approaching the southern tip of the moon where the vents were strongest. In response, the propulsion engines flared a bright white, and the station listed upward and away from the surface. The makeshift incubator had begun its climb away from the dangerous vapor bursts. It was now or never.

Using the control panel and the shuttle's built-in AI, Di brought up a virtual display of the ship's projected trajectory. It also overlayed the station's trajectory, pinpointing a spot of potential impact some four- or five-hundred meters away. A handy countdown timer appeared as well, giving her just over one minute to prepare before locking everything in and bailing. It could do all but pilot the ship itself (a feature that would have been much appreciated in their current predicament).

With no time to lose, Di sprinted back toward the tiny closet where Emma still lay unconscious and unmoving. She conveyed a mental command to her suit to assess Emma's of any breaches or malfunctions. It wouldn't do for her to launch them into the vacuum of space in an effort to save Emma only to lose her from a pin-sized hole leaking all the suit's oxygen. As her suit performed its functions, she gripped Emma beneath the armpits and hauled her into the hallway toward the cockpit and the emergency hatch set into the floor.

All clear, her suit's voice said in a falsely cheery tone. *Ms. Taylors' suit is performing at adequate levels.*

Di gritted her teeth against the pain of her broken and battered body. Every bone, every muscle, every tendon burned and ached. Hell, throw her skin into that camp as well. Every surface and part had morphed and coalesced into a single ball of agony. All but her right elbow, for some reason. That had somehow remained unscathed, though there was still time.

Glancing down the short hallway toward the view screen inside the cockpit, she saw the counter drop below twenty seconds. Gingerly dropping Emma to the floor, she hobbled her way toward the control panel and poised her hand beside the ignition switch. Three buttons flashed repeatedly as indicators of what systems needed prepping before launch. With five seconds to go, she pressed two and waited. The timer hit zero, and she hit the third. A new timer began counting down, giving her their window of escape.

"Bring the shuttle's display to my HUD," Di said, subconsciously reverting to vocal commands. A virtual display of her view out the cockpit appeared in the bottom corner of her vision, including the countdown. Less than forty seconds. She limped back to the hatch, placing trembling hands on the lock.

Despite her leaps and bounds in addressing her phobia of space, forced or otherwise, the thought of opening the ship to the void terrified her. You didn't just undue decades of a rational fear's grip on your psyche with a few proud moments of overcoming that fear.

You don't have to leave. A captain goes down with their ship, don't they?

Di's resolve hardened. She refused to let anyone dictate what she could and could not do, not even her own subconscious.

With a muted thunk, the emergency hatch unlocked. Flashing yellow lights flared to life along the hallway accompanied by a shrill warning chirp. The hatch slid open revealing a small compartment just big enough for the two of them to fit, albeit uncomfortably cramped. Di hopped in and dragged Emma's limp body behind her.

"This would be a bit simpler if you were conscious, you know," Di muttered, sliding the hatch closed and relocking it.

Pressurized air hissed as the tiny space equalized in preparation for their departure. She maneuvered herself into a seated position bringing Emma between her legs like a toddler in a carrier. A much larger, unwieldy toddler. Extending the safety tether from her suit, she wrapped it around Emma and herself several times before securing it to the eyelet at her waist.

Di checked her feed from the cockpit, noting the countdown timer. Ten seconds to spare. She flipped the protective cover and hit the release button, grabbing Emma tightly to her chest. The bay door beneath them slid silently away, opening their cramped cubby to the vacuum of space.

Silent alarms flared to life from the cockpit overview. The station was turning, moving itself gradually out of the shuttle's trajectory.

Seven seconds.

"Shit, shit, shit," Di spat. She glanced down at the terrifying view of Enceladus far below her, triggering both vertigo and hyperventilation at the empty expanse.

Six seconds.

If she didn't move now, the shuttle would slam them back in its acceleration, trapping them in the emergency hatch with little hope to eject. She doubted she had enough time to seal the hatch, unhook Emma, and alter the course to still intercept the station. Options were few and far between, shrinking by the second.

Five seconds.

She could abort. It was a simple killswitch command, something her suit could communicate to the shuttle. While a complex calculation to alter the course of the shuttle was too much, stopping it altogether was a built-in safety mechanism. It would give her time to get to the cockpit and...

And do what exactly? By the time she got herself back to the cockpit, their window of opportunity would be gone. The station would be entering the safer tail end of the vent gathering up millions of biological bombs. Her ship had no weaponry, illicit or otherwise. They could leave to get help, to fix their communication array and notify military, but at that point the station would be lost to the infinite expanse of space. It gave the Omega Parasite time to evolve, to learn.

"Screw that," she said. Twisting and tucking her lugs beneath her, Di launched herself headfirst out of the shuttle as hard as she could, angling herself toward the moon and in the direction of the nose of the shuttle. She only hoped she had given herself enough time to get clear of the boosters.

A flash of silent, bright white light was followed quickly by the Katana's shuttle rocketing forward toward the station. Despite the distance, Di felt the heat wash temporarily over her suit before it automatically compensated to protect her. That ship was cooking, and it was locked in. Unfortunately, it was now locked into a spot slightly off from the center of the orbital station's arm.

There was no time to waste. Di engaged her propulsion

pack, angling herself toward the rear of station and its thrusters that were currently pushing it out of her shuttle's line of impact. Her HUD flashed a warning. Battery percentage officially dropped to one percent. It should be just enough to get her in position.

As a grunt in interplanetary construction, she had worked on plenty of structures. Freighters, support and transport shuttles, even a few stationary waypoints. She had also worked on orbital stations. Every station was outfitted with adjustment thrusters. Small engines to alter the position of the station, most often used in cases of emergency where impact with a foreign object was imminent. The fine details escaped her, as she wasn't an engineer. She couldn't explain the reasons behind the thruster angles or the necessary speed to alter the trajectory of a station so large. What she *did* know, however, was that every thruster had a supply line. Power, fuel, it didn't matter. Cut that line, the thruster was dead.

The orbital station loomed large in her view. There was no way in hell she could outrun the shuttle, but if she could just get close enough...

Her propulsion pack sputtered, going silent. A large flashing green 'zero' let her know the obvious fact that the pack was dead. It didn't matter. In space, she had no air resistance to slow her down or gravity to pull her in the wrong direction. All she needed was a clear line of sight.

The shuttle was closing in on the station. If Di didn't do something now, it would miss the station's right arm completely.

She could barely make out the right-most thruster pushing the station out of the shuttle's trajectory. It had not yet reached a speed that would carry it completely out of harm's way, but it wouldn't take much longer.

Reaching toward the holster on her thigh, she pulled her pistol out and checked the chamber. Her final bullet sat ready and waiting. Di stretched her arms forward, right hand holding loosely on the grip with the left wrapped tightly around the right. The trigger felt firm beneath her quivering pointer finger. This shot would have been impractical with a fully scoped rifle. With an inaccurate pistol it was borderline impossible, but it was all she had.

Her helmet zoomed in as far as it could, though her target was still miniscule. Di sucked in two deep, calming breaths. The universe owed her this one. She *would* make the shot.

You've never been great with a pistol, she thought, causing a moment of hesitation. Her confidence dimmed as her brain tried to calculate the likelihood of success. Her pistol drooped in her hand, despair threatening to overwhelm her once more.

You've got this, Di.

She startled at Gene's baritone voice in her mind, but felt her nerves settle and her mind clear. Her lips turned up in a bittersweet smile at hearing him one last time.

She sighted down the length of the gun and gently squeezed the trigger. At the last second, she adjusted slightly to the left. The trigger depressed, muzzle flashing briefly, pistol kicking against her bent elbows. The opposite force expelled from the gun slowed her slightly, though not enough to halt her forward progress toward the station and the thermal vents. The bullet was away, disappearing against the deep black backdrop of space.

Di held her breath. She had absolutely no idea if her shot was true. For all she knew, it could have already pinged harmlessly against the hardened steel of the outer hull.

A dim flash burst beside the two rightmost engines, and their white-hot glow rapidly faded to a dull blue. Di sucked in a shuddering sob. She had done it. By some miracle, she had hit the exact spot to disable not one, but two course correction thrusters.

The station twisted lazily and rudderless as the shuttle rocketed forward. Her eyes were glued to the small feed from her former cockpit as she forced herself to take shaky breath after shaky breath. It would be close, even with her incredible shot. The shuttle's engines flared brighter, and her helmet dimmed automatically with the sudden blast of light.

The shuttle's impact was breathtaking. With its added boost of speed, it collided solidly with the outer edge of the rightmost arm, ripping out a massive chunk of twisting metal and debris. The shuttle flared with a brief, bright orange before the vacuum sucked away all the oxygen from the explosion. The station lurched solidly toward the surface of Enceladus as it attempted to limp its way free from utter destruction. It did it little good.

As it entered the space above the southern pole of the moon, a violent burst of vapor and particulate rocketed from the surface and collided with the damaged right arm, sheering clean through it. The length that had been engulfed by the geyser had disappeared completely leaving nothing but shards of glinting metal spinning out into the void. A few moments later as the station floundered, another forceful expulsion enveloped it completely, shredding it to billions of unidentifiable pieces.

Di laughed. A hearty, exhausted chuckle. It was over. She had done what she set out to do. She had avenged her crew, the ones lost to the evils of the parasite, and saved the rest. Well, she had saved two. She felt a twinge of guilt as she glanced down at the still unconscious Emma strapped to her chest. She would unfortunately share in Di's fate. Another casualty to her captain's inadequacies.

The vents loomed closer. At Di's current trajectory, she would hit the vents in only a handful of minutes. She didn't let her mind dwell on what that would do to her when it had so entirely and utterly annihilated a million-metric-ton space station. Her only consolation was that it would be so fast, she doubted she would feel a thing. That would be nice. No more aches, no more pains. No more guilt. No more suffering. Just an instantaneous evaporation into nothingness.

"Capt... -ome in..."

"It's done, Hazel," Di responded, closing her eyes. "It's over."

"I... vents are... incoming."

"I'm sorry I couldn't give you the documents on the Omega Parasite, or what Paragon did. Still, your eyewitness account will be important to keep others from coming back to Enceladus."

"Don't be... coming... -old tight." Hazel's comms cut in and out, further interference caused by Di's proximity to the vents and the clouds of icy particulate.

Di wanted to say more, to apologize. The words caught in her throat. She was just so tired. And so done. Before, when she had contemplated ending it, it had been empty and meaningless. Giving up. Now, in the aftermath of near impossible odds, her sacrifice would mean something.

The CS Katana suddenly loomed large in her vision as it slid from below her feet, rear bay doors opened invitingly. With the deftest maneuver Di had ever seen, Hazel matched their speed and eased the ship around their floating bodies, enclosing them in the safe confines of her beloved ship.

"We're cutting it close, Captain. It's gonna be a little bumpy."

The bay doors gently closed, initiating the ship's artificial gravity. Di hit the floor with a painful thud, trying her best to twist Emma out from directly beneath her. The Katana pulsed with turbulence for a brief moment before settling.

Di reveled in the silent familiarity of her ship. This was home. She was home. Tears flowed freely down her cheeks, a mixture of joy and sorrow. Her brain felt muddled. Conflicted. So much loss and pain, but she had survived. Hazel, Lucas, and Emma. All safe aboard the ship.

They should never have come here. It was plainly obvious

in hindsight, as most 'revelations' tended to be. Di doubted the guilt would ever completely leave. Under her direction, she had gotten half of her crew killed. Gerald, lost below the waves. Gene, mutated to a monster. Gayle, left to take her own life because of Di's cowardice. Their faces hovered before her, accusatory eyes glaring.

You left us.

You abandoned us.

This was your fault.

Your fault.

Di's head pulsed painfully behind her temples. It was too much. She hurriedly unclipped herself from Emma and rolled to her hands and knees, stomach heaving sharply. Nothing came up but flecks of spittle and a thin line of burning stomach acid, but as it quickly cleared it gave her momentary relief from the nausea.

"Captain?" Hazel's footsteps thunked closer, but Di held up a hand in warning, eyes squeezed shut.

"Don't. Not yet."

"Captain, you're hurt. We need to get you to the medical—"

"My suit was exposed to the parasite. Emma's condition is unknown, but she was exposed as well. I want quarantine until we can confirm we're both clean."

Hazel's footsteps thankfully stopped. She knew protocol. Though not through firsthand experience, she also knew the dangers of what this parasite posed. "Yes, Captain. Initiating quarantine protocol." Her footsteps faded followed by a hiss as the loading bay was sealed.

Di rolled herself onto her back and opened her eyes. The piercing glares were gone, but she could feel them in the back of her mind, lurking like shadows. She doubted she would ever be rid of them. She wasn't certain she deserved to be rid of them.

"I caught an emergency distress beacon after making contact with you," Hazel said through personal comms. "It's Roberts in the escape pod. Looks like the bastard survived."

Of course he had. The man was the human embodiment of a cockroach.

"We'll head toward him, though his ejection took him pretty far out there. With our ship as battered as it is, it might take us a few hours, may half a day to catch up to him. Should give us time to evaluate you and Emma, get you cleaned up."

"Thank you, Hazel." There was a pause, a moment of hesitation before she managed to choke out the words she was desperate to say. "I'm sorry. I'm so sorry."

"There's nothing for you to be sorry for, Captain. You did everything you could." The line went quiet.

Di sat up, glancing toward the unmoving form of her assistant pilot laying sprawled on the metal floor of the loading bay. Whatever was wrong with her, whatever John had done, it hadn't yet turned her into a mindless, bloodthirsty host. Maybe he hadn't done anything at all. They would know soon enough.

Shakily and with great, painful exertion, she hauled herself slowly to her feet, wandering over to the viewport beside the bay door. Enceladus, Saturn's icy moon, loomed large in her view. Spouts of vapor emitted periodically from the southern vents. Debris floated lazily in the vacuum, scattered throughout the area. The twisted remains of man's outpost on the moon. She followed the remnants of the interplanetary elevator with her eyes and imagined she could see the tiny speck of grey where the surface station sat below, though it was impossible to make out anything through the constant haze of the moon's atmosphere. A microscopic grave marker for the ones lost below.

Though they had escaped with their lives, their mission wasn't over just yet. She had vowed to expose Paragon for the monster it was, for the monsters it had knowingly unleashed. The bastards would pay for what they did, and she would see it done personally. She fantasized about bringing those responsible to justice, hearing the names of her dead crew on their lips before ending them with a bullet between the eyes. Hell, maybe she'd start with Liam Roberts.

Her lost crew, ever hovering in the fringes of her thoughts, seemed to approve, though their accusatory eyes remained fixed on her soul. It wouldn't bring them back, but it just might let their souls rest in peace. It was the least she could do for her friends. Her family.

Enceladus, with its bright white, icy exterior and its fetid, rotten core, slowly receded as they limped away with the bedraggled remains of a once-glorious crew. Di prayed to whatever god would listen that it would be the last time she ever had to set eyes on that frozen hell.

ACKNOWLEDGEMENTS

I'll be honest, this is a little surreal. Ever since I was a little kid, I have dreamed of looking up on my shelf and seeing my name on the spine of a book. To think that moment is actually here is wild.

This book has been bouncing around for nearly four years, so there are plenty of people I need to thank without whom this book would not have been possible. If you're expecting your name and you don't see it here, I'm so sorry I forgot to include you. Feel free to shoot me a nasty text.

If you saw the dedication, you know I owe a lot to my wife, Carlie. As a busy home school teacher/wife/cook/career nurse/housekeeper/mother-of-four, she still found time to read early drafts and let me bounce plot ideas off her when she could have been catching up on much-needed sleep.

My mom, Julie, has always been a huge supporter of my little side project writing hobby, and she was more than willing to read all the early drafts (despite hating the horror genre). Her excitement on what would happen next often gave me the confidence and drive to keep writing.

My dad, Chris, is a big Stephen King fan, so I knew I needed his approval. Thankfully, he chewed through the draft I gave him pretty quickly and seemed to enjoy it. Good sign.

I need to thank the additional people who were willing to read beta/early release copies of this book; Spencer Judd, Miss Kate, Kalon Gluch, Talia Gluch, Spencer Doty, Colbie Monson, Parker

Christopher, Sue Turner, Shelby Ivory, Dawn Meehan, Janeil Jones, Lisa Olsen, Traci Suman, Haley Lichtie, Andrea Sam, Nicole Skowronek, Jandi Carter, Julie Springer, Ashley Williams, Sherri McKenna, and Kimberli Berrett.

A big thank you to the artist for my fantastic cover art, my sister-in-law Talia. This is, shockingly, her very first book cover. I hope there are many more to come.

Although my kids, Carson, Colton, Connor, and Charlie, are a little too young to read this one, their love of reading and constant curiosity is an inspiration for me. It's a reminder of what it felt like when I was a kid picking up a new book for the first time and starting off on another adventure.

My third-grade teacher, Ms. Wilhelm (who later also became my junior high art/photography teacher), saw me writing away in a notebook when I was supposed to be reading in class, but she enthusiastically encouraged me to keep writing. It's taken me awhile, but I've finally found something that's hopefully worth publishing.

I have to throw in a cheeky thank you to Brandon Sanderson. I don't know if I ever would have set off on this writing journey without his vast bibliography and his living example of the joy writing can bring (even if it's only ever seen by a handful of people).

As a bit of a catchall, I'd like to thank the rest of my family and friends who are always cheering me on and lending me support.

Finally, I have to thank you, the reader. For those who know me personally and picked this book up as a favor, those who may have been given this book by one of my friends or family, or those who randomly came across this book and decided to give a brand new, self-published indie author a shot, I thank you.

(I know there are very few people who actually look at the acknowledgments of a book, so I know anyone reading this is especially dedicated. Thank you again and again. Your support means everything.)

Author Bio

Chase was born in the good 'ol 90's in Idaho, but he grew up in Utah where he was constantly getting in trouble for reading (and sometimes writing) in class. He was obsessed with books like the Redwall series by Brian Jacques, the Dragonlance Chronicles and Dragonlance Legends trilogies by Margaret Weiss & Tracy Hickman, and Harry Potter.

Chase took time away from his studies to serve a mission for the Church of Jesus Christ of Latter-Day Saints in Taiwan. He returned and completed a Bachelors of Art in Mandarin Chinese with a minor in Communication. He then attended law school and received his Juris Doctorate, and is currently a practicing attorney.

Chase married his wonderful and gorgeous wife Carlie who, after months of putting up with his nonsense, finally succumbed to his incessant begging. She is a registered nurse and works with blood cancers on the bone marrow transplant unit. They have three wonderful boys, one very spoiled little girl, and currently live in Utah.

Some of Chase's favorite authors and influences are Brandon Sanderson, Dan Wells, J.K. Rowling, V.E. Schwab, Robin Hobb, Brandon Mull, Margaret Weiss & Tracy Hickman, Eric Nylund, Martha Wells, Robin Hobb, Jim Butcher, and Andy Weir.